A
PARISIAN
from
KANSAS

PHILIPPE TAPON

A

PARISIAN

from

KANSAS

A WILLIAM ABRAHAMS BOOK

DUTTON

DUTTON
Published by the Penguin Group
Penguin Books USA Inc., 375 Hudson Street, New York,
New York 10014, U.S.A.
Penguin Books Ltd, 27 Wrights Lane, London W8 5TZ, England
Penguin Books Australia Ltd, Ringwood, Victoria, Australia
Penguin Books Canada Ltd, 10 Alcorn Avenue, Toronto, Ontario,
Canada M4V 3B2
Penguin Books (N.Z.) Ltd, 182–190 Wairau Road, Auckland 10, New Zealand

Penguin Books Ltd, Registered Offices:
Harmondsworth, Middlesex, England

First published by Dutton, an imprint of Dutton Signet,
a division of Penguin Books USA Inc.
Distributed in Canada by McClelland & Stewart Inc.

First Printing, March, 1997
1   3   5   7   9   10   8   6   4   2

Excerpts from "The Love Song of J. Alfred Prufrock" and "The Waste Land" in
COLLECTED POEMS 1909–1962 by T. S. Eliot, copyright 1936 by Harcourt
Brace & Company, copyright © 1964, 1963 by T. S. Eliot, reprinted by permis-
sion of the publisher

 REGISTERED TRADEMARK—MARCA REGISTRADA

LIBRARY OF CONGRESS CATALOGING-IN-PUBLICATION DATA:
Tapon, Philippe.
    A Parisian from Kansas / Philippe Tapon.
    p.   cm.
    "A William Abrahams book."
    ISBN 0-525-94239-4
    I.   Title.
    PS3570.A5678P37   1997
813'.54—dc20   96-30724
                                                                  CIP

Printed in the United States of America
Set in Bembo
Designed by Jesse Cohen

PUBLISHER'S NOTE
This is a work of fiction. Names, characters, places, and incidents either are the
product of the author's imagination or are used fictitiously.

This book is printed on acid-free paper. ♾

Kings no more merit a stone mark of death than
do the least men: dark princes, white queens,
dukes of great might once dead, in balance weigh
not light feathers more than their poor squires,
nor musicians and makers of lyres, all of them
likened when naked, strong and weak, lusty and
wretched, each of them barring exception equal
by human condition.

—Jean de Meung

para los ñoños

CHAPTER 1

I first met Darren not long after I had finished my studies in Paris. It was summertime; the days were warm, and slow, and idle, and I had a friendship with Jean-Baptiste, who was Darren's closest friend.

"I can't wait until he comes back," Jean-Baptiste had said, three days before. He showed me pictures of Darren and of his family while we idled away time in his flat. He had a whole album full of photos of his visit to Kansas.

"This is Darren," Jean-Baptiste said, pointing out a handsome but emaciated youngish man with unruly blond hair. "And this is his mother," he said, pointing out a grotesquely fat dark-haired woman piled in an easy chair. "And this is Darren's dad. He's every bit as solid as he looks." Jean-Baptiste's spoken French was quick to the point of being incomprehensible. "And this is me," he said, showing me a picture of the least likely thing I expected to see on a snow-covered farm in Kansas: a Parisian, with neat elegant glasses and delicate hands.

There were more photos: Darren and Jean-Baptiste behind a barn; Darren and Jean-Baptiste eating fried chicken; Darren and Jean-Baptiste in blue parkas standing before a snowplow. A family portrait: Darren, thin as a fence post, behind his parents and three siblings. Darren and his little sister were slender, but any two of the others would have easily burst the big door frame.

"They are a *bit* large," I said.

"The picture makes them look smaller than they are."

"No," I said incredulously.

"Yes," said Jean-Baptiste, still speaking quickly, "and look at this. This is an aerial view of the farm."

An enterprising pilot had flown over all the farms in the county, taking photographs and later selling them to the farmers. The photo of Yew Tree Farms showed the Swensons' dairy, barn, silos, and white clapboard house in the vast Kansan atmosphere. Everywhere around was a flat barren snowscape.

I said, "Can you—"

"What?" he said.

"Can I ask you *when* did you go back to visit?"

"We went back in January."

"Has he changed much?"

"No, not at all. He's better now. He's starting to gain weight, he says. In these pictures he's—he's as thin as *anybody* can ever get."

In one of the photos he looked skeletal, a human coat hanger.

There was another one, his legs crossed, the big chin jutting out, squinting in the porch sunlight.

"And he used to be so big. You can't imagine, Philippe. He was . . ." Jean-Baptiste sucked in air and made a futile gesture with his hands, the kind you make to describe a riverbed or a tremendous animal.

"He was *baraqué*." He meant very big. "Huge," Jean-Baptiste said, looking at the photograph as if the flimsy, puny thing could never, should never even pretend to contain an entire human being.

"And here he is at K.U." There he was, smartly dressed, with a foot atop a stone, as if he owned the empty football stadium below him. There was a slight smile on Darren's face.

For me, who had grown up in America and come to Europe, there was a pleasant ambiguity about Darren's appearance. He looked American, certainly. There was that gesture, the foot atop a stone, the half-backward look at the camera. But there was something *else* too. There was—how shall I describe it? A glimpse of something that was so out of place near a Kansan football stadium that it arrested my attention. A look in his eye, the shape of his peculiar smile—neither coming nor going—which hinted of irony, of cynical wit, of café chic.

"That's a nice pair of shoes he's got," I said.

"He dresses very well. But he has very little clothing. You'll see, when he arrives. He has much less than I do."

"Jean-Baptiste, no one has as many clothes as you do!"

"You'd be surprised! I've seen people who have entire rooms as wardrobes."

"I'll listen to you once you've gotten rid of your"—I counted—"five, six, *seven* pairs of shoes."

He rolled his eyes but conceded the point.

Jean-Baptiste's flat was a small studio, a student's pad. He had taken pains to give it a colonial flavor: mounted butterflies in glass frames decorated the walls. He'd found a wicker bookcase and had laden it with all his unread books; among them I spotted *Sur la route* and *Le Soleil se lève aussi*. Hanging on a wall was a pith explorer hat. He never wore it himself, but he thought it gave the tiny room a South Pacific look.

There was a silence.

"Was Darren already sick when you met him?" I asked.

"Oh, yes. He told me he was sick the day I met him. It was very clear from the start."

"When did he get it?"

"Nineteen—nineteen-eighty-eight," he said, hesitating. "He was twenty-four."

"Oh," I said, and grimaced a little, quite involuntarily. "Twenty-four," I repeated.

"Young, isn't it?" Jean-Baptiste was at least twenty-two himself.

"God, horribly young. Too young to come down with something like that."

"And do you know who gave it to him? His best friend."

"Oh," I repeated. I grimaced again.

"When I met him . . . when I met him . . ." Jean-Baptiste said, "I knew he was going to be . . . very . . . I was . . . he was . . . just right." He was staring into space. "But now . . . he has one . . . year to live maybe. I can't . . . I won't stay to watch him die. I have to get on with my own life. I have to . . ." He broke off. Then he made a curious remark. "I think it's proof of my strength that I can leave him now."

Everyone suspects himself of at least one virtue, and this is mine, a small one: I will never willingly destroy another person's illusions. So, faced with Jean-Baptiste's inflated rhetoric, I said nothing. But I thought: you poor pompous son of a bitch.

"He was my closest friend," Jean-Baptiste said.

And probably still is, I thought.

"He meant everything to me, once."

And still does, I thought.

"But life goes on," he said.

And death goes on, I thought. Death goes on and on. I wrote that in the novel I wrote about Darren, much later.

Jean-Baptiste and I had met at a boring cocktail party given by some rather pretentious graduate students attending our school. At that party, Jean-Baptiste was a courtesy guest—that is, he was introduced politely and then no one spoke to him. I was another such courtesy guest. It was not until I was paid the compliment of a conversation by our fat host, all hot from his recent acceptance at his huge, perfectly *wonderful* big school, that Jean-Baptiste and I actually met.

"Yes," our host was saying, "it is a perfectly *wonderful* start to my career. I can *choose* to do anything I want, now—really, I can. . . . But enough about me. Tell me: what do you, Mon*sieur* Tapon"—it was a courtesy, among these students, to use last names—"what do *you* intend to do with your little life?"

I looked this pompous jackass straight in the eye and said, "Why, I intend to write novels about—successful people."

"Oh, really? I can't imagine it."

"You can't imagine? Why not? Are you not a writer?"

"Monsieur Tapon, I *am* a writer; I *have* written; indeed I *shall* be published. Please count on that. I have written many essays and a modest historical article or two."

"How successful of you," I said. He inclined slightly at the waist.

"It is nothing," he said.

"No," I answered. "I mean, it's obviously just a start. Will you write more, do you think?"

"Of course! But not novels. You see, I have this theory which may interest you. Novels are, I admit, amusing. They are light, imaginary—diversions from real life. But they never represent reality. Imagination is not as true as real life. That is why the novel, as a form, can never be as great as the history or the essay. What do you think?"

"I think you're full of—wit," I said.

"So then, Monsieur Tapon, tell me: why do *you* want to write novels?"

"Well, it is very simple. Because I have to," I said, smiling.

"What?"

"I have to," I said, again.

He looked at me blankly, saw my smile, then excused himself suddenly and left. Jean-Baptiste (I did not know him then) had watched the whole thing. He came up to me now.

"Bonsoir," he said.

"Bonsoir."

Jean-Baptiste glanced at our host across the room, and said, "What a perfectly *wonderful* party. Don't you think?"

"Yes. Isn't it."

"I really am having the time of my life."

"What a coincidence. So am I. Cheers." We touched glasses.

"Ah—may I ask you—?" he said.

"Philippe," I offered.

"Jean-Baptiste," he answered. "Philippe, do you *really* intend to be a novelist?"

"Sort of," I said. "But really, I only say that to be charming. You know, I try to be charming, at parties like these."

"Oh, please, Philippe, I implore you to be charming—but please save your charm for our worthy host. I certainly don't deserve it."

"I say, Jean-Baptiste. You are a frightful bore."

"My apologies. Now may I ask, Philippe: what do you really want to be?"

"What do I want to be? Hmm. Rich, I suppose? Happy, perhaps?" I thought a bit, but nothing came. "I don't know," I said.

"Don't people who don't know become novelists?"

"No, not me."

"Why not?"

For a moment I hesitated. To give a straight answer was tricky. But this fellow seemed curious about me, and I liked him. I looked into his honest, triangular face and slowly said, "I think being a novelist is much, much too public. A novelist has to reveal himself to everybody—gooseflesh-naked. Then he has to get his friends to reveal all their secrets—and then betray them too. And it helps, these days, if he describes, in detail, all the hard sex he's ever had."

"Sounds like a very interesting life," Jean-Baptiste said. "And you won't do it?"

"Not if I can help it." I sipped my drink. He continued staring at me, unwavering. That unnerved me somewhat, so I said, "Let me make you a small confession." I cleared my throat. "I've already tried, you see. This summer, I tried to write creatively, but I couldn't. I can't. I may know how to write, I may have a style, but I can't really imagine things very well. I can't describe anything, except what's actually happened to me. But I don't want to write about that, because that's cheap and shabby."

"Aren't you being a bit snobbish?" he asked. "After all, everybody else does it."

"I won't," I said. "Never. Because, you see—I'm too moral." I smiled. "I'm American, you know. And as you know, all Americans are so very moral."

"You're *American*?" he asked.

I nodded heartily.

"But—you speak French so *well*. You *look* French."

"Yes, amazing what an act I do put on. I so enjoy pretending to be what I am not."

His stare took on such a crazed intensity I had to wonder if there wasn't something a little sinister about him.

"My best friend is American," he blurted out. "And he's coming to Paris. Quite soon."

"Oh? What's he like?"

"He's like you."

"Like me? In what way?"

"He's a novelist."

"A novelist!" I narrowed my eyes. "How many novels has he written?"

"Well, that's just it. He hasn't written *any*."

"None?"

"No. No, not one. Zero. He says he's given up. He says he hasn't got enough time. He can't write anyway."

"Why not?"

"Style. He wants to describe what has happened to him, but he hasn't got a style. And you can't say anything without that. You need technique."

Now I was piqued. Mine is a terrible, irrepressible curiosity about techniques—and styles—and lives—of other writers; so I tried to pry, in a modest manner, about this writer's style problem. But Jean-Baptiste would reveal nothing, except the writer's name, the name of his friend: Darren. Jean-Baptiste said he wouldn't talk of Darren at this party, but he suggested that, perhaps, if I wanted to, we could talk about Darren, and about his style, later.

By a strange coincidence, Jean-Baptiste lived only a few minutes' walk from me, along the Left Bank. He lived in a studio; I lived in a *deux-pièces,* a two-room flat. Jean-Baptiste and I were about equidistant from the Pont des Arts, the footbridge that joined the Cour Carrée of the Louvre and Saint-Germain-des-Prés. It was a romantic part of town, or at least it was to me, and I never tired of dawdling on the thin planks of the Pont des Arts, leaning on its narrow iron balustrades, and watching the evening sun slowly redden as it dipped into the water. The evening after Jean-Baptiste and I first spoke in his flat, after he showed me the pictures, I went to the Pont des Arts and watched the tourist boats blazing up and down the Seine, shining their secret-rending lamps deep into the old, cracked masonry. I watched these bateaux-mouches until late at night, and thought about Jean-Baptiste's story—about how he and Darren had met. I tried to imagine them meeting in Paris; I tried to imagine them going to Kansas; I tried to imagine Darren.

Darren landed in Paris the next day. In the afternoon Jean-Baptiste left a message with my concierge, telling me to be at his studio around ten. That was a night in July, with warm air—air you could kiss—so I went, slowly walking past the churches, observing the gray saints and the brilliantly lit-up crosses capping the white spires. There was an intensity in the air that night, as if it were the last night of summer. Slowly I sauntered over to Jean-Baptiste's flat, past his concierge, rang the doorbell—but no one was there. I sat down to wait, waited ten minutes, waited some more, then growing impatient, I got up and began wandering in the area, and wound my way, as I usually did, to the Pont des Arts. There, in front of the Institut de France, I saw Jean-Baptiste. But he did not see me, at first; he was transfixed, watching a man walk on the balustrade of the bridge.

Like a tightrope walker, like a dancer—Darren—for it was he, was balanced on the iron railing, with the swirling river beneath; there were people staring, and the lamps of the floating bateaux-mouches fixed him whitely in the darkness like an aerial acrobat; powerful halogen glares caught and framed his slender figure as he walked, long arms outstretched, the entire length of the bridge.

"Jean-Baptiste!" Darren called out, over the whoosh of the waves. "Jean-Baptiste! I told you I could do it!" He stood still. He looked about at the rosy darkness crouching over Paris, and then, like a bird alighting, gracefully hopped onto the pavement.

Jean-Baptiste rushed up with me just behind. "Darren!" he cried. "Darren! You could have died doing that!"

"Died? Me, died? Ha! Well, hmm—well, *yaass,* I suppose you could say I could have died, that's so, Jean-Baptiste, that's so." His French was incredible, an outrageous mixture of campy Left Bank affectation and Kansan drawl. "But—*so what?* I'm ready. Why not now? On this bridge? Why not now, beneath this sky? Good—God! Look up! Look at the stars! Look at the *moon!*" he said, pointing up. I looked up. I could see no stars, but the moon was full and high and white. "Full moon!" Darren said. "You know what *that* means, don't you?" He wailed like a wolf. "Arrooooooooooo!" Then he lowered his voice to a hoarse whisper. "Now, fellow travelers, do you know where the *lowest* part of the city is? Do you?"

"Darren, this is Philippe," Jean-Baptiste said, trying to introduce me.

"Philippe, do you know where the *lowest* part of the city is? Do you?"

"No," I said.

"Well, come on then! Follow me!"

And, pushing me like a pawn to another square, he grabbed my arm and walked me off the bridge, down towards the river.

"Now, Philippe," Darren huffed, breathlessly, excitedly, as we walked downriver. "What—is on—our left?"

"Saint-Germain-des-Prés."

"Yes! Now what is in Saint-Germain-des-Prés?"

"Shops? A school?"

"No! Not just antiquity shops! Not just a school! The *best* antiquity shops in the world! And the most perfectly *wonderful* school—*in!—the!—world!* Right?"

"Yes, I suppose so."

"So—what is down here? BENEATH this bridge? BENEATH this wonderful neighborhood?" By then the three of us were standing beneath the Pont du Carrousel, at the mouth of the tunnel, which gaped awfully like an open maw. Inside it was dark, dark, dark.

"I don't know," I said.

"Your WORST NIGHTMARE!" Darren yelled, and he wheeled and stepped into the darkness inside.

The tunnel looked at least three hundred meters long. I could see, even from its mouth, that there were alcoves all along its length. Inside it was impenetrably black. But Darren was already inside, waving us to follow, already a shade of dark gray moving through darkness. Jean-Baptiste and I looked at each other. Then, we stepped forward.

I missed the first step, and nearly fell on my face; I staggered forward, much deeper inside than I wanted to; my throat gagged at the sudden reek of shit and piss and rot; the bottom was slippery, the walls coated with liquid; and in the darkness, Darren was standing mesmerized, looking at a wall—into a crowded alcove.

"Look!" he whispered hoarsely. "Listen!"

I tried to steady myself and listened, at first, to nothing. Then, slowly, from a hole in the wall, came guttural grunts, exhausted panting, moans and groans. There were male shapes inside that hole, crowded over each other, whispering, sucking.

"See that?" Darren said. "Hear that? *Arrooooooooooo!*" he howled again, and his cry dissolved in a cackle of maniacal laughter. Suddenly he was gone inside the alcove, and all was quiet. Then, booming, came his voice: "SLUTS! SLUTS! Yer all gonna DIE! *ARROooooooo!*" and then I suddenly saw his blond and silvered smile, laughing and laughing; laughing, he made his way out of there for the far side and led us out the tunnel. Coming out of there, I again missed the step.

"Christ, Darren," said Jean-Baptiste.

"Oh, please, please, that's *nothing*. I've seen lots worse than that. *Lots* worse. Ah, it's so good to be *back*! Give me reality! Real! Reality! Uh-oh. Philippe, are you all right?" He put his hand on my shoulder.

"I'm fine."

"You don't look fine. Is Gay Paree a bit too much?"

"I'm fine," I said. But I was off balance, and could almost feel him pushing me. "I'm fine!" I said, although I felt the ground was unstable and continually tilting.

"Now, isn't he the sweetest little fellow in the world?" Darren said to Jean-Baptiste. "Look at how he's holding himself together, even though the discovery of this morass of sin just beneath his doorstep has horrified him. Look how he takes it all in, look how he will not let himself lose his dignity. But now— you keep your judgments to yourself, right? No judgments now, right, Philippe?"

"No, Darren. No judgments."

"Show compassion."

"Compassion. Right." My brow was awash in sweat. I closed my eyes.

"Poor Philippe. I'm sorry. But Jean-Baptiste told me you were a *writer*! I wanted to be a writer myself, once. Now, of course, I'm only a fallen angel. Oh, the stories I've seen—and could tell, if I had the *time*! I thought writers were people who had *seen* things. Haven't you *seen* things, Philippe?"

"*Now* I have," I said. I opened my eyes.

We were standing still, the three of us, outside the mouth of that tunnel, the smell of urine drifting by, while boats swept the lonely wharves, illuminating the Louvre with their pure white beams.

"Please, Philippe—I'm sorry. May I offer you a cigarette?" Darren said.

I had never smoked seriously before, never. But now—I looked at that white cigarette before me, protruding from the pack, coolly inviting. It looked clean and good. Suddenly it was between my lips and I was drawing it to life with Darren's prof-fered wind-swept flame. We walked along—westwards, away from the quais. I walked in the middle, between Darren and Jean-Baptiste. Not far off, I heard the gentle tinkling of the Institut de France's nightly chimes.

The next night, the three of us took a corner table at Finnegans Wake, a pub not far from where the river ran, and Jean-Baptiste and I tried to drink our black beers while Darren told amazing story after story after story. I had the impression that the bar was bending its ear to listen, and when the bartender unlocked the door to let us out, it was long past midnight.

We walked back along the river. As we approached the Pont du Carrousel, I could see, from far away, the mouth of that dark tunnel. Darren had been dominating our conversation all night, but now his voice rose even higher, until he seemed to beseech the sky. "Oh, if only I could find someone who could under-stand my story, write it down. You see, I want to leave some sort of legacy behind. But I can't do it by myself. I need a writer."

I knew it: it was an invitation. I could feel what he wanted me to say. I could not tell whether he knew I knew. But I decided to play along.

I stopped dead. "Darren," I said. "*I'm* a writer."

He stopped in midstep. Jean-Baptiste stopped. Darren looked ahead, and then slowly, like a statue rotating on its base, he turned to face me. "Ohhh . . . how right you are, Philippe. I forgot. You're a writer," he said. Our eyes met. "But, Philippe—sorry. You can't do it."

"What?"

"You can't do it. I can tell."

"What do you mean, I can't? I have a good style. I can describe your life's tragedy."

"That's just it, Philippe. You want to write about the tragedy of AIDS and all that sad-sounding horseshit. You want to write about Darren, the AIDS Case. You know what you are, Philippe? You're conventional, you're stuck-up, you have no imagination. My life is not about tragedy; my life is about *life*. My life is about *living*. I don't want to hear about AIDS. That's why I don't want you as a writer."

"But—Darren—what do you know about me?"

"Jean-Baptiste told me a thing or two."

"Darren, I can write. Believe me. I can write well. I can write about your life, the way you want it written. I can write about *life* and *living*. What do you mean, Darren, saying I can't? Is that some sort of bait?"

"No way, Philippe, I'm as straight as the surface of the earth. But honestly, I'm not sure you are. Why should I make you write my book?"

He was playing with me: I could feel it. But something made me take him seriously. I wanted to say: because you're running out of time. I wanted to say: because no one else will. I wanted to say . . . but I couldn't, because . . . because . . .

Jean-Baptiste was a fastidiously correct young man who upheld the standards of Saint-Germain-des-Prés. His every hair was gummed in place, and in his physical appearance he was aquiline and Parisian. His eyeglasses—delicately trimmed wire things upon which floated two thin discs of glass—were enough to impress local shopkeepers.

Jean-Baptiste knew how to impress local shopkeepers, since he was a shopkeeper's son; his parents had a shop on the Quai Malaquais behind which Jean-Baptiste lived. With his twenty-four shirts, twelve pairs of trousers, and bewildering collection of chic cuff links, chic socks, and chic ties, he cut quite a figure in the *quartier,* all the more so because he understood the rules of Parisian elegance, and kept his best elements almost but not quite out of sight. He held his head back, walked quickly, knew the ins and outs of Paris, and spoke and dressed like a local representative of the *jeunesse dorée.*

This member of the *jeunesse dorée* and Darren had met in The Trap, one of the most sordid clubs in Paris. The club had a back room, dark and smelly, for those customers in a hurry. But Darren and Jean-Baptiste didn't meet in there, exactly; they met in the main room, a relatively civilized chamber lit in blue and red.

"The moment I saw him," Jean-Baptiste had recalled, while lying on his bed, staring meditatively at the ceiling, "I knew it was him. He knew it was me. It was one of those strange

moments when two persons meet and they feel destiny irresistibly taking control."

Jean-Baptiste had told me that story in his room, while the
night chimes of the nearby Institut de France tinkled. That was
the night I had really started imagining Darren: not only imagining his nice shoes and wry smile and café chic, but imagining
also just how his lifelong collections of photographs, journals,
tape recordings, café-chic clothing, and his vast accumulation of
stories, could have all been yoked to his immense ambition—to
turn the raw material of his life into a novel.

We had sensed that ambition in each other, and that ambition lashed us together. He had the material, I had the style—
and together, we had a novel. We both needed a novel, and he
felt his need as strongly as irresistible destiny. My need was
strong, too, though right then neither of us knew just how
strong. So on the quais, below the tinkling bells of the Institut
de France, near the sulfurous glow of the Pont du Carrousel,
next to the hell-hole filled with shuffling darkness, my lips
opened, and I slowly, finally answered him:

". . . Because, Darren. *You have to.*"

Darren said he would think about it. So much for irresistible
destiny, I thought, and went to sulk in my darkened flat. But the
next night, he turned up at my door. The deux-pièces was
habitually a mess, but that day it was particularly bad, with the
kitchen sloshing with dishes and what looked like the contents
of a dresser spilled all over the floor. Darren paid absolutely no
attention. He came in, swept T. S. Eliot and Ernest Hemingway
off my bed with a grand Swedish hand, adjusted the lonely lightbulb of my gooseneck lamp for maximum dramatic effect, and
waited for my full attention. He cleared his throat. Twice. Then
he said:

"All right. It's you. You can write my novel." At that instant
the lightbulb burst, leaving shattered glass everywhere. Darren
laughed softly, and he added, "Or do you think perhaps God
doesn't want you to write it?" A shard lay hot against my
trousers; I flicked it across the chair and onto the floor, where it
wouldn't burn anything.

"Well, Darren . . ." I said, in complete darkness. "Maybe

this is God's way of telling me No. But who knows what God wants?"

"I do," Darren said. He thought. "He's telling you to go ahead."

We really did say all those things, and that really did happen. At least—that's what I'm writing. *You* can believe what you want.

Certainly Darren was surprised when, much later, he read my description of our conversation that fateful night.

"Is *that* what I said?" he asked.

"Well, sort of," I said.

"Are you writing what we *really* said or what suits your purposes?"

"Both. Neither. I don't know—whatever sounds right."

He still looked puzzled. "But I am not that bossy. In fact, Philippe, I wasn't going to say anything at first, but now I must protest. You make me look like a—like a religious prophet."

"That is exactly what you are, Darren."

"No—no, no, no! I hate those sorts of people; I left those kinds of morons in Kansas. I'm not that way at all, I'm a Parisian. Look, Philippe. This is *my* novel. Yours has to be an honest portrayal."

"It *is* honest! It's honest because it's intense, more intense than real life."

"*Screw* intensity! Look: in that conversation we had, you were more positive about the project. *This* dialogue, the way you've written it, makes you look—overwhelmed."

"No, it doesn't, Darren." Then, reconsidering, I said, "Well, maybe it does. But the thing is, when you asked me, 'Do you think perhaps God doesn't want you to write it?' I immediately thought of when Gatsby asked Nick Carraway, 'What's your opinion of me, anyhow?' Nick was a little overwhelmed, and I thought as the narrator in my book I should be overwhelmed, too."

Darren looked completely befuddled. "But are you writing about *life* or about *literature*?" he asked.

"Life," I said. "*And* literature. I don't know. Both."

"Well," he said. "Can you write about . . . about *me* in a way that ties into literature, but subtly, delicately, so that it weaves right in?"

"That's what it's supposed to be about," I said.

"All right. Good."

That was *months* later. We really did have that conversation. Sort of.

And I wrote *that* months later. Darren hadn't arrived in Paris yet, and I was only looking at his photograph, in Jean-Baptiste's room, imagining him, while the bells of the Institut de France tinkled. Jean-Baptiste was on his bed, looking meditatively at the ceiling.

"When I introduced Darren to my friends," he was saying, "they thought he was extraordinary, unbelievable. They said, 'God, Jean-Baptiste, where did you find him?' "

At The Trap, was the answer, but Jean-Baptiste didn't say that. He merely shrugged and implied that his social connections were exalted, the natural result of elegant dressing and an excellent address on the Quai Malaquais. It *was* an excellent address, in a way: it was near The Trap. It was also near the Tuileries. Sort of. That's what I'm writing. You can believe what you like.

But Jean-Baptiste was talked about a lot more by Darren's friends than by his own. The reason was this: Darren had a lot more friends than Jean-Baptiste. Jean-Baptiste was so fastidiously correct he had driven away all his lycée friends but two, and he'd made no others. One was a girl who had been in love with him. When Jean-Baptiste had explained, politely, in a letter, that she was simply not his type—which, as it turned out, she wasn't, because she was a girl—she sent back a clipping torn out of a girly magazine and scribbled: "Here is your kind of girl, then. I'm sure she is in France somewhere. Good luck finding her. [signed] V——."

"A horrendous fag hag," Darren later called her. "A clumsy lamprey."

Jean-Baptiste's other friend was V——'s boyfriend. He'd written a long letter to Jean-Baptiste on the occasion of Jean-Baptiste's departure for Kansas—the time when Darren and Jean-Baptiste returned to Immaculatum for what was to be Darren's big homecoming to his family farm. Darren was to tell his parents he had been HIV-positive for six years and that he had perhaps three years to live.

Jean-Baptiste's friend Jean-C—— knew that, but he wrote a solemn letter telling Jean-Baptiste how to behave:

Well Jean-Baptiste, I do hope that you know what you are get-
ting into. Certainly since you have now come out, and have
decided to follow your friend Darren to Kansas, I can no longer
give you what I consider to be proper advice as to your behav-
iour; but I do counsel you, and I think I speak not only for
myself but for all of us and of course for V——, that you not
get carried away in the heat of passion and that you do practice
safe sex.

And so on.

Jean-C—— had been dating V—— for two years and, it seemed, had not yet slept with her.

"What a lot he knows about the heat of passion," Darren said, later.

And so on. I never met Jean-C—— nor V——. I did meet many of Darren's friends, particularly Marzenna and Francesco. Almost as soon as I had met them I decided they belonged in the novel.

"They do belong in the novel," Darren said later.

I agreed. I later showed portions of dialogue to Marzenna and Francesco, so they could make corrections. Marzenna protested when she saw the first line she spoke in the book.

"I didn't say *that*! I never would have said that. And besides, I'm not that elegant, Philippe."

"But you are, Marzenna. You have the admiration of everyone who meets you." She was easy to admire. Even Jean-Baptiste admired her—and she didn't at all look like the girl whose picture V—— had torn out of a girly magazine. Jean-Baptiste admired her so much he thought Marzenna was the one woman he would like to kiss.

"Too bad she's married," said Francesco, her husband.

"It would be the first person he's *ever* wanted to kiss," said Darren.

Jean-Baptiste had told me about that difficulty of his. Jean-Baptiste had never kissed anyone, anywhere—well, on the cheek, maybe.

"He's never committed a *single—sexual—act,*" Darren said. "All he does is sleep with people. Literally. *Sleep* with them," he repeated in disgust. "How can anyone just *sleep* with someone?"

"Well," I said, "Look at Jean-C——. He can't even sleep with V——."

Darren rolled his eyes. "I don't understand people like that."

"People like that don't understand *you*," I said.

During the course of writing the novel about Darren, I made a lot of outlines. The best outline, or at any rate the prettiest, was drawn with colored pencils on a sheet of bristol board. The paths of the main characters roared around on the page like the tracks of slot cars. Darren was orange, and when he went to Grenoble, he pulled away from the five other slot cars that were his family; then he joined them briefly, went to New York, partied, rejoined them briefly; then he returned to Paris, met me, and that's where the orange line made a loop-the-loop—it was supposed to be a self-referent novel.

" 'Self-referent novel'?" Darren asked me. He wasn't literary, but he was neither impressed nor incurious about the jargon I sometimes used.

"A novel that talks about itself," I said.

"You think that will make for a good story?" he asked.

Yes, I said; I said I thought it was even *branché*.

"Well," he said, "don't do anything just because it's fashionable. This is going to be a high-class novel, not just *branché*."

Being "plugged in" could have been one of Darren's strongest points. But he preferred quality over fashion at all times in his life. Not just in novels: but in cafés. One afternoon, while I was racing the slot cars of his life around on the bristol board, studying the albums of his photographs, and listening to the recorded monologues of his fortuneteller, Darren asked me to put the colored pencils aside to go try a new café he'd seen.

"Oh?" I said. "Which café is that?"

"Café Marly, in the Louvre. Let's see what it's like."

"Right *now*? I'm a little underdressed. I can't even fake being chic."

"Don't worry," he said.

"I'll feel like an idiot," I said.

"No you won't. You will not," he said.

But I *was* underdressed. My extra large sweat shorts had served duty in wrestling practices, and my sneakers had pounded miles of stadium turf. I wore a collared shirt in deference to Parisian sensibilities—though that collar was nearly frayed away.

"*Don't* worry," Darren repeated. "I can fake enough chic for the two of us." He laughed at that. It was a ridiculous thing to say, but it was also true. He wore a burgundy-colored corduroy suit that softly meandered round his body. It was also true I was wearing my sneakers without socks.

So in we went. Darren ascended the staircase leading to the terrace with imperial grandeur, looked around sniffingly, decided the inside might be better. From the outside you could see the glass pyramid of the Louvre and its mighty fountains roaring.

"Come," he said.

Inside, chairs seemed to have flowed into liquid shapes. Pretty people sat around molybdenum tables finished to a dull gray matte. Inside each table was a vase and inside each vase was a pure red rose. Vast windows commanded views of the Louvre's statuary. The walls were shiny black and blue with gilt *boiseries*. On a gleaming teak chest, pinned on their rosewood sticks, were up-to-the-minute editions of *Le Monde,* the *Times,* and *Die Welt.* A waiter in an impeccable white jacket noticed me. I tried to fit as much of my body as possible into my shirt, which too late I realized was not tucked in.

Completely insouciant, totally unaware of my exposed knees, Darren said, "Let's see the menu," and plucked it from a sleek mantelpiece. Even the roses seemed to be staring, but Darren read with as much concentration as if he were in a library.

"Not too bad," he finally announced. "Like to have a drink?"

"However you like," I said.

So we did. Darren went outside and chose a warm sunlit table. I sat so as to hide as much as I could of my shorts, sneakers, and calves under the table.

A waiter materialized next to us. *"Monsieur?"* he asked.

"Deux monacos," Darren said without looking up. The waiter saw him rolling what Darren called an Amsterdamer Special, which required a cigarette rolling machine, French paper, Dutch tobacco, and Jamaican weed.

"Oui monsieur." The waiter nodded crisply, turned, and shot through a velvet curtain, which billowed behind him.

"It's *very* nice," Darren said, taking a puff and stretching out like a cat in the sunlight.

"Yes," I said, feeling like an idiot.

"I like it quite a bit. No street noise."

That was true. The Café Marly was in the Cour Napoléon of the Louvre, so the only noise was the pleasantly roaring fountains around the pyramid. Motorcars seemed miles away.

"The *provinciaux* like it," he said, and blew smoke towards two ladies behind me. He showed such scorn for those ferociously overdressed provincials that he made *me* feel chic for dressing like a slob. I thought I might let them see one of my bare knees.

"I *like* it," Darren repeated.

"It's full of interesting people," I said.

"Oh yes."

"You'll meet someone here," I said.

"I hope so. Well—I know I will. The question is, will I like him? Will he like me?"

"Prince Charming?" I asked. "Of course he will. It'll be love at first sight. It'll be a fairy tale."

Darren had a fantasy—a very precise fantasy about his own Prince Charming. In the novel that I was going to write about him, I told him the climax would be the fulfillment of his fantasy. But I didn't exactly know what the fantasy was, yet, or even what the fantasy man was like, and I had to know what he was like before I could put him in the book.

"The fantasy man . . ." Darren inhaled thoughtfully. *"Garçon!"*

The garçon bearing the two Monacos rushed past us absentmindedly. Darren looked disgusted, and made sure the overdressed ladies saw him.

"What an idiot," he said.

I pulled out a little brown notebook and warmed up my fountain pen—the one I am using to write this, months later.

The waiter came back.

Darren asked in a hurt tone, *"Vous m'avez oublié?"*

"Non, monsieur. Bien sûr que non."

"A little confusion, perhaps."

"Very little, monsieur. Don't you know—it happens *even* to us. *Even* here," he said, with a wry smile. He put down the drinks and the bill.

The Monacos looked delightful. Overhead I saw a full moon in the blue sky. I held one up and looked at the pyramid through a rose-colored glass.

"Thank you, Darren. *A ta santé.*"

"*A la tienne.* A pleasure."

"Your fantasy, now."

"Yes. Now the fantasy man is about thirty-five, maybe forty, good-looking, masculine. From a *big* family. Titled, probably. Certainly old, old money. Speaks French but also very good English. *Hôtel* in the *seizième.* Gay, of course, and also HIV-positive, but his family doesn't know a thing. And I'm the one—I'm the one who gets called in to break the news to everybody."

I wrote everything down, using the fountain pen I am still using to write these words. I did not smile.

"Well," I said, "I think meeting him, and telling everything to his family, should be the climax of the book."

"Um," he said.

"Don't you think so?"

"That's your business, not mine."

I was supposed to be the expert in climaxes and narrative techniques and allusions and all that. Darren said the "technical aspects" of the book, as he called them, were mine to handle. But the novel about Darren was my first novel, and I wasn't sure I knew more about how to write a novel than he did. I originally wanted to tell the story from the point of view of Jean-Baptiste; and the results would have been very different.

THE MOST INCREDIBLE PERSON I KNOW
by Jean-Baptiste Duvet

Darren Swenson is the most incredible person I know. We met in November 1992. We met in this horribly sordid bar, which I won't talk about. But when I saw him I froze in place. I knew at *that* second he was the man of my life.

We talked all night, and it was a very special relationship from the very start. He was a father figure. I wanted to spend all my time with him.

I decided to go with him to Kansas. He had to visit his parents. They already knew he was gay, because when he came home for Thanksgiving in 1988 he told them. But what he didn't tell them was that he already had AIDS. That January he was going back to Kansas to tell them everything—and he was taking me along. I was 21 years old. He was 29. When we showed up on the big farm porch, with me beside him, his father said:

"What the HAIL is John-Batiste doin' HERE?"

And so on.

Years later, after Darren died, I received a phone call. It was Darren.

"*Salut* Philippe!" he said.

"Darren?!"

"Hi!"

"What—what—what?!"

"Where do you think I'm calling from? I'm calling from heaven. I'm using a pay phone. My old AT&T calling card *still* works!"

"Christ, Darren—"

"The connection's great, isn't it?"

"What?!"

"Relax. It's me."

I showed that passage to Darren at Café Marly, and he read it and read it again. He wasn't sure about it at first. Then that night he burst into tears thinking about it. He decided we should prolong it.

"How's your fantasy coming along?" I asked him.

"Fan-TAS-tic. I live in a château now." He was giddy.

"With who? What's his name?" I couldn't believe I was talking to him.

"Oh, Philippe, he's incredible. His name is Laurent de Saint-Satyre."

"Well well. Darren strikes gold again."

"I can't believe it. It's too good for words. He's *so* handsome. And he's got such a *big*—"

"I know," I said. "How is heaven? I guess you don't have to worry about AIDS anymore, huh?"

"Oh, you do."

"What?!"

"It's just like earth. The thing is, you won't be happy as a human being if you're in a blob of amber. You'll never be happy if you're immortal. So it's all out here: diseases, war, the whole bit."

I let out a breath of total shock and outrage. My lips moved; I tried saying various things; I couldn't say anything.

"There's supposed to be another heaven after this. But it's more of the same, only better. Actually, that's what this heaven is like: more of the same, only better."

"Better what?" I managed to say.

"Better moments. Better appreciation. The higher you go, the more you appreciate, I think. Real heaven is when you're really sensitive to everything around you. Hold it—wait—is the connection breaking? I—"

Then of course the connection broke. You can only talk to heaven once in a blue moon, looking through a rose-colored glass.

I showed that passage to Darren. He liked it, and said we should put it in the novel. Then he took another sip of his Monaco. He hailed the waiter, who was young and good-looking.

"Would you mind if I asked you a question?" Darren asked.

"No monsieur, of course not."

"What time do you open?"

"Oh, well, eight, eight-thirty; depends on how spiffy we are. We are always ready by a quarter to nine, you can count on us for that."

"Grand. I can have breakfast here, can't I? How much is it? Is it expensive?"

"For a man such as you? No, not at all. A trifle. Eighty francs."

"How very reasonable."

"Sir, in all Paris you could not find a better way to uselessly blow eighty francs first thing in the morning."

"Grand. You are terribly kind. Thank you."

"It is nothing. But I want you here, tomorrow, first thing. And don't forget your cigarettes," the waiter said, striding away.

Darren beamed at me. "Isn't this *great*?" he said.

"This is *great* stuff," Darren said, looking over what I have written. He read exactly what you are reading now, sort of. "But it hops around a lot," he added.

"I know, Darren, but that's how *you* tell stories. When you tell me about your life, you don't describe everything that's happened in strictly chronological order, do you?"

"No, I guess not." He still looked puzzled. "But do you think the readers will follow it?"

"Darren, if you can follow it, and if it pleases you, and if it pleases me, then what else matters?"

"The fame," he said.

"The prestige," I said.

"The *money*," we both said, together, understanding each other and laughing like schoolboys.

Darren said, "I think we should call somebody, get a bit of dialogue in."

"Who do you want to talk to?"

"Jean-Baptiste?"

"You *always* want to talk to Jean-Baptiste."

Darren and Jean-Baptiste met when Darren was already dying—well, in this book we were *all* already dying, but Darren was already dying in a very visible way. By December 1992 Darren had lost sixty pounds. Even more annoying for him, his libido had disappeared; he didn't feel the desire to *do* it with anybody anymore. His going to The Trap was kind of like a kid going to a candy store without any money, hoping that someone would give him something for free. But one night, Darren did get something for free: Jean-Baptiste, who adored him instantly. They never made love, so their relationship settled into something like father and son. Darren didn't want to make love. Or rather, he did want to, but he couldn't want it badly enough. His sick biology did not want sex. It was a case of not really wanting what he thought he should have wanted.

And then there was Jean-Baptiste's peculiar style of sexuality: the kind that never commits sexual acts. So their relationship was not physical: aside from a few nights they spent no more sexually than a boy sleeping with his father because of night-mares. Despite Darren's scorn for such things, they only *slept* together. Darren considered his friendship with Jean-Baptiste extraordinary, as if Jean-Baptiste were really his son. He was quite mystical about it. I asked him about his mysticism.

"All you have to do to become really mystical," he liked to say, "is to get AIDS."

Of course, at that time, when I was writing the novel, Darren was thirty and Jean-Baptiste was twenty-two. Jean-Baptiste sometimes acted, mystical relationship or not, like an impulsive adolescent looking for that special something. Shortly after I started writing the novel, which was shortly after I met Jean-Baptiste, Jean-Baptiste left for Australia. He had been plan-ning the move since before we had met, and it was a permanent move, he said, although I didn't believe it. Nor did I believe it was a "proof of strength," as he had pompously called it. He went there to try to settle down with a forty-something-year-old man fabulously in love with him. The forty-something-year-old man was so fabulously in love with him he had bought a do-it-yourself hair lightening kit, and so inept he had turned his entire scalp bright orange.

"What a queen! *What—a—fag!!*" Darren said, later.

Darren had immense dislike for queens, queers, dressed-up hysterical fags, transvestites, transsexuals, and everything except for what he called a "normal gay man." He probably never real-ized to what extent he, as a member of a minority, was unsym-pathetic towards other minorities. Or rather, he *did* realize it, after he read that passage you have just read.

"Am I really that bad?"

"Almost. But at least we know what you like."

"I'm just awful. All I want are big beefy boys with *big—*"

"I know," I said.

Later the subject came up again.

"Why do you suppose I'm such a size queen?" he asked. "Why is that?"

"Farm life?"

"Can't be—" he said, with what appeared to be incredulity. But then his face melted into an absolute smirk, as if he had just asserted his membership in the society of those who came to sex hard and fast. "Do you think we should mention my earliest experiences in the book?"

"Your *earliest* experiences? What, with Alex and the boys?"

"No, even before that. With the baby calves."

"With the baby calves. Well. I certainly think it's a funny story."

"I'm not sure I can put it in," Darren said.

"I'm sure that's what you told Alex. Well, I say put it in. As long as you put it in with good taste."

"I'm not sure you can talk about things like that in good taste."

"Oh yes you can," I said. "You can talk about anything in good taste. Just because you guys were leaving sheep children all over the landscape—things with one hand and one hoof— doesn't make it vulgar."

Darren laughed so hard he closed his eyes. I laughed too. Baby calves were obviously one of those farm things you sometimes did and never mentioned. I'd never had sexual relations with an animal, and I had no idea what it was like. The closest I ever came was reading a description of a woman attempting sexual intercourse with a Shetland pony. And that was two degrees removed—quite tame, really, next to what this former farm boy had seen and done.

"Fourteen years old, wild to couple. Oh well," I said.

Oh, well. I decided to put it in, but not mention any details.

CHAPTER 2

In my younger and more vulnerable years my rugby coach
gave us some advice I've remembered ever since. He used to
give this advice to the entire team on the pitch, during a
game, just after we'd score a try.

"Bears, the score is *still* zero-zero. Get in there and score for
the first time."

Our coach did *not* like complacency. Of course, at the end of
the game he really did rack up all the points, and we really won,
because we weren't complacent, and our points did add up.

So when Darren asked me how I would start the second
chapter of the novel about him, I said, "The score is still zero-
zero." And he would have had to read the second chapter to
understand, as you will. He read almost exactly what you are
reading. Almost.

It worried Darren, a little, that this was my first novel. I'd
written a long poem and a play, and I wasn't complacent about
them; Darren wasn't complacent either, sitting underneath the
immense sunlit arches of the Café Marly, gazing at the plumes of
water-smoke that surrounded the glass pyramid in the court of
the Louvre, but he was happy, and maybe a little too comfort-

able. I had read him the first chapter, which I had just written, and he was surprised and delighted. That was his first reaction. Now, at Café Marly, he was having his second reaction. Things that hadn't rung absolutely true the first time were turning very dissonant very fast.

"It's too gay," he said.

"What? The whole chapter?"

"Yes, it's entirely too gay," he said.

I paused. I held my breath. I clenched my teeth. I looked at the table and tried to smile. It came out all crooked.

" 'It's too gay,' " I repeated.

"Don't you think so?"

"Quite honestly, that's the last criticism I expected to hear, from you."

"But look, Philippe. Jean-Baptiste isn't homosexual, and that's what you make him out to be. You said: 'If it isn't true, it doesn't belong in the book. The only thing that matters is that the whole book feel true.' That's *what—you—said.*"

"Well, Darren. He *did* sleep with you. He *did* declare himself a homosexual. He may be wrong, but he *did* say it. He wants everyone to think he's a homosexual, so can I be blamed for thinking that? Can I? I don't want to hear any more of it, Darren. *I'm* writing this book, not you."

Darren looked at me. He looked at the faraway fountain spreading its white plume in the sky. Then he looked down at his cigarette-rolling machine.

"All right," he said. "Excuse me. I'm leaving. You can figure it out. Do what you like."

And he got up and left.

No, he didn't.

That's what would have happened if we were living life like Neal Cassady and Jack Kerouac in Denver: but we weren't. What actually happened was this.

Darren said: "It's entirely too gay."

And I said: "What?"

And he said: "I don't want it to be a 'gay' novel. I want it to be about other things. There's so much to bring out, other dimensions of my life, and you haven't touched upon them at all."

And I said nothing. I took a deep breath.

Darren continued: "I mean, don't you think so? Isn't that what you want? You don't want a gay novel, right?"

And I thought: Well, I've used every trick I know to keep all the gayness I could out of the book. But it does seem difficult to write a non-gay novel about someone as gay as *you*, Darren.

But what I said was this: "Well, I can change certain things."

"Like what?"

"Like Jean-Baptiste."

"Make him less gay?"

"Yes."

"Okay?"

"All right?"

"Yes."

There was a silence. He saw I was upset. I saw he saw, and he saw that.

So we apologized to each other, for the rest of the afternoon. Our first argument was a draw. At least, that's what I say it was: you can believe what you want.

Darren liked the rugby idea because he had once played rugby himself. He had been a star athlete in high school, had won the Most Valuable Player award in football, had set the high school record in the shot put (a record that still stands today), and in college, had recruited the biggest, burliest, best-looking football players into his fraternity. The fraternity loved him at first. They voted him most outstanding citizen, made him an officer, and Darren was a big hit at all the parties. They were about to elect him president when they found out he was gay, and threw him out.

Oh, well. It was a hard blow, but Darren pulled himself up by his bootstraps. He must have told himself, start over: zero-zero.

He had learned to play rugby his junior year abroad, in Grenoble. He showed me the photos. They were impressive. Darren was an impressive-looking youth, with big strong arms and a neck as thick as a bull's.

"You can't imagine what he was like, Philippe . . . he was *baraqué*," I could hear Jean-Baptiste saying, while I was looking at the photographs.

Darren had always played football and the other varieties of our nervous, sporadic games. Grenoble was his smooth introduction to the uninterrupted fluidity of a European forty-minute half. It was like trading a bouncy bumpy speedboat for the languor of a ninety-foot yacht. He found he loved it.

"When I arrived in Europe," he said, "it was like discovering where I really belonged." We were in my room when he said that, in my deux-pièces in Saint-Germain-des-Prés. It was an ideal flat for a writer. There was a bed and a desk, and the desk was bigger than the bed.

"Did you love it from the very start?" I asked, taking notes in my little brown notebook.

"There was love from the start. But there was great difficulty too. I had to persuade Professor Flewelling to send me to France, even though I could barely speak French. I only started learning when I was nineteen, and at twenty I wanted to go. It was an incredible year. When I got on the plane to return, I remember hoping it would be hijacked, so that I could stay in France.

"But of course it wasn't. And so I arrived in Kansas. And that was my first homecoming party. All the aunts were there. All the uncles were there. Wayne the Pain and Marge the Barge were there."

"Wayne the Pain?"

"And his wife Marge the Barge."

"Should I take notes?"

"Yes. This is a good story. Wayne and Marge owned this lakeside house in the Ozarks. Every year they went waterskiing. One year he was towing Marge around in the lake and she capsized. There was this other boat that was right behind, and I guess the driver was drunk, because he ran right over her. And then—he circled and I guess he didn't see her, or was *really* drunk, because he ran over her *again*."

Darren was laughing his head off. So was I. It was a lousy thing to laugh at, but we felt lousy: Darren felt lousy for having such relations, and I felt lousy for Darren.

"So from then on she walked dragging her foot behind her, like a barge. Anyway, they decided they wanted to See Yurop. This was when I was in Grenoble, so I went to meet them when they arrived in Amsterdam. They were going to tour

Amsterdam, Bruges, Cologne, Heidelberg, Interlaken, Luxembourg, and Paris—in eight days. And when we met them at the airport—I was with Patti and Ward—Wayne the Pain had a huge cowboy hat, cowboy boots, a pipe in his mouth, and they were dressed in Wal-Mart from head to toe. She wore polyester floral.

"And Wayne saw me at the same time I saw him. And he said, 'Darren, how the hell arya!' And I said, 'Ah'm great!' Ward and Patti, who were with me in Grenoble, just stared. They just *stared*. Ward was a nice refined Georgetown boy and Patti had been in Europe for a year. And then there was Wayne the Pain and Marge the Barge, plucked straight out of Kansas.

"First I had to check them into a respectable hotel. Ward and Patti and I were going to the youth hostel—which was a huge pot palace, you could smell it as you walked in—but I thought that Uncle Wayne and Marge were slightly more re-*fined*. I found a one-star hotel on a canal. Then Wayne saw his room. And then he said—I swear—'Are all the hotel rooms in Yurop so *small*? And so *expensive*?' And I was just about to let him *have* it and then Patti—thank God—said, 'Actually, Wayne, you're very lucky. Darren bargained for you downstairs. Isn't that great?' And then he asked me, 'Did ya, Darren?' And I said, 'Yes.' And then he apologized in his huge hefty way. 'Ah'm sorry, Darren. Didn' mean ta hurt yer feelings. But the room is so awful small, compared ta America. Marge, this must be what they call *culture shock*.' And she said, 'Yep.' "

Darren was still laughing. I was laughing and trying to take notes at the same time; it was hard. Darren went on.

"But the best was yet to come. Years later, when I got back from Paris, they found that dear Darren was a 'gay-boy' and HIV-positive. And they said, 'Well, and after his folks put him through school, and made all those sacrifices. Look what he's done to 'em now. Just one more slap in the face.' After I had put *myself* through school, thank you. Then Pete, my brother-in-law, had Hodgkin's disease, so there were two sick boys in the family. Wayne sent a long letter telling us 'how sorry we are to hear that Pete's got this terrible disease' and so on. Not a word about Darren. Darren didn't exist." He looked at the floor. "Dear Uncle Wayne. Oh, he was one obnoxious bastard."

I reclined in the chair, and sighed. "God," I said, "should I put that in the book?"

"What—about Wayne the Pain?"

"The whole thing. But especially the way you finish off. I'm looking at my notes, and they say, 'Oh, he was one obnoxious bastard.' Should that go in?"

"It's strong, isn't it?" Darren asked me.

"But it's true."

"But it wasn't, Philippe, not really. Wayne called up when I was staying in Kansas and he asked me how I was. I guess his conscience overpowered his Tuff Kansin Morls. He called and said, 'At least yer home eatin' all that great food!! You'll be able to put on some weight!!' And me ready to vomit.

"But his heart was in the right place. Just a little small."

I kept on scribbling and scribbling in my notepad.

"You were saying," I said, "about your homecoming. You know, the novel is structured around your three homecomings, and this is the first."

"Well, structure and all that is your business."

"So what happened, at the homecoming from Grenoble?"

"Well"—Darren took a puff from an Amsterdamer Special—"there was this huge family reception; all my relatives were there, including Wayne and Margie. Wayne kept saying, 'Eat all yer mom's great food, Darren!!' And she was asking, 'What about the *culture shock*?' I had just come back from staying with the Sansons, and we had been eating good, healthy French food all year. And then my mother brought out this huge vat of country deep-fried chicken. Philippe, there was grease everywhere. The bottom of the pan was a puddle of lard. And everyone just reached in with their hands and just started tearing away the food with their teeth. I felt like I wanted to vomit. Grease—mastication—saliva. Blergkh."

I looked up from my notes.

"You don't like your mother's cooking very much, do you?"

"*Not* really."

I thought hard about what I was going to say next.

"And you don't like your *mother* very much, do you?"

Darren looked at nothing.

"Darren, do you hate your mother?"

Darren said nothing.

"All right," I said under my breath.

Darren sighed, and he began, "Philippe, my mother is this four-hundred-pound monster who does nothing but sit all day in her chair. You saw the pictures."

I had.

"She spends *forty* dollars a week on *cigarettes*. She drinks coffee from morning till night. She—" Darren looked around helplessly, searching for the expression, the anecdote, that would illustrate.

"Sometimes she gets up from the table—she gets up, she takes a couple of steps away, and then she farts. Right in front of everybody. When I was in Kansas she told everyone, 'Come visit Darren, before he dies.' Now, Philippe, that's the kind of mother I have." He was desperate and a little angry I'd made him say such a thing.

Okay, Darren, I thought, I'll say nothing.

In conversation at Café Marly the next day, Darren asked me how I'd written up that story.

"Wayne the Pain and Marge the Barge? I just went from memory and my notes."

"You changed a lot from the first draft."

"That's true. A lot of it was sweet but unnecessary. Like Fitzgerald. On the other hand, I got rid of all the allusions, which is too bad."

"I wish I understood all these allusions," Darren said.

"Don't worry, old sport."

"What?"

"Don't worry. You're worth the whole lot of them put together."

I thought it was my obligation to keep him confident and bubbly all the time, like the huge fountain behind the Café Marly that spewed and spewed water into the air.

Darren asked me, "How do you—when you're writing, how do you know how to write dialogue? Like in this passage, you say, 'Darren was laughing his head off.' How do you decide to put that in?"

"Well, *I* was laughing when I was writing that paragraph. I was laughing so hard I was having trouble *writing*. I wrote that sentence to calm myself down."

"And you say, 'I reclined in the chair.' Did you really recline at that moment, when I told you the story in reality?"

"I don't remember. I *did* recline when I finished that paragraph, and I didn't know what to say next, so I wrote what I had just done: 'I reclined.' Then there were all the pauses when I got up and went to the kitchen, but you can't notice those, I think."

And I reclined in my chair, in my quiet deux-pièces in Saint-Germain-des-Prés. I wondered what Darren would think when I showed him the imaginary conversation we were going to have in twenty-four hours, near the roaring fountains of the Café Marly.

By now I had a fairly good idea of how I wanted to structure my novel about Darren. I had decided to write it from his point of view, and in the first person: "I, Darren Swenson, was born . . ." and so forth, and I thought it would be divided into twelve chapters. Multiples of three were his homecomings: so chapter three, homecoming from K.U. in 1982; chapter six, from Grenoble in 1985; chapter nine, from New York for Thanksgiving in 1988; and chapter twelve, from Paris in 1993. Chapter seven would be the mystical, spiritual chapter. I needed material for that chapter and so when Darren proposed that I accompany him to see Rosita, his tarot card reader, I agreed to go.

Rosita Sosostris was perhaps the best tarot card reader in Paris, and she liked Darren; he had seen her twice, and she had refused all payment both times. Darren and I took a taxicab to see her. The taxi driver was very nice.

"Excuse me, monsieur," Darren asked as we roared down the quais with the massive glass domes of the Grand Palais off to our right, "do you mind if we eat in your car?"

"Not at all!" he said.

"How nice," Darren said to me. We wolfed sandwiches we had bought on the rue de Buci. Darren, as always, had paid for both of us.

"Thank you," I said.

I thought, is it possible to write objectively about someone who treats you to breakfast, lunch, and dinner?

Is it possible to write objectively?

I thought about that as we turned right into the Place de la Concorde. We flew through, hearing the rubbery sound the pavestones make under turning wheels. My mind was working on how to put the fortuneteller in the story—Rosita, the Parisian tarot card reader. Darren opened the window and the wind roared in. I watched the stately columns of the Hôtel Crillon glide by. The marble seemed to glow from within; you could see the sevenbranched candelabra, and the yellow artificial flames flicker. Then we drove up the uncertain half-deserted streets (for it was August) towards the chic area around l'Opéra. Finally we were there. It was a handsome building, all dressed up for the belle époque. Darren paid the taxi driver, who thanked him heartily for the tip. It was easy to make friends in France, and Darren certainly knew how.

We walked through a little door which was cut into the frame of a larger door. The hallway was dark and damp. At the doorbell's ringing, a little woman appeared. She was dressed all in black and her short hair hugged her skull. She smiled at both of us.

"*Bonjour, Darren,*" she said.

They touched hands and he introduced me. She held out her hand, and I took it; her touch was very, very soft.

We went in. Incense burned, and the perfumed smoke rose lazily into the coffered ceiling. The candlesticks were dull bronze. It was dark. There were glinting reflections everywhere.

I palpated my blazer pocket, which held my notebook. I whispered to Darren, "Should I take notes?" Rosita was showing the previous visitor out.

Darren shook his head.

So I didn't. So I paid extra attention; I knew I would have to write later from memory only.

I sat down on the couch, moving aside weird and holy books to make room for myself. Pictures of animals decorated the room, and shadows swam in the unreal light. On the walls were giant reproductions of the cards of the tarot: Force, the Moon, the Sun, the Emperor. I was looking for the Card with No Name when Rosita came in.

"How are you, Darren?" she asked again.

"I am extraordinarily well."

"I'm pleased to hear that," she said.

She drew the mystical cards from underneath the table.

"Now. What are you here to see me about?" she asked.

"Well, I have come to ask you about several things."

I looked at him, then at her. She did not take her eyes off Darren. He sat up in the high-backed chair, and drew a breath.

"Could you tell me about my physical health?"

I pressed my lips together.

"Your physical health," she repeated. "Draw seven cards, please." She spread them out in front of him, face down. Darren's finger hovered over the center of the pack, then began swooping down on cards. She pulled them out and flipped them over before her, working from the center outwards, and calling out their names.

"The Tower of Destruction, upside down. Death. Force. The Lady. The Pope. The Hanged Man, upside down. The Star. This is good news, Darren. Death here signifies a change, a change for the better. You were very sick last year, were you not? You told me you had problems; your doctor—Doctor Daly, was it not?—said that you were so dehydrated when you arrived at the hospital you nearly died. But you didn't. I see great changes ahead. The Tower of Destruction upside down represents a *métamorphose* of your life. The Star. That is hope, Darren. Hope for change, a positive striving, moving upwards out of your sphere to where you want to go. Where do you want to go?"

"I want to live," said Darren.

"You will be born again. I see a renaissance. Force. The Lady. I see the presence of a maternal figure. I see maternal love, allied with spiritual and worldly advantages. This will be confusing: you have been too long without a positive maternal figure. This will change. It is a change for the better. I see solitude in your past, change in your future. The Hanged Man represents you in the present. You are upside down and will be righted."

"Philippe"—Darren said, lifting a hand to indicate me but still looking in her direction—"has been a strong protective figure. He's been very maternal, taking care of me, encouraging me. Is that it?"

Rosita smiled at him. She didn't look at me.

"Stronger," she said. "Give me another question." She slapped the cards into a long drawn-out fan.

Darren looked at her. He hesitated, and then began, "Philippe is writing a book. It's a book about my life. What we'd like to know is—is how the book will turn out, what the prospects are for the book."

"The prospects for your book? Very well. Seven cards, please."

Darren drew the cards out as before.

"The Lovers. The Moon. The Hermit, upside down. The Fool. The Magician. The Wheel of Fortune. The Emperor. These three upside down. Very strong worldly cards, Darren. Fame, prestige, and money." She smiled; Darren smiled; even I smiled, alone in my corner. "But the lovers at the center, and right side up. This is the bond between you and Philippe, a very strong spiritual bond. It is at the center of the book; this is good news. And look! Here on the card of the Moon, which is also right side up, are two dogs, together howling at the moon, at the heavens, a spiritual presence. This is you and him, together. There are pairs everywhere, here. The Magician and the Hermit; these are natural complements. This represents the act of writing: in the Hermit much solitude, much; and the wizardry of writing in this, the Magician. And look! They are upside down together. Now the Wheel of Fortune. This represents health, the accumulation of power, the playing of wagers. The Emperor, he crowns this set of cards; he is the fulfillment of your worldly desires. This is good fortune, Darren," she told him.

"Good!" Darren said.

"But as I said, at the center of the book is the relationship between you—and you—together." She indicated me, with a hand gesture more felt than seen. "Now, your next question. Ask me what you wish to know."

"My next question has to do with Jean-Baptiste."

"Ah yes! Jean-Baptiste. How is he?"

"He's fine. He's doing well. He's leaving us, soon."

This was shortly before Jean-Baptiste had moved, permanently he said, to Australia.

"What do you wish to know about him?" she asked.

"How do you see our relationship? How should I treat him? You know our bond has become increasingly spiritual. I'm the father figure he's been looking for. He's like a son to me now."

"I know. I know." She looked down at the cards meditatively. I thought of Jean-Baptiste, spending the evening with the photograph album.

"Seven cards, please." She put her hand on each end of the little table and watched him intently.

Darren drew out the cards and she began flipping them immediately. They shone under the lamplight.

"The Sun. The Chariot, upside down. The Empress, Temperance, both upside down. And upside down, the Tower of Destruction. The Fool. The Hanged Man. Great changes; great changes, Darren; things will not be as they were before. The Sun is the card of growth, of maturation, of pushing upwards and outwards. It is the force that shoots the seeds from their sockets, drops the fruit from the tree. It is life, moving outwards and pushing onwards to create more life. The Chariot: voyages, trips to far-flung places. The Empress: the world. Temperance, upside down: this is no temperance; this is sudden decisions, quick movements. I see travel. For you, it has already happened. You have come to Paris. For him, it is just beginning. You must let him go, Darren. You are the bow that shoots forth the arrow. He is the arrow, and he must fly. He is a fool, too, as you can see"—she pointed out the card before him—"but a fool must go his own willful way. The Tower upside down augurs changes, but they are changes for the better. The Sun is at the center. Let him go, Darren. He must go to grow."

Darren looked at the cards. I looked at the sibyl. She looked at Darren.

"Is that all right?" she asked. "Is that what you expected?"

"Yes, it sounds right," he said. "My whole life is full of changes. My health, this book—and now this."

"Life is always changing, Darren. It is only when you die that change stops. You look well."

"I'm better than I was before, don't you think?"

"Before you left for Kansas? I should say. There was nothing but gloom there. You look better. You feel better, I wager."

"I do. Can I ask you one last question?"

"Yes, of course."

"Can I ask you about my spiritual health?"

"Your spiritual health? You're fine, Darren. You're f—" She caught herself telling the future without the aid of the cards. Then she smiled at him. "I don't need to look at cards to tell you that. You look well. You are well. Your friend will write the book, and you will live your life."

She stood up.

"Could I pay you?" Darren asked, placing a large note on the table.

"Oh no, Darren. That's far too much. I'll take half and that will be plenty." She changed the note and showed us to the door.

There was a tall English-looking gentleman wearing pin-stripes and glasses behind the door, resting on a furled umbrella, waiting.

"Bonjour, madame," he said, with an execrable accent.

She acknowledged him with a smile.

Darren said good-bye; so did I. She stepped back; the gentleman looked at me with a backward half-look, and then she closed the door on them both.

"Was he American, or British?" Darren asked me.

"I have no idea," I said.

We walked down together towards the Champ de Mars.

All that was a month ago. Today I wrote what you have just read, and tomorrow Darren and I will go to the Champ de Mars again. We'll see the immense pylons of the Tour Eiffel anchored in the ground, the intricately wound latticework and wire. It'll be a hot day and we'll lounge in the shade.

"How did you remember all the cards Rosita pulled out? Or did you make them all up?" Darren will ask me.

"I made them all up. I chose what I wanted. So I wasn't playing with a full deck, I'm afraid."

"I do remember that business when she started telling me about my health even before she looked at the cards."

"Oh, she did better than that."

"What?"

"I'll tell you later," I will say.

And Darren will ask, "When you write, do you try to actually reproduce what we said?"

"How should I know? I'm not writing this book. *You* are. Because *you* are living it."

And Darren will say, "I am? We *both* are." The pivotal point of our friendship: something will click.

At least, that's what's scheduled to happen.

When Darren saw what was scheduled to happen tomorrow, he said, "That's *great!*"

"You like it, really?" I asked.

"It's fan–TAS–tic," Darren said. "I'm so pleased with what you're doing. I am very, very pleased."

I liked to hear him say that. If I wasn't going to dedicate the novel about Darren to my father, I would dedicate it to Darren. He needed it as much as anybody, except perhaps myself.

"Do you think," Darren asked, "Rosita actually reads what's in the cards, or . . . what?"

I let out a breath of amazement. "Well, Darren," I began. "I think it's fair to say she says what you need to hear."

"But do you think the cards can be read objectively?"

"Darren, listen to this trick she did. At one point she turned over the card of Death. But she immediately covered it with her hand and told your whole fortune with the six other cards."

"You won't say she did that in the book, though."

"I *do* say it. Sort of."

I thought, Rosita was wrong for trying to hide the card of Death. Death is a good card to pull out for someone looking for objective truth. No matter how your life is going, you can expect to get involved with death at some point. In fact, death had already gotten involved with one of Darren's friends: John Leadman, or *Dead* John as we called him. *Dead* John became a kind of pep-talk phrase between the two of us.

"Oh, well," I'd say. "We're all going the way of John."

"*Dead* John," we would say together, and laugh.

John Leadman had been Darren's best friend, and, it seems, had given him AIDS. Not on purpose: nobody gave someone else AIDS on purpose, except the Devil, but he was one character I wanted to keep for later in the book. *Dead* John, like a good many well-educated self-made Wall Street whiz kids, refused to believe that he could do anything wrong, or even get sick or slow down. So he behaved as if he were immortal. He didn't know, and he didn't want to know, either. When Darren told him they were both HIV-positive, John said no, no, it couldn't be.

"I'm pretty sure it was him," Darren told me. "But it would've happened to me eventually. I was getting it left and right. And I knew what I was doing; I knew the risks I was taking. But I was just obsessed by sex then."

I believed that about Darren. Before he became too ill to want it, sex was the one holy and important thing in life, although he had to sweat and curse to make a living and so on. Darren did eventually manage to combine work and sex, but only much later.

And as for getting sick, Darren said: it was destiny. He was going to get it, as surely as the sun sets in the evening.

"All this talk of free choice," he said in disgust. "Makes me want to vomit; worse than greasy chicken. What can I choose, really? Can I choose when and where I was born? How I grew up? And doesn't everything kind of follow from those things? If things had been different in the past, then things might be different in the future. But you can't control the past; you can't even repeat it. Don't you think so?"

What I said was: "I have no idea. Perhaps."

What I thought was: I do not know. How free are we? Can we control the past? Even in the present, can we be free? When our psyches force us to haunt the streets, the bars, the parties, the silent beaches, the deserted neighborhoods where nothing grows, the stinking quais where the streetlights blaze, all to seek the one truly holy love affair—until we find it, are we free, at all?

Darren had been looking for the one truly holy love affair his whole life, ever since he charmed (even at fourteen he was charming) a baby calf into providing non-dairy services. Of course, he couldn't fall in love with a baby calf, but, as it turns out, he couldn't fall in love with anybody, except his fantasy man.

"I have never found true love. And you know why not?

Because I have always refused to compromise my standards," he said.

He obviously hoped I would congratulate him. Instead I stared hard at him. "Your standards are not the reason," I said.

"They're not?" he asked. "What is?"

I thought about what I was going to say. "Love," I said, "breaks whatever standards you care to set. And besides," I added, "you should talk about all the friends who've fallen in love with *you*."

Darren would have liked to talk to one of those friends, perhaps to Dead John, to see what falling in love was like, but John Leadman was dead. For John, who had been born into poverty, who had put himself through high school and two expensive degrees, who had grown up calculating everything just to survive, the love he had for Darren was as close to true love as he ever got. Then he died.

When the good-looking and doomed (we are all doomed, but John was particularly doomed in this story) John and Darren spent Christmas in a secluded cottage in 1987, John made dinner.

"When I saw the main course, I about *died*," said Darren. "John had taken the meat dish straight out of a can. But the wine was very, very good. It was a wonderful Margaux with overtones of walnuts and a gorgeous, silken finish. It made you want to have a good time. You lost all your inhibitions and threw caution to the winds."

After the meaty dinner they went to the Christmas bed and Made Love. It was fabulous, Darren said. It felt like something was beginning—and it was.

After writing that story, I made yet another outline of my novel about Darren. This time it was a kind of geometrical drawing with boxes inside of boxes and arrows pointing everywhere to show the hierarchy and compartmentalization of a self-referent novel. Then I threw it away. I was getting worried about my lack of outline; I had no idea how to begin this novel about Darren, let alone how to end it. So I gave up on outlines for a while and went to listen to music at the Virgin Megastore, which is ten minutes from where I live. Listening to music I broke down and cried in the store, but I had a handkerchief, so I was all right. But I did feel badly about Darren. That evening when we went over the text of Rosita's visit I said, "Darren, I'm sorry for the foolish grievance I held against you yesterday after-noon."

And he said, "Don't worry. I believe in you."

We really did say that to each other.

Sort of.

CHAPTER 3

Darren Swenson had once been shot-put champion of his high school. That title meant a lot to him, then; now, not so much. He had since put it into its proper place, and generally forgot it. He did not forget, however, the feeling of praise, of greatness, of having been the best in the world at something.

"When you're sixteen," he said, "the *world* is your little high school, your family. The farm. The chores."

But even then Darren knew there was more to life than that. In 1978, when Darren was fourteen, Grandpa Anderson thought the future shot-put champion should have a larger view of life than the one provided by lowing cattle, baby calves, and the flat atmosphere. He took Darren to Washington, D.C., for two weeks, so that the boy would be suitably impressed by the political center of the United States. Fourteen-year-old Darren sent home two postcards, one each week—the first of the White House, the second of I. M. Pei's East Wing of the National Gallery with its pyramidal skylight and its underground restaurant. The first message read:

Dear Mom, Dad, Sharon, Sherrie, and Davey:
How is everything. I am doing great. I went to a movie today. And I got grandpa a belt buckle with the Washington oblisk on it. We went to the fancy shopping center and had a lot of fun. I have been laying around lately which I enjoy.
Love,
Darren

Washington was the first big city Darren had visited, and his first intimation that just beyond that flat horizon was something, something achievable, attainable, which could be grasped by a hand that was just strong enough.

"Darren loved it!" Grandpa Anderson said upon their triumphant return. Darren himself had come back as churlish as a boy entering puberty—which he was.

"Darren, go see how the cows are doin'," said his dad.

"Aw Dad, do I have to?"

"And check on the baby calves, too."

"Yes, Dad."

Darren's father, Al, wanted to hear more about how much the boy had liked the city, but out of his earshot.

"Can't understan' it, m'self. It's so dirty and crowded. How can *anyone* like it?" He meant the city.

"Wail, *he* did," said Grandpa Anderson. And as though they would confirm his opinion, he asked to see the cards the boy had sent home. Al pointed to the cards displayed on the mantelpiece.

Grandpa Anderson was a wise old man. He read Darren's message:

Dear Mom, Dad, Sharon, Sherrie, and Davey (last because he picks on me):
I am leaving. That's all there is to it. I am leaving Kansas, cows, pigs, all that. You can keep me in Immaculatum while I'm growing up, but I am leaving as soon as I can. You'll see why, someday. Someday you'll see why the city is better than the country. I'll prove it to you, someday.

That's what wise old Grandpa Anderson saw, but he was too

wise to say much or do anything except silently resolve that nature take its course.

"See," he said, smiling, giving it back to Al, "he liked it a lot."

"Wail, I guess he did."

"Hail," said Darren's mother, who was a little bigger than normal but still nice-looking, "I'd like to go there m'self. But it's too crowded and it's way too expensive."

"Oh, it is." Grandpa Anderson knew, because he'd been around. He would get around a few more years before a stroke would take him away to the largest underground restaurant ever built. He would die in a hospital with large windows—large windows probably not unlike the large windows in the hospital Darren went to, the Institut Pasteur in Paris, when a swelling inflamed his calf, just as I began writing this chapter.

I was carrying things he needed up to his room. A lot of what I was carrying was writing material, like a bubble jet printer, and it seemed to weigh as much as a human limb. I imagined, as I climbed the stairs, that I was carrying Darren's amputated leg in a leather satchel. When I opened the door, he looked awfully sick and tired.

"Hello," I said.

"Hello," he said.

We had had a huge argument, and hadn't spoken in three days. I had been brooding and sulking in my deux-pièces when Darren had sent me word that he was being treated at the Institut Pasteur for what appeared to be a viral infection inside the calf muscles. A chance existed they would have to amputate. Then I thought, argument or no argument, the sick merited sympathy. Not just the sick: the well, too, but especially the sick.

So when we said hello to each other as I entered his room, I counted his legs: two, sticking out from under the hospital gown, plus the imaginary one I was carrying in my leather satchel.

"I brought you what you asked for," I said.

"Oh?"

"Your bubble jet printer. Paper. The extension cables. Weighs a lot, all this."

"I'll bet. Am I a bitch to make you carry all that?"

"*I'm* the bitch," I corrected quickly. "How are you? Not too frayed?"

It had been a really big argument we had had, or rather, it was a bazooka tirade from me. It had happened at Café Marly.

"I'm fine. How are *you?*"

I sighed wistfully. "All right," I said. "Chapter three isn't going too well. I've lost the freshness, the self-referential feel. You know, this latest turn in your illness sort of colors the book."

"Well, we can't do anything about it. Let nature take its course." He meant the virus. He rolled himself an Amsterdamer Special. It was cut at the ends, and its edges were as flat as a Kansan horizon.

"What's going to happen?" I said.

"Hell, I don't know. They may have to cut the damn thing off. I just don't know."

"Well," I said, trying for black humor, "if they *did* cut it off, you wouldn't be so tempted to go to The Trap. And you'd cut more of a figure at Café Marly."

Darren looked at me in that way of his when he was contemplating something too wicked to enjoy and too enjoyable to resist. "I *would,* wouldn't I? I wouldn't even want a prosthetic. Just the stump!"

I decided later that I would write up that conversation, in my deux-pièces in Saint-Germain-des-Prés. I thought it would show Darren looking brave.

But at the time I was speaking to Darren, I was still handing him over all the little things he needed for work. He had asked for address labels of a very particular size—exactly 14 centimeters by 6.5 centimeters—so that they could be used as labels on the back of a Café Marly postcard. He was going to send a spectacular change-of-address notification: his new *carte de visite,* with addresses in Paris, Amsterdam, New York, and Kansas, and a postcard with a greeting on one side and a picture of Café Marly on the other. The picture showed a view of the I. M. Pei glass pyramid from the restaurant.

Grandpa Anderson was too dead to receive the postcard and the new *carte de visite,* but no doubt that wise old man would have known what it said, really:

*How is everything. I am doing great. I went to a movie today. I
bought a friend a belt buckle with an obelisk on it. We went to
the underground restaurant and had a lot of fun. I have been
laying around lately which I enjoy.*

Love,

Darren

That wise old man knew how to read between the lines. I
could only speculate on how the *carte de visite* and the Café
Marly postcard, with its picture of the pyramid and the fancy
restaurant, would be interpreted by the others. Dead John
would have liked it; one of the last photographs I have of him,
quite sick and tired-looking, is of him and Darren seated next to
the pyramidal skylights in Washington.

The rest of Darren's friends would express their admiration
vigorously.

"*Darren! strikes! again!*" Steve Johnson, the painter, would say.

"Ha!" Darren would roar, imagining Steve.

"Darren is *just too much,*" would say James.

"Ha!" Darren would roar.

James Dawkey would have a hard time explaining the over-
sized *carte de visite* and the Café Marly postcard to his friends,
who thought *they* were refined and original.

"Good God," I imagined them saying. "Addresses in Paris
and Amsterdam and New York *and* Kansas?! Who is this guy?"

"Well, Darren's that way," James would say. "He started out
in Kansas, but now he's in Paris."

When I interviewed James, he would look at me, not shifty-
eyed, but with a certain distance. And he would comment on
what I said, and then he would look slightly upwards, as if at a
disembodied face floating before him, which no one but himself
could see.

"I think . . ." he would begin, "Darren was *born* enjoying
those things. He certainly wasn't trained to enjoy them, because
they didn't exist when he was growing up. Have you ever been
to Kansas, Philippe?"

"No."

We were in his place on the Ile Saint-Louis. It was a silent
two-bedroom apartment in a good part of town. A tall lamp
quietly illuminated the corner. On the walls were framed

turn-of-the-century prints he had bought *chez les bouquinistes* on the Left Bank, when he lived with Darren on rue Duroc.

"Kansas is this huge, flat pit," he said. "I went in winter, and it's a waste land. You can see for miles, and there's nothing to see." He stopped himself as if he had already said too much.

I sat still as moss, waiting for the rest. He sat upon his couch, long legs complexly folded, looking out in front of him.

"Would you like a drink?" he asked me suddenly.

"No, thanks."

"Well, I'll have a drink. Very wise, you know, when talking about Darren."

Disentangling his legs, he got up, walked with long steps (for he was tall) to the kitchen, let fall ice cubes which plopped tinklingly into a tumbler of whiskey. He sat down again and took a sip. He looked upwards, a little. He was again looking at that mysterious disembodied face. "Darren and I first met at a rock concert in New York."

"In the crowd?" I blurted out.

"In the crowd," he repeated. "It was an English band, Go East Young Man, or something like that, I think. We met in the crowd. And we hit it off right away. Darren was—have you ever seen Darren at a concert? Or at a disco?"

I shook my head a hair's breadth in either direction. This was enough for James, who continued. "He's"—he smirked a little—"quite *liberated*." And he chuckled, nearly imperceptibly.

I smiled to encourage him. He had one of those voices with the law in it—leathered and plush. It sounded lovely to me. It was a voice full of compassion and sympathy—but dignified. He continued. "Now, I'm not liberated—certainly not me—but he was. We balanced each other out. We hit it off very well, right from the start." The invisible face had become totally engrossing. He lifted the whiskey to his lips, and said, "We began to see more of each other—"

Just then the telephone rang. Rang, and rang again. It was Darren.

"Hi, Philippe," he said.

"Hi, Darren."

"Am I interrupting anything?" he asked.

"No," I said, "I've been expecting you to call." And with my moving fingertips I silenced James.

"Well, they cut into the leg and they *still* don't know what's going on."

"Oh no," I groaned. "How can they *not* know?"

"Some technician left early. Now they're saying the leg is full of blood."

The leg was all puffed up; it was so swollen it looked like one of Darren's normal legs, the ones he had before his seventy-pound weight loss. It was his hypothetical leg, the one carried in a leather satchel, or written about in a book.

"God," I said. I tried to cheer him up. "Well, in a grim way, it's good news. If you'll excuse my being so cynical, if the technician left early, it means that it's nothing urgent."

"Or maybe he went home knowing it *was* urgent. Now *that* would be cynical."

"Yes."

He sighed wistfully. "Oh well. I don't care. If they want to cut it off, let 'em cut it off."

"Here," I said, trying to cheer him up, "I have something to read to you." So I read him chapter three, starting from, *Darren Swenson had once been shot-put champion,* up until the point James said, *"We began to see more of each other—"*

James, sitting in the margin of this conversation, was still quiet.

Darren thought it was good, but that the part with James was "a little slow" compared to the rest. So I said I'd work on it. Then I added: "I'm having a great time here."

He said: "Good! You finish up what you're doing."

"Right. Bye. Take care of yourself."

"Take care of *yourself,* Philippe."

"Take care," I repeated to him.

"Right. Bye."

We really did say those things to each other. Well—sort of.

When I hung up, James asked, "Is he all right?"

"Sort of," I said.

James took a deep breath, and tightened his lips. He stared at the disembodied face. The ice in the liquid was absolutely still. There were no sounds. We stayed in that position for so long that I was sure the evening was over. I started thinking about James, this six-foot-seven deep-voiced man who swore in

his dreams he was always a woman being made love to by
another man.

"He swears he was born in the wrong body," I remember
Darren told me, in the opening days of our relationship, when I
was busy gathering facts and vignettes about the 120 persons I
would use to populate the novel.

"How did you two get on?" I had asked Darren about
James.

"We got on fine. He followed me from New York to Paris,
and we shared a flat on rue Duroc. At least, we did until he
walked out leaving me with five thousand four hundred francs
to pay in rent."

"Five thousand four hundred francs!" That was a lot of
money to me.

"Five thousand four hundred francs." It was a lot to Darren, too.

"What happened?" I asked. "Troubles in bed?"

"Philippe, we never even slept together. We had separate
beds. Each of us did our own thing. We never included each
other. Well—maybe just a little." He smiled his bashful-dwarf
smile. "Oh dear," he said. "But it was just a little."

"Why do you like him, Darren?" I asked.

Darren thought. "Why do you ever like anybody? Oh, I
suppose he was a refined, sensitive boy. Mystical and idealistic,
too. He was looking for the special something, all the time, and
so was I. I was looking for true love, and he was looking for a
job." Darren snorted. "I broke his heart. He's still looking for
that job, I hear." He looked up, at the past. "He's still looking.
That makes two of us."

James was still looking away. Then he interrupted my
reverie by opening his lips, as if about to speak.

But no sound came out; I listened hard, thought he might
try to speak again, but he closed his lips, and what he was about
to say was uncommunicable forever.

I do not know if Darren, even when he was fourteen years
old, with his thick fingers wrapped around the pink paps of
those old farm cows, squirting down into a bucket the white

milk, feeling it stream past the life-lines of the palms of his hands—I do not know if even then he was planning to affect people the way he affected James. Doubtless, as he pulled and tugged and squeezed the teats, he was thinking of things else-where—the action was so repetitive, so repetitive, that his active mind could not *but* wonder if there was something *else*. Real dreaming was harder, with the furred belly mashed against his face, the acrid stink of the urine, and the sour smell of the pissed-on barn hay. But Darren didn't just milk the cows, he also drove the big tractor across the land, even at fourteen, and that was where he started looking out at the horizon, and really wondering and dreaming about what lay beyond it.

For the Swedish settlers that were his ancestors, that flat horizon, as level as silence, held all the promise in the world. It was an uncorrupted fresh start. The absoluteness of the landscape promised an absoluteness of life: here, in such a place, it seemed possible to begin at zero, again, and consciously move in a perfect way to the perfection that was God, whose perfection that flat horizon only reflected.

Darren's reaction to the landscape was one of disgust. No: not of disgust, initially, but of tremendous dissatisfaction. For him, the edge of the landscape represented the edges of the wings of a stage, and everything that was interesting happened behind it.

"Darren!" his father would yell. "Ya finish milkin' the cows?"

"Yep!" Darren would say.

"Ya done stackin' the hay?"

"Yeah, I done that, too," Darren would say.

"Ya clean up the barn?"

Darren would try to think of an answer to that one. But this time his father was quicker.

"When yer done cleanin' up the barn, come in the house. I got somethin' ta show ya."

"Aw, Dad—"

"Just do as I say, Darren. When yer done, come in the house."

And Darren grumpingly marched to the barn and uncoiled the thick yards of the mighty hose, turned it on, and blasted it into the barn. As the gush of water hissed from his hand, he thought, Is there anything *besides* this? Is this *it,* for me? And the beam of the water spray slid the cow plops along the floor, blew away the hay, and smoothed the wet wood. Then he turned it off, looked at the barn, and heard the trickling water dripping into little puddles. Better, he thought, and went inside under a sky pouring itself into a violet dissolve.

"What?" he demanded, bursting into the kitchen.

"What, *Dad,*" corrected his father.

"*What,* Dad?" said Darren, exasperated.

Al Swenson looked at Lilian, who glanced at father and son, shifting her eyes from each to each.

"I do hope this is a good idea," said his father.

"I know it is," said his mother.

"C'mere," said his dad, and walked into the living room. Darren followed him. Right in the middle was a brand-new piano, shining black and ivory. It looked enameled and bright. Fourteen-year-old Darren froze in the door.

"Well, go on," said his father, no longer able to contain a grin. "Try it. Sit down." He waved at his son impatiently. "Go on, play; we got it for you. Play!"

Darren said, "What a story, Philippe. What a story."

I said, "Isn't it great?"

"What a story!" Darren repeated. "God! I wish it *had* happened to me!"

"Yeah, well. But that's the way it happened to *me* when I got a piano, in reality. And since we both started playing the piano when we were about fourteen, I thought I could describe what happened to me as happening to you."

Darren looked up, out his big window in the Institut Pasteur, and said, "Well, you've got quite a dad for him to rig a surprise like that."

"I know," I said. "I've decided I'm going to dedicate it, this novel I'm writing about you, to him. 'For Dad,' I think I'll say."

Later Darren, sitting up suddenly in his chair at Café Marly, having read over what I have just written, exclaimed, "Well, damn it, Philippe, who do you *think* I'm going to dedicate this book to? My father, that's who. Put that in. My father is my only hero, Philippe."

"Relax, Darren. I already have," I said.

Darren worked hard and happily on his piano, practicing his scales and exercises. He moved on to more difficult pieces like Beethoven's *Pathétique,* and of course he could always appreciate what he couldn't play, like the *Emperor* Concerto.

"My favorite recording was by Dinu Lipatti," he told me.

There was good reason to like it: Lipatti played with astonishing depth of feeling, yet never lost control of the piece's majestic dignity. He never once confused starchness with dignity, or mushiness with feeling. Lipatti had a brilliant piano career, then died of leukemia when he was thirty-three, in 1950, thirteen years before Darren was born.

Seven years *after* Darren was born, Kenny Moore, a family friend, died, also of leukemia. Darren could hardly remember Kenny, but he later learned that Kenny had been the best high school soccer player Immaculatum had ever known, and that at college, Kansas City State, he was the captain of the team. He had a bright corn-fed smile, a strong, lithe body, and a sunny disposition. He was twenty-one when he died.

"So it goes," Darren said.

Kenny was not only the beloved son of Keith and Doris Moore; he was the beloved son of Kansas City State, and every year after he died, before the annual soccer match between Kansas City State and their archrivals, B—— A——, there would be a ceremony to commemorate the incredibly premature and unnecessary death of Kenny Moore. Most deaths are probably premature and unnecessary, to somebody anyway, but Kenny Moore's was particularly so.

When Darren and I were in the opening days of my writing the novel, and I was doing research on the 120 persons who would eventually populate the book, Darren called Doris Moore, who was an old, old lady, and who cared for Darren like a son.

"Hello, Doris?"

"Hello?"

"Doris, it's Darren."

"Hello! How are you? Where are you calling from?"

"Paris!"

"Oh, very nice. When did you get there?"

"I left Kansas then spent a few days in New York. I'm having a wonderful time."

"Good. You *sound* well."

They went on talking; Darren, as if to a mother that might have been his, and to whom he spoke openly and without fear of judgment; she, as if listening to a son she thought might have been hers. Their conversation was full of might-have-beens, and could-have-beens, and although they never mentioned what life might have been like if only Kenny hadn't died, or if only Darren hadn't started dying, that was the real subject of their discussion: their patience with dying.

Then Doris said, "I spoke to your mother."

"Oh really."

"She was complaining about some aches and pains."

("She's *always* complaining to other people about her aches and pains," Darren said later, bitterly. " 'The problems of being obese.' As if anybody cared. As if anybody was doing it to her except herself." I wrote that down; it seemed important, like the center of the plot of the novel.)

"Mom's always complaining about her aches and pains," Darren told Doris. "Oh, but you should have seen her *this* time, Doris, after I told them." He meant after he had told them he had AIDS.

"Mm-hmm," said Doris, audibly nodding in agreement.

"She called up everybody to tell them how badly I was doing. 'Darren is really ill; we're not sure he's going to make it through the summer. You come visit him while he's still alive.' It made me sick, Doris."

"Midwestern frankness," I joked, but Darren didn't hear me because he was listening to Doris.

"It was worse than when I went back in 1988," Darren continued, "when I told them I was gay. When I told my whole family."

"Oh yes," Doris said, "I remember that. Well, we each have our way of dealing with the bad things that happen."

"I know, Doris," said Darren. "But in the end we'll all be judged on how we deal with the negative."

I rolled my eyes. The gospel according to Reverend Darren. Reverend Darren hath spoken. All bow.

"That's true," said Doris.

After his homecoming for Thanksgiving in 1988, Darren told his family he was gay. Two years before, he had told his mother, and she had sent a letter to his New York address. To be fair to Lilian Swenson, she did her best in what she considered to be a negative situation. The letter was partially sympathetic to what, for her, was his wildly different style of living. But it was this *partial* sympathy that was their tragedy. Darren wanted uncompromising love. Darren was a relentless, obsessive perfectionist for whom one hundred percent was scarcely good enough. So, when his mother wrote that she was not one hundred percent satisfied with his style of living— nor would she lie to him about accepting it, "for lying is a sin"—then he was stung to his core. Darren convulsed. All he could think about was the pain, the imperfection of his life, and how nothing could be done to change things: for his mother would not change her views on queers, and Darren was one hundred percent queer. It revolted him that she drew an impossible line between his sexuality, which he couldn't help, and her morals, which he couldn't change. So, stung and angry, this is what Darren thought he read, when she wrote him that letter:

Dear Darren:

Yes it is still <u>dear</u> Darren even though you call yourself gay now. See, I can use that word just as well as you can: gay, gay, gay, gay. Even though I think you are making the biggest mistake of your life, and our lives, when you choose to be homosexual. Darren, I can accept a lot of things about you but I cannot accept that. It would be a lie to say that, and I will not lie, for lying is a sin. Your homosexuality is a curse on our family, Darren. Your father would never recover from this and Davey and Sharon and Sherrie would hang their heads in shame, shame, shame, shame. Now, I want you to be happy—but I will not be happy with this decision. You telling me you are gay is like telling me you have cancer. Cancer! CANCER! Do you understand? It is like telling me you are going to die.

And so on. That was not what she had written, exactly. But that was exactly what Darren felt he had read.

And Mrs. Swenson didn't know her son was already HIV-positive when she wrote him.

In her letter, she tried to be honest and courteous. But
Darren needed a lot more than honesty and courtesy. He
needed, and wanted, uncompromising love, love that was one
hundred percent true, unadulterated and with no fine print. She
gave him some love: but not all of it. She held back her complete approval. And why? Because Darren had made a lifestyle
choice. Evidently, he had *chosen* to be the way he was; he had
chosen to besmirch the family honor, *chosen* to humiliate his
father, mother, brother and sisters, and *chosen* a lifestyle that was
like cancer. She was opposed to this choice; Darren was a free
man, and an adult, and he could certainly *choose*, she thought,
whether to sleep with a man or a woman.

"You can't choose to be gay," Darren said, "any more than
you can choose to be born in Kansas. Oh, you can run away
from it, at the start, but you can't run away from it forever. All
you can do is accept it gracefully, like you accept aging, or
dying, or getting fat when you're old. Why not say that old
people *choose* to be fat?"

Why not? Lilian Swenson weighed 400 pounds. Darren
weighed 160, down from 220, about as much as Sherrie. Al
probably weighed 270. Sharon and Davey both weighed about
350. Evidently, they all *chose* their body weights, along with
their respective sexualities.

Things like this passed through the minds of Doris Moore
and Darren when Doris said, "Oh yes, I remember that," and
when she said, "Well, we each have our way of dealing with
the bad things that happen." She was probably thinking of what
she had felt when the doctors told her that her twenty-year-old
son had not more than one year to live, and how she had
braced herself for his death, but Doris was too old and too wise
to say anything about that. So she nodded silently in agreement
when Darren said, "I know, Doris." And she agreed with him
when he said, "We'll all be judged on how we deal with the
negative," except that she would have added, "There is no
judgment, only living with the consequences. And we only
rarely choose the consequences; the consequences choose
themselves." But she was too old and too wise to say that
either.

★ ★ ★

Much later, I was thinking about the novel in my little apartment in Saint-Germain-des-Prés when the doorbell rang.

"Hello?" I asked through the interphone.

"Open up!"

"Who is it?" I asked.

"John."

"John who?"

"*Dead* John."

There was a silence.

"Excuse me?" I asked.

"I'm coming up! Someone's letting me in. I'll be right up!"

I looked around. What! It wasn't Darren's voice. Who the hell—I looked over the balustrade of the staircase. Someone in a leather jacket with a crimson scarf was moving up the staircase, fast. I turned around and suddenly he was in front of me. It was Dead John, standing before me, in Paris.

"Hi," he said. His accent was American, his voice strong, his hair jet black. "Can I come in?"

I stared at him, my eyes wide open.

"Only for a few minutes, okay?" he said reassuringly, and then walked through the door, the way dead people walk through doors.

"I like it," he said, speaking of my room. "I like it. Small, but cozy." He looked at the bed and clucked his tongue in the Parisian way, click-click-click. "Awfully small bed. Must be kinda uncomfortable, for two."

He looked around. The room was a mess, as usual, and all my chairs were stacked with clothes or books. He moved aside a copy of *Four Quartets* to make room for himself on the bed, and sat down. He settled in, his feet square, and folded his hands in between his knees.

"Now before I forget," he said, "can you say out loud, 'I am writing a book.' "

" 'I am writing a book,' " I repeated, feeling like an idiot, closing the door behind me.

"Louder, man."

"I am writing a book!"

"Louder, man, much louder!"

"I AM WRITING A BOOK!!"

" 'Kay. I have to do that because they only give us permission to drop in on artists who are trying to make us come back again. We also get to drop in on people who remember us, for better or for worse. The artist loophole is good, isn't it?"

I nodded weakly. I swallowed. "Yeah," I said. I stared at him.

"Can I have a drink?" he asked.

"What?"

"Can I have a drink?" he repeated, with a hopeful smile.

"Uh—what would you like? I have milk, orange juice, water . . . ?"

"Brandy."

"I don't think I've got any brandy."

"Water's fine, then."

"Paris . . . tap water?"

"Yeah yeah, that's fine."

I filled up a glass and gave it to him. He drank.

I cleared my throat. "To what—what—what brings you here?"

Dead John spoke very intensely; he knotted his brows and thought. "Well, Darren always blabbered about Paris. I thought I should visit some time. You have his Paris pictures?"

With a motion of the hand I showed him where the photograph albums were. Dead John looked much stronger than he did in the last photos. I thought of Jean-Baptiste who had shown them to me, far away in Australia, looking for true love on the other side of the world.

"Why don't you visit Jean-Baptiste?" I asked.

"Too far away. And he doesn't know me." He shook his head slightly, indicating the photograph album. "Later. Some other time." He cleared his throat noisily, drank some water. "Now. The reason I'm here, is because I saw you writing about this business of free will and free choice. Well—" He hesitated, picking his words with care. "Don't overdo it. We do kind of choose to be who we are. But a lot of the choosing is done for us, if you know what I mean. Nice water." He drank. "I mean, do you think I *chose* to die? I had a lot going for me. But—shit happens. And a lot of shit we think we bring down upon ourselves—well, we don't. Not all of it. And don't give yourself credit for all the good things that happen either. There. That's the message."

He put down his glass, blew out air through his lips and cracked his knuckles as if he had finished a Herculean task. "God, I need to get *laid,*" he said.

"Do—do you want some more water?" I asked.

"Uh—yeah. Yes please." He called out to me while I was in the kitchen. "I mean, you do understand, that's the message for your book. Well, *one* of the messages. It's just a suggestion. But *this* message is from the *Owner* of the big underground restaurant. Take it or leave it."

"I'll put it in the book, definitely."

"I mean, what else have you got? How else are you going to explain Darren's illness and his life? With—temptation? With—the *Devil*??" he asked leeringly. He leaned back, slit his eyes. "Actually, I've met the Devil. He's not that bad." He looked at me sternly and seriously, as if giving me some really good advice. "And *he's* a good lay," he said.

"I'm putting him in my book, but later."

"You should. He's not good-looking, but he's soooooo charming. Watch out, Phil, or you'll be on your back in ninety seconds."

"*Is* the Devil responsible?"

"Oh, hell, who knows?" He lowered his voice to a whisper and pointed upwards. "Even *He* doesn't know, or if He does, He's not letting on. There's some sort of bug in the master program and instead of having this Final Judgment, when everything stops, it just loops over and starts again at zero. He can't figure it out, and all this omnipotency shit is just a cover-up. He *made* the Devil, don't forget. Don't put that in your book, if you value your life."

"I won't. Well, I'll allude to it, maybe."

"Well. Don't insist on it. And remember." He looked at me sternly. "*Datta. Dayadhvam. Damyata.* The only thing you need to know. Didn't like poetry when I was alive, but O how I care for it now. Stay cool. Try not to be too mean to anyone in the book. But if you got to—you got to, right?" He tapped me once on the shoulder, as if passing on a thought. Then he downed his glass again, zipped up his bomber jacket, and said, "Gotta run. Say hi to Darren for me. And don't believe everything he says. See ya."

"Good night," I said, but the door was already closed; he was already gone, leaving me alone in the unquiet darkness.

CHAPTER 4

Darren's mother, Lilian Swenson, had once been considered a dead ringer for Elizabeth Taylor. She certainly
had the perfect skin, the spectacular violet eyes, and the
jet black hair. She was elegant, too, and wanted her children to
be elegant, especially Darren, who from the tenderest years was
bright and good-looking and hardworking and friendly. During
his school years, friends called him "Mister Perfect."

But although Darren was the high school valedictorian,
football star, star pianist, actor, singer, class president, and the
longtime holder of the school record for the shot put, Darren
hated Immaculatum High School. Those stupid small-town
honors, he thought, were only his ticket out. Not just out: up.
On that brilliant commencement day in 1982, when "Mister
Perfect" glittered with every school trophy, pin, ribbon, and
award in existence, Darren felt like one of God's chosen, summoned upwards. He felt divine—or at least perfect.

He would have become complacent; he was, in a way; but
along with his unassailable feeling of being the best in the world
(the world being Immaculatum High School, class of '82) went a
grand and regal generosity. Darren gave everyone some of his

super-abundant spoils of victory. It was an easy way of making friends. Friends were what Darren used to protect himself from himself.

"If you can't take care of yourself," he would say, "no one else will."

Only once in a while did his inflated sense of self creep out from behind his blond head. When he was about fourteen, the King of Sweden himself came to visit Lindsborg, a nearby city. Dad wanted to go see the King, and so did Mom, and so did Dahlia, Darren's grandmother. That left one space in the car, and Davey was the eldest.

"*Noooooo,* Mom," Darren wailed. "*I* should go."

"What's that, Darren?" asked his mother.

"*I* should see the King."

"Now why is that?"

"Well—*I* got all the good grades. Davey's grades were not so good. And—Mom—I'm in all the plays. The King will like that. And—*Mom*"—each syllable was like a caterwaul—"I'm the one who *deserves* to go."

"Oh, dear," Darren said, when he read that, sitting upright in his bed at the Institut Pasteur. He shook his head sadly and smiled. "I was such a wicked boy."

"You were a good boy," I said, looking out the huge bay windows that gave onto the courtyard. "With a slightly wicked side. You knew what you wanted. You didn't lie to get it, but you did present your side of the truth."

Darren looked at me, teeth on his lower lip, a little smile creeping into his face. "Oh, well," he said. "I never said I was perfect."

That reminded me of one of the comments I had made in my bazooka tirade at Café Marly. I had said, with my eyes as wide and fiery as hot plates on maximum power, "Darren: you just haven't *figured it out.*" I put a maximum amount of emphasis, and of spit, into those words as I flung them across the table.

"Philippe," Darren said, "I never claimed that I had." He was scornful of my anger, which made me more angry.

"Darren, you lying sack of shit!"

He looked at me incomprehendingly.

"You *just don't get it!*" I said. Then I said the thing I'd been waiting to say, the feeling I'd been hoarding.

That feeling had been in me a long time, ever since I'd met Darren in fact, when I became conscious of the unassailable sense of superiority that surrounded him. "I'm the most interesting person here," he seemed to say, all the time, and sometimes he did say it.

"When I was with John, in New York, we talked about *me,* because we both knew *I* was the interesting one." And he smiled.

He had said that just a few seconds before I hoisted my verbal bazooka to my shoulder and fired.

I must admit my method of dealing with an egocentric person was not ideal, particularly when that person was the hero of my book. It would have been easier to have said, maybe a few hours after I had met him, months earlier, "Darren, I wish you would stop saying that you're always the most interesting person around for miles! The rest of us think we're quite interesting, too, but we don't say that because we think it's sort of a silly thing to say."

Then Darren would have said, "Oh okay," and continued thinking he was the most interesting person around for miles, although not saying that in front of me.

The difficulty for me in dealing with Darren's big ego was that I could not bring myself to break his illusions, at least not in reality. But I could *write* about breaking them, in a work of fiction, and then show him what I'd written.

"I suppose," he would say, "that this is your way of trying to improve me. Making me read about it afterwards will help me become a better person, hmm?"

He really was saying that, and a lot more, when I arrived at the Institut Pasteur to see how his leg was doing.

"Do I really have a big ego?" Darren asked me, looking up from the manuscript.

"No, not really."

"Yes I do, you lying bitch. Philippe, you need to tell me these things earlier."

"I told you as soon as I could."

"What, in Café Marly?"

"No, right here. Right now."

"Where?"

"On this *page* you're reading."

"Oh! Oh, well whatever. I don't understand this novel sometimes."

"Sometimes I don't understand you. But I'll tell you why I couldn't quite bring myself to criticize your ego earlier. I rather admire your honesty. You only state quite openly what a lot of us believe about ourselves, but are too well bred to confess."

"I'm not well bred?"

"Not well bred enough, obviously," I said with a smile.

And I wrote *that* one morning before I went to the Institut Pasteur to see how he was doing.

Darren's leg was hugely swollen. Paradoxically, it looked normal, like the leg that should have belonged to someone of his size and frame—his hypothetical leg, the leg he would have if he hadn't gotten AIDS.

"They thought it was phlebitis at first. And that had me worried, because as soon as they say phlebitis they say hacksaw and tourniquet. Then they changed their minds and thought it was a lymph infection. That was better. Then they found *blood* inside, and did an *échographie,* and it turns out the muscles are torn to ribbons inside."

"How did you do *that?*" I asked.

"*I* don't know. Anyway, now it's full of blood. And they still don't know what it is. Oh wait. Here's Doctor Daly."

Darren had told me about Dr. Daly. He was a very handsome, easygoing young man with charming little wrinkles around his eyes. Darren was trying to fall in love with him.

"*Bonjour, Docteur Daly,*" he said, as the doctor stepped in. The doctor winked at me. I did not wink back. I was not going to interfere with Darren's love life.

"*Ça continue, oui?*" Dr. Daly asked Darren, touching the swollen limb very lightly.

"*Eh oui. Ça continue. Ça ne dégonfle pas et ça commence à faire mal.*" Yes, Darren said, the swelling continues and it's starting to hurt.

"Have they given you analgesics?"

"Yes. Not enough, though," Darren said, and smiled. Darren always wanted more analgesics, in case his prescription Prozacs and Amsterdamer Specials didn't do the job. Darren put on his sweetest face. "Can't you give me just a few more painkillers?" he pleaded.

"I'm afraid not," Dr. Daly said with a smile. Dr. Daly suspected Darren of wanting to hoard analgesics—for the day when he would want to kill quite a lot of his pain, all at once. "I am sorry," Dr. Daly said, "but the hospital's policy on euthanasia is quite firm." He meant absolutely not. They would only let nature take its course. *"Bon,"* he said, to change the subject. "We are going to do another biopsy and see what comes out. There wasn't enough fluid last time."

"Not enough fluid? You took out 10 cc's."

"Not enough. There are many tests."

Darren looked at me, skeptical and exasperated.

"Bon. Ah—" he said, thinking of something. *"Mauvaise nouvelle."* Bad news. "I have again had problems with that nurse—the old one."

"Oh yes." Dr. Daly shifted his feet, nodded. "She's a problem."

"She has no right to make comments on what I did to get in here. It is none of her concern. If she doesn't like—who I am—let her leave."

"Yes. I am sorry. The policy of the Institut is that whatever the nurses' private views, they are to show compassion for all the patients—whether they be homosexuals, drug addicts, or whatever."

"Good. Sarcasm is not compassion."

"Absolutely. You should complain. With a letter." And he explained how he wanted the letter written, to chastise this rude and unsympathetic nurse.

Dr. Daly said good evening charmingly and exited into the corridor.

"What a hunk," Darren said.

"He's a nice guy," I said.

"I'm trying to fall in love with him," Darren said.

"Well, do. He deserves to be fallen in love *with.*"

"When are you going to write about the rest of your tirade at Marly?"

"In a while."

"Well, do it. I want to read about all the other nasty things you said."

"You will, Darren. But I have to build structure around it first. Preparations for writing and all that. Outlines."

"Oh, of course. Have you got an outline for the novel? One that you like?"

"Yes, in fact. I've decided that the start of the novel should be—you're going to laugh—you, and Rascal."

"Rascal! The raccoon?" Darren exploded laughing. "Why not with Star?"

"With the horse? The filly? That came later, didn't it? You were fourteen when you started riding the horse."

"Not exactly."

"Not exactly fourteen?"

"Not exactly *riding*."

"Right. I got that." I grinned. "*All* will be made clear. Now—about Rascal the raccoon. Judging from your photographs, he was the first living thing you really cared for, outside your immediate family. You saved this animal, fed it, raised it, sent it off into the world. A little bit like you did with Jean-Baptiste."

"Yes!" Darren was surprised. (And again when he read this, later.)

"He was also very much your imaginary companion. I remember that when I was a kid I endowed my animals with immense amounts of human personality. My brother and I buried our dead goldfish, for Christ's sake."

"Instead of flushing them down the toilet, like I did, when I was staying at Jean-Baptiste's."

"Well, that was two weeks ago. My brother and I were eight or nine when we were giving our dead goldfish a proper burial."

"What would you do?"

"Stick them in a little black box, dig a hole, and bury them. We marked the grave with a popsicle stick bearing their names, but I think that those graves got ripped up by one of the gardeners. Of course, if we'd been really chic and modern, we would have cremated them."

"Like I will be," Darren said.

"Like I will be, too. We're all going to get it."

"Hopefully I won't get flushed down the toilet."

"Hopefully if someone does flush you down the toilet,

they'll wait until you're dead. That was an awful way to get rid of goldfish, Darren."

"I needed the counter space and that damn aquarium was taking up too much room!" Darren said, in between happy gasps of laughter.

"Well, Jean-Baptiste won't be happy."

"I'll buy him some other ones. Goldfish are easy to replace."

"Perhaps. But Rascal was not. Looking at the pictures, I think he was your secret confidant, your best friend, in a way, the only being who really understood you. At least, you thought so. And then what happened?"

"He ran away. Nature took its course. Raccoons can be good pets when they're growing up, but then they run away when they get older."

"Kind of like you."

"Kind of like me."

"Yeahp," I said, practicing my Kansin drawl. I had to get ready to learn how to speak like a *Kan*sin ta do ma big showdown scene, when Darren got home to tell his folks he had AIDS. "That's goin' to be the end of the book," I told Darren. "Now I just need a middle."

"Grenoble," Darren said. "Junior year abroad, first time in Europe; I had my mystical experience in that English pub, the whole bit. That should be the middle."

"And the end?"

"When I go back to Kansas to tell the folks that Dear Darren is going to turn into *Dead* Darren."

"Yes, I think we can save that for last."

I did decide to save that for last.

Darren's Grenoble experience was going to be the center of the novel. It was going to be hard to write about. My father was a Frenchman expatriated in America, and I grew up thinking of France as an area more or less contiguous to California. I had visited, seen the French houses where my ancestors had grown up, looked at the cities and countryside where they had worked, visited the French churches where they had been married, and seen their blue tombstones in the French rain.

Darren had a different experience. When he was twenty, Europe had no boring casual familiarity; to him, it was holy, and secret, and closed, like a tabernacle. As a twenty-year-old in his sophomore year, he was determined to open that tabernacle and step inside it. And that was what he told Robert Flewelling, his advisor.

"You can't go, Darren. You'd be a fool to go," he said.

"I've been studying the language real hard, now. I don't speak perfectly but I can certainly get by, Professor Flewelling."

"You can ask for bread in a bakery, if that's what you mean." That was true; Darren knew that *pain* was bread in French. And pain in French was *douleur*. The professor sighed. "You're pushing very hard for something that's very doubtful, Darren."

"I know, but I want to go."

"Well—if you absolutely want to go—"

"I do."

"If you absolutely want to go to France, you shouldn't go to Paris. It's very expensive, for a start, and the Parisians will eat you alive." Professor Flewelling looked at his student over rimless spectacles, similar to the ones Jean-Baptiste wore. "They will, Darren. Maybe later they won't. Maybe later you'll be eating them alive, for breakfast, lunch, and dinner. Maybe later you'll be telling Parisians what to do, and they'll do it, because they find you *so* charming. But right now," Professor Flewelling paused for emphasis, "you're a twenty-year-old with one year of French, who's never left Kansas—excuse me, who's left Kansas once, for a two-week vacation in Washington, D.C."

Darren smiled. Professor Flewelling knew him well.

"You should go to Grenoble. It's not as expensive, and it's much friendlier. You will have fun in Grenoble, whereas you'd have a lousy time in Paris. You'll like Grenoble, and you'll be readier for Paris when you decide to go there and take it over."

Darren smiled again. Professor Flewelling was always right.

So Darren packed his bags, and left for Grenoble: left behind the farm country, left behind the flat landscape and the violet dissolving sunsets; left behind the fraternity and the beer busts and the easy ladies, and the Droopy Drawers Party, and the Barn Party, and the Zombie Party and the Winter Formal; left behind the family reunions at Yew Tree Farms, with Lilian his mother, Al his dad, and Dahlia his grandmother, all asking, "What the *hail*'s he goin' to France for?"; left behind his little sister Sherrie, who'd been chosen homecoming queen and was romancing fra-

ternity brother Jeff, whom Darren liked; left Rascal behind—
Rascal, no doubt making more little raccoons somewhere in the
Kansan night. He left all that behind and came to a city that rose
before him, looking brown and holy.

When he arrived, and looked down upon the city from his
view in the student flat where he lived the first few days, he
thought he was looking down upon Mecca. As he wandered from
streets, dazed, unbelieving, he lifted his eyes, and he knew he'd
discovered a Promised Land. He raised a quiet hand, and conse-
crated everything, invisibly. It was all holy to him now. At first
every aspect of it seemed sacred. Everything was worth pre-
serving, and he saved everything, as I was ultimately to describe:
cartes d'identité, stubs of train tickets, shop receipts, photographs
of everyone he'd eaten with, chatted with, bumped into, seen;
the streets, the shops, the monuments, the views. Europe lay
before him like a fantastically beautiful body, and he didn't
know where to *begin* making love to it.

Later, of course, he would think of Grenoble as a pleasant
little provincial town with a pleasant little provincial bour-
geoisie, that came and sat near his usual place at Café Marly from
time to time and looked horrendously pleased. *"Provinciaux,"*
he'd say, rolling his eyes. He was not as snobby as people said he
was, although he was a colossal snob.

"Darren's a bit of a snob, isn't he," said Andrew, with whom
I conferred frequently about the novel. "He doesn't have to call
my relatives 'white trash.' "

"That's true," I said. "He could have been more subtle, but
he had confidence in you and your self-esteem. So he gave it to
you straight."

"Well, he's still a big snob."

"Actually, he's related to more white trash than you've ever
met. 'White trash'—at least, that's what he calls them," I said.

"Sounds like he has a problem accepting where he's from."

"He's always had a problem accepting where he's from."

The truth is that Darren Swenson, of Immaculatum, Kansas,
had sprung from his conception of himself. He thought from the
very start he was *not* a farm boy, and his fertile imagination had
had difficulty accepting his mother and father as his true parents—unless he thought of them as accidents between him and
his true ancestry, which was closer to the King of Sweden. From

the very start, Darren was convinced that *he* was different (and much more interesting, for *miles* around), and that sense of difference was the keystone in the cathedral of self-belief he erected around himself. Some people thought it was infuriating; I certainly did, and told him so, rather tactlessly, at Café Marly. His closer friends thought it was charming.

"You are harsh with him," said Marzenna, to whom I read the passage just before this one. It was the second thing she had said about the novel I was writing.

"I know," I said. "I do care for him, but that doesn't mean I can give him the uncritical love of a mother."

"Even a mother can't give uncritical love," said Marzenna. "But there are good ways and bad ways to give someone love that is also critical. Don't you think, Francesco?"

"*You* can say or do whatever you like, Marzenna," said Francesco.

"I know," said Marzenna.

She had said that in the Institut Pasteur, while we were crowded around Darren, who had his leg all swollen up; it was filling with blood and lymph, but the doctors couldn't figure out why. We were listening to me reading the passage I have just written, and everybody was laughing, trying to understand how a self-referent novel about life and death actually worked.

"I don't know how it works," Darren said. "Philippe knows how it works. As long as he gets the story told, I'll be happy."

"How does it work?" asked Marzenna.

"I have no idea," I said. "I will tell you that those hard words about Darren being a colossal snob came out of Maugham, even though the sentence construction came out of chapter one of *The Sun Also Rises,* and the business about Darren springing from his conception of himself came out of *The Great Gatsby*."

"Ha!" said Francesco.

I tried to begin reading again. "Well, that's enough reading for—"

Darren interrupted: "Philippe and I hit upon a philosophy about what to laugh at in the novel."

"Oh really?" Francesco was a philosopher himself.

"We decided we can laugh at *death,* but *not* at people's pain."

"Seems like a fine philosophy," Francesco said.

"In a few years it'll seem like all the other fine philosophies I've had," I said.

"Well, in a few years it won't matter," Darren said.

"Correct," I said. "*Heureusement*. Imagine if you had to live forever. You'd be visited by all your friends," I said, thinking of Dead John.

"Philippe, I think you may be going crazy," Darren said.

"Just wait," I said. "All your friends are beginning to visit me. I'm trying to have conversations with them even when they're not there. They're always alive, in front of me, when I'm writing."

"Getting difficult to tell when life begins and literature ends?" Francesco said.

"Exactly."

Darren was a little bored by all this. "Oh, did I tell you, Francesco, Marzenna—" His hand covered his mouth; I knew he was about to say something really wicked and enjoyable, and I also knew what it was. "Somebody just *died* next door," Darren said, giggling, twisting, his laughter barely under control. It was really very funny that someone had died next door while we had been playing Bronski Beat on Darren's boom box. I doubled over laughing. "There were all these people milling around," Darren said, "looking gloomy and depressed. And then Philippe came in and said there were two people outside my door who were crying into handkerchiefs. And I said, 'I told you the fucker died *right next door!*' " He practically had to shout the words to get them across, he was laughing so hard. Darren and I continued laughing and tried very hard to get our breaths back.

"Oh well," he said, sighing longingly. "The nurses say somebody croaks every week or so. They laugh at it, too. What else can they do? Constantly mourn? What about the living? Why should we celebrate the dead more than the dying? I'm going to die; I accept that. Just no pain, God, please. Philippe, thanks for the plastic bag."

I brought Darren plastic bags because he said he might eventually use one, when his illness was unbearable and he was away from adult supervision.

"Here you are, as requested," I would say, handing him a bright blue plastic bag.

"Oh, Philippe, you don't ever stop being kind," Darren would say.

"You need a sense of humor in this life. This will be a very funny novel about death."

I smiled at him. So did Marzenna and Francesco.

Then in front of all of us, Darren suddenly winced. Winced, and winced again.

"Darren?" I asked. "Something wrong? Pain?"

"No," he said. "I'm trying to fart."

Marzenna and Francesco thought that passage was hilarious. I had been reading them the parts in the novel where they spoke. We were crowded around Darren, who had his leg all swollen up; it was filling with blood and lymph, but the doctors couldn't figure out why. We had just listened to the passage I have just written, and everybody was laughing, trying to understand how a self-referent novel about life and death actually worked.

"I didn't say that!" said Marzenna.

"You make me sound like an idiot," said Francesco.

"I like it," said Darren. That pleased me.

Marzenna said, "It's bizarre how you wrote that *before* we got here. You were describing a scene that was *going* to happen. We were listening to ourselves being described in the present, by a document written in the past."

"Deep, isn't it?" I said.

"Wait," said Francesco. "I *still* sound like an idiot. I should be saying that, not her."

"Well, say it then," I said.

But he only smiled, shrugging off his chance to say something clever. "No. I'll only succeed in sounding like an idiot."

"But you're not an idiot, Francesco. You're incredibly intelligent and you must have a very special physique to satisfy Marzenna, that's for sure."

Darren had told me in between this scene and the previous one to compliment Francesco at least once or twice on his intelligence. I threw in the compliment on his anatomy for good measure.

"Nevertheless," Francesco said, smiling, "you make *her* say all the clever things."

"But I *do* say them," Marzenna said.

"Not in real life."

"But in the novel I do."

"I haven't finished the novel yet," I said. "I'm still writing it. I may decide to edit both of you out."

"Well, you should at least mention Marzenna's irritating habit of pointing her finger at people."

"I will," I said.

"Like this," he said, and demonstrated.

"No, not like that, like this," Marzenna said, and demonstrated.

Just then the phone rang. Darren answered it. It was Jean-Baptiste.

As always, he spoke incredibly quickly, and there was only his chipmunk-like high-pitched squawking on the other end of the line. He was complaining about Australia, and his decision to go there.

"Well, Jean-Baptiste," Darren said, "that's life. You *chose* to go, so now you have to live with the consequences."

Jean-Baptiste squawked something about how he couldn't have known . . . had to find out . . . something else, incomprehensible.

"Well, tough," Darren said, sharply. "You have to make the most of a negative situation, that's all."

Marzenna and Francesco and I looked at each other. Reverend Darren hath spoken. And Reverend Darren was often most critical of the people he most loved.

Someone knocked on the door. It was James.

"That's just it," Darren was telling Jean-Baptiste. "You *can't* start again from zero. You can't just change countries and expect to start all over again, Jean-Baptiste. You have to work with what you have."

"Wouldn't you like to have said that, Francesco?" I said.

"Shh!" said Darren. "Look—Jean-Baptiste. I have four friends here, and James just walked in. . . . Yes, James. . . . So take care of yourself, because no one else will, certainly not that orange-haired queen you decided to . . . Well, tough. As soon as he gets his normal hair color back, I'll stop saying he has orange hair. Right now, he does. So: *no sympathy.* . . . Jean-Baptiste— no—no—listen. . . . All right, I'm sorry. We'll talk later. *Sorry.* Bye. Bye-bye. Bye."

He put the phone down. "Hello, James."

"Hello, Darren." They kissed a pair of times, on the cheeks, as some Frenchmen do. James said hello warmly to Francesco and Marzenna, and shook my hand. Then he turned to Darren again.

"Jean-Baptiste still giving you problems?" he asked.

"He never stops," Darren sighed, a little wistfully. "Oh well. This is what I get for adopting him. And now he runs away."

"How are things down in Australia?"

"Let me see. . . . At first it was terrible. Two days later it was great. Then two days later it was awful, again. And the next day was fantastic. I lost track of what happened after. But ever since I sent him some Prozac he says everything is perfectly *fine*. But he does want to come back. He's coming back next month. That means he lasted one month and a half."

"But he was expecting to stay for a year! For life!"

"Yeah, well—life is full of surprises. Look at *me*!"

"I am looking at you," he said tenderly. "You look good, Darren."

"What a sweetheart you are, James. How are you? How long are you here for? Why'd you come so all of a sudden?"

"Well, Philippe sent me some pages of his novel, and I found he said we met at a Go East Young Man concert, which is not true at all; it was a classical music concert."

"Big difference, James. The net result was the same. As I remember, you were on your back *that night!*" Darren roared laughing.

"Are you high?" asked James.

"*Am* I high? Just a little bit," said Darren.

Marzenna and Francesco and I looked at each other. Francesco tilted his head towards the door, which sort of suggested we should leave Darren and James alone for a while.

"Darren," I said, "I think we're going to get some Chinese food. Do you want any?"

"Chinese?" Darren said, looking up. "No, not for me. James?"

James shook his head, a tiny elegant shake, his eyes closed, the corners of his mouth turned down.

"All right. We'll be back before eight."

"Have fun. Take care," Darren said.

Marzenna, Francesco, and I exited his room, passed the room next door with the dead body, and made our way through corridors and down flights of stairs until we were in the rue de Vaugirard.

"Thanks," said Francesco, "for letting *me* give the signal for us to leave. That makes me look intelligent, at least just once."

"You're welcome," I said.

We entered the Chinese restaurant. We were the only ones there.

"You've given us quite an honor," said Francesco, "to be a part of your novel."

"I have to write it first," I said. "Actually—I have some questions to ask both of you. Research."

"Research?" asked Marzenna.

"Yes. About your wedding."

"*Our* wedding?" Francesco and Marzenna looked at each other, surprised.

"Well, yes. There are only going to be two weddings in the book. Yours—and Darren's. Yours was the real thing, with bells, and robes—and true love, I think."

"There were no bells," said Marzenna.

"But there was lots of everything else I mentioned," I said. "I hope. Ah—Francesco, now *I* sound like an idiot."

Francesco looked at me with wide eyes.

"Anyway," I continued, "I need to do research. I've seen all the pictures—Saint Nicholas Cathedral and all that. Marzenna looked beautiful, and you looked handsome, Francesco."

"Oh, thanks."

"Well. So Darren was there. He thinks it was the most beautiful wedding of his life. Of course, compared to his own wedding, it probably was."

"Darren's wedding was *very* interesting," said Marzenna.

"I wasn't there," said Francesco. "But I would have liked to have been."

"Do you know the story?" Marzenna asked me.

"I know the outline. Tell me what you know."

"Well," said Marzenna, "Darren decided—this was in 1990—that he wanted to live, and work, in France. He needed a *carte de séjour*. And the easiest way to get one was to marry. So he placed an ad on the Minitel. 'American, 26, desires marriage to French woman.' Two girls answered; the first wanted money."

"People always want money," I said.

"Don't write she said that," said Francesco.

"I won't," I said.

Marzenna continued: "So—Darren decided to marry the second girl, who didn't want anything except to get married. She lived at Choisy-le-Roi. And that's where they got married."

I was still scribbling notes. "Who was there?" I asked.

"Mostly men," Marzenna said.

I looked up. "One of the problems with this novel," I said, "is that most of the characters are men. I need some women characters."

"Here's one," said Francesco, pointing at Marzenna. We both laughed. Marzenna rolled her eyes.

"Anyway," she continued, "I was the only girl there, except the bride. Marie-Espérance had gone to a lot of trouble to look nice. The wedding was a big, big day for her. It *convenienced* her enormously to get married, not just to an American, of course, but for social standing."

"Did she know about Darren?" I asked.

"Oh, she knew everything. Darren was very clear about that."

The pot stickers arrived.

"Merci," we said.

"Then what happened?"

"Nothing, really. Well—at the wedding, Darren acted like the *man* of the house. He was something to see, that day. He looked like a man—no mannerisms, no affectations—just opening bottles, and acting like a *man*. It was just an act, but it made you think of what he could have been, if things had been different."

"What could have been," said Francesco.

"What could have been," I echoed. "And then what happened?"

Marzenna smiled. "Nothing happened. They never slept together, not even the first night. But actually, for a *mariage blanc,* they treated each other quite well. They invited each other out, and to each other's parties, although she always felt out of place among his friends."

"I have a hard time imagining what she's like. I have a hard time imagining a woman who feels unmarriageable—" Then I bit my tongue, thinking of a past girlfriend. I felt my past poking into the moment like an unwanted person suddenly turning up at my door. I tried to say something, anything, to rid myself of the uncomfortable feeling. "She wasn't unattractive, was she?" I asked, just to say something.

"Not at all," Marzenna said, politely pretending not to notice my malaise.

"She found her husband on the Minitel," I repeated, stupidly.

"You can find almost anything you like on the Minitel," said Marzenna. She did not look at Francesco; it would have been humorous if she had.

I returned to our other topic. "And after she found Darren, she gave up trying to fall in love, forever?"

"No, she didn't. Not at all. Last year she found a man she says she's in love with, and who's in love with her. She's asking Darren for a divorce. She didn't give up on the search for true love at all. She just got married for convenience. You see, Philippe, the problem with their marriage—besides the obvious one—is that he was prejudiced against her from the start. He said she was white trash, because in his fantasy life he wanted to get married to somebody from a vastly superior stratum. He was disappointed by her because she was normal—quite decent, even."

"And what was wrong with that?"

"It fell short of his fantasy world. Everything falls short of his fantasy world. That's why he's such a snob."

"He's not a snob!" protested Francesco.

"Noooooooo!" we all wailed together, and laughed.

"A snob—him, the son of a Kansas dairy farmer. Why is he such a snob?" I asked.

Marzenna answered. "But he's not a snob, really. He likes saying those things because he thinks it makes him sound urbane. But in fact he's always comparing his whole life to his ideal life, an ideal life he made up when he was a boy. And even now, years later, it hasn't changed; it's still the sort of ideal life that a seventeen-year-old boy would be likely to make up. Europe, prestige, glamour, castles. That's what he's looking for, constantly looking for: to fulfill those dreams. That's why we can't really call him a snob."

The pot stickers were untouched.

"He's like a little boy who doesn't want to grow up," Francesco said.

"I'll say!" I said. But if he was haunted by an imaginary world, that explained his friendship with James. "Do you know James well?" I asked.

"He's a nice guy," said Francesco. "Very nice. Head in the clouds, a little, but pft! that makes him charming."

Marzenna smiled sweetly. "Another one looking for the end of the rainbow."

"I heard he was looking for a job."

"That also. He's always out of money."

"Huh!" I said. "I know about that!"

"He cares for Darren very, very deeply," said Francesco.

"But," said Marzenna, "Darren doesn't quite care so much for him. Not in the same way."

The end of the rainbow always falls where you are not, I thought.

I said, "Still, I think it's good that he comes to see Darren."

"Yes. Especially now," said Francesco.

We all frowned. We knew what had been mentioned, even though it hadn't been mentioned, really.

"It happens to all of us," Francesco said. "Sooner or later, it happens to all of us."

He really did say that.

Sort of.

CHAPTER 5

I started writing chapter five in my deux-pièces in Saint-Germain-des-Prés. In my solid hiking boots and lined flannel shirts, I was walking from the bedroom into the living room, and then back again, and then into the kitchen and the bathroom and then out again; I was walking—long distances, longer distances, and the carpet became a kind of gravel, and the ceiling became a kind of sky, and I was walking down the driveway of Yew Tree Farms, on a cold November day.

The Swenson family house was a white clapboard two-story ship in the middle of the tanned Kansan sea. The house had strange rectangular portholes, squares oddly balanced on their corners, cut around all its long walls.

I rang the doorbell. I was wearing boots and my favorite lined flannel shirt—what I usually wore in Paris. I had left boot tracks up to the porch, and the marks they left in the ground were the only familiar things in the landscape. I waited for the answer and shivered.

I was about to ring the doorbell a second time when the door handle turned, and huge Mrs. Swenson stood before me.

"Hello, Philippe."

"Hello, Mrs. Swenson."

"Come in," she said, sadly, and averted her eyes.

I came in, clutching my worsted cap in my hands, close to my chest.

"Your trip was fine?" she asked me. She was dressed in a purple shirt, and wore rouge on her cheeks, a little lavender on her eyelids. Her skin had a brilliance to it, like the snow on a hill after the first snowfall.

"Yes," I said.

"No problems?" she asked. She began to busy herself with tea things and coffee things. Making an effort to look only at her, I followed her from the kitchen into the living room: past pots and pans and knickknacks lining the walls, photographs—photographs of Darren, fourteen years old, smiling, wire-framed farmer's glasses, a big-striped gray tie.

"No, Mrs. Swenson, no problems."

There was a silence. She sat down in the easy chair I had seen in the pictures. It was a dark beige color.

(I was sure it was beige. In fact it may have been red, but beige seemed a more *appropriate* color.)

She leaned back in the beige chair, as far as it would go, and I stared at that hippopotamus neck—it was not a neck, it was where the blob of her head met the blob of her body—and I shuddered. The size of her!

She caught me staring. "You look hungry," she said.

"Oh! No, I'm fine."

"Have some coffee, tea. Have what you like."

"May I serve myself?" I asked.

"Nothin' easier than self-service," she said. I began to fiddle with the tea things and the coffee things, propping one knee against the small table. My hiking boots had pressed indentations in the brand-new carpet that still smelt of plastic. I was afraid I had dirtied it. Hoping she would not notice, I moved my hand—to me, all of a sudden, a very small, thin hand—slowly down to touch my boot track in the carpet.

"Don't worry about your tracks," she said, startling me. I drew my hand back. "They'll disappear," she said.

I turned to look at her, but again she averted her gaze, and in her clear eyes I thought I saw many swimming reflections, all the little thoughts, the little lights in the room and the pale light from the great windows.

I said nothing and poured myself some coffee. I added milk and it turned a pale gray color.

"Would you like some, Mrs. Swenson?"

"No thanks—Phileep. And you can call me Lilian. Now say: have I got your name right? Pronounce it 'Phil*eep*'? Phil*eep*?"

"Yes," I said. "That's me." I had the coffee mug in my hand, the coffee still spinning round and round inside the mug. I glanced about the room for a place to sit. There was the deep-looking sofa, covered with a homemade shawl. There were six hard chairs at the big round table, where the Swensons ate, played poker, and did their taxes. There were three black wooden chairs with cushions machine-stamped with a fading yellow design; they looked unused, too fragile for the fat. I decided on the big, deep sofa, and I sat in it—it gobbled up my buttocks and nearly hauled my feet off the ground.

"So—Phil*eep*. Darren says you're his ghost writer. That you're writin' his biography."

"Sort of."

"Darren—*deserves* a biography? He hasn't lived all that long. Do you think he *needs* a biography?"

I sipped the coffee. "Your coffee has a nice flavor," I said.

"I—why thank you," she said, and she seemed very pleased, and smiled. Her eyes crinkled up the corners, and her chin stuck out; I could have sworn it was Darren's chin for one second, and then it fell back into the flab. She said, "Don't know about you, but I like good coffee."

"Me too. Darren too," I said. I looked at the walls papered with dark brown—at the photographs, the awards, the certificates, the ribbons encased in gold-plated frames. On the dark-colored shelves were ineptly assembled model airplanes, painted rocks, pincushions, raggedy dolls—one of them with bright orange hair—little rhinestone-studded mirrors, strange unstoppered perfume bottles. There was a framed print of a well-known painting.

"You lookin' at that? It's a Mo-nay," she said. "Bought it on our honeymoon in Paris."

"That so?"

"Yep. And those there are the children's old toys," she said. I was disconcerted by her ability to see what I was looking at.

"Really," I said.

"Know the children?" she asked me. "Darren's mentioned 'em?"

"Yes. Davey is the oldest," I said. Mrs. Swenson was suddenly looking at me with full-blast intensity. "Then there's Sharon," I cautiously continued, "Darren's twin sister."

"Now, Philippe, let's test you. Who's older, Sharon or Darren?"

"Ah . . . I don't know, Mrs. Swenson. I never thought it mattered. Who's older?"

"Just testin' you. Go on," she said, and her gaze became absolute, interrogatory. "Keep talkin'."

"The youngest is Sherrie. She's married to Pete. Sharon is married to Wade. Davey is married to Susie. Darren . . . is married to Marie-Espérance."

It was too late: I had said it. Lilian fixed me with a formulated phrase.

"That so?"

I wriggled a bit. "Yes—yes—it's marriage. They're married."

"You call that marriage?"

"Yes, ma'am, I do."

She turned away, muttering *tut-tut-tut* in a disapproving way. "You Europeans. I bet you think anythin' goes. But I'm not so sure. I'm not so sure. Maybe you'll say I am backwoods and old-fashioned. Say it, if you like. But Darren's 'marriage,' as you call it, is a crock. Lord help me for saying so."

"Mrs. Swenson—" I hesitated. She looked at me, her eyes like talons, ready for one wrong step, one unguarded revelation of my actual position. "It suited them both. Marie-Espérance wanted it. They both . . . *chose* to enter it." And I immediately cursed myself for being a fool, using that word *chose* in the wrong way. Now she would use it against me.

She said, "So he—he *chose* her? And *she chose* him, too?"

"Well—sort of, ma'am. Yes. They *chose* each other. They wanted marriage."

"What they get married for if they don't want children?"

"In truth . . . Mrs. Swenson . . . I think Darren married at least partially to please *you*. To not be a disappointment to you.

But he could not love his wife, that was simply not in his nature."

"His *nature*? Fine word. What's it mean?"

"I'm not sure," I said.

"Think you do, Philippe."

You fat bitch, I thought, I'm not playing these sorts of games.

"Yes," I said. "You're right. I do. I believe—I don't believe your son *chose* to be gay."

She looked at me, hard. "Gay?" she repeated. She sighed. The sigh was like steam escaping from an overheated pot. "*Chose* to be—gay," she said. "So." I felt something inside her unlock. "So tell me, Philippe—if my son, Darren, is *gay*—if my son, Darren, has sex with *men*—then why did he *marry*? Why did he marry—a *girl*? Why? You're his biographer. Why?"

I cleared my throat. "For papers to live in Europe?"

"Ohhh. For papers. I see. To live in Europe. It's so simple. Need papers to live in Europe? Marry somebody. Right outta the blue. Doesn't matter who she is, what she is, we don't know, we don't care. Pick her in a phone book, say 'Let's get married,' get a lawyer, sign papers, say vows, shake hands and walk away and you are married. Just like that. Isn't really *hick*-style marriage, but Darren isn't a hick, is he? Not like his parents. We are hicks, aren't we, Philippe, don't you think? You don't think we're hicks? You don't? Well then tell me, Philippe, if Darren was born into Kansas—if country was his home—if he was born, raised, and happy here—then tell me, *why* did Darren have to leave for *Europe*? Tell me, why—what in heaven's name did Darren J. Swenson have to do in Europe? In *Paris*? What does a *Kansan* have to do with *Paris*? What does a son of Yew Tree Farms, born here, bred here for four generations, raised here, made here—for four generations—why should he, all of a sudden, have to live in *Europe*? Why'd he have to—why make such a hypocrisy of marriage—to be—what he wanted, 'a Parisian from Kansas'?"

She kept staring at me. I said nothing for a while. Then I cleared my throat, cautiously. She said, "So? You have an answer?"

"No," I said. "I don't. I don't know why he had to become 'a Parisian from Kansas.' "

She answered right back. "You don't know? *You don't know?* What kind of an answer is that, you 'don't know'?"

"I'm sorry, but I don't."

" 'I'm sorry.' Well, that's swell. I'm sorry, too, Phili*ppe*." She contained herself. "You don't know. But of course not—after all, you're just writin' a biography. What do you know? What do you know, Philippe? D'you even know how to milk a cow?"

"What?"

"I said, d'you know how to milk a cow?"

"No."

"No, you don't. D'you know how to reap a crop?"

"No."

"D'you know how to drive a tractor?"

"No, Mrs. Swenson, I don't."

"Darren was drivin' a tractor when he was twelve—maybe earlier. Now what makes you think you can understand a boy like that, a boy so different from you in every respect? I can see you're not a country boy. I don't hold that against you, by the way, I don't suppose you *chose* to be a city kid." She smiled at me, and I smiled lightly back.

"And you are all right, I suppose. You didn't waltz in here expectin' favors. I was afraid you were goin' to be like some greedy lawyer, askin' questions and takin' names. I thought that's what Darren wanted. I was sure Darren wanted that. But I understand it: you're only askin' questions for your biography. Not for blame. Interestin'. Very interestin'." She broke off, and looked into space almost dreamily. Then, in front of me, she farted—quite loudly. Then she sighed. "I don't know," she said. "You and Darren. Must not be easy, bein' with Darren, satisfyin' his every fancy, always bein' pleasant. Darren isn't always that pleasant. Darren always wants things, and Darren is always *sure* he knows what he wants. Don't you think?"

"No."

"You don't think so?"

"No."

"Didn't Darren send you to show us bein' awful? Prove how dumb and ignorant and awful we are? Find fault with everythin'—with the house, the farm, the accent, the people—didn't he?"

"No."

"Tell the truth."

"Then yes. Darren did want me to prove you were awful. He did. He does."

She stared at me, and her eyebrows came apart. She looked away from me very sadly. She said, "Does he really." Then she said, slower and softer: "Does—he—really."

She continued: "Philippe—now—let me ask you. Answer honestly. I don't care what you say, but answer honestly. Do you think we're awful? Do you? Do you think we made a mistake, bringin' Darren up? Did we go wrong, somewhere? What could we have done better? We don't have ten million ways of raisin' children, Philippe, please understand. This is hard country out here. We raised Darren the best we could. With fear. Fear of God. And good morals . . . discipline. We gave Darren so much love, you can't comprehend what love I gave him. Did I go wrong, doin' that? I don't know, Philippe—I just don't know. We tried our best, you must believe me, we tried our best. Does Darren think we deliberately screwed him up? Does he?"

I said nothing.

"Maybe we are old-fashioned and backwoods. Maybe we aren't the free-thinkin', free-livin' people Darren's grown accustomed to. But it's workin' for us, it always has and always will. But we *tried,* Philippe. We *tried.* When Darren gave up farm work, we let that pass. When Darren left for France, we let him go, and when he came back a snob, we let that pass. When he made us say he was gay—that was hard, Philippe, but we said it, we admitted it to everybody. When he threw Jean-Baptiste in our faces, that day he came back—we let that pass. But now— he wants to prove to the whole wide world how dumb and ignorant and awful we are. When you know we are not. Why? Why do you encourage him?"

I said nothing.

"You don't know him very well. He's a spoiled brat. We must have spoiled him; it must be my fault. We tried to raise him hard. But damn it, he's got *charm,* Philippe. He got used to gettin' what he wanted, and never could take no for an answer. Ever. Don't you think so?"

"I thought it was the illness that made him difficult."

She inhaled deeply with a sigh that was more like a suppressed sob. "The illness. Yes, that's a nice way of puttin' it—the *illness.*" She looked at the floor, at the carpet and the worlds deep down below. "No. The illness only made things worse."

We were silent a long time.

"But Philippe—you still haven't answered my question," she said. "Do you think it was right—that he got married?"

"Well—Mrs. Swenson—" I began, faltering, "I think it was legal."

"Oh! of course it was legal. Anythin's *legal,* so long as a lawyer's alive. But what's legal isn't always *right.* Suppose I'd put Darren in an orphanage, adoption, soon as he was born. The law of the land would've made it legal. But the law of God would make it wrong. Now, was Darren's marriage *right?*"

I hesitated.

"Was it?"

"No," I said. I looked down. "But, Mrs. Swenson—it was the best—Darren could do. I think—truly."

"What do you mean, 'best he could do'?"

"I mean he could not have gotten married any better, and maybe it was better, given what he wanted to do, to marry, rather than stay single." Her gaze was both maternal and contemptuous. "But I really don't know," I added. "I'm uncertain about what was *right.*"

She shook her head and scowled at me. "Philippe—anyone ever tell you, you are *confused*? About certain facts of life. Tell me this. How many teats has a cow got?"

I lowered my eyes, feeling ridiculous, and said, "Six?"

She smirked. "No. Don't be ashamed—you're a city kid, after all. You know other things. But: Philippe, d'you suppose that *we* can afford to live, not knowin' the basic facts of life?"

"No."

"Do you think we have the luxury of questionin' everythin', the way you do?"

"No."

"Do you think runnin' a farm is like writin' a biography, where if there's doubt, you just make a footnote? If we get it wrong, Philippe, if we don't know the answers, we starve. We have to make decisions, and stick by those decisions. Plant or don't plant. Harvest or don't harvest. Reap what you sow. Do you know what that means? Do you?" She softened her voice. "Do you know what that means? Do you?"

A long long wait. "No."

She seemed satisfied by this answer.

"Now. I am goin' to tell you what I think. Life round these parts is too hard. Too hard for biographies—too hard, Philippe, for anythin' but solid, no-nonsense people. There's no room for screwball marriages." She looked towards the desk, at the photograph of Al Swenson, who looked tough and rugged, deep blue overalls under deep blue eyes. She kept talking. "That's not to say every marriage round here is fair and square. Some are as fake as a three-dollar bill. But most people round here—almost everybody—marries for love. And that's quite lovely, I think. So what I hate is that Darren, who didn't have to marry, who didn't want to get married, married—a girl—for *papers*. For *work* papers. So he could work in France, as an alien. Among people who were not even his friends."

"Some of us are his friends," I said.

"I know you say you are a friend. I know. But tell me this. Be straight, Philippe. Why are you writin' Darren's biography? Just 'cause you like him? Or for money?"

"A bit of both," I said.

" 'Cause after you write the book, you're gonna sell the book, and it's gonna make money. Right?" she asked. "Who gets the money?"

"Darren and I will share."

"Wail, I know that without you, there'd be no book. You're the writer. But don't you think—that Darren is puttin' *all* of himself behind this book? Don't you think, when all is said and done, it's *his* book?"

Just then the screen door opened. Heavy, gruff, and hearty, Al Swenson, covered with the cold, came in, and the wind howled around the door.

"Hello there!" he said.

I stood up.

"Hello, Mr. Swenson."

He immediately fixed me with an intelligent, clear blue eye and said, "Now then, my name is Al. Everybody calls me Al, and you will, too. Now. I'm afraid that Lilian here has *tried* to explain I don't know how many times just *how* to pronounce your name. But for the life of me, I can't. Now, so as not to embarrass you with my god-awful illiterate pronunciation, may I just call you 'Phil'?"

"Al," I said, "*please* call me Phil."

"Awright, Phil. Phil, have you had coffee and things to eat? 'Cause I'm gonna have some."

Lilian, for the first time, lit a cigarette, and I could hear the flint itching against the tungsten as Al helped himself to a great sandwich. He took three huge bites and the thing was suddenly gone.

"One of my boys told me I et like a hog once," he said, "an' I had to beat him for it. Trouble is, he was right. And you know what? I *still* et like a hog," he said, and gave me a mayonnaise-and-mustard smile. "Which of the boys told me, Lil? D'ya remember?"

"It was Darren," she said.

"Oh, of course. It was Darren." He chewed with his mouth closed, masticating thoughtfully. "You're writin' Darren's book," he said.

"I'm trying to."

"Hard work?"

"Desk work."

"That can be the hardest work of all," he said, and wiped his lips. He looked at me straight. "What do ya think of Darren?"

I felt pushed back by the intensity of the question. "That's a—rather big thing to ask," I said.

"Your answer don't have to be big." Our eyes met for an instant.

I said, "Darren got a disease which he didn't deserve. And—it's unfair."

"Ya mean—the disease is unfair."

"Yes."

"Yeahp. Unfair. When your health gives up on you—" He shook his head sadly. He sighed deeply. He had a thinker's reserve, and said in a monotone, "Now we're gonna wonder for years about what might've happened—what he could've become. Don't you think?"

"What might have happened?" I repeated.

"Yes."

"Only God knows what might have happened—Al. I don't know." Then I remembered his first question, about what I thought of Darren. "Certainly Darren is generous, and sincere, and brave, and he loves life."

"Yeahp, maybe he loves life a little *too* much—you know." He bowed his head and stiffened his lips. "You two get along?" I nodded. "Pretty well," I said. "Not perfectly, but well."

"Wail," Al said, "ya take the good with the bad. Nobody's perfect."

"Some people are," Lilian said suddenly. "Some people are tryin'. Don't you think so, Philippe? Don't you think some people are really, really good—almost perfect?"

"I don't know, Lilian. I suppose a saint can be better than other persons, but you have to be dead to be a saint."

Al snorted as he went into the kitchen to look for some more food.

"Hey, are ya religious, Phil?" he asked me from the kitchen, fixing himself another sandwich.

"I'm Catholic by birth."

"Wail, that's good," he said. "Its good to have religion. It's damn useful, for when times get tough. Damn useful."

I thought Lilian had turned to look at me. But instead I saw her attention fixed at some point far behind me, far away, on the past, on what might have been. I noticed something in her expression suggesting she bore some terrible scar, lacerated through her whole soul. Then she realized with a start I was looking at her face, and had seen all the unconscious expressions that had passed over it silently. I quickly glanced at the piano.

"Do you know who bought him that? I bought him that," she said, with forced jollity. "You shoulda heard him play. He played Beethoven's *Pathétique*. And he played *Für Elise*. He woulda been a great pianist. He *was* a great pianist," she added, correcting herself. "Do you play?" she asked.

"No," I said, lying.

"Darren said you played," she said.

"I used to."

"Give it up?" she asked.

"Yes."

"So you mighta been a great pianist, too, eh?" she said. "Eh?"

"Might've been," I said.

Lilian got up, heavily, and waddled towards the kitchen.

Just then the phone rang. She picked it up.

"Hel-lo. Oh—yes. Yes, he's here. What's the rush? All right, you don't need to shout. Philippe—" she said, "it's for you. It's Darren."

I took a deep breath, then lifted the receiver to my ear.

"Darren," I said. "I've been expecting you to call."

"Really? Why? What's going on?"

"Your parents. *Very* interesting."

"So you're getting an idea of what it was like, growing up in that shit-hole, huh?"

I closed my eyes when he said that and thought of Al and Lil, together in the kitchen. "I have an *idea,* yes. But I wouldn't call it a *shit-hole,* Darren." My eyes remained closed; I did not even want to imagine what his parents were thinking, hearing me talk like that. "However, Darren, I am researching and imagining, imagining a lot, and everything is going quite well. What's up?"

"Philippe, I just spoke to Jean-Baptiste." His tone was funereal.

"Yes?"

"Philippe, he just dumped me."

"Really?"

"He said he doesn't want to see me again."

"Really?"

"What a bitch he is. He said, 'Darren, I just can't take your illness.' Oh, Philippe, it won't work between him and me. It just won't. It *can't!"*

"Is he still in Australia?"

"Yes! He called me collect *from* Australia to dump me."

"What did he say, Darren, exactly?"

"He said he wants more independence. He says he can't deal with me and my *maladie* anymore."

"Is that what he said?"

"Ye-e-es," he said, stretching the word out.

"Well," I said. This was only the fourth time Jean-Baptiste had dumped Darren in two weeks. And this was only the fourth time he had called me, when I was working, to complain about the dumpings. "Darren . . ." I began. And I gave him the best speech I could. "He's too young to know exactly what he wants . . . he's like a restless boy, he needs to explore, but he'll be back. . . ." And so on. Darren seemed to be better after a quarter of an hour of this.

"Thanks," he said, finally. "I needed that. How are *you*?" he asked, with interest that sounded a little forced.

"Ah . . . I'm fine. The usual. You know."

"Good. Oh, Philippe, I've been thinking about my mother . . ."

"Yes, so have I, Darren."

". . . and I've decided that you are going to *burn* her, Philippe. Write everything up, Philippe. Every one of those pages is a log you're going to use to *burn* her."

I took a deep, deep breath. "Oh-kay," I said. "You want to listen to your parents?"

"Listen to them? Right now? I really don't feel like it."

"They would like to talk to you. Here's your father, Darren," I said.

"H'lo, Darren? . . . Yeahp. Yeeahp. . . . Oh yeah, he's bein' fed, he looks kinda skinny. . . . Don't you worry 'bout that. He'll get everythin' he needs from us. . . . Awright, yep. The doctor takin' care of ya? . . . Wail, let us know. . . . We miss ya, son. . . . Right. Yeahp. Yeahp. Uh-huh. Good. . . . Good. . . . Great! That's great! Awright now. Here, I'll give you back to Phil. Here ya are, Phil."

"Here's your mother, Darren," I said.

"Hel-lo. How are you. . . . Fine. Fine. Yep. Yep. . . . Oh, not too bad. Philippe says . . . He's very nice, Darren, I don't need to be told who he is; I can figure that out by myself. . . . Of course! Of course! Why are you worried? Darren, you don't need to tell me what to do. . . . Darren, if I said that to you. . . . Awright. Awright. Wail, tell us when you do. Talk t'ya soon. Let me pass you back to Philippe. Here's Philippe."

"Yes, here's me," I said. "All is well. . . .What? . . . Oh. Very good. Glad to hear it. . . . Let me know when, then. Thanks. Okay—bye."

And I hung up the farm phone—an old, rattling contraption colored beige (how appropriate, I thought).

As soon as I replaced the receiver, the phone rang again. I picked it up. This time it was *my* mother, which surprised me, because she wasn't in any of my outlines or in any of my plots or in any of my character notes.

"Mom?" I asked.

"Yes, Philippe, it's *Maman*. How are you?"

"I'm fine."

"What are you doing so late?"

"Writing."

"The novel about Darren?" she asked.

"Yes."

"How is poor Darren?" she asked.

"He's still at the Institut Pasteur. But he's getting better."

"And how is your novel going?"

I smiled. She was so concerned for me and my novel. "Ah, it's going well," I said. "I was making up a scene about life in Kansas when you called. I was pretending I was actually in Kansas. I'm at the point now where I have all sorts of fragments, completely disordered. But it's not a novel, and it's starting to worry me. I could just throw them all together, I suppose; it would make for a very modern novel."

"Oh! A modern novel. How impressive!"

My dad came on the line.

"Allô, Philippe?" he said.

"Hello, Dad."

"So now you're in Kansas!" he said.

"No, not really," I said, smiling.

"What's going on?" He was being witty with me. I could hear him grinning. I liked to hear him grinning; he was old, with the sicknesses of old age, but he still grinned a lot. I grinned right back.

"Well, I'm pretending I'm in Kansas with Darren's parents; I'm pretending Darren has called. All my phone calls are pretending."

"I don't get it," said Dad.

"In the book," I said, "phone calls are my way of getting people to say things I don't want to say myself."

"Such as?"

"Well, you have to say it."

"Say what?"

"You have to say, for example, that Darren takes an obscure view of his mother."

"What?"

"He wants me to be very negative about his mother."

"Be careful about criticizing his parents," my mother said.

"I'm trying!" I said.

"Darren will never be a likable hero if he can't get along with his parents," she said.

"He does get along. With one-half of them."

"Which half?" asked my father.

"His father," I said. "But he really *hates* his mother."

"That means he loves her, but can't show it because he's too angry at himself," said my mother.

"*You* tell him that," I said.

"I will!" said my mother cheerfully. "Let me talk to him! No, that's not my job. But somebody should tell him that he'll never be a hero if he hates his mother."

"But Darren can't take the *least* criticism," I said. "He winces if he even thinks you're going to contradict him."

"Blergkh. People like that are so tiring," said my mom.

"Speak for yourself," said my dad.

"René!" she said. My father laughed.

Mom returned to the main topic. "He's very demanding, isn't he?" she said.

"Yes."

"And he wants his parents to be perfect, doesn't he?"

"Yes. He doesn't say that, of course, but that's what he wants."

"Well, nobody's perfect, right?"

"Yes, but—Mom, his mother weighs four hundred pounds; she's really pushy and bullying sometimes. She can be charming, but it's only to get what she wants."

"And Darren is not like that? Not at all?" She let *that* criticism sink in. "Tell me, Philippe—does she love her son?"

"Her heart is all screwed up; she can't display the least affection—"

"Does she love her son?" my mom repeated.

I paused before answering. "Yes," I said.

"Well, then you can tell her to lose some weight, maybe, if she can; sometimes it's biological, you know, maybe she can't help being fat. And you can tell her to be nicer to people, if you think she'll listen. But you can't blast her, Philippe. Or if you blast her, you must blast Darren too. Because it's far more hateful for a son to hate his mother than a mother to hate her son. Who's sacrificing who, here?"

"Darren wants to sacrifice *her*."

Dad said, decisively, "Well, tell him to do it in his *own* book. *You* be fair to everybody, and if Darren doesn't like it, tough. 'That's the way the cookie crumbles,' tell him."

"Platitude number fifty-five." My brother had come on the line.

"Hi, Francis!" I said.

"Hey, Philippe. How goes it?"

"Writing away."

"So what's with this Darren dude? He wants to be the hero of his own *Star Wars* epic?"

"Something like that."

"He wants to be cast as Luke Skywalker and his mom as Darth Vader, huh?" He did Darth Vader breathing into the mouthpiece and the three of us laughed. "Come with me, Darren, and we shall rule the galaxy as father and son! Mother and son, whatever. That makes *you* Han Solo, the mercenary writer. Chewie! Prepare the Millennium Novel for writing! Warp factor five!"

We were all laughing hysterically.

"Philippe—Philippe—Philip. Now listen. You will never be a great writer if you follow the advice of some asshole who's never read a novel in his life. 'An expert in the art of bad writing'—that's what he is. Write it as *you* see it, Philip. It's gonna be a shit novel if you let Darren use it as a weapon against his family. You write it so that it's *true*." That was a favorite quote from *Garp*.

I breathed in heavily. "Oh-kay," I said.

"Why are you letting this guy control your life?"

"I don't know."

"Or your writing?"

"I don't know."

"Tell him to fuck off and write his own novel. If he doesn't like it"—he imitated Bugs Bunny—" 'Ahhhhhh, git outta heeere.' Tell him to shove your book up his ass."

"Francis!" said my mother. My father laughed.

"He might like that," Francis said.

"All right, enough, Francis," said my father.

"Is Darren tiring?" asked my mother.

"Exhausting," I said. "For him, every moment is the most important moment in the entire history of the universe, and every ten minutes we all have to stop what we're doing and listen to his account of it. And of course he is at the center of his entire mystical galaxy."

"*Only* the galaxy? What about the entire gossamer fabric of spacetime?" said my brother. "His ego can't be *that* big. Gee, maybe he's humble after all."

"He calls me three times a day sometimes to let me know the secret state of his mind. If I don't drop everything to listen, I've committed treachery. The third time he calls to *apologize* for the first two times. He tracks me down and calls me at my *friends'* houses, *after* midnight, 'to see how I'm doing,' he says, when he just wants to talk to me, wants to see if I can talk to him politely even after I've told him I'm not available."

"This guy is complaining about his *mother*? He's lucky you don't blast *him* to smithereens."

"I know."

"Does *he* know?"

"No."

"*Tell* him. In one way or another."

"I'll write about it in the novel."

"Good," they said together, in my deux-pièces in Saint-Germain-des-Prés. What would my parents say next? I wondered.

"You missed *Brideshead Revisited* again," they said.

"Not again."

"The *'Et in Arcadia Ego'* episode, again! Antoine B-B-Blanche," said Mom, laughing.

"Do *you* have a stuttering character in your novel?" asked my father.

"B-b-bye, Philippe," said my brother. He thought *Brideshead Revisited* was b-b-boring.

"Bye!" I said. Then, to my father: "No, I don't. . . . But I could make one up."

Make one up?

Not long after I began writing the novel about Darren, as I was walking up and down the banks of the Seine, reciting *The Waste Land* to the seagulls, hearing the slippery sodden leaves underfoot, and no other sound except the murmuring of surprised passersby, a man stopped me. He wore a cashmere overcoat and a tiny orchid in his lapel, and sported an immaculately trimmed beard. It was Antoine Blanche. "My d-d-dear," he said, in an Etonian way. "Follow me." He took me away from the banks, up the embankment, down the rue de Seine, past the squares Honoré Champion and Georges Pierné, with their smiling statues and twinkling fountains. With his heels quickly clicking on the pavement, he pointed out every art gallery, every boutique, until we reached the café called La Palette. In a flurry of motion Antoine removed his coat, hat, sat down, made love to everyone with his roving eyes, ordered four "Alexandra cocktails," and began lecturing me on my recital of *The Waste Land*. But he tired himself and quickly changed topics.

"*N-n-not* so hysterically. Keep the dignity, rather. But—enough. I am not here to discuss thoughts and theories which you have forgotten. I am here to warn you: to warn you against a peculiar variety of American charm, lying in wait near you, fondling you, caressing you, exciting you. Charm is your enemy, Philippe. It blights, it kills, maims, destroys. It withers even the fairest lily. *Et tu*. Philippe, why are you not drinking? You do not like brandy Alexanders?"

I looked at them. "They look pretty."

"They are not only *pretty*." But I sipped one; it was disgusting.

"No? *No? I* shall drink them, then," he said.

"One.

"Two.

"Three.

"Four.

"Now," he said, his lips still shiny and moist, "about *Monsieur* Darren Swenson. The P-P-Parisian from Kansas. What a charming sobriquet, to be sure! What do you think mine would be, if he chose it? The P-P-Pederast from Windsor? But you are injured by my humor. You love him, do you not? But of *course* you do. It is written on your every feature, you poor boy. Sympathy and compassion for the sick and the dying. Ah! What greater love than love for fellow man! Well, b-b-be the martyr if you like. But how will you stop *yourself* from being sick? How will you stop *yourself* from dying? It is not wise to have unending

compassion for him. You're not his nurse, *Monsieur* Tapon.
You're not his servant. You're not even his boyfriend, *Monsieur*
Tapon. You are that rarest of things—an artist. Tapon. What a
b-b-brutal name you have. Is it real?"

I told him. He looked at me steadily and I was sure he would
roll his eyes in disgust, but he didn't.

"*Mister* Swenson is a f-f-farm boy who lives in Paris. He has
traded the sow for the Seine. And his principal weapon in this
city is his deb-b-bilitating charm—charm which *he* thinks entitles
him to everything. Well, give him what he likes, but not *you*.
Because, for all his v-v-vaunted intellect, Mister Swenson is really
brilliant in only one department, that of recruiting novelists. We
may not accredit him with a literary understanding, *much* as we
love him. Could we, now? My dear, he could hardly tell you the
difference between the *Bhagavad-Gita* and the *Kama-Sutra*. He is
a featherless chicken, but one who thinks he can fly because he
found some eagle feathers in a Grenoble street one day. And one
day he will return to his chicken coop, 'Kansas,' or whatever
horrid place spawned him, and look himself in the mirror, if he
p-p-possibly can. Till then *don't* let him think his borrowed eagle
feathers make him better than you, or entitle him to tear your
manuscript with his prehensile claws. You and he are b-b-both
going to the long home. As did the Reverend Mr. Eliot, my
dear, whom I am glad to see appearing in your work, however
briefly. But don't let him hurry your journey; it would not be
worthwhile. One last word. I neither know nor care, what you
do in your divan or bed. But try to exercise some caution. One
must be so careful these days."

Night was falling. He rose, leaned forward and kissed me
once on the forehead, turned, and disappeared in a flash of cashmere and orchids. I was so dazed that for a while I couldn't
move. But when I rose to pay for the brandy Alexanders, I was
told Monsieur Blanche had taken care of everything. I looked
around, but he was quite definitely gone. The air was very still.
The telephone was pressed against my ear.

"I'll send a manuscript as soon as I put it together," I told my
parents. "Right now all I've got is a big mess, fragments."

"That's fine. Keep at it. And take care, Philippe," my mom
said.

"We love you very much," they said.

"I love you," I said.

"Good night," they said. "Ta ta."

"Good night," I said. "Good night."

Thus ended the surprise conversation with my family, which was not in any of my outlines. It had been a surprise when it happened, happening right before my eyes. The phone call had just been in my imagination.

When I showed Darren the work of the past couple of days, which was from the opening of chapter five until the top of this page, he was a little upset.

"I don't get it," he said. "Why are you so angry, all of a sudden?"

"I'm not that angry. But I am irritated at suddenly becoming your confidant, ghost writer, male nurse, and errand boy all at once."

"Philippe, why don't you *tell* me when I become too demanding?"

"Then I upset you. It's your nature to ask and keep asking and asking and asking, and it's my nature to give, give, give until I explode and take back everything I believe is mine."

"Yeah, I know all about that," he said with irritation. "I was the target of that Café Marly ambush."

"And I suppose you think it's very easy to keep you company when you need company, and lend at all times a sympathetic ear to your problems. How do you think it is to spend all day with the photographs, trying to feel every emotion of your life, and then describe your life with the greatest possible sympathy, not just for you, but for everybody, and to fritter away my nerves that way, then when finally I get some rest, who calls but *you* on the damn telephone to ask for yet more sympathy?"

"I do plenty of things for you, Philippe."

"And I do plenty for you. Tit for tat. But—you give a lot, just so that you feel justified in asking for things later. That's not sympathy, that's calculation. True compassion is when you give without expecting anything in return. But sometimes I feel I give you a lot more sympathy and compassion than you give me."

Darren was quiet. This was obviously what I had wanted to say at Café Marly, but had been too tongue-twisted and angry to say coherently.

"Of course, you are sick and I am well. And the sick, I think, always merit more compassion than the well. And believe me—believe me, I try to give you everything I can. Even so . . ." I sighed heavily. I paused and collected myself for what I was going to say next. "I'm ambitious. I want to become a writer. That's my sickness, if you will—why I need, why I have to write this novel. We both need this novel, but I think I deserve it less than you do. How much I deserve, I don't know. I need sympathy from somebody, clearly, but I can't force you to give it to me, or it won't be true. I think—I think—that the reason you love Jean-Baptiste so much is because he, without having any reason to, suddenly gave you all of his compassion, without expecting anything in return. He loved you. And since this is not something you were used to, you loved him for it. And—and—and—you know the rest." I collected myself. I breathed in, breathed out. "I'm sorry I have to say it. It's very formal, I know, but I have to say it this way." I was referring to my solemn language about sympathy and compassion and the mechanics of love and so on.

"It's all right. I'm sorry I pushed you into this," Darren said.

"We're a good match in a lot of ways, you and I," I said. "But—what I think you must realize is that when I'm writing about somebody, they're *always* with me, in some way. I am always talking to them, trying to understand. And I am always exercising restraint, controlling myself. Otherwise too much anger would spill out, and I don't want the novel to be angry. Although . . ." I covered my forehead and my eyes. It was very difficult to talk to Darren this way. But he was so self-centered that he couldn't see when he exasperated others. That was Darren—a chicken, believing he was the most exotic bird for miles around, flapping and strutting around in the coop while the others kept their wings politely folded. But I didn't say this. What I said was, "We're a good pair—but you can't expect me to write this book and serve as round-the-clock agony aunt *and* as an errand boy *and* as a dinner companion, whenever you feel like company. Imagine that you were writing a book about Jean-Baptiste and he called you with a complete mood swing every four hours. Your patience would run out. You'd be harsh with him. But . . . maybe you're the reason I'm writing . . ." I broke off, shaking my head. It seemed all too much for me; I didn't understand it.

When Kenny Moore had died, when Darren was seven years old, Darren had not been invited to the funeral. He was told he "wouldn't understand." The idea was, I suppose, that adults understood death and children did not. I'm not sure adults really understand death. Perhaps adults are merely familiar with it. Some adults, like Doris Moore, were certainly familiar with it. She was eighty, and had lost her son when he was twenty-one. Darren was becoming familiar with death because of Dead John. Jean-Baptiste and I were becoming familiar with death because of the future Dead Darren.

I didn't say these things, but this was what was going through my head. I looked at him with the thousand-mile stare I had learned in the army, the stare that says nothing. It's a good stare to have, especially in the HIV wing of the Institut Pasteur.

"All right, Philippe," Darren said firmly, after a long pause. "I understand you better. I don't understand everything about you, but I understand more."

"I'm sorry; this whole chapter is momentary anger and frustration. You're charming, Darren, and right now, you want a book. You'll get it, but it'll be better if I'm not doing the work of four persons trying to keep you happy."

"I am really sorry, *really* sorry, to have wound you up this much. Leave me alone. Go away. Do what you like to make yourself feel better."

"I need to get a part-time job; my money has nearly run out."

"Well, do. You need to get some financial stability."

The phone rang. Darren answered it, and looked surprised. He handed it to me. "It's for you. Some guy named 'Darren'?" I frowned and put the receiver to my ear.

"Philippe? It's me. Can you do me a favor? I need you to go to Café Marly to pick up the postcards for my change of address form. It's very important; I need them ASAP. Can you go, you think? What are you doing this afternoon?"

"Nothing. Working."

"Working on *what*?" he asked. That made me angry. The other Darren, the one on the hospital bed, was in the margins of this conversation, but receding further and further away.

"I'll give you three guesses," I said, bitterly. "*What* could I be working on?"

"Are you angry?" Darren asked.

"No, I'm not *angry*. *Why* should I be angry? You only interrupted a conversation I was having."

"Oh!" he said, surprised. "I'm sorry." He assumed that my friends were his friends. "Who are you talking to?"

"None of your business."

"All right," he said soothingly. "All right. I'll get someone else for the postcards." Then, as an afterthought, "Oh, Philippe! Very important. D'Annunzio called."

"Oh, really?" Paul d'Annunzio was ninth in the New York plot outline, eighty-third on the master list of characters.

"We talked for *two* hours," Darren said. "I could *not* get him off the phone."

"Really? I can't get d'Annunzio out of my *flat*."

"What?"

"He always seems to be here, clamoring for attention. I'm going to have to write about him at some point."

"Is that who's there?"

"No. I'll write to you about it later."

"Well, you do that. Finish up whatever you're doing. Don't work yourself so hard. I think you're driving yourself crazy with this book sometimes."

"I'll tell you all about it *later*."

We said good-bye and hung up.

That was it for my hospital scene with Darren. Ruined, of course.

Later I could tell Darren *what* he had interrupted, what he always interrupted, when he called me. While he was sitting in the Institut Pasteur, next to the big windows, I would read him chapter five, all the way from the beginning up until the point you are now reading. And Darren would be shocked and upset and laugh and cry and look at me as if he understood a little better what I kept beneath my folded wings.

"It's good," he said.

"I'm sorry it's so formal, but I have to say it this way." I was referring to having to tell him what I thought about him in a novel, instead of screaming at him on the telephone like normal people.

"Well, keep going," Darren said. "Looks like Paul d'Annunzio's up in the next chapter."

"Oh, yes. Life in New York for a twenty-two-year-old. Definitely."

"And, Philippe—?"

"Yes?"

"I promise I won't call you anymore with hysterical misinterpretations of Jean-Baptiste's phone calls."

He really did say that.

I stayed up late last night, changing dialogue and scenes, rewriting and revising. I got to bed at dawn, exhausted. At ten o'clock, the middle of my sleep, the phone rang. It was my mother again.

"Mom?"

"Philippe? It's your mother."

"Yes, I know."

There was an unnatural pause.

"It's about your father. His heart—"

"No."

That's what I feared I was about to hear when I picked up the receiver.

But what I heard was this.

"Philippe? It's Darren. You're not going to believe this. After our last reconciliation, Jean-Baptiste—again—has finally broken all the bounds of human decency. He called me up and said the most awful, awful things I've ever heard in my life. I've abandoned him forever. I simply cannot, cannot take this kind of abuse."

What I thought I should say was this:

"Darren, take it easy. You're feeling tense because of that leg."

What I felt like saying was this:

"Darren, you promised!"

But what I actually said was this:

"Darren, *fuck you.*"

No, I didn't. The telephone receiver was not against my ear. The telephone receiver lay on its hook, on my bedstand next to my bed in my deux-pièces in Saint-Germain-des-Prés. That phone call had just been in my imagination.

CHAPTER 6

Imagining something is better than remembering something," I said. I was speaking to Darren in his room at the Institut Pasteur. Through great windows glum light poured; the clouds were low and white-gray. I could see the petunias outside, purple and blue.

"I know," said Darren, "but I still think it'd be good for you to visit New York and meet my friends."

"I'm doing all right so far, I think," I said.

"You're doing a great job," said Darren, "but maybe it would be even better if you met them."

"Might cramp my writing," I said. "Besides, I'm not sure I *want* to meet all your friends. After everything you told me about Murphy Stavros, I think I'd be better just imagining him."

"Oh, God. Stavros. *She* was something."

I smiled. "No, I think I better stay away. I am very happy in my deux-pièces in Saint-Germain-des-Prés."

And I *was* very happy, when I was writing that.

Then Darren said, "But don't you find it easier to imagine somebody if you meet them? It's easier to imagine Francesco and Marzenna now that you've met them, isn't it?"

"Now that I've met them I'm not imagining them any-more," I said. "I'm just describing who they are." That was true. I'd read them the passages where they appeared in the book, in reality this time. Francesco had recommended a few changes to "Francesco," who he thought appeared somewhat stupider than himself. Marzenna tried to say nothing whatsoever about how I described her, because she was afraid that, whatever she said, I would use it in the book. What she didn't realize was that what-ever she *didn't* say, I would *also* use in the book.

"Marzenna was so silent because she was afraid you would start commenting on her marriage," Darren said.

"Why not comment on it?"

"I don't know," Darren said, doubtfully, shaking his head. "None of our business?"

"Well, I'll describe their marriage ceremony, compare it to yours. True love versus convenience."

"Yeah, you can do that," Darren said.

Of course, Darren never said such a thing. I had imagined him saying it, that's all.

The next day Darren invited Andrew, my literary friend, and me for sushi lunch. Eating sushi with him while he was bedridden at the Institut Pasteur was a complicated affair. I had to dig through the mess in my room until I found the blank checks he gave me for just such occasions. Then he would call Matsuya's on rue Guisarde and would order sushi for three. Andrew would come to my place, I would read him some of the fragments that were developing into a novel, and then we would walk over to Matsuya's to pick up the sushi and metro to the Institut Pasteur.

Andrew was very pleased with the fragments I read him. "God," he said, "a self-referent novel! Every time you change levels, I feel like—*whoosh!*—I've dropped into hyperspace."

But later I read *that* sentence back to him, and he corrected me, saying, "No, I never said that. I said, 'Now that you're writing a self-referential novel, when I'm with you, I feel like there are fucking cameras everywhere.' *That's* exactly what I said." That *is* exactly what he said, in fact; I wrote that down almost as soon as he had said it.

And I wrote *that* down almost as soon as I had finished revising the rest. I wanted our conversation about a self-referential novel to sound absolutely *true*. We had that conversation right before our sushi lunch with Darren.

Andrew and I entered Matsuya's, where a lovely lady in a simple dress brought me the sushi in a blue plastic bag, which I would give to Darren as a special gift. She asked me, "Darren is well? He has energy?"

"Oh, he has plenty of energy," I said. He had so much energy, in fact, that the doctors had given him Lexomil to dampen the lift he got from the Prozac. It was supposed to even him out to the point where he almost felt like he wasn't taking drugs at all.

"Good," she said. I filled in the blank check signed by Darren. The cashier smiled at me. It was so easy to make friends in France. All you had to do was spend a little money. Darren spent a lot of money at Matsuya's.

Andrew and I, carrying plastic sushi boxes, descended into the metro and rode through its tunnels and rattling caverns.

"What'll happen to the names?" Andrew asked me.

"We may have to change some of them," I said.

"Oh, that's awful. The novel works because you know the people are real, not imagined."

"Yeah, well. People will just have to make believe."

Then it was our stop. It was drizzling lightly when we came out to the rue de Vaugirard. We walked past the dour concierge, past the leafy and charming interior court, and up the stairs to room 29.

Darren was in good spirits when we walked in. "Hello!" he said.

We both said hello enthusiastically and unpacked the sushi. There were mountains of it.

"God! Thanks, Darren," said Andrew.

"Yes, thanks very much, Darren," I echoed. But as I said it, I asked myself, is it possible to write objectively about someone who buys you lunch?

"Is it possible to write objectively?" I said aloud.

"Of course not," Andrew said confidently. "All writing is opinion."

"But surely some people can give you a more objective view than others," I said.

"I'm not sure anyone has ever been objective about anything. Certainly not about someone else's life." I admired Andrew's philosophical asceticism.

But Darren had his own opinion. "The day I first met Martin Fogel," he said, referring to his psychologist-palmist friend in New York, "he told me, 'You are from another world than the one you were born into.' And it was absolutely *true*."

I looked at Andrew with a raised eyebrow.

"It *was*," Darren insisted. "Martin saw so many things. He saw Jean-Baptiste in my future, when I was only twenty-six. He said I would have problems with my central nervous system. And I did. He said that at age thirty I would be working on a *creative project*." He emphasized the words. "And, Philippe, *I am*."

I said, "Yes, you are."

"So you see."

He was certainly working creatively: he had the portable computer, the bubble jet printer, the cellular phone, and the electronic organizer, to prove he was busy; he had read twenty pages of my manuscript, adding marginal comments to describe himself, such as "he was so solidly built and rugged, like the Kansan farm boy that he was, and yet an air of refinement was present as well." He had created a sensational *carte de visite* which he had tried to make refined yet unpretentious. In fact, it was rather the opposite, but I didn't tell Darren that.

Nor did I look at Andrew. Nor did I raise an eyebrow. I wanted Darren to believe in himself; it did him good; it was necessary for his health. My problem was that Darren believed in himself too much. He believed himself a competent editor, though he had never really read a single novel. In fact the first novel he began really reading was the one about his own life. Somehow it held his attention in a way all the others had failed to do. He edited the first twenty pages with so much enthusiasm that I hesitated about handing over any more material, for fear of any more enthusiastic editing. I feared for the manuscript in his hands; yet I also feared for Darren's happiness. In the end, I thought then, I would give him the entire manuscript, including this passage, and would let him have his way on anything I thought was reasonable. That had been our informal, lightbulb-breaking deal, when we were projecting the yet-to-be-written novel. It was my literature; but it was his life. His enthusiasm notwithstanding, I believed he would listen to me about writing, if not about life. He did not care, deep down, about demonstrating himself to be literate. That was my ambition, we both thought. What Darren Swenson really wanted from me was nothing less than unquestioning devotion. That, and a 1,000-page masterpiece about his life.

His life had been the subject of other analysts: before Madame Sosostris, there had been a futurist-psychologist and palmist, Martin Fogel. A few years after he'd been diagnosed as HIV-positive, Darren spoke to Fogel for an hour on a bench in Central Park, across from the mammoth apartment building where, on the second floor, he had a small, rather gloomy consulting room. But Darren preferred the sunlight and Fogel said, Awlright. Once they were established on the bench, along with Darren's recorder, Darren recorded everything they said that day.

Four years later, the tape of their conversation was in my deux-pièces in Saint-Germain-des-Prés. On a quiet night, when the moon was full and bleached white against a deep blue city sky, I popped the cassette into the recorder and pressed Play. Suddenly, the sounds of New York: the jug-jug-*spat!* of a nearby motorcycle; laughing children, hiding excitedly, a calliope playing, and overhead a circling seagull. I listened closely to Martin Fogel, as Darren must have listened, four years before me.

"Let's see both your hands please," he said.

"Now, in this setting. The first part of the reading, I am going to read your conscious self. Then your subconscious personality, then I'm going to read your life.

"Now the hand folds into a map, a very clear map. The elements: the top part of your hand is your emotions. How you express and do not express your emotional self. The most important part of your hand is earth. It's your personal Garden of Eden, where you pray and where you make things work for you or not work for you in the material world.

"Here: fantasy. Dream. Water. And this is air. Naturally the water mixes with the air and is nourished by the earth. And this is fire. Fire in my system speaks of time, actually—realms of time. This is the lake of fire. This is your own personal influences. Philosophical influences. World of intellectual endeavors."

He paused again. Children laughed and I heard a nearby seagull.

"Which is your working hand?"

"My right," Darren said.

"Your hand is crossed between the artistic hand and the working hand. Now is a very good time for you to work. Throw off certain doubts and fantasies of the past—that kept you back, kept you from going forward, held you mired without the benefit of mind. You have to get rid of certain nagging aspects of doubt. Bubbles that form on your mind. You're starting to become a person of mind. Doubt—have to smash it. Confidence above all. See it clearly. Visualize. Give it a blue color, a black color, a negative color. Then eclipse it with a positive color. You must allow this to become true, to become real.

"Now—you like your freedom, actually. But when people tell you what to do, you don't like it, you fight it. You have to visualize—see yourself submitting humbly to other persons in your life. Very ambitious person, actually.

"You're sentimental, *too* sentimental. Present in check by the past. Past memories. Sentimentality, nostalgia. You tend to repeat certain negatives in the past, relive them over and over.

"You love one way and express it another. People think they know you and they don't. When people love you they find out you're a different person than they thought you were. You need to be with people who are essentially non-threatening, who allow you to express yourself as you really are. You try *hawrd* to be accepted, but try as you may, you cannot be accepted. You're in another world. You're an inside person. Very emotional. This is the hand of a very emotional type of person. Moody. And this is where the negativity begins to rise. Anger. Hardness. When people do bad things to you, you give it back to them three times. That's why it's important for you to release that energy. Dancing; dancing is very important for that hardness, that energy. That hardness *blawks* the sun in your life, keeps it from rising, keeps it from shining, illuminating people around you. Because you're not a materialist. You're an idealist."

Blawks: I liked that word. I had a vision of Darren's sun, *blawked*, unable to shine.

"Complicated relationships with older people, authority

figures, traps. You need to be with someone who needs you. You need to be needed. That open part of you, in conflict with the careful part of you. Jupiter with Saturn. You need—someone who demands from you, emotionally. This will make you—this will make you grow. Because—it's more who you really are. Very hard on yourself. Guilt. Feel very guilty.

"You get caught in a rut. Boxed in a corner. You live very much in your mind. Your mind gets stuck. Same thoughts over and over. How old are you?"

"Twenty-six," said Darren. Then he made a curious remark. "I am a bit older than I should be." He meant he expected to die aged thirty-three, although Martin had no idea about that, yet.

"You're going through a change in your life. Suddenly, it seems to you, hey, the things I thought guaranteed success and order, don't. The logic is upset; it doesn't guarantee anything anymore. This causes stress, anxiety. You have to work to change the past outlook to let the future become reality.

"This is the hand—this is the hand of an obsessive personality. When things don't go right in the material world, there is confusion and anxiety. You *luxuriate* in past notions, past feelings. But the conflict is still there. Now your psyche is resolving the antagonism—that's one of the reasons for your positive maturation."

"You said—problems with the older person? Will it be resolved?" Darren said. "You see, it's probably my mother."

Martin paused. "A very deep attachment. More linked to your heart than you realize. But—doesn't allow to grow. You can see yourself, you have—have had a lot of—you were very hard on people you loved the most. It's negative. You lost that bond of passion. Your mind is saying, 'My intellect is hungry now. My intellect is thirsty now.' But you can change it. You have to confront people with logic and not with passion."

After a pause, Martin started on the other hand.

"*This* hand is *very* different. Many roads, many directions. A lot of anxiety, here. Now you're dominated by the idea of *destiny*. The idea that, hey, if *I* don't get it right, it's not going to be right. The universe is not a friendly place. In the past, you would depend on the fantasy and excuse yourself from *the work that had to be done*.

"Betrayal, very important in your life. Subconsciously, you

view that older person in terms of the past. Important to work
out the negatives. As a way of cleansing. In the past you were
much more physical. But you cannot *luxuriate* in certain aspects
of the past.

"You meet people—and you're expecting to feel disappointed by them. You go against your own judgment. You
expect too much from people. Getting depressed—and liking it.
Getting hurt by somebody—and liking it. Negative tendencies.
Blawks the sun in your life.

"I'm going to read your lifeline now," Martin said. There
was a long pause. I heard the cry of the seagull, the children
shouting. Then he spoke in a much more solemn tone.

"Before you were born, at the time of your birth, you were
very different from your parents and you were very different
from the place you were born. So you felt the difficulties. You
felt it especially in terms of your father. From one to five you
needed a lot from him. You couldn't shift into your mother for
some reason. Five to eleven, not your reality. Feel trapped. Nine
years old, internalized feelings. From thirteen to fourteen, not in
your reality. Fourteen, older person tries to help you. Fifteen,
sixteen, getting worse—frying pan into the fire. Smoke is really
rising. Fantasy world. High energy levels. Authority figures are
attracted to you and you need to be attractive to them. Eighteen,
high negativity, negative influence. Nineteen, twenty, you're not
even there. Twenty-one, big change. Twenty-two, twenty-
three, twenty-four . . . twenty-four, strong influence, new
reality. Realize you have to change, twenty-four. Two different
lives. Feel the doubt here. Twenty-seven, you want to trust
someone. Twenty-eight years old—balance rising. You find
yourself *blawked* for some reason. Twenty-nine, you feel much
happier. Thirty, destiny. Creativity. Impulse. Thirty-two, thirty-
three, financial problems. Thirty-three, water, fire, mixes with
smoke, there's trouble for you. Thirty-four, financially an older
person. Work, job, career. Thirty-eight, good times, two lives.
Thirty-nine, grief. Sick. Forty, forty-one: sad time, bad time.
Negativity rising. [indistinct] two lives. Forty-seven, forty-
eight—big life change, like at age four. Forty-nine, real balance
between work, job, career. Younger person very important in
your life. Lots of younger persons. Your child. Or if not your
child, someone who you think will be your child. Fifty, fifty-

five, fifty-nine—death in your life; not yours. Sixty. Child in tension in your life."

He ended it.

Darren asked, "So you see children as important?"

"It's a process for you," Martin answered. "You need to have a child."

"I have very strong paternal instincts," Darren said.

"Extremely strong. Paternal relationships."

"But I have to ask you this. Because—you see, I'm gay. But will I be able to have a child?"

"I know you will," Martin said. He hesitated a half second. "But—you need to find a woman to share that reality."

"Will there be harmony between these two lives? The true, sexual self and the need to have children? Is that deep love—is it with a woman? Is that possible? Is that in my lifeline?"

"That is all possible."

"In my lifeline? You said it's long."

"You have a long lifeline, but that doesn't necessarily mean a long life. When it's over, I'm sorry pal, you're out of here. We're all out of here in this life. Nervous system problems. I see the body has a poison. Nerve endings, the way the heart relates to the head."

"Really?" Darren asked, very interested. "You see—I have a medical problem."

Martin said, more slowly, "I can see that. I can see there's a problem. But I don't see your life ending. You know it won't."

"But—with a long lifeline—?"

"Doesn't necessarily mean. I had a friend with a very long lifeline. And he killed himself, last year."

"And that's fine."

"No, it's not fine. Because it didn't have to happen. . . . Now that you told me you have a medical problem, I'd recommend something for your nerve cells. Your blood cells."

"Do you think my medical problem is spiritual?"

"Definitely."

Then Darren asked a series of precise questions.

"Do you see my hands as strong and positive?"

"I see *this* hand as strong, positive. This *other* hand—*chaos*. Confusion. Subconscious."

"Do you see a leader in me? Do you see me becoming a positive force for others on a *mass scale*?"

Listening to the tape, I found it incredible that Darren would say this, and I could tell that Martin was having trouble conjuring a diplomatic reply; perhaps he shrugged his shoulders. But nothing could stop Darren.

"Am I a pure person?" he asked. "How can I deal with those that are not pure?"

Martin thought about that. "They're a part of your journey," he said.

"I could never go back to Immaculatum, Kansas. My mother—"

"Hold it—I think you have to resolve certain things with your mom."

Darren seemed not to have heard him. "It was very interesting to hear you say that I was 'born in another world.' From day one, being a pure person—is that it?"

Martin said, "To deal with people who are not pure, your mind has to take responsibility."

"Do you see me being polluted by the negative people around me?" Darren asked.

"You can—there's a tendency—in the past you were polluted by people around you. You were completely taken off the road. Your destiny—"

"It is *all* destiny," Darren remarked, decisively.

This stunned Martin, who fumbled a bit. "You must—if you take out the clear pure vessel and somehow dash it, and muck it up, and pollute it a bit, you have to fill it with the most high . . ."

This remark so puzzled them that they both fell silent.

Finally Darren said, "There is something that is troubling me. Intellectually I have arrived where I am without reading. And that's scary. What should I read?"

"The classics," Martin said.

I smiled, alone in my corner of my deux-pièces.

"I've read them all, in a superficial way, in college," Darren said.

That nearly made me stop the tape.

"Homer," Martin said.

Hurray, I thought.

"The Bible," Martin said.

Hurray for the old book, I thought.

"You see," Darren said hastily, "I grew up on a farm. There was no tradition—"

"You don't need tradition to read the Bible."

"But I don't approach it in a religious way."

"Well—that should be the point of *life*," Martin said, a little wounded. "The great books should be the *pillars* of your life. Many of the great questions appear in literature. Especially the Bible."

"I have never read the entire Bible."

"Well, get started."

"But—I have, already. The day I read the first paragraph of Genesis—I was filled with so much emotion that I started crying. I could feel something there. And I've come so close to God. God in my own sense. Not God in my own spirit."

"But—as of—what you need that is—I'm *trying* to make you understand that you *need* the Bible as a bridge. We all need that to elevate our spirituality."

"Should I read the Saint James Bible?"

"Sure," Martin said. "You're bright enough." I could have sworn I heard him break into a ghostly smile. "Read, and pray. Prayer. Prayer is the end of it. It's all prayer. Prayer is essential."

"Yeah," Darren said, seeming to agree. "Yeah. How can I meet the right people?"

"How do you meet the right people?" Martin repeated, uncomprehending.

"I've not been able to meet intellectual people," Darren said.

"The road to those people, essentially, is love. If you show love for those things, those people will make themselves known to you."

This put Darren in a reflective mood. He said, "I've been searching, for years, for something higher. I just spent—five days in the hospital because of my—diarrhea. And I felt a change through me this time. I spent five days feeling the elements that were created first—water, light, and air. And the doctors said, 'Your T-cell count is at twenty-seven. Your blood work is perfectly healthy. We don't medically understand why.' But *I* understand why. It's my *mind*. It's my *spirit*. When I sit, in a smoky room—"

"You're smoking?" Martin broke in. "You should feel ashamed of yourself."

"Now, we all have vices. I know I'll never sit on the right hand of God. But I don't feel guilty because I light a cigarette in the morning."

"Well, get into flowers."

"But up until this point I've been very lucky. They checked my lungs five, six times and everything's healthy—"

"That's not the point," Martin said.

"I know, I know. Am I in tune with what I'm doing?"

"Why do you doubt it?"

"I don't! I don't! Okay—I do. I had no spiritual or emotional support growing up. I was plopped into Kansas—"

"For a reason."

"But I feel so much more *myself* in a café in Berlin or Paris."

"The *Old Testament*," Martin repeated, slightly exasperated. "And Homer," he added. "And maybe—a little closer to home, a little more accessible—some of the better American classics."

I smiled when he said that. He really did say it.

Sort of.

The tape stopped with a clunk.

Of course, the conversation didn't exactly happen that way; I was trying to make an objective account.

But of course it couldn't be objective. I had no objectivity, in any philosophical, ascetic sense. I had only a sense of what was right and what was wrong, and that was as personal as a fingerprint. But I was beginning to feel that even that sense of right and wrong was changing as I was writing. At first, in the book as in real life, I had tried to show the greatest possible amount of compassion for Darren—not criticizing him at all. And of course the criticism I felt brewed and boiled and rose until it burst in that devastating tirade, that day at Café Marly.

That day, the sun was shining. That day, we were drinking Monacos. The fountains played in the sunlight; the ice glittered in my glass. I had already said a lot of nasty things that day. Now I fired my last, most wounding words into Darren's surprised face.

"Do you know why you've never fallen in love, Darren? It's because of your *egotism*. You're so *full* of yourself. You're so *in love* with yourself, that you've never been able to give yourself over to anybody. Your *ego* gets in the way of everything."

I stared. "*Have* you *ever* fallen in love? *No.* Because you've *never* stopped putting *yourself* at the center of your whole world. Everything turns around you, for you. Falling in love is when everything turns around the other person. But you've never gotten that far. Darren Swenson—his own pure made-up North Star in his own made-up gossamer-fabric Kansan fucking space-time."

I was not even making sense to myself anymore.

Darren looked at me with absolute incomprehension. "You've—you've gotten quite *mystical,* Philippe," he said, trying to break the tension.

"Fuck your humor. Excuse me. I appreciate your attempt to calm me down," I said. "But I can't. Not right now."

"That's all right."

I tried to say something, and couldn't.

"Are you feeling better?" Darren asked.

"No."

"Can I help?"

"No."

"Well, do you mind if I go to the bathroom and vomit?"

"Go right ahead."

So he got up and left.

I felt badly for him. He didn't deserve that outburst, and I could have told him what I thought with a lot more tact. Marzenna could have shown me how.

"You're such an *enfant gâté,*" Marzenna had once told Darren. She meant he was a bit of a spoiled brat.

If I had said that, Darren would have rattled off a merciless farm-boy schedule of pushing, scrubbing, hoeing, driving, pulling, milking, and cleaning, from 6:30 in the morning to 6:30 at night, every morning and every night, ever since he was four-teen. And I would have had to agree that anyone doing that amount of physical work could never have been spoiled.

But Marzenna, merely with her eyes and understanding smile, would have disarmed Darren of that reply. "Yes, you worked," she would have seemed to say, "but isn't the *essence* of being a spoiled child the feeling of being special, perfect, pure?

And tell me, Darren," Marzenna seemed to say, merely with her smile, "if you didn't feel that when you were a child?"

Then a kind of you-sure-got-me-with-that-one look would enter Darren's face, and he would smile sheepishly. It was true: even while he was pushing, scrubbing, hoeing, driving, pulling, milking, and cleaning, he felt like the most special, perfect, pure child for miles around—if not the whole world.

"When you're fourteen years old," he had told me, "the whole world is the farm and the high school." He forgot to add: And I was at the center of it.

It was this colossal sense of self-importance, of destiny, of ambition, that drove him out of Immaculatum, out of Kansas, out of America even, and into Café Marly, where he was looking for the hypothetical Prince Charming with his castle and his title and the end of the rainbow falling into his pocket.

"Just you wait," he said. "My life is like a novel." It certainly was; I was writing it that way.

"But it's not a sad story," Darren said.

"It is too a sad story. You die at the end."

"We *all* die at the end! The point is *how*! And I'll tell you, Philippe—and I'm quite honest—I've never been happier, never felt gladder to be alive, never felt better, spiritually. This disease—believe it or not—is a positive development in my life. Where would I be without it? How could any of this—these wonderful people that I know, these great things I'm doing—have happened without it?"

When he said things like that, I had trouble believing him. Those things sounded absurd. I searched for his cynical wit, but it didn't seem to be there; there was nothing but a fiery sincerity, and boundless optimism. But then he said, "Of course, it'd be nice *not* to have hemorrhoids and diarrhea *at the same time,* but there you go."

I smiled at him. He was really very brave.

"Well," I said, smiling, "it won't be such a sad book. We'll put in some *great* sex scenes."

"Yes, please. You know, when Murph Stavros called me, he said that's all he's interested in reading, those *great* sex scenes."

"Great," I mumbled. "Tell him to read chapter eleven, the descent into hell."

"With the Devil?"

"With the Devil. With Murphy Stavros himself. Do you remember when he said, if you ever ran out of material, you could use his life?"

"Yes, I do."

"Well, I'm going to. The Murphy Stavros Chapter."

"Hallelujah," Darren said. "The Murphy Stavros Chapter. I can't wait. But, Philippe, you also have to describe *my* life in New York before I met him. When I was gettin' it and *gettin' it.* Every night, man." He lifted his legs in the air and let his tongue loll as he rolled back and forth in his hospital bed. "*Every* night," he repeated. "Two or three times a night, and sometimes during the day. My libido, man, it was something. You could not imagine it."

Of course, I *had* to imagine it. I had to imagine him cruising bars with names like The Trap or The Spike or The Big Hungry Come.

" 'The Big Hungry Come'?" Darren asked me when I showed him that passage. "Where did you get *that* name?"

"I made it up," I said. That was true; I had. But it wasn't true that I had shown him that passage. I hadn't shown Darren anything I had written for nearly a month. The reason was that he was still in the hospital, and I felt the newer, more critical chapters would not raise his morale or help his recovery. It was also true that he'd loaned me money. My savings had finally run out and I'd asked him for 2,200 francs, to pay my rent, while I looked for a job. He lent me the 2,200 francs and threw in another 300 for good measure. I figured that if he was buying me breakfast, lunch, and dinner, inviting my friends and me for sushi, and lending me money besides, I'd better keep whatever nastiness I had to myself—at least until I could pay him back.

CHAPTER 7

My bank statement showed a balance of 798 francs. I got out my checkbook and credited Darren's check, and discovered I had a balance of 3,298 francs. That was enough for a month.

I was not the only one to benefit from Darren's generosity. Jean-Baptiste once had a phone bill for 11,000 francs—three-quarters of Darren's monthly income. Darren, who wanted to act French and make a beau geste, paid the entire bill. Jean-Baptiste, who *was* French, did not bother paying him back. He went to Australia instead. Darren drove him to the airport, and then offered to pay the excess weight charge for Jean-Baptiste's baggage. That would have been another 2,000 francs. But in the end he did not pay it because the airline agent found him so charming.

Jean-Baptiste called frequently from Australia—every four hours sometimes. Things down there were either utterly fantastic or utterly abysmal. Either way he said he was coming back. He said he hadn't found a substitute for Darren, at least not in the shape of his forty-year-old Australian with orange hair.

Before Jean-Baptiste had left—during the time he was making that pompous declaration about how strong he was to abandon Darren and seek true love in Australia—he had nevertheless joked about what a poor substitute the orange-haired man was going to be. Darren would make a face thinking of the Australian.

"*What—a—fag!!*" he said. "*What—a—queen!! But*—this whole Australian thing is necessary for Jean-Baptiste. If he doesn't do it, he'll always regret not having done it." And Darren was confident that Jean-Baptiste would return to him. " 'You can't run away from love,' " Darren said.

That was a Bronski Beat song:

You can't run away from love
You can't run away from love
You can't run away from love

a song that in the heady, drug-driven vigor of the '80s in America, had all the discos dancing, shaking, moving, breaking, and in the city of New York, where the biggest, wildest, most intoxicated discos were, it was to those words that Darren shook and moved.

Picture New York City by night: high above the city, see the surface glittering out of a humid night: note the office windows winking, the suspension bridges lit like lakes of electric fire, the tyrannical pulse of city streets below, beating.

Descend lower: descend only: into the city of New York. Between dark buildings where you see night workers sweeping: through dark avenues lit by lamps glowing electrical red, down streets full of tanned young men wearing white T-shirts and jeans, women walking quickly, guards in front of bars: walk down Christopher Street, clogged with traffic, where the drivers of cars hail through open windows the smiling handsome boys, who lean in windows, and ask for lights. A match is struck, a cigarette is lit slowly, someone draws in smoke, and says thanks with a big smile. Izod is hot tonight. Walk down the sidewalk cluttered with madly chattering old men, young men, men in between; excited debutants their first night out, old men intoxicated by the promise that tonight, anything could happen—anything could happen, with no particular wonder.

Step up to a door: boldly go in past the sour-faced and handsome bouncer, past the kind old lady checking leather jackets and giving away condoms like candy. The condoms are in a glass bowl, the kind used to hold jelly bellies or candies at the optometrist. Adjust your eyes to the darkness: blink at the blue light: enter wavering, like an uncertain reflection, onto the first dance floor. Someone slips by you, looks at you, is gone. You look behind you, and he's gone.

The music blares

. . . oooooOOOOOAAAAAAAA BABY!
My heart is full of love and DESIRE FOR YOU!
So come on down and do what you've GOT TO DO!

And now someone on the floor has GOT IT and he's lifting booted feet, leather feet, his arms are wrapped around someone else's bare neck; next to you, there's an eighteen-year-old boy with hair combed as perfectly as in ancient Egyptian paintings, and his face is the face of a statue. Move onwards: move outwards: step through the Palladian door, under the arcades of phosphorescent light, the strobe lights flashing by moments holding each suspended in a stranger's glare. Move: move: feel the rhythm: feel the drums. Stranger, you too, you too can dance; you too, you too can feel it FEEL IT. Let yourself be swept into the crowds: wave your arms: raise them—high, high, high over your head, over others' heads, swinging back and forth like excited metronomical sticks. Too soon, too soon, you catch the glimpse of someone you like; he's stopped dancing: he's looking at you, stunned, stopped. Your heart is pounding. You too, you too like him: he's close to you and turns, heads away, past the arcades into the lowest chambers.

Descend lower: descend only: follow the traces of where you think he's gone, following him the way you follow a salmon leaping through a phosphorescent sea. Past the lonely-looking faces at the corners of the bar: past the desperate-looking faces licking their lips in the corners of the bar: through the blue light, through the miasmatic colors and globes suspended above the staircase, look at the blank-looking faces swirling back the way you came. Descend: the steps go on forever.

Now here is a darker room: weave your way through wet hard bodies mashing together, feeling before the feeling begins, touching in place, waiting, watching and waiting. Look at the barman: barely twenty-one, hair cut short, skin like a china doll and yet blue. Move: move: push onwards through a sea-change of weathered and leathery faces, old faces, young faces, mustachioed faces, bald faces, hairy faces, smooth faces, everyone looking for companionship, everyone clustered around looking for love.

> Pushed around shoved around
> Always a lonely boy
> Run away run away run away run away

Push onwards: deeper: deeper into the heart of what you have come for: past the two men nuzzling and kissing: past the pair of jeans pressed against the other pair of jeans against the wall. Through the black hole: through the dark door, where dark men covered in dark anonymity watch, waiting for a sensual touch, an ambiguous brushing of a hand against a hand, for that invitation meaning love was a dark hair's breadth away: or if not love, then sex. You hear someone at the back GETTING IT and someone behind him giving it. Move, move forward: advance to meet it, to see it, in the dim flame of a lighter: not him, not him, the boy you were looking for, the man bent over, inhaling. Then the flame goes out: and there is only the harsh breathing. Sudden in a touch of warmth there is a hand on yours: the boy you followed is here beside you, glad you followed him. He turns his face to yours, and you turn to kiss his lips. . . .

That was almost how Paul d'Annunzio had met Darren. Paul had been the man in the arcade, and Darren, the dancer, when they met in The Saint in New York only a few days after Darren arrived in the city. He was twenty-two. Darren had descended upon the dance floor feeling quite liberated from every Kansan rule. Gyrating wildly, like an overwound mechanical toy, he caught the attention of the thirty-year-old tall stranger with flowing hair.

"*She* can dance," said d'Annunzio to himself. He brushed a lock of flowing hair and moved onto the dance floor, where Darren, smiling and waving big-hippily, was at the center of an admiring throng, dancing every which way.

"She can *really* dance," said d'Annunzio as he stepped into the circle of youths, with the suavity of the elder cowboy visiting the young bucks. Paul knew how to move fluidly, and he glided up to Darren. Their eyes caught.

"Hel-lo, *girl*," Paul said, loudly.

That greeting astonished Darren. He smiled lightly and sort of nodded to him, in time with the music. He kept on shaking and moving, though inside he was flustered. The stranger had challenged his masculinity. His reaction was automatic; he wanted to show this stranger that he, Darren, was a man and could take it like a man. But he also liked the idea that someone wanted to take him like a girl. In time to the music he put on brakes and swerved, elbows pistoning, teeth down on his lip, head rocking and rolling, hips swiveling for the stranger:

. . . oooooOOOOOAAAAAAAA BABY!
You started this fire down IN MY SOUL!
Now can't you see it's burning OUT OF
    CONTROL!

They left The Saint together.

"Do you want to head up to my place?" Paul asked him, in the New York City street, while the orange lights blazed gaudily on.

Even then Darren had his conception of himself figured out precisely. To the outside world, he was just another Kansan country boy, come to a city of heartbreaks to eke a fortune out of the asphalt. Inside, though, he felt as if he were marching to the drums of destiny, alone in front of a vast column. The ferocious indifference of the world, of New York, to that drumbeat did not discourage him. He believed that the outside world would soon cooperate, and would reward his faith in himself with fame, prestige, and fortune, would make him a leader on a mass scale, and would give him a permanent seat in a chic underground restaurant with a view of an I. M. Pei pyramid.

But he knew better than to explain any of this to Paul d'Annunzio, who, Darren could see, had been around New York a while and was no believer in Midwestern prophets. Darren thought that explaining his massive destiny would be a little silly, given that right now he lived on Cranberry Street in Brooklyn Heights, in a tiny flat equipped only with a single gray bed and a sad pressboard nightstand.

So instead, he smiled—he had discovered people liked him when he smiled. "Let's go to your place," Darren said. So they did. Riding through the subway's rattling caverns, past the hobos and the filthy and stinking mutilated veterans in olive drab, they went up towards the West Side, where the numbers and apartment prices rose dizzyingly.

Darren's imagination bubbled in anticipation as the subway rocked him from side to side against this man's foppish body. Into whose arms had he fallen tonight? Some millionaire playboy living on inherited money? A famous artist? If the subject of art came up, he would feign cool familiarity by nodding gently. His mind raced forward with such imaginative speed that when Paul d'Annunzio finally opened the door on his small but well-appointed studio, Darren had to fight himself to not show he was disappointed, almost angry, because the flat was much smaller than he had imagined. D'Annunzio, meanwhile, had expected Darren to fall flat on his face in amazement at his highly disciplined chic. But Darren was groping for words only to conceal his disappointment. (He later had to grope to remember just what those words were.)

"Not bad," Darren said, finally, trying to be generous and coolly urbane at the same time. He sat down on a black leather couch. But the stronger emotion confronting him was that this pathetic flat was much less than what he had imagined for himself. Darren would forever find himself confronted with the sense that his whole life was somehow much less than what he had imagined for himself. Chester Hyland would almost shatter that masochistic pleasure in disappointment—almost, with a château on the Riviera and a collection of sports cars big enough to fuel the fantasies of a hundred randy adolescents. Alone

among the people he had met, Chet Hyland was *almost* equal to
Darren's fantasy man. But, for Darren, almost wasn't good
enough. Chet had neither a European title, nor much land, nor
even much of a sexy body, and all were imperative, for the fantasy. But Darren admitted that the château on the Riviera was
impressive.

"It's not *too* bad," he would say, later, trying to sound coolly
urbane and generous at the same time. "But you know,
Philippe, the Hylands are not *that* wealthy. I doubt they're even
in the top twenty in America." And so on.

But Darren's chance to snub poor Chet Hyland came later.
For now, Darren was sitting on a leather couch, staring at the
disciplined chic of a smooth flat on the Upper West Side.
Crystal goblets glittered on the black matte table; a delicately
spun vase stood like a sleek statue in a discreet corner.

D'Annunzio brought out two bottles of red wine. "Château
Margaux?" he asked. "Or Saint-Emilion?"

"Oh, Margaux, of course," said Darren quickly. D'Annunzio smiled. What confidence! What a command of French!
Indeed, for Darren, Grenoble had paid off handsomely. Not
that Darren could *tell* a Margaux from a Saint-Emilion. With
Vicki and Ward and Patti and all his other Grenoble friends,
he had drunk plonk all year, although he had gathered vague,
nebulous convictions about what was good and what was not.
But Darren had correctly guessed that d'Annunzio was enough
of a snob to offer only good bottles, and Darren also knew,
from France, that in such situations any answer was the right
answer, as long as it was decisive and delivered with supreme
Gallic haughtiness. Darren could imitate supreme Gallic haughtiness with ease.

So they drank the Margaux. There was lots of caviar and
smoked salmon in the flat, and they ate that, too.

"I work as a caterer," Paul explained. He had waited for the
exact moment to say that, pressing a redolent piece of goat
cheese onto a piece of bread dipped in olive oil with his thumb,
and shoving it all into Darren's hungry mouth. To Darren,
primed on a bottle of French wine, never did "caterer" have a
more delicious sound. And by "caterer," d'Annunzio meant
"caterer to the *rich*," and thereby made himself smack of elegant
parties, of champagne, of contacts with the remote and

powerful. If Paul was not, Darren decided, a millionaire playboy living off his inheritance, he could at least provide introductions to such playboys. And Paul certainly knew his way around food.

And around other things. After he finally got around to *giving it* to Darren, which he did much to Darren's pleasure, they lay in bed, smoking lazily and watching the fumes ascend to the ceiling. Then Darren experienced an awful feeling.

"What about the big A?" he asked, trying to appear nonchalant.

"Oh, God," Paul groaned, as if Darren had broached a very boring topic. "Overhyped media bullshit. They make it sound like the plague. It's actually *very* hard to get, Darren. You have to get fucked and fucked and *fucked* to get it."

"But what about you? What about what we did right now?" asked Darren, his heart racing, because getting fucked and fucked and *fucked* was exactly what he liked doing best.

"What we did right *now?*" asked Paul. "*I'm* negative. What about *you?*"

"Yeah." Actually, Darren didn't know; he *reckoned* he was negative. But he didn't want to know, really.

"Well, then we can do whatever we like, right? *Girl?*"

"Okay," said Darren, relieved.

So later they fucked and fucked and *fucked* some more. But there was a difference. Paul enjoyed giving it. Darren enjoyed *getting* it.

"Yeah, lust," Paul said, after their second time, watching the cigarette smoke ascend again to the ceiling, "it's something. If you like getting it, then you better insist on a condom. And remember to insist. Because, girl, after a few drinks, a few grams of this and a few grams of that, you'll say, what the fuck, I want to live a little. And you'll do it, and you'll break all the rules, and you'll like it, because—if you're lucky—you'll have tempted fate and won. And that, man, is a better feeling than sex. Some people can't help tempting fate. But—*but*—fate is bigger than you. Even you, Darren. Even *bigger* than you."

Darren was big, with tremendous golden thighs and a bar-reled hairy chest, shoulders strong as tractors. And he remembered the huge flat landscapes of his youth—landscapes he had filled, and even outgrown. How big could this teeny-weeny virus be, compared to those? "Yeah, you better watch out," Paul said. "Sometimes you'll just want to have fun, and one thing will add up to another, and you'll want the best food, and you'll drink the best bottle and order another bottle after that, and before you know it, the bill's come in and you can't afford to pay. And you only get so much credit. So the trick, if you want it all," and Paul spoke like someone who did, "to live fast and eat well and get those girls, girls, girls—is to *reckon correctly* how far you can really go."

After that, for two years in New York, Darren lived fast, ate well, got girls, girls, girls, and reckoned correctly. But then Darren *got it,* all of it, from John—*Dead* John. Initially he kept quiet about it. Somehow, however, Paul found out, and he gossiped about it incessantly. At a party at the brownstone in which Darren lived with his Kansan painter friend Steve Johnson and his Grenoble friends Patti and Ward, everybody knew a matter of minutes after Paul's arrival that Darren was HIV-positive. Darren forgave Paul in small pieces, but never entirely, for that indiscretion, and they stopped speaking for years—until Darren, from his bed in the Institut Pasteur, called Paul's old New York number, and tracked him down to Venice, Florida. From there Paul called him, speaking for two hours at the most expensive rate. Darren was thrilled.

"Two hours," Darren kept repeating.

We were in the Institut Pasteur, at nighttime, and the big windows were closed. The rectangular room was lit with fluorescent bulbs that gave it a cold, medical atmosphere. Darren's leg had been operated on, and the surgeons had cleaned up all the pus and left a four-inch scar with a drain running into a bandage around his shrunken calf. The thigh looked as thin as an arm.

I'd fetched him Chinese food for dinner. "You're sure you don't want any?" Darren asked me.

"Very sure," I said. I had decided that my tantrums and mood changes were at least partially provoked by changes in my blood sugar level. So in Darren's company I now ate nothing and drank water only. The system had been working so far. I got him food; he gave me material for the novel. It was a simple exchange of values.

"I'd rather eat than write a novel," I said, humorously. "Eating hurts no one—no one human, anyway. Writing a novel—you can hurt a lot of people."

We both knew what I was talking about.

Darren replied, "The only person this is going to hurt is my mother."

"I'll try to be fair to everybody," I said. "I'll try to be objective." That seemed easy to say.

"But Rosita said—and these were her words—*Il faut la sacrifier*. She has to be sacrificed. Those were her exact words. She really said that, Philippe."

I took a deep, deep breath, and said nothing.

I tried to imagine Lilian Swenson hearing that news. I had seen the photographs of when Darren and Jean-Baptiste had returned to Kansas. In those photographs Al Swenson looked stoically resigned. Darren looked exultant, happy that he had finally unburdened himself of his heaviest secret, and sorry that it had caused such sorrow, and trying to show that he didn't feel sorry, and trying inside to feel no sorrow at all. Lilian Swenson was the same: she was trying to show no sorrow, and even to feel no sorrow: but in every photograph I could see that the news had broken her. She tried bravely to hide the enormous mourning she stored up in her heart as soon as Darren told her he was going to die. In every photograph she felt herself physically sick, as if the best, most essential part of her had been cut out.

I had once told Darren, after looking long and hard at the photographs, "Darren, I think you hurt her in such a way that part of her will never get up again."

"You think so?" he had asked me rather hopefully.

"Oh, yes, Darren. I think a part of her will never live again."

He had tried to smile with pleasure, at first, and then found he couldn't; so then he had looked away, confused, wondering why her grief gave him less satisfaction than he had expected. I thought I knew the reason, but I said nothing more about it, although at that point it began to haunt me.

And if it haunted him, in the Institut Pasteur, he said nothing about it either. Instead he said, with typical showmanship, "My gorgeous friend Catherine Lancaster is going to be at

Café Marly at half past eleven tomorrow morning. You and Andrew are invited."

"Oh!" I stood to attention with mock respect. "*Lady* Catherine Lancaster, cousin to Chester Hyland," I said, sounding off like a majordomo at a ball. Of course this had to be Darren in his grandiose, teasing mode. But his smile was so confident and innocent, I thought it might be one of his fantasies turning into reality. "Is the heiress in Paris?"

"No, in London."

"How is she getting here? Flying?"

"Hitching a ride on Daddy's jet."

"Chic. How charming. Practical, too, I suppose."

"Oh, Philippe. We talked for an hour, catching up—it's almost a year since we've seen each other. And she's going to be here tomorrow!"

"Meeting at the Marly?"

"Yes."

"Say the time again."

"Eleven-thirty."

"How are you getting there?" I asked.

"They're letting me out for the day. I can get around on a crutch, or in a taxi. They don't want me to, *but*"—his eyes twinkled and he threw back his head coquettishly—"it's been too long since I put in an appearance at Marly."

The next morning I was walking quickly to Café Marly, retracing the route Antoine Blanche had taken from the Seine to La Palette. I was walking quickly because I'd overslept (as usual) and did not want to be late. I walked across the Quai Malaquais, not far from the building where Jean-Baptiste lived, on the ground floor, and where Andrew lived, on the seventh floor. Neither would be home right now; Jean-Baptiste was not due back from Australia for a few days, and Andrew would be at Marly to meet us. I crossed the Seine, walking on the Pont des Arts, looking at the barges being towed low and flat as they passed underneath the bridge. The river looked nice. Far away the sun rose and the day prepared itself for heat, though there was still a pleasant early-morning feel in the air. The big rectangular façade of the Cour Carrée raised itself before me. I crossed the Quai du Louvre, watching for careless, hurried drivers, and walked into the Cour Carrée. It was completely quiet except for the simple splashing of a fountain. I turned leftwards and saw the I. M. Pei pyramid partially hidden by the grand archway. It was always pleasant to see the pyramid.

I passed underneath the soaring arches, vapor-cleaned to the color of early autumn, and noticed that the stone on top resembled many-petaled flowers six feet across. Then I entered the Cour Napoléon. The fountain splashed merrily, shooting great spume into the air. I wove through a throng of gaping tourists clustered under the arch of the Pavillon Richelieu, and entered the arcades of Café Marly. It seemed like a long, narrow, high-ceilinged chapel, with the stained windows not yet installed and white light streaming through; at the end of the arcade a perfect circle was cut out of the stone, and the pure blue sky was behind it.

Darren was sitting in his usual place. Andrew, who was leaving for America in a few days, sat opposite him. Catherine Lancaster had not yet arrived.

"Hello," I said, as I took the chair next to Andrew.

"How are you," said Darren.

"Hey," said Andrew. He was from the West, like myself.

"You're looking well," I said, to Darren.

"I feel good," said Darren.

"He looks really good," said Andrew. Andrew had more sympathy to give than anybody I'd ever met. I was sorry to see him leave Paris.

"Andrew," I said, "why are you leaving Paris? You're going to make this place feel like Dresden after it was bombed. Nothing around for miles."

Andrew smiled. "But at least your shower will get a rest."

Andrew's flat had no shower, and he used my flat when his boho stink became unbearable.

"Hey," I said. "My dirt is your dirt."

He laughed.

Darren impatiently tapped ashes and attempted to finish the conversation they had been having when I arrived.

"Andrew, I don't care about the stairs. It's just for two weeks or so. I'll sacrifice my leg—it's no big deal."

I immediately knew what they were discussing.

"*No,*" I said decisively. "Out of the question." Darren had more or less recovered from his leg operation and needed a place to stay once he was released from the hospital. Jean-Baptiste had made clear, from Australia, that Darren should *not* try to share the tiny studio on the ground floor of the Quai Malaquais. I had made clear that I would prefer *not* to share my deux-pièces with Darren and try to write a novel about him at the same time. It was true that a few days after I met Darren, I had trusted him with the keys to my flat and put his sleeping bag in the living room; that arrangement had lasted three weeks. Marzenna and Francesco were a possibility, but Darren thought he'd be imposing and besides they were too far away from Café Marly. That left Andrew's flat on the Quai Malaquais, which he was vacating. It was a splendid little *chambre de bonne,* although it had no kitchen and no bathroom and was on the seventh floor with no elevator. To get there one had to ascend one hundred twenty-three steps up an incredibly steep staircase. The idea of Darren climbing those steps was intolerable to me.

"No way, Darren, you'll stay with me. We'll figure out something." I meant that I would figure out a way to lodge him and still not lose my temper. Darren considered my tantrums an intriguing, though inconvenient, side effect of my "artistic temperament." For me, the possessor of this "artistic temperament," my tantrums were a damn nuisance. Darren did not have an "artistic temperament," but he did have hemorrhoids and diarrhea at the same time. That was certainly a damn nuisance. We both had to be careful of what we ate. He could not eat just anything, for fear of exciting something down in his bowels, and I could not eat anything in his presence for fear of exciting something down in my soul.

Andrew thought all this was funny—in a rather grotesque way.

"You two," he said, "are almost entering a kind of symbiosis."

"Oh, Lord," Darren groaned.

"I hope not," I said.

"I suppose I should go to the bathroom now," Darren said. We all laughed at that.

"*Can* I live in your flat?" Darren asked me.

"Yes," I said. "Not for forever, but for now."

That pleased Darren. He had not wanted to ask me to lodge him out of consideration for me. On the other hand, he knew that I would not refuse to offer him the floor space, particularly if the only other available lodging was a room in the sky with a one-hundred-twenty-three-step staircase. That was what the comment about "sacrificing" the leg had been about. It was a comment calculated to elicit my sympathy, and although I saw it as that kind of calculation, I also saw that his need for a place to stay was real. Also, I owed him twenty-five hundred francs. And I still hadn't found a job. So I was being calculating myself, by inviting him to stay. No one is pure, I told myself, not in this life, and certainly not in this novel.

"Philippe," Andrew said, "do you remember that kid we saw the other day in the metro? The one that looked as if he had Down's syndrome, but sort of didn't look like he did?"

"Yes."

"Well, I don't think he has it. I saw him yesterday on a metro platform, counting money with his street-urchin friends. He looked as healthy as you and me and—" After an infinitesimal hesitation he included Darren with a nod. "I think he fakes it to get more money. You were right."

Was I? Had I said that? Who was right? The kid needed the money; he got more sympathy if he looked sicker than he was. And he didn't actually lie. He did, in a way, but it was justified; without acting, he'd get less money than he needed to live, and he needed to live. The question turned around and around in my head.

"Here she comes!" said Darren.

The three of us turned to look down the arcade. Walking with a great deal of movement, a smartly dressed woman wearing black sunglasses was approaching us fast. She wore a black bodysuit. She was built with the curves of a racing yacht, and you missed none of it in that bodysuit.

Darren waved his arms as if he were waving from a dock to a friend on a boat. "Catherine!" he cried. "Catherine!"

They embraced under the columns. She turned impulsively to me and gave me *quatre bisous,* two pecks per cheek, changing each time. She was so pleased to be in Paris she was giving everyone twice the normal ration of feminine affection.

"Catherine, you've just kissed Philippe—and this is Andrew," said Darren. She gave Andrew four kisses, too. Andrew smiled at her.

"How *are* you?" asked Darren, speaking in French.

"How are *you*?" she replied, in her transatlantic English.

They embraced again.

"Oh, I've missed you," she said.

"I missed you, too."

The waiter came up. *"Madame, messieurs?"* he asked.

"Un café," Darren said, his hand still in hers.

"Un café," Catherine said.

"Un café," Andrew said.

"De l'eau," I said.

Catherine wore her black sunglasses with great elegance. She had rosy cheeks, with high lovely cheekbones, and a fantastic smile. She and Darren looked at each other lovingly a long time, as if they could hardly believe they were in each other's presence.

"So how are you?" asked Darren, again. "What are you doing?"

"Oh, the same thing as ever," she said.

"Still looking?" asked Darren.

"Still looking."

"That perfect relationship?"

"The perfect man. Where is he?"

"Why don't you go for Marzenna?" Darren asked. "She's a nice girl, don't you think? Don't we all think?"

"No, I mean with a *man,*" she said, laughing.

"Oh," said Darren, as if she had broached a boring theme. "But you do like Marzenna."

"I do."

Darren, Marzenna, and Catherine had been so close that Francesco, the odd man out, had called them *les trois copines*—the three girlfriends.

"*Still* looking, eh? But I bet you get the big trick all the time."

Catherine laughed, confused by the speed of Darren's serve. She saw I was smiling.

"So, Philippe, how do *you* fit into this?"

"He's my ghost writer," said Darren.

"Hello," I said.

She looked at Darren. "You told me *you* were writing your novel."

"Well," Darren said, "I'm getting a little help."

"Well, whose work is it? How will it be presented?"

I stared hard at a point just beside her.

"We haven't decided that," said Darren.

Andrew pulled out a notebook and a pen. He began drawing sketches of everyone present. I continued staring.

"How's K——?" Darren asked. K—— was one of her former boyfriends.

"Oh, God, he's well set up. He's working for Chet in New York."

I pulled out a notebook and a pen. Andrew kept sketching, his eyes flashing back and forth between the three of us. While Darren spoke of K—— and his friends, I wrote in my notebook, "K—— a true friend Chet H. he knew Dead John working in NY."

"Who's 'John'?" asked Catherine.

"He's the gentleman who . . . most likely . . . whatever. He died a year ago." Darren hesitated; no one looked comfortable as he said it. I looked away down the arcade. Supplies for the restaurant were arriving and the marble floor had popped open to reveal the dumbwaiter beneath. For a moment I could see the café's inner workings.

"And he knew Chet?" Catherine asked.

"Definitely. You know, Jean-Baptiste will be weeping that he's in Australia when you're here."

"I like Jean-Baptiste."

"He absolutely adores *you*," said Darren.

She looked at him. "You're the one he adores," she said. She kept looking at him. "You look great."

They embraced again. Their hair was catching the light. Darren had lovely hair; it rose dreamily above his head and shone like gold in the sunlight. Catherine's hair was silky and brown and it fell over her shoulders like an oriental canopy. I enjoyed looking at her. Andrew's hair was gummed down backwards over his head and he continued looking at both of them, sketching.

"What happened to that girlfriend of yours?" Catherine asked. "The one with the cancer problems?"

"Marie-Thérèse."

"Marie-Thérèse," she repeated, remembering.

"Marie-Thérèse is now having big gynecological problems. They just diagnosed her as having some big cyst down there. And they told her, 'Well we kind of know what's going on, but we'll tell you about it later.' So she went off on her vacation, and the only thing she could think of was what was wrong with her. But they wouldn't tell her. Fucking doctors."

"Why wouldn't they tell her?"

"They didn't know, they said. And they didn't want to scare her by telling her what they thought it might be. As if telling her nothing was better." Darren shook his head. "Long-term illness. Just can't get it out of your mind."

Catherine understood this comment and looked at Darren with enormous concern. She had an expressive, true face and even under the dark sunglasses you could see the movements of the little muscles beneath her eyebrows, which revealed concern and the effort to control it.

"Oh, I do miss you, Darren," she repeated.

"I miss you, Catherine," he said, and put his hand on her knee; she touched him on the shoulder. I noticed she had a little cut on her finger near the cuticle. She had started to nibble it, half-desperately, when Darren had begun talking about Marie-Thérèse's health problems and about how the "long-term illness thing" made them much closer in a way no healthy person could understand.

Then she noticed his gold ring, positioned near her knee. "Are you *still* married?" she asked with a laugh.

"Do you know where I bought this ring?" He paused for effect. "Christopher Street." We all laughed and I rolled my eyes. "I just changed it from one hand to the other, and voilà."

"What about *her* ring?" Catherine asked.

"She brought her own," Darren said, laughing.

"I still can't believe you didn't wait for me," said Catherine.

"Girl, we waited thirty-five minutes for you. That's as much as anybody ever gets."

"Not long enough," said Catherine.

Andrew looked at them carefully, craftily, and I looked at Andrew. He put away his notebook and pen. It was getting near time for lunch, and time to go. We paid the *addition*. Café Marly was very expensive.

As we walked down the sunlit arcade, Darren decided it was time for a photo shoot. Andrew volunteered.

"No, don't, Andrew," chided Catherine. "You should be in the pictures, too."

"No," Andrew said. "It's all right. I'm the man behind the camera." Unfailingly generous as always, Andrew took pictures of the two of them proceeding down the narrow café, Darren on a crutch, one of his arms in Catherine's. There was an enormous smile on his face, and he looked like he was leading her down the aisle of a narrow church. They were moving towards the disk of blue sky cut into the end of the arcade. Andrew took photographs using both their cameras, diving into nooks and behind tables, trying to get the best shot. Then Catherine took pictures of us. Some of the patrons seemed to be a little annoyed.

"Let's get out of here before they kick us out," laughed Darren.

Andrew said good-bye: he had packing to do.

Catherine, Darren, and I walked out to the rue de Rivoli, where Catherine signaled for a cab. She would take Darren back to the Institut Pasteur, and then go on to Roissy airport. Darren had nudged me and quickly explained she was going to take a helicopter to Chet Hyland's pretty little château—a pleasant night on the Riviera.

Walking by myself through Paris, I felt amazed by Catherine. As I arrived in a familiar spot, the phone rang. It was, of course, Darren, again. And I, of course, was in my deux-pièces—and so forth.

"So! What did you think of her?" he asked me.

"Oh, beautiful lady. I don't know what to say. Could she kidnap me, you think?"

"Afraid not. She doesn't trust writers."

"What a shame. I'm trying to decide how to fit her into the book."

"I don't really think she belongs in the book."

"She doesn't? Why not?"

"She doesn't really belong in my life. It's just—well, you know. She's a *girl*."

"Well. Tell her I'm sorry," I said. "But it's—too late."

"What?"

"Yes. It's definitely too late. I've just finished the chapter where we meet her. And it's one of the best chapters in the book."

CHAPTER 8

Reading over what I have written so far, I see that I have given the impression that I was either totally sympathetic or totally critical of Darren. On the contrary, I was neither—or rather, I tried to be both. In the beginning, it is true, I tried to show as much sympathy as I could towards him, because I was writing for him, and writing any condemnation of his life made me feel guilty. But not writing a condemnation where I thought one was deserved made me feel angry, and overwhelmingly irresponsible: not a good condition in which to write. So the work advanced by spurts and starts, sometimes coasting for twenty pages in a day, sometimes stalled for weeks at a time.

"It's emotional diarrhea," I told Darren. "I have no control over it. Sometimes pages and pages just pour out of me. Other times I'm like a dry well."

I was speaking with him at the Institut Pasteur. It was a glum afternoon and dead light seeping from the big windows gently illuminated the room. Darren was sitting on the toilet and grimaced as he poured and poured waste into the bowl.

I stood in the bathroom doorway and watched him. His legs

were dangerously thin, with all the veins popping out; the side of his face was scarred with persistent pimples.

I stood in the doorway, hands in pockets, and kept talking blithely about writing a novel and how important it was not to get complacent—either in literature, or in life.

Darren wiped his ass and dropped the paper between his legs into the bowl.

"Hemorrhoids—*and* diarrhea," he said, looking at me. "Isn't that *special*? What an *appropriate* punishment."

I knew this mood of his. It was my job to get him out of it.

"*No*, Darren, it's not. It's just the way things happened. You got picked for bad luck, that's all."

Darren looked at me. Then he flushed the toilet and hobbled over on his good leg to the bed. He was not wearing any underwear so as he crawled onto the bed he raised his ass in the air and I saw his hemorrhoids bulging out. They looked like the two halves of an angry red moon. But I kept on speaking as before.

"There are many people who are going through this, and much worse, who have done nothing to deserve it. And in my mind, this is something that has happened to you, not something you deserve."

"Yeah, I know," said Darren settling into his bed, and pulling the sheets over himself, "but it's hard to believe, sometimes."

I paused. This was one of his more delicate moments. "No, Darren. Your friend Marie-Thérèse—do you suppose she deserved cancer? And Kenny Moore? Can anybody who dies of leukemia at age twenty-one deserve to die? How can anyone even suggest that? These things just happen and happen. You may as well ask why you were born gay, or on a farm, or . . ." My lips nibbled nervously. "What will people say? Some people will say, 'Well, Darren *chose* to fuck without a condom, so he deserves it.' And I suppose those same people will say that Marie-Thérèse *chose* to live in a city, which she *knew* was full of carcinogenic agents, but she chose to take the risk. Never mind that she loved the city and loathed the countryside. She chose to do it, some people will say. But what can you say about Kenny Moore? 'Bad genes'? He was carrying leukemia inside of him from the moment he was born. 'It was destiny. Bad luck. He

didn't deserve it, but, when his parents married, they should
have known.' Is that what some people will say?"

Darren looked at me, his sad, pockmarked face staring out of
his glasses. What I was saying sounded resoundingly hollow to
me, but Darren wanted to hear me say it.

"What will they say?" I continued. " 'Darren did it to himself.' All these other people, it *happened* to them, but you got
yourself into this? No, Darren, it's more complicated than that.
There are forces in your life much greater than your own free
will. What's your will up against your *lust*? I suppose 'you want
what you want,' too. Well, people who tell you that are plants
telling mammals what their appetites should be. Straight out of
Garp. Free will, my arse."

Darren read over that passage when he was much better. He
read it while puffing on an Amsterdamer Special and looking
out at the I. M. Pei pyramid, saluting the white-jacketed waiters
at Café Marly. He said, "You sound more mystical than I am—
philosophical, almost."

I was opposite him, hearing the familiar fountains gush on.
"I'm not really mystical."

"But you are, Philippe."

"I hope not. *Your* mysticism is enough for two persons."

I was glad I had only imagined that conversation. I was
waiting to pay off my twenty-five-hundred-franc debt to Darren
before showing him any of the sixty further pages I'd written
under the imaginary title "The Limits of Compassion."

By now the novel was well under way. I had filled three and
a half little brown notebooks with dense scribblings, built a
twenty-page outline with various genealogical tables, chronological tables, all sorts of tables, filled up pages and pages with
anecdotes and vignettes and stories about his life. I had listened
to the tapes of Martin Fogel and studied Darren's gigantic collection of photographs. My favorite photograph was one of
Darren with a little girl from Grenoble, Amandine Sanson, on
his lap. The picture showed Maurice Sanson, the girl's father,
taking a picture of Darren. It gave me a great idea: the novel
would be like a picture of a man taking a picture of Darren.

"A self-referent novel!" I said.

"If you say so," said Darren.

"Fiction that talks about fiction."

"But *this* fiction is supposed to be a true story."

"Well of course it's a true story. But it's *true* in the sense that every part of it feels true. If this conversation we're having, for example, feels true once I write it up in the book, then I'll put it in. But if it doesn't, I'll revise it, or I'll make it up."

"You wouldn't make up conversation between us, would you?" Darren said.

"Of course not."

Of course, I was in my deux-pièces and you know the rest. There was a big mess everywhere, a pile of dirty dishes in the sink, used glasses on all the tables. Then the phone rang. But it was only a wrong number.

"I've stopped," I told Darren, in reality, on the terrace of Café Marly. I meant I had stopped writing. Darren wore a polo shirt and fancy clip-on sunglasses. I also wore fancy clip-on sunglasses in an effort to look *branché*. He smoked an Amsterdamer Special, watching the delightful fumes fly away from him and into the pleasant breeze that blew around us. "I have to find a part-time job," I told Darren, "or I'll be so deep in debt that I'll need a full-time job to get out of it."

"Well, then you should stop writing and look for a job."

"I *am* looking for a job, and I *have* stopped," I replied, a little irritably. But I held myself back and smiled at him to show I was not about to lose my temper. "See?" I said. "No food, no tantrums. I have wonderful self-control when I'm hungry. *Dayadhvam.* You're right; the skinnier you are, the more mystical you get."

"Look at me."

"I am looking at you, Darren. But you're not that mystical. You're just appallingly sentimental, like Gatsby. He never loved Daisy. He loved her disembodied face."

"Are you all right?" asked Darren.

"I'm fine. This hunger works, I'm telling you. Beautiful self-control. No energy."

And that was how it was. I stopped writing, stopped in the middle of this sentence in fact. I did not start again until I found a good part-time job with a bank; by then I would be several thousand francs in debt, which I would repay in a little less than a year. During that time Darren remained in the hospital, and when he wasn't calling me with up-to-the-minute reports on the state of his soul and of his leg drain—attitude self-checks to which I listened with what I hoped he would perceive as great interest—he called up nearly everyone he knew in America. Well—everyone he *liked*.

"I called my Uncle Milt, and Jack and Lois Webster, and Pat and Carol Boeh, and Pat and Blake Stephenson. They were wonderful."

"Great! What did they say?"

"Oh, they were just wonderful."

"Isn't that fine! What did your Uncle Milt say?"

"Oh, he was wonderful. I told him about the book, and I said I had a ghost writer. And he said, 'Oh Darren, you don't need to tell anyone that.' "

"Fantastic!" I said.

"And he told me how important the book is. Philippe—this book is going to change a lot of people's lives."

Never shatter another person's illusions, not even those fed by Prozac and Amsterdamer Specials. So I said, "Of course it will, Darren." And for all I knew, it would.

"It *will*," Darren said. "This book is going to be a work of art."

"We'll see about that when I finish it."

"When *are* you going to finish it?"

"I have sketches and drafts, now, lots of them. I've got ideas for a few titles and a few fairly large fragments."

"I'd like to see them."

"They're based on that monologue of yours we recorded, the first night we worked together, at my place."

"Which monologue was that?"

"The four-hour one."

"Oh, of course! Great. Good work."

"What else did your Uncle Milt say?" I asked.

"He said to go right ahead and burn my mother. I'm through fighting it, Philippe. The axe is going to fall and it's going to fall hard. Oh, and I spoke to Frank and Wendall—"

More maternal uncles. The roster of Darren's extended family had taken up pages and pages in my notebook.

"And they said to burn, burn her and Dahlia. They're the ones who're going to get it. Because they deserve it."

"I see."

"And he asked me if I was going to say anything nasty about him. And I said, 'Of course not, only about Mommy dearest. And of course about Grandma Dahlia.' "

"And what did Jack and Lois Webster say?"

"Oh, I told them they were already in the book!"

Which they weren't, I thought, but I guess they are now.

"And they were speechless. So I explained that since they picked up Jean-Baptiste and me at the airport when we arrived from Paris, and drove us to Immaculatum, they play an important part, don't you think?"

"Oh yes." I had decided to exclude the Websters from the book, because I already had seventy-five characters too many, but now that they had been told they were in the book, hell, I thought, why not put them in? I was trying to show a little of that endless Kansan generosity. "I had meant to put them in all along," I said.

"And I told the Boehs they were in it, too."

"Great!" I said. I hardly knew who the Boehs were, except that they were "wonderful people," like all the wonderful people in wonderful Kansas.

"They were wonderful about it. They asked when the book would be coming out."

"What did you say?"

"I said next June." We were in October.

"Great!" I said. Thanks, Darren, I thought, it's not like you're putting me under any pressure or anything. "Oh, I read your notes."

"Good; what did you think of them?"

We meant Darren's notes for the book.

As I sit here at Café Marly looking out at the pyramid, the fountain, and the Eiffel Tower, one can't help but be humbled by its grandeur and beauty. After four years of searching I have finally found the café that pleases me in almost every way. The ambiance and "cadre" are nearly exactly what I have been looking for.

"I thought your notes were very true," I said, "and that always makes for good writing."

"I don't think they have a high literary value."

"No one knows what makes for literary value," I said, and changed the subject. "Who else did you call? What did Blake say?"

"Blake said to *write the fucking book.*"

"And *who* did he direct that comment towards?"

Darren laughed. Who was writing this book, anyway? It was writing itself, I supposed. I certainly felt I'd surrendered to it, and to Darren. It was awful; it was like watching a friend become a master and finally a tyrant.

"Anybody else in the book?" I asked. Darren took a perverse pleasure in constantly adding to my list of characters. It now ran to a hundred and seventy-five entries, for a book I had described as "between the length of *The Sun Also Rises* and *The World According to Garp.*" That meant a new character every 2.4 pages, on average.

"It'll make a great movie, won't it?" Darren asked. "A cast of thousands. Just think about it."

"I *am* thinking about it, Darren," I said. "Believe me, *I am.*"

Darren had asked me several times if the book could be made into a movie. I had replied yes, very firmly. Movies meant more prestige, fame, and money.

"Who do you think they'd get to play me?" Darren asked. "I wouldn't want just anybody."

"Brad Pitt? Is he handsome enough?"

"Sure. They can get some young unknown to play you."

"Oh, I won't be in it. I'm the man behind the camera."

"What'll we call it? Hey, I thought of a title for the book. How about 'A Parisian from Kansas Searching for Dot Dot Dot Question Mark'?"

" . . . ?" I raised my eyebrows.

"It's just an idea."

"I'll give it a thought. Something like that, anyway," I said.

"It goes with the theme of the book. I think. What is the theme of the book?"

"Death," I said. "And lust."

"Why *lust?*"

"All right—lust and mysticism."

That pleased him. "What else?"

"Europe versus America. The country versus the city. Sympathetic people versus not-so-sympathetic people. The symphetic people are the good guys in the novel. The not-so-sympathetic people are the bad guys."

"Like my mother," Darren said.

"Like your mother," I repeated. I wet my lips quickly. "There are also four levels of plot. The first is your life. The second is the development of the novel about your life. The third is"—I inhaled—"the gradual realization of how much you resemble your mother—something you accomplish through the writing." I paused. Darren did not seem shocked. It was safe to go on. "The fourth is a system of allusions to favorite books of mine—you know, *Gatsby, Sun Also, Road, Garp.* Commentary on the American Dream, et cetera."

"Do you think there will be a reconciliation between my mother and me?"

"No. I think you may come to realize that in her own supremely tactless way, she adores you. But you two will remain enemies until the end."

"Yeah, that sounds right." He sighed. "You know, Davey once said, 'Darren, you're always bitchin' 'bout Mom but you're actually the one of us who's most like her.' "

"Well," I said, "maybe he has a point. Your brother has a good heart."

Davey was a friendly, likable oaf. He assured Darren he was ready to take the first plane out to Paris, although he didn't know what a passport was. But he was Darren's only brother and although he didn't understand him he loved him. "He loves you in the best way," I said, meaning the simplest.

"So . . . four levels of plot," Darren repeated, conscientiously. "Any more?"

I looked hard at a point just beside his head. "None that I'm aware of."

"What about allusions?" Darren surprised me; he really had done his homework.

"Allusions are just phrases borrowed from other works. It's a way of calling up ghosts of authors, making dead people speak again. The book is full of ghosts. My job is to keep everyone alive, forever."

"Like that man waiting outside Rosita's office."

"I imagined him, yes. But it felt right that he should be there. Doesn't it? Isn't fiction great? You can rearrange anything that didn't happen right the first time." I looked at him fondly and then sadly. "I hope they find a cure," I said.

"Yeah, it's the least we can hope for," Darren said.

I looked at him some more. "You are going to have one *good* funeral, man. I'm going to give you one hell of a funeral oration. I'll compare you to Kenny Moore."

"But I'm not sure Doris would be happy about that."

"Well, tough. Kenny died slowly and lingeringly and young, and that's how you're dying."

"But I'm not sure how Doris would feel."

"Oh, God, we'll change the names then."

"What?" Darren asked.

"*What* what? The funeral in the *book*."

"Oh! I thought you were talking about real life."

"No, silly. God knows what I'll say in real life. I meant the *book*."

"Oh, then say whatever you like. Let them *have* it."

"I figure after the funeral you can come in and comment on it. Anything in particular you want? White horses? White maidenly boys? Bronski Beat?"

"What a hip funeral that would be."

"You could make a video to tell us all those things you could never tell us while you were alive."

"What a great idea!" Darren said.

"You should make the video now, while you're healthy. Later you'll be slobbering and skeletal and you won't be so photogenic. Whereas now you look great."

"Philippe, you are such a *bitch*, I swear!"

"Aren't I, though? But I'm honest."

"Honesty is the most important thing."

"Honesty," I announced rather pompously, "is the basis of all good friendships. You have to know when not to use it."

Darren howled at that. We both did.

Somebody knocked on the door. It was Marzenna and Francesco. They visited Darren nearly every day.

"*Bonjour,*" said Francesco, and shook my hand. Marzenna gave *deux bisous* to both Darren and me. "*Ça va?*" she asked.

"*Je vais bien!*" exclaimed Darren. I liked to see him in good spirits. Visitors always put him in good spirits. They had brought some *tartes Tatin* from Mulot's, which no one could resist, not even me.

"What were you discussing?" Marzenna asked with a sly smile. Ever since I had read her the passage where she first appeared in the book she'd regarded me with wary amusement.

"My death," said Darren cheerily.

"Charming," said Marzenna.

"This morning I had the most wonderful conversation with my father," said Darren.

"Oh really? What did he say?" asked Francesco.

"He said that as far as he was concerned, *I* could choose to die wherever I wanted. And I told him that afterwards *they* could do whatever they wanted with my body. That was the arrangement."

"Very nice," said Marzenna.

"I told him that I would get cremated here and we would send the ashes to Kansas via UPS. It'll be cheaper that way." Darren doubled over in laughter at that one.

Marzenna thought it was a horrible thing to say. "Darren, you didn't."

In between gasps of laughter, Darren nodded achingly, his mouth in a happy grimace. Then he eased up, let the laughter out with a sigh. "No, of course I didn't."

Marzenna rolled her eyes in relief.

"Too bad," I said. "Well, in the book I'll say you did."

"Philippe and I have been talking a lot about my death. We have this kind of grim slapstick humor going on. Don't you think?"

I looked at Marzenna and Francesco. They obviously thought we were *both* sick.

"I think it's very American," I offered. "Also, I have to. I have to imagine what the future is going to be like. Or at least, what it could be like. So—the funeral, in Kansas. And his family will be there, and I'll be there, probably, and Jean-Baptiste."

I looked at Francesco as if to ask whether he would be there, too.

He looked at me. "Is this in real life or in the book?"

"That, Francesco," I said, "is the first really intelligent thing you've said in the whole book."

"Thank you."

Over Darren's shoulder I saw a face in the Plexiglas window of the door. The door was a little behind Darren and off to his right. The face looked vaguely familiar; it looked white and pressed up against the Plexiglas. In slow motion I approached the door, until I was so close I could hear the hissing voice on the other side.

"Open it! Let me in!" hissed the voice on the other side.

"No. Not now. Not yet," I said, holding the doorknob firmly.

"I have as much right to be in this as you do!" the voice commanded. "You open this door right now!"

The three others were looking at me as I stood there with my hand on the knob.

"You have to turn it to open it," said Darren.

"I know," I said, not taking my eyes off the slit eyes that watched me from the other side of the Plexiglas.

"Who is it?" asked Darren.

"You let me in, do you hear?" said the voice. Of course I knew who it was.

"Who is it?" repeated Darren.

"Someone . . . who doesn't belong here right now." I put my face against the window, with my hand still on the door handle; I felt it moving with incredible force, the metal sliding through my tightened fingers despite all my effort. I tightened my grip as hard as I could, and still it slipped, slipped irresistibly. I grimaced. The door was opening!

"*NO!!* NO! NO! NO! NO! NO!" I had dropped to my knees. The door was wide open. But there was no one there. I was crouched down, panting like an animal, my hands underneath my armpits, my head ticking from side to side.

"Philippe! Are you all right?" cried Marzenna.

Francesco rushed over to help me, put his hand on my shoulder. I drew back from it, the way a snail retracts into its shell when touched.

"*Ça va?* What's happening to you? Tell me!"

Darren looked at me, helpless in his bed. "Francesco, let him go." But even he was shocked. This was my worst one yet.

"Dar . . . Dar . . . Darren . . . tell . . . tell . . . tell them," I managed to articulate.

"Philippe's having one of his attacks," Darren said, making an effort to sound grave and in command of the situation. I had placed an arm over my head, another over my face, as if to fend off a swarm of bees; I was still on my knees, curling up into a ball.

A nurse ran over to help me.

"No . . . not . . . noth . . ." I managed to say. My eyes were shut tight. I felt I had been caught by a blinding spotlight.

"He's having some sort of psychological attack," said Francesco, trying to explain.

"Does he need to be taken outside? How can I help?"

"He needs to be left alone," Darren said. I had actually curled into a ball, my head between my knees, my elbows gripping my knees together, my hands holding my head. "Philippe," Darren asked, "do you want to go outside?"

"Y-yes," I said.

Gradually, slowly, Francesco and the nurse raised me to my feet, and although I never removed my hands from my skull, they managed to take me down the lift into the warm greenhouse at the end of the nice pavilion where Darren's room was. I did not want to sit down. I started walking around in the greenhouse. With automatic lips I started reciting. I found that to be very calming. Twenty minutes later a concerned nurse came in to see how I was doing. I managed to smile at her sufficiently to reassure her, and after she went out to the corridor I continued reciting:

> DA
> *Datta*: what have we given?
> My friend, blood shaking my heart
> The awful daring of a moment's surrender
> Which an age of prudence can never retract
> By this, and this only, we have existed
> Which is not to be found in our obituaries
> Or in memories draped by the beneficent spider
> Or under seals broken by the lean solicitor
> In our empty rooms
> DA

And so on. After I finished reciting I felt much better. I was able to remove my hands from my skull. I mounted the steps and shyly said hello to the nurses at their station. They smiled wonderfully. It felt good that they seemed to care for me. I walked into room 29, making very little sound. Francesco and Marzenna were still there.

"So?" Darren asked. "Feeling better?"

"Much," I said.

"That was a good one," Darren said.

"Good one yourself," I said, shaking my head, grimly amused.

"What happened?" Darren asked.

"I don't know. I just—lose control, sometimes. I'm working too hard, writing too much."

"You should take it easy, then," Darren said.

"That's just it, Darren. I can't. The writing has possessed me to the point where I just can't stop. It's beyond my control. It's like being alone every evening, and what can you do? It's like—lust." I looked at him helplessly.

"Fucking *lust!*" said Darren.

"Fucking *writing,*" I said. But he'd succeeded in making me smile.

Francesco asked me to sit in his chair and I did. "I'm going to stop being so secretive," I said. "Soon—maybe tomorrow—I'll show you some fragments I've been working on these past few weeks. You'll see why I've been shy about showing them. Oh, it's been awful."

"Are you going to be all right, Philippe?" Marzenna asked. She put her hand on my arm, and it felt good lying there. I smiled to let her know.

"Much better, thank you," I said.

"Now you see what I mean when I say I drive Philippe crazy," Darren said.

"I see," said Marzenna.

"We are too close," said Darren. "It's unhealthy."

"Fucking men and their homoerotic relationships," I said, joking.

"Fucking *men,*" said Francesco, and we laughed.

I felt tired. "Well, Darren. I think that's enough for one evening. I'm going to walk home and try to turn in early."

"Do you want a ride or anything?" asked Marzenna and Francesco in unison. "We go right past your door."

"No," I said, "but thank you anyway."

"Philippe?" asked Darren. "Can I ask you one thing?"

"Yes."

"I'm sorry if this will upset you—but could you tell me just what you saw in the door that made you freak out?"

I looked at him. "The bad guys," I said. "Good night."

And I descended the steps into the rue Vaugirard, where a thin drizzle was just beginning. I looked right and then left: I had to remember which street led home since they looked almost the same for the first few blocks no matter which way you went. I turned right and began walking up the wet rue de Vaugirard, past a square where young students were frolicking, wearing their boots and comfortable checkered lumberjack shirts. I passed the Necker Hospital—POUR LES ENFANTS MALADES, said the sign—and kept on walking quickly, watching the Fifteenth Arrondissement turn into the Sixth. Stores selling carpets and auto parts became twinkling clothing boutiques selling thin women's shoes and many-latched purses. I turned into the rue de Rennes and was walking near Saint-Sulpice, where I knew Catherine Deneuve lived, and whenever I was in that area I hoped I would glimpse her. Then I walked across the great Boulevard Saint-Germain, and at night the cars seemed further away and more gentle, and I crossed the sidewalk separating the two terraces of the Deux Magots, where many expensively dressed people smiled at each other and studied passersby with a critical eye. I felt briefly studied and then was through, bearing rightward into the rue de l'Abbaye, that passes near the serene and elegant Place de Furstemberg, which I love. I stood for a moment looking at the street lamp with its four big lights. Then I saw Darren. He looked strapping, and was dressed in a beautiful blue suit. His lovely Kansan wife held his hand admiringly and together they stood admiring the Place. He had become a very successful businessman, with the most prosperous dairy farm in all Kansas, and his wife was his high school sweetheart, a girl with pure and innocent eyes. Darren Swenson was clean-shaven and tall, and his shoes were very shiny, and his wife adored him, and he was adored by his four children, who were all star students and star athletes and star musicians and wonderful people.

From behind me I heard some shouting, "Yes! *Yes!* Man,

you sure can GO! *Whooooooeeeee!*" then the shamble of frenzied footsteps. They were two Americans getting drunk and kicks in Paris, chasing each other through the Place like dingledodies, on their way to the Pont des Arts, maybe.

I turned back to look at Darren and his lovely wife, but they were gone.

It had been the hypothetical Darren and his hypothetical wife and his four hypothetical children, the one everybody but Darren had dreamed about.

I felt badly for Darren. It seemed so unfair somehow. Not the least of the unfairness was the way I needed to be so alone to write his novel, however much we enjoyed each other's company. I felt I had left the Institut Pasteur abruptly. I thought that at any moment he might collapse once and for all. So I turned around and began walking *back* to the Institut Pasteur. The drizzle had stopped, and the way seemed shorter this time. At the door of the hospital I had to be a little insistent and cross with the doorman, because it was after hours, but he let me in eventually. I crossed the red brick court and went back up the staircase to room 29. The night shift had taken over, and they didn't recognize me or say anything when I crossed the hall to room 29 and opened the door. The light was on. I walked right in.

In his bed was a huge four-hundred-pound bloated form. It rose under the covers like a tumulus. I recognized it immediately. I stopped in my tracks. I tried to speak. I heard myself breathing.

"Hello, Philippe."

It was Darren's mother.

"Where's Darren?" I finally asked.

Her answer was said in a kind of imitation joyful manner. "He's back at home, darlin'! He and I have changed places. He's at home, doin the cookin' and the cleanin', and ah'm here gettin' service for a change. I never tried marijuana before, but oh how I like it. Very good stuff. Very good." Her body was monstrous and enormous; the sheet bulged as if covering a mound of earth.

I was very confused and said nothing for a while. Then I said, "Stop."

"What?"

"Stop. Stop it. Stop it now. Please—get out. Get out."

"Ah'm here to stay. You can't get rid of me. I'm Darren, honey. He's me."

"Get the *fuck* out of here. Get *out* of my fucking book. Get out of my *fucking* LIFE!"

"Philippe! Philippe!" I heard behind me.

I turned around. I was on my knees, in the Place de Furstemberg, my knees wet in the street oil and water, my head and hands pressed up against the big elegant lamppost, which felt pleasantly cool against my forehead.

I turned, but there was no one there.

In my deux-pièces, I decided I should stop writing. Tomorrow I would show the fragments I'd worked on to Darren. He would be glad to see them, and I would be glad to show them to him.

The Man Behind the Camera

Listen to what the tape recorder said when I pressed PLAY:

Philippe—you must believe what I tell you. I've never started a project with more hope. I know we've only known each other—what? three days? But I feel there's a special, spiritual bond between us. That bond is going to move us forward. It *is* a crazy project, isn't it? You writing a novel about my life. Well. This is only the most recent crazy thing I've done.

So this is for the tape.

My name is Darren J. Swenson, and I was born not far from Immaculatum, in Kansas, and grew up under flat horizons in prairie fields and with pigs. I came from a fifth-generation Swedish family: the Andersons, who married the Swensons—good stock, honest and hardworking people; they were the founders of the Crane Hill Swedish Lutheran Church, which is a very tough church indeed. We're the oldest family in that church.

The house I grew up in has been the Swenson house for five generations now. There were additions made, and of course my mother bought furniture and bought furniture—wall-to-wall furniture, now—but it was always the same house, with the same photographs in the same dining room—photographs that we kept adding to and adding to. My photographs are all over the walls— always wearing my farmer glasses and my fan-TAS-tic polyester suit.

Being born into all that was another world. My father knew from very early on I was *not* going to be a farmer. He knew I wasn't tied to the land. But he still made me work and *work*. Oh, it was good for me. Once—I was eleven—I was standing next to the tractor, my eyes fixed on the fields, and my old man, who was about a quarter of a mile away, yelled, "Darren! Bring the tractor over here!" knowing full well I'd never driven it before. But I gingerly climbed in and figured out how it worked and touched the gas pedal for real for the first time in my life and drove it over to him. There was the *biggest* grin you ever saw on his face. But then there was all the milking. I milked cows at six-thirty in the morning—every morning—and at three in the afternoon—every afternoon. Milking cows in the milk barn that was full of cow plops and piss and it just stank. Then the others took over so I could concentrate on studying; I learned to play the piano when I was fourteen. I would go over to Mrs. Effland's house, just down the street, and I learned *Für Elise* and the *Pathétique* and spent hours sometimes talking to her. I was her favorite student. That wasn't very hard. There were about twenty students in my high school class—most of them with big shoulders and hairy tongues.

I knew, almost as soon as I knew there was someplace else besides Kansas, that I wanted to be someplace else. Day in, day out, watching these damn cows, staring at their black spots, smelling those cow plops and all that pissed-on hay, and then driving the tractor and just looking at that flat, absolutely flat horizon and thinking, I am getting the *fuck* out of here. I can even remember the exact moment.

I was sitting in the hay meadow—there's this special spot where the ground dips a little, so it's shielded from the wind, a little, and no one could see me from the house—and I was sitting there, having my great big fifteen-year-old thoughts, when I looked up at a plane. It was slicing the sky into halves, a long white plume across that blue sky. And I thought, that plane is leaving Kansas, and one day, I'm going to be on it.

But that all came true much later. In the meantime, waiting for my time to come up, I milked the cows, and did my studies, and ran track, and played football, and smiled all the time, and just counted the days. I felt so much smarter than all the adults there. Immaculatum was big enough for them; it wasn't big enough for me.

So I was very ambitious. One year I gave a recital of the *Pathétique* at the school hall. It was a winter night. I'd gotten to the fast part and suddenly—*pop!*—all the lights went out. Some sort of electrical failure. I just kept on playing. I played in the dark without missing a note. Then they put on the lights and I still kept on playing as if nothing had happened. Everybody oohed and aahed and just *stared*. Valedictorian, Athlete of the Year, Musicianship Award—you name it, I got it. For what it was worth: remember, this was a tiny hick town in the middle of nowhere.

I was so, *so* bored. There was absolutely nothing to sink myself into. Well—almost nothing. I discovered early that the lips of the baby calves were at just the right height for li'l adolescent me. They did a very good job. Then there was Star, our favorite filly. Not just mine—also of a friend called Alex. Oh dear. We'd take turns getting behind her and just banging away. That was actually the first time I touched another man's dick—because sometimes someone else had to ease it into the horse.

So—*aside* from that, there was nothing to get my juices flowing. There were no books. There was no culture. So I thought, Darren, work, work, *work,* and get the fuck out of here. So I seemed a lot older and more responsible than the other boys. I was always the one who bought the liquor. And when the schoolteachers found out Darren Swenson had been—horrors! *buying liquor*—they actually smiled, and thought, thank God he's not as straight as we thought. Of course, my mother was very unhappy about it. She wanted me to be "Mister Perfect."

Yeah, well. Nearly everybody else called me Mister Perfect. On field trips strangers thought I was the teacher. And when I told my football coach I felt picked on and all alone, he said, "Darren, you're right and they're all wrong." He meant all those dumb Midwestern boys. "Just keep driving on. You're right and they're all wrong." I remembered that.

Yeah, I was Mister Perfect. I had no accidents. No illnesses. No pimples even. Compared to my poor brother, who just sort of chewed his cud through his high school years—my family knew he was going to be a Tuff Kansin Farmer almost the minute he was born—I really *was* perfect. Best of show all around. Moo.

The day I graduated everybody wanted to shake my hand. "You stay in touch, now. Y'hear? We want to know what's gonna happen to ya." Grandpa Anderson said he was "lookin' forward to sendin' ya postcards at 1600 Pennsylvania Avenue, Darren!" And my mom told me that day, "Darren, you are my A-number-one son." I remembered that. She wasn't big on compliments, but that day she told me, I was *the* jewel in her crown.

I was gone like a shot. K.U. was about three hours' drive from Immaculatum and I could not wait. But almost as soon as I had arrived I had a letdown. My dad had told me, "Darren, yer eighteen. Ya go to college, fine. But there, yer on yer own." And there, at K.U., instead of friends, I found all these stupid, snotty rich kids, who didn't have to do anything to stay enrolled except not drive their cars into the fountains—and some of them could not even manage that. And me, pinching pennies as a hospital orderly, working graveyard shift. But I thought, well damn them, I'll play the game anyway. Because what I had, and these boys didn't, was *charm*. I had plenty of that.

Entry into society was through a fraternity. So spring term '83 I pledged Tau Omega Rho—they turned out to be the biggest band of dingbats I ever met.

But not at first. At first these guys seemed nice, seemed sincere. Those first few friendships seemed really, really deep. So when we pledged together, put our hands together on the old sword, I took the vows seriously, for I truly thought we would all be brothers, for life. I knew I was as smart as the smartest of them, I was just as good, even though I didn't have their money. Or their family. Or their sexuality.

I did everything in secret then. My first time was a lurid, lurid old man. Then there were bathrooms in the student union that were pretty busy. But mostly I kept cool, even dated girls, some of whom I really liked—although I couldn't even dream of having sex with them. One girl fell head over heels in love with me. She adored me. She thought I was so *cultured*. I took her to a K.U. Symphony concert—the *Emperor* Concerto was the centerpiece—and picked her up in a truck. I don't think she even noticed. Sad, sad case. Anyway, I had to dump her when she became too insistent, and some guys at the fraternity even thought I was a bit of a ladies' man. I did nothing to stop this rumor. In fact, I rather liked it.

There were endless parties, parties, parties, beer, beer, beer, vomiting, vomiting, vomiting. It was gro-*tesque*. There was always someone on the steps late at night, head between his knees, puking his guts out. Then there was the Droopy Drawers Party and the Barn Party and the Zombie Juice Party—each one another scantily-dressed excuse to cram as many people as they could into those awful-smelling rooms. I chatted to all the girls and ogled all the boys. Faking and pretending, waiting to be accepted.

I had just one friend at the frat, Jeff. I liked him, he was tolerant, he knew about me and had sympathy. Jeff started romancing my sister Sherrie when she came up to K.U. Sherrie was a bright girl, and she thought that Greek scene was absurd beyond belief. She cut out after her first year when she saw that attending school was like being a cow prepared for insemination—which well-bred man would she marry? everyone asked. She married Pete Schmidt, who never left Immaculatum, and now she milks cows twice a day, and that's enough for her. Do you know that my family has milked those damn cows twice a day, every day—I mean, every single day of the year—for sixty years? They're up at four-thirty most mornings. I think they've missed maybe four, maybe five milkings in all that time.

Anyway—K.U. was getting just as boring as the milking and I wanted a break. I also wanted something to distinguish myself. In Kansas, at the fraternity, I was at a disadvantage. They were urban boys; I was a goofy hawr-hawr-hawr farm boy. I wanted a do-it-yourself pedigree. Out of Kansas, I thought, I would get to play on a level playing field. Out of America, I thought, the differences between the rich boys and me would be wiped out; we'd all look and sound alike to strangers; getting ahead would be purely a matter of savvy. Maybe it was something Grandpa Anderson had said; maybe it was something I'd read in a book. But I decided on France. I'd never been, didn't know anyone there. But by becoming French I thought I could distinguish myself. I started French lessons, could just about imitate the sounds you make when you're supposed to be asking for a *baguette*, and I told Robert Flewelling, my advisor, that I wanted to go to France. Professor Flewelling said this was like a twelve-year-old insisting he wants to drive. I said I'd been driving since I was eleven. He smiled, put in a plug for me, and I got admitted to the American Studies program at the Sciences-Po in Grenoble. I scratched together the money for a flight and was off. I told myself, that'll show 'em, when I get back.

But when I arrived in France, it was like heaven. It was like Oz. I couldn't believe it. I really couldn't believe it. The towers, the monuments, the manners—the manners! That was what got me. The way you asked for bread, the little ceremony you went through to buy cheese, the little things you said—it was like a grace note, a light note, on everything. It turned the *quotidien* into something that was a daily amazement.

Then there were the French. I got along so well with everybody. In Kansas everyone pegged me in a farm-boy stereotype. Here I could make myself up as I went along. A couple of weeks after I arrived I met Francesco and Patti and Ward. But more importantly, the school lodged me with the Sansons, who were wonderful, and had a wonderful house and wonderful children. And that was where I learned to be sophisticated. The parents and I put away a bottle of wine every night, and we talked in French, about absolutely everything.

Soon after I moved in with them, I had an experience that—so long as I live—I won't forget. It'll sound trite to you. But I felt what I felt just as clearly and tangibly as I feel the flesh on my skin. I was in a pub in Grenoble. It was an afternoon, and there was stained glass behind me, yellow stained glass, so the light came in over my shoulder with little drops of red and dark-lined shadows where the iron cut up the light. There was a barman wiping down his bar. He wiped from side to side, then leaned against the bar. There were no other customers. And I thought, well, this is kind of sad, let's have some music. There was a jukebox at each table kind of like in American diners. It sort of made me feel at home, except that I felt better in France than I did at home. And I put some francs into this machine and wound her up. I can't remember exactly what I listened to or in what order. Although I do remember that I chose "I'm Still Standing" by Elton John.

Anyway, the music came on, and I had a pint of beer in my hand. And all of a sudden I was just taken—seized by this series of extraordinary realizations—I can't explain it all—sal-*salvation,* feeling much much bigger than I was, escaping—I felt my soul

physically get larger—just breaking time barriers and space barriers, moving onwards and outwards. It was just—I can't explain
it—it was just too big, it was like stepping into the presence of
GOD, it could only be. And I felt at that moment this feeling of destiny taking over. Things just fell into place. And like, when after you
come down from visiting the observatory on a very tall building,
you come down home to earth, so I felt like I was descending back
into my body, the flesh that held me. But for an instant, the instant
it lasted, I was just VAST on a huge scale, like on a mass scale, and I
knew—there's no stopping me and the rest of my life. There's no
stopping. It was the moment I realized what Martin Fogel would
tell me years later—"You were born into another world." It was a
spiritual world, and I could see it, I felt it, for the first time. The rest
of my life was clear. The die was cast.

Of course then there were more mundane matters. There were
my studies, which I did a little of—not a lot. *Mystical* Darren was
too busy talking to God on the white courtesy telephone to bother
with mere studies and problem sets. So my grades were pretty bad.
Also my French was awful, particularly compared to everybody
else's. But there was also the social game. Darren got introduced as
the witty, eccentric farmer boy, Mr. Child of the Universe. Everybody thought I was so *exotic*. "Oh, you must meet Darren. He's
from *Kansas*. Apparently he knows how to milk a cow." Some of
these urban sophisticates didn't know how many teats a cow had.
Four, by the way, Philippe.

But despite their ignorance, they were so nice. Ward was from
Georgetown. Patti was from Brown. They treated me as an equal,
but that was where I felt the power of the East Coast, and of course
of old Europe—not Grenoble but Paris. The truly grand people
were in Paris. Paris was refined by tradition, not because of pretension. That was what I detected right away—tradition. I understood
the refinement. Others only understood the pretension, like Vicki.
But Vicki was still a good friend, because she was from K.U. and
very understanding. I told her I was gay and she just shrugged. "Part
of life." That was the other thing I liked, the tolerance of the homosexuality, so different from the hellfire and damnation back home.
At the frat some guy had been seriously hazed because someone
else said he'd been seen cruising the bathrooms. Europeans were
more casual about that, and less casual about food, or manners, or

buildings, with their stone architecture full of scrolls and timpani and frolicking monkeys.

None of us wanted to leave. At Christmas my mother sent me all her love, pleading I come back. I didn't want to. I really wanted to prove how grown-up I was, how good, how far I'd come up in the world. And another thing—I felt so much more free in France, that I decided this was my home. Home was here. I started trying to figure out some way of staying out here forever. Of course my mother sent me a gift packet from the Boehs—this gooey, horribly sugary American candy. And she said, "Merry Christmas, Darren. (This is a lot harder job, emotionally, writing this than I ever dreamed)."

Anyway the candy was awful and I think I threw it away. I used to really enjoy receiving things from my mom—always took it as expected, even automatic—but then I hadn't gotten *back* from Grenoble, hadn't told her what was really going on, not yet; she hadn't written me off, not yet. . . .

So I spent Christmas with the Sansons and it was the most wonderful Christmas of my life. Because my birthday was around Christmas, everyone was just magnificently generous. I didn't feel like a guest at all. I felt like I was a member of a family.

Then later Wayne the Pain and Marge the Barge came to visit. Cousin Jacquie came to visit—a forty-year-old come-lately-to-California bimbo still looking for *Mister Right*. What a fool. People like Wayne and Margie and Jacquie were just bad reminders of what was waiting for me when I got back home.

Well, I did get back. Mom was standing in front of the house like a fort. They had been preparing the homecoming since *Christmas*, for Christ's sake. They had invited absolutely EVERYONE. All Immaculatum was there. And the more I saw the more disdainful I became. I was having trouble hiding it. "Darren, you've come back weird," my mother said. How could I not? There was fried chicken dipped in grease, those rich sweet salad dressings. I think she'd started getting really fat around then. She must have been close to two-fifty—eating like a sow, putting on those pounds. Sharon and Davey each weighed a quarter ton. "Hey, Darren, why do you like France?" everybody asked. "Well—" I said, "let me see. Where shall I begin?"

Where *could* you begin? Where could *anyone* begin? More

than ever I felt out of place. I wanted to tell Mom, to show her, I'd outgrown her, moved past her, past Immaculatum, but I couldn't, somehow; I didn't want to hurt her—not yet. She kept repeating, kept repeating, "Darren, deep deep down, you're still only a farmer boy, and that's what you'll always be." Oh God, that made me angry. How dare she tell me who I was? How dare she? When she didn't know the half of it? What was really happening, of course, is that she felt me breaking away and she didn't want to be left behind. More than ever I felt I was tied to Kansas only by a crazy accident of birth.

So there I was, staring at the bottom of this vat of chicken—there was at least an inch of grease down there if a drop—thinking, how am I going to get *out* of here? I had people to see, things to do, worlds to conquer. And I had that strange urge to be where I was not.

When I got back, K.U. seemed more stifling than ever. I got away every chance I got—Kansas City, mostly. There was a bar there that attracted both straights and gays because it had really good music.

> We're not at all blameless
> Our prices are shameless
> We do remain nameless
> So come and have fun

That was me, in the discos, dancing, my arms like excited metronomical sticks, my body shaking and moving. "Hi there!!" I would call out when anybody cute passed by. But that was all I did back then.

Back at the fraternity parties, Vicki came along sometimes and played the part of a long-lost girlfriend whose love for me had not quite been extinguished. We'd flirt, for the cameras of course, snapping away those pictures. Everyone thought we were such a handsome couple. We were, too—for the cameras. Although I think Vicki liked me a little more than she let on. She liked sexually ambiguous men. For a long time her boyfriend was this completely androgynous long-haired blond boy who liked to wear blowsy clothing that just sort of—blew *around* him, I suppose. It was slightly oriental. His parents worked for an airline, so he always got free tickets to go to New York, and then to Paris, where he'd go for a weekend—to get his hair trimmed. Then once the androgynous boy went to Italy—he told me this much later—sat down next to a stout middle-aged businessman. They sat together for a long time and then the train went into a tunnel. For some reason the lights didn't come on. So this boy sucked off this businessman in the time it took to get from one end of the tunnel to the other. I'm not even sure the businessman was gay. But this boy looked so *much* like a girl, and the blowsy clothing just sort of hid everything, I suppose.

In my last year our numbers were down and I got picked as rush chairman for the frat. I went at it full blast. The football players were the hardest group to recruit, because everybody wanted them, so of course I went after them with a vengeance. And I got a lot of them to sign on. There was Paul, this huge linebacker, and Chuck, the Californian quarterback, who had arms—Jesus!—biceps like cantaloupes. They were really, really nice to me—much more comprehending, in the end, than the grim and hungry types who weren't sure what they wanted, sexually speaking. These other guys would go to the mixed bars and fuck up other people's lives. There was one guy, he was jealous of me—Judd Tallworth.

God only knows what he wanted in bed. Judd spotted me in the mixed bar in Kansas City. He saw my ass dancing with *men*, he said; he said he'd seen me dancing with *men* at the Twist and Shout. He made an effort to tell everybody at the frat. That was his revenge, for having heard "Isn't Darren interesting?" once too often.

The fraternity officers couldn't believe it. They said, "Gay—him? No . . ." But the rumors started multiplying until other fraternities heard about it. That was what did it. Because I'd just been chosen rush chairman, and because they were even thinking of making me president—and because I was well known to the other fraternities—something had to be done.

I had never lied to anybody, not in so many words. It had been *understood* that I was heterosexual, and I let this understanding persist, living the rest of my life with discretion. After all, if I went dancing in a mixed club in Kansas City on my own time, what the *hell* was it to them? They'd never asked me if I was gay; I'd never said no. They asked me now. And I thought, either I'm going to spend the rest of my life hiding and denying, or I'm going to come out with it. I had no choice about whether I was gay or not, but I could choose to lie or not. I decided not to lie. So I said, "Yes, I am gay."

Well, that did it. That was what they couldn't stand. That I'd been seen dancing with men in a mixed bar—okay, you were drunk. It won't happen again. But to say, in the face of the officers, "Yeah, I'm gay, what're you going to do about it?"—that was what they couldn't stand. So they had a special emergency meeting just to throw me out. They were going to do it with great pomp and circumstance, for maximum humiliation. I was supposed to hang my head in shame and walk bowed out, escorted by two persons to make sure I wouldn't come back.

But I wasn't ready to do that. So when they asked me if I had anything to say, this is what I said.

"My friends know I'm gay, and have been gay since I joined this fraternity. People who care, who live up to their promises, don't need my talk. You others, who want to go back on what you swore the night we pledged, need a little talking-to. You need a lot more than that, in fact. You need a scapegoat. You need someone to blame for abusing sympathy, for letting you think I was a normal person and not a sexual pervert.

"A sexual pervert? Is that what you call me, you educated Kansan minds? You go out and have party after party and fuck every girl you can, boast about it later. This you consider normal, as long as marriage vows have not been taken. As long as there are no promises. But you promised *me* something, let me remind you. You promised we would be brothers, for life. And now?

"What frightened fags you are. You call me coward? Me? I have stepped up to the truth and faced it. What are you going to do? Live in fear the rest of your lives.

"What do *you* know about homosexuality? None of you probably have a single openly gay friend, except me, and you're getting rid of me. Too scary. Not conventional. Well, hedge-clipper brains, perhaps, people are worth knowing even if they aren't crewcut Kansans in blue blazers, swearing by a skinny Christian god by day, and getting roaring fucking drunk by night.

"Do you think I *chose* to be gay? Do you think I chose anything about who I am? Some of you will say, 'Yes, very well, Darren. We're sorry for you. But you should not have chosen to join Tau Omega Rho. We don't allow those things here. We have traditions.'

As if I knew all about myself, when I joined. And why tradition? It's always been done this way, so that's the way it'll always be? Fat lot of good you would have been, when the Americans decided being a British colony was a bad tradition. Fat lot of good you would have been, when Columbus decided the old sea routes were a bad tradition and had to be scrapped. It's not tradition. What counts is compassion. What matters is sympathy. Instead you're hiding behind your flags and your beer bellies and your spray-painted coat of arms. You hide, because its easier than thinking by yourself, or feeling for yourself. You throw away three years of friendship—like that? You abandon your friends—like that? What a heartfelt pledge! What good brothers you all are!

"Witch-hunters! I doubt you can face yourselves. But I'll have nothing to do with such cowards, such criminals. So I resign. I resign from this fraternity. Take your fucking vows of friendship and brotherliness and shove them up your ass. Good-bye."

That was it; I walked out of there. There were hoots, cheers, jeers, and even a few boys in tears. I was a star for one second. I didn't care. I was through with the frat.

Of course, they still went through the business of formally kicking me out. Later, one of the football players—they were actually more sympathetic than most of the others—was driving me back and said, "Darren, are you really gay?" And I said, "Paul, if you take your dick out of your pants, either my hand or my mouth will be on it right away." And he said, "Oh okay. . . ."

I liked that speech, if I may say so, although there was one inconsistency: I'd suggested at one point that an eighteen-year-old might be a little confused, sexually. Not me. I had known, probably since I was about fourteen, that I was one hundred percent gay.

But oh well.

I had to go back home that Christmas with *this* hanging over my head. My mother knew, I think, but she said nothing; my father didn't know. I think.

It was a very quiet Christmas dinner, restrained, especially between my mother and me. Some of the fraternity brothers stayed close to me afterwards, like Jeff. But most of them just pretended that I didn't exist, never did exist. They just wiped out three years of friendship like that.

When I saw people—the young, the privileged—capable of

that, that was my sympathy taken from the world. From then on I was out for myself. I no longer wanted to be hurt. I wanted to get away from these sick hicks, pull away from the roots. I became hard and everything else became surface, surface, surface. I bought my plane ticket and three days after I graduated I flew to New York City.

No One Is Pure

I arrived in New York and loved the racy, adventurous feel. I found a flat on Cranberry Street in Brooklyn Heights, and took to the city like a duck to water. The Saint was my first grand discovery. On the balcony, on a good night, it would be jam-packed with hundreds—*hundreds*—of men fucking, sucking, ducking, and doing everything else they did. You'd be gettin' it almost as soon as you stepped off that staircase, sooner if you got lucky. I was big and good-looking and young and cute and I was gettin' it almost every night.

Two weeks after I arrived I met Paul d'Annunzio. I also found a crappy job, getting shat on from a great height by M.B.A. types with designer suspenders, but I told my mom all was well. I was *branché,* I told her. I was plugged in. But my getting plugged into New York was what she feared most, so she flew over to visit me.

I decided Mom should meet Paul. He was in fine form those days, sending back expensive bottles of wine with a look of disdain, signing overdrawn checks with a grand flourish, and running his hand through his long, permed and dyed hair.

We met in the Palm Court at the Plaza for tea. She shook hands with him as quickly as possible, to pretend he didn't exist, and tried to talk to me. But he just kept pushing his way into her face with comments like, "You have a *very* fine son, Mrs. Swenson," and smiling horribly as if to say, "And he has a very fine ass." Then when she tried to ignore him completely, Paul asked the waiter to bring the prearranged "gift for Madame." So the waiter, wearing impeccable livery and white gloves, came back with an expensively wrapped box of chocolates. Paul said loudly, "Oh, PLEASE, Mrs. Swenson, you must EAT THEM HERE. After all, this is your FIRST TIME at the PLAZA. You CAN'T buy these chocolates in KANSAS." People were staring from the tables around us. Paul looked absolutely unflappable; my mom turned red. I made a heroic try not to laugh. My mom opened the packet and said, "Thank you, Paul," with an effort.

Afterwards the chocolates disappeared. "Maybe she ate them all herself," Paul later said. "Good. That sour sow will think of a faggot every time she eats a chocolate."

But the real sparks were yet to fly. The next day I invited Mom to dinner at my flat.

"Now Mom," I said, "there's something I want to tell you."

She said, brusquely, "Some things are better left unsaid."

And I said, "No, Mom, you're going to listen to this.

"I'm gay."

And I told her who Paul was. I told her how I'd gotten thrown out of my frat. I told her I was gay, gay, gay, gay, and had zero, zilcho, absolutely no interest whatsoever in girls. Before I finished she fired back.

"Darren—now you listen to me. You listen good. Don't you ever *dare* come home with news like this. Don't you ever *dare* tell your father. You will destroy our family, Darren. You're just—your generation, you, that's all you do, go from one quick high to the next. Always lookin' for the next high, to fill up your empty lives, aren't you?"

"We're not talking about my whole generation, Mom. We're talking about *me*."

She cut in, saliva flying. "Don't you ever *dare* come back to Kansas with this. Don't you ever *dare* come back with Paul d'Annunzio or anybody like him. I cannot accept this part of you, Darren. This part of you is *not my son*."

Then came the compassionate letter from Kansas, saying being gay was like having cancer. Well—there's a moment in your life, in every person's life, when you need one certain person to be there for you. And if at that moment, she's not, you never forgive her. Or him. That year in New York I needed love. Or even just understanding. And at that moment, when she could have given me a fair hearing, tried to sympathize, or just *tried* to control herself—she said I *was not her son*. Oh, she was so kind.

I went back to Paul, and he just laughed in my face. "All of us have got one asshole parent. Deal with it, Darren. Go to The Saint if you want love. Oh, that reminds me. I've met somebody new. Sorry. you know how it is."

Dumped by Mom and dumped by Paul—I hung my head in the darkness of my sad flat, and after putting up with shit at work for what seemed an interminable time, I went back to The Saint. Fucking, sucking, ducking, doing everything else I did. One time I hooked up with Lon Panofsky, a cocaine fiend. He was good for a few weeks, but snobby, stupid, and helpless without the Bolivian marching powder. When he was high he used to say, "A cure is on the way," or "Just don't come inside of *me*," or the old classic, "I swear I'm negative." This time I dropped *him*.

I had boyfriend after boyfriend after boyfriend for months and months and months. Then at the opera I met James. We made eye contact in the lobby. I could tell he was a nice boy, a shy boy, and I played my farm-boy-fresh-out-of-Kansas melody on the marble steps, and then marched him off to bed. That fling lasted three months—off and on, before he started complaining about not seeing me enough. He started leaving these half-hour messages on the answering machine, saying he wanted to move back to Chicago with me, buy a house together, come out to our parents together, God knows what. I was twenty-three. This is ridiculous, I thought, and besides we're incompatible in bed. Somebody has to *give* for the other to *get*. So bye-bye James. I broke his heart, the poor fool.

And then—I met John Leadman. Poor James had invited me to work out at his gym, in the hopes of getting me excited again, but as soon as I laid eyes on this stranger with the squash racket I felt the pricking down there. James was oblivious, looking at himself in the mirror, going up an imaginary staircase. In the locker room, this stranger and I exchanged glances, then names, then phone numbers. Weeks later, after I gave James his walking papers, I went to John Leadman's apartment.

Well, well, well, I thought—Darren has struck gold. This was not an overdone pretentious caterer's flat, with Brancusi imitations flopping in the corners. Nor some artsy-fartsy opera lover's loft, with cockroaches creeping and a refrigerator that coughed to a stop twice a week. No, this was a penthouse, upper Sixties, windows everywhere, a view of the park, a grand piano, Renaissance prints, pine floors, white walls, dimmer switches, and a Zen pebble garden in the middle of the vast central room. Everything was in the open. I couldn't believe it. And John—God, was he good-looking. Thirty, dark, muscular. I sat down in a sofa made of wires; quite comfortable. And I thought, *this is the man.* But then I looked at his collection of paintings and etchings—and they were all of women. I looked at the printed invitations on the mantelpiece—all from women. His pictures pinned to the cork message board—they were all of him, always with women. And I thought, what is going on here?

"Perhaps you would like some brandy? Perhaps a cigar?" he offered me.

"Sure," I said.

The brandy was old and the Havana was pure as a sunset. He sat down in front of me, in one of those chairs you find at MoMA.

"I choose not to smoke myself," he said. "But I thought you might like it."

"Have you ever smoked?"

"No."

"You should try it," I said. So I gave him the cigar, and he drew on it, and coughed noisily.

"First time?" I asked him.

"Yes," he said.

"It gets better the more you do it."

As I finished the cigar, he asked me whether I liked Renaissance paintings. I had no idea what the hell he was talking about but I repeated certain names, saying I liked this more than the others, found such-and-so divine, found such-and-so a little false. We kept on like this for a couple of *hours,* and I was beginning to wonder if I had the wrong man. He'd not made a single move on me. But then conversation got around to Michelangelo. I asked him if he'd visited the *David.* With a bowed head he replied he hadn't. But I had, Eurorailing from Grenoble.

"It's impressive," I said. "Beautiful statue." I lit another cigar and said boldly, "Turns me on, actually. I like that boy. Thank God Michelangelo liked boys, *too.*"

John lowered his head. I think he actually blushed.

There was no more ambiguity now. I stepped over to him and put the cigar away. Yeah, I thought I'd smoke something else of his.

That was how it started.

"This is only my second time," he confessed.

"Yeah, well, show me how it's done."

I was sure he'd turn into a bull and ravage me. But Mister Renaissance, with his pecs and his Harvard M.B.A. and all that, simply couldn't get it together in bed. You'd think the business of tab A into slot A would be easy. But he simply could not. He slipped and fumbled and missed. Our first night was a failure. The second night as well. Third night got a passing grade. But Mister Phi Beta Kappa never managed more than a C+ in what really mattered to me.

Still, I was so impressed by him, at first. He was dealing mortgages, making millions on the Street. He had properties everywhere, including a handsome little cottage in Connecticut. At first I thought he was from a very grand family. But gradually the illusion started falling apart. Little things gave it away. He was obsessed with cleanliness and appearances, and he would talk about anything rather than where he was from. He was from a lower-class background, as it turned out. The art, the furniture—all that was bought, not inherited, and he relied on gray-flanneled good-taste people to make his choices for him. And when drink loosened his tongue, he dropped the affected lockjaw fake-aristocratic diction and started speaking more like an Italian-American, with rough, leatherjacketed diction.

Heaven help me—he was *so* bad in bed. It got frustrating; we'd argue; and one night I left his flat, pent-up as a boiler, and got released at The Saint—again. He was really mad when I got back.

"Darren—what is this? You and I—we're a *couple.* That's what I thought we were. You and I are going to beat loneliness by being together. And we're *not* going to cheat on each other. We're not going to need other people. How could you need anybody else? Aren't I enough?"

"No, you're not enough!" I said. "You think you have it all. Well, you don't. You're far from perfect, John. You think having money and degrees is everything. Well, it isn't. You need certain other qualities, too, which you *ain't* got, John."

"Well, then *teach* me, Darren. Teach me."

So we'd start again, but it was hopeless; it was like trying to make love to an ostrich. He put his head in the ground every time things went wrong. And things went wrong so badly.

Yeah, things definitely went wrong with John. For Christmas 1987 we went to his country cottage—the love shack. John brought the wine, the food, the candles, the egg cups, even. He set the table as if for an ambassador and took pictures of everything. He wanted everything right, for what I suppose was some sort of consummation ceremony. Outside he bravely wore a leather jacket and a crimson Harvard scarf, the combination of who he was and who he wanted to be. He even asked the neighbor if he would mind taking pictures of us, kissing, in front of the porch, as we entered the cottage for that Christmas night. Oh, John.

We drank. We ate. We drank some more. We got into bed. I had some poppers; John tried them. One thing led to another. He said he wanted to please me, was ready to do whatever it took. Well, I thought, if we're going to do it, let's *really* do it. C'mon, John. Let things rip. So that night John and I fucked and fucked and *fucked.*

Yeah, that would have been a fine night.

That night John wanted me to promise never to leave him.

"What?" I said.

"I want us to be together forever," he said.

"John, you're asking for the impossible. I'm barely twenty-four years old."

"Well, I'm thirty. I want us to be together, forever. I want us not to leave each other. I think now I've got the right to ask, Darren. Stay with me, and you won't ever have to work. I can work for both of us. I can provide everything you need."

Everything except one thing, I thought.

"If we stick together," he kept saying, "the wolf will never come to our door."

"What wolf?"

"The AIDS wolf, Darren. I don't want to go out hunting, humiliated, try dozens of men and not be happy. I don't have to.

I have you. If we stick together, nothing will never come between us."

"That's if we stay together."

"Well, I'm willing to stay with you."

I was silent. It was a really awkward moment. I sort of sighed
and pretended to acquiesce. John really thought he was God's gift
to a man like me.

After Christmas we went back to the city. I dropped John off at
his flat—and then he made me promise never to leave him. It was
very dramatic.

"Promise me, Darren, you'll stay with me. I want this promise
from you. I want this promise from you, now."

"John," I told him, wearily, "I promise to stay with you as long as
I can."

"Let's shake on it," he said, manfully. So I did, feeling fake as a
three-dollar bill.

After I left his flat, I went back to The Saint, and my promise
was blown as quickly as the rest of me. After that things got even
hairier. John began sending me these word-processed letters,
twenty, thirty pages long, sending me catalogs, describing vacations
we could take together, countries in Europe that might get us married, God knows what. After a while I felt trapped.

"John, I think I've had enough. I want an open relationship."

"What's an open relationship?" he asked.

"It means we love each other, but as far as sex goes, we don't
have to remain faithful."

"Absolutely not. Darren, you're not cheating on me?"

"Not exactly."

"What do you mean, not exactly?" he demanded.

"I think about it."

"Well, stop thinking about it."

So I stopped thinking about it, and just started doing it without
thinking.

Sometime in June '88 I looked in the mirror one morning and
saw that my eyes were yellow. I also puked in the toilet for no
reason. A little worried, I went in for some tests. They drew blood
and told me to come back in a week. I did some research during
that week and came back confident.

The doctor called me in to her small office, sat me down, closed the door, and opened my folder very cautiously.

"Mr. Swenson," she said.

"Hello."

"Do you have any reason to believe you may have a disease?"

"Yes. I've done some research, and I believe I have hepatitis."

"Well, you're half right. You do have hepatitis. But I'm afraid you also tested positive for the HIV virus."

Calmly she explained what the HIV virus was, what the margin of error was for the test, how I would be retested, and what I should do. She gave me a three-page pamphlet, *Live With Hope*. She told me all about the hepatitis; I wasn't listening. I thanked her very much and very seriously stepped outside, feeling the entire weight of the world on my shoulders.

I went home to lie in bed. Strangely, I smiled in the dark, and I said to my soul, "Tick. Tock. Get a move on. Now the clock is truly ticking." Even more strangely, I had a sudden sense of freedom.

But I still had to tell John. I invited him to dinner at my house. I lived then in a house which I shared with some friends. Patti, from Grenoble, lived there, cooking up a storm, chirping at how great life was in the Big A; and Steve Johnson, my painter friend from K.U., painted late at night. He said he was trying to catch the fleeting nature of time.

John and I had dinner in the house one night when the others were gone. I said, "John, there's something I have to tell you."

"You've been thinking of what I said?"

"I certainly have."

He leaned back in his chair, unsure of the outcome. Would I say, yes, I want to marry you and love you forever? Or would I say, no, I'm too young, I think I can get a better deal?

Instead I said, "John, I'm HIV-positive."

"What?"

"I tested positive for the HIV virus."

"When?"

"Last week."

"We haven't seen each other for a week."

"John. The virus incubates. A lot longer."

"How long?"

"Years."

"Years!"

"Yep."

He was looking at me, his mouth tightly set. There is no confusion like the confusion of a simple mind.

"John. I think you should get yourself tested."

There was a long silence.

"I don't believe you," he said. "I don't believe this. You're using this as an excuse to get away from me."

"No, John, believe me. This is no excuse."

"You're lying."

"Not about this."

He was silent a long while.

"I can recommend a good clinic," I said, helpfully. "It's free."

"How can you tell you have it?"

"You can't. Not at first. Later the virus will come out of incubation. This is quite hard for me, too, John."

He looked as if the entire world had fallen down before his eyes. "This isn't happening, Darren. This is *not* happening. This cannot happen to us—this kind of thing happens to other people."

"It's happening, John. Face up. This is reality."

"No. This isn't happening. You haven't said a word of this."

"I'm sorry, John—"

"*Not—one—word.*"

Dinner proceeded in silence. The next week John still did not take the test. I stayed in my room, not telling anybody, feeling the sweats, feeling awful. The entire house seemed much more empty, and I felt like an animal in a cage, panting, straining, seeking, where's the lock? where's the key to get out of this? And the rest of the world smiled sarcastically, and the bright, sunny day was a mockery, just laughing at me.

Some time later, in the middle of the night, I got a phone call. "Darren. It's John. Come over to my flat. Right now."

"John? Do you know what time it is? It's three a.m."

"Right now, Darren. Big news."

So I got up, dressed, and took a cab to his flat. The entire flat was crowded with medical journals, reports. John had been digging through libraries, getting absolutely every piece of information about AIDS that existed.

"I've been misdiagnosed," he said. "Happens rarely, but I'm

sure that's what's happened to me. I'm going to get retested. I was really worried for a while—here're the books to prove it!—but I'm sure you got misdiagnosed too. That clinic makes lots of mistakes, Darren."

I sat stiffly in the couch and stared at him. He kept talking for ten minutes and then stopped, and looked at me, waiting for my answer. I said, "John—no."

"No what?"

"You're—seeing things."

"No, I'm not, Darren. I'm not. I know what I'm doing. Misdiagnosis, Darren. It's that simple."

"John, I've already been tested twice. I've *got* it, John. Get that through your head."

"No," he said. "We're both fine."

"John, damn it, I have the paper. I have it in my wallet. Do you want to see it? Look, John. Look. What does that word say? Positive. That's what it says. It means *infected*, John."

"NO, Darren. It's a lie! It's not true!"

"YES, it is true. You have to take action, John, and not just deny it!"

"NO! It's NOT true! You DON'T have it, do you understand me? It's a lie! A lie! It's NOT TRUE!"

Then he broke down and cried, fell to the floor, looking for a hole to crawl into. And that smooth, clean flat laughed at him. Everything was in the open. I leaned down to touch him.

"Don't!" he screamed. "Don't. Don't! Oh, God!" he wailed. And he opened his mouth, as if to scream, kneeling, but I saw his mouth open, no sound coming out, held open for a time, and then he collapsed back down.

Of course, his retest showed up positive. Instantly he became a monk. He refused to see anybody, do anything except work. All he read were medical journals; he went to Mexico, smuggled the interferon, the lipids, the works. He had the money for it. Meanwhile, I was determined to let nature take its course. He was trying to fight it with drugs; I was trying to fight it with a good attitude. So I took my antidepressants and got into smoking. Maybe that was why I started having symptoms before he did. I started getting the diarrhea—small at first, then more and more chronic. For a while John looked fine, looked healthy, took care of himself. On August seventeenth, he collapsed in his flat. Two weeks later he was dead.

That's why I don't think I infected him; he died barely eight months after our Christmas love party. To die that fast, he had to have been further along than me. His first lover infected him, surely. It's also possible he killed himself with a drug overdose. I think that's why I'm still alive; I loved life more.

So it goes.

The week after he died, I was alone in Central Park, watching the mothers with their children, the babies, the young men jogging, the young women. . . . I remember thinking, all of us have only one chance to do what we want to do. I remember thinking, life is short; the clock is ticking. And I remember feeling a still, strange sense of calm, of resolution, of hope. Suddenly I was grateful for all I had. For I still had life. It was a great moment. Thank you, Prozac.

Then it was Thanksgiving, and I had to go home. The Midwest stopped still for Thanksgiving—we'd even missed a milking once, on Thanksgiving Day. It was also the day of family values—of thrift, clean living, honesty, and goodness.

I no longer wanted to lie. So I wrote to my mom: "Either *you* will tell Dad I am gay before I arrive, or *I* will tell him when I'm there." I actually thought this was the gentlest way to start breaking the news to him—because telling him I was gay was nothing compared to what I would have to tell him later.

Mom protested, so I repeated my offer—or my threat—over the phone. "*You* tell him, or *I* will." So she told him.

A long letter arrived from my father. It said, "This is the worst thing that has ever happened to me in my life." I wrote back, "If this is the worst thing that has ever happened to you, you are a very lucky man."

He didn't write back. I didn't call, and no one called me. I went to Kansas not knowing whether they would accept me. So I made arrangements for Jeff, my old fraternity brother, to pick me up in Kansas City and drive me to Lindsborg. We talked all the way. Ol' Jeff had a big grin under his Jayhawks baseball cap. "Oh, boy, Darren," he said, "oh, boy. You sure know how to get things right down to the wire." And I was trying to smile, while inside I felt like a dead man. I watched the endless rolling away of houses that seemed to cruelly smile at me. Jeff had gone on to bigger things in

Kansas City. Judd Tallworth, I learned, was in an investment bank somewhere, screwing people endlessly, again (some things, and some people, never changed); Paul the football player didn't make the pros, and was traveling around the country, trying to find himself. As Jeff talked cheerfully on and on, I still felt like a living corpse and tried to hide it. "I wish Sherrie had married you instead of Pete Schmidt," I said. "Oh well," he said, "can't have it all," and he smiled that tight-lipped smile of his. He was married, too. But true love had not faded. "Sherrie," he said, "was a farm girl, deep down inside. The city just wasn't for her. So if it makes her happy to milk cows and live on a farm and do all those farm things, hell! what can I do? Can't teach an old dog new tricks, eh? But I wish her well, all the same. She was one lovely girl." And he drove on in silence, thinking of what might have been. I was thinking, too.

Finally we arrived in Lindsborg. I called my dad on the phone. "Dad?" I said. "It's Darren. I'm at the Lindsborg bus station. You can come pick me up, if you like." "I'll be right over," he said. Jeff and I shook hands and he left.

Then my father arrived, in his big truck. I watched him get out, and he saw me on the steps. He came up to me, straight on, no bullshit, he shook my hand up and down and said, "How the hell arya, son?" I might have said, "In bad shape, Dad," but he hugged me, hard, and stopped me from saying anything. I could feel his old hoary weather-beaten face pressed tightly against my smooth skin, and I felt his strong arms hold me with all their might.

We drove back in silence; what little conversation we had was mostly monosyllables—yeahp, nope. But my father and I have always been unusually communicative in a reserved way.

Things had changed at the farm. My favorite filly Star had died, I was sorry to hear about that; and Rascal was gone, of course. Sherrie was pregnant with Pete's child; Grandma was in a wheelchair; my twin sister Sharon had gotten married. Davey was dating somebody. Everyone looked a little older.

And then there was Mom—friendly as a battleship. She stood on the porch and turned her head like a turret. "Darren's here!" she called out, as if firing a shot across my bow. There was some quick chitchat, and we went inside—the carpets were the color of a shadow. Then we sat down to eat, eat, eat: we stuffed ourselves with stuffing, sugary turkey, sugary salads, sugary fruit, gallons of ice cream—all served on plastic plates with orange flowers. Then the juicy family talk: "Frank and Wendall bought a new trailer." "Uh-huh?" "And took out those scrubby shrubs." "Uh-huh?" "Really looks nice." "Yeahp." "But Madge has got that pesky new weed now, and then there's that god-awful bacteria, turnin' them udders black." Oh God, I told myself.

"You're awful quiet, Darren."

"I'm tired, Dad."

"How's that job?"

"Interesting. I can't complain."

"Good."

"Y'know, Darren," my mother said. "I've been thinkin'. Think you might find some interestin' opportunities up at Kansas State. Business program."

"No, Mom. It's not interesting."

"Why not?"

"Kansas State does *not* interest New Yorkers."

"Why not? Didn't you have a friend who had a business degree? Darren?"

"Yes. I did."

"And?"

"He—had a Harvard degree, Mom. Not Kansas State. It's like the difference between being alive and being dead."

"You make it so, Darren."

"Oh, shut up, Mom." And I got up from the table.

"Darren, you've been *weird* ever since you got back from Grenoble. Ever since—" But I didn't hear the rest, because I locked myself in my room and cried.

And of course there was the charade of my parents continuing to pretend I was heterosexual. They asked, "How is *Miss* Vicki? Your old friend?" You mean my old fag hag, I should have answered.

And underneath *that* was their unforgiving reproach. I could see my mother thinking, his *dick* got the better of him. I could have been something, but my *dick* got the better of me. And of course I felt no more in control of my dick, and my life, than I felt in control of the earth's rotation.

In our house the word "gay" was never mentioned. Darren's

homosexuality didn't exist, had never existed, and would never be allowed to exist. Nothing was wrong with me. Except my laziness.

At lunch the next day, my mom said, "Darren, you're nearly twenty-five years old. You can't go round any longer expectin' to stumble on the great gold mine. You have to give yourself some kind of *destiny*, Darren—or you won't amount to anythin'. You have to have direction. If not, you'll drift like a leaf in the wind. You'll be tempted by whatever."

I did not answer. I just boiled in silence. She was one to talk about temptation, with her three-hundred-pound belly. She never met a donut she didn't like. Ah, sin, sin, sin. The Devil is everywhere. Everywhere. I just met him at the wrong time.

Then at dinner Mom and Dad brought up the subject again.

"Darren, is there any future in what you're doin' at that office?"

"Dad—the partners are all millionaires."

"Think you'll make partner, Darren?"

"Dad—I've got to try."

"Yeahp. Got to try."

"You better do more than try, Darren," my mother said. "You better *succeed*. If you work there, you better be the most outstandin' employee there. You better be the apple of your boss's eye. You better make partner, and do everythin' you have to do to be a *success*."

"Well. Perhaps, *Mother*, there are more important things in life than your country notion of *success*. Maybe it's more important to *enjoy* life. Maybe it's more important to have a good life—a worthwhile life. Even a *fun* life."

"A *fun* life? That's your answer to our upbringin'? Throwin' away your father's work, throwin' away all the time we spent on you, to bring you up right? For a *fun* life! Our upbringin' in our faces, that's what your life's about. Do you know what you are? You're a spoiled child. Yes, spoiled as sin."

"Yes, God damn it! I am spoiled as sin! And I don't want anything to do with your goddamn Kansas State, or your fucking business courses, or your goddamn farm! I want to live! I want to live just because it pisses you off, Mother!"

"Darren!"

"I don't give a shit what you or any other fucking person thinks of me! I'm tired of success, I'm tired of all your *hick*, backward,

ignorant ideas on how to live my life! Shut the fuck up, you bitch!"
And I stormed out.

That was how the crown jewel cracked. That was how I got
thrown out. That was how we both started looking for something to
replace each other with. She found she liked putting things in her
mouth—fattening things. Food became her best friend. Like
Darren before he was gay, food was perfect. It didn't fight back.
Unlike Darren, food didn't become homosexual, all of a sudden.

But I liked putting things in my mouth, too—big fat juicy
things. I loved getting them inside my mouth.

That homecoming was dark and wounding and purposeless.
There was no compassion for me in Kansas. So I went back up to
New York, intent on really living. The clock was ticking, remember.
And when I got back to New York that time, I met the Devil.

The Murphy Stavros Chapter

A few nights after I got back, some friends and I were driving down towards Christopher Street, when from behind we saw this car coming up. It was a small car with California plates and the mad Ahab at the wheel had been weaving in and out of traffic, not pausing for anyone or anything, but weaving, honking, and blazing out on the road as if he were hunting an animal. He got right behind us, gave us a long honk *EEEEEEEEEEEEE!* and then with unbelievable sureness cut out, drove up on the curb, yelled at us, "*FAGS!*" and back down again. I could see he was wearing sunglasses and there were five other guys crammed in there with him. Everyone was a-chortling and they all looked ripped. Then the driver sped on, weaving in and out of traffic like it was an obstacle course and everybody else was standing still.

"*Who* the *fuck was that?*" asked someone in the car.

"Just mad, man, just mad," somebody else said.

I drove on and, unbelievably, found a parking space only twenty yards from The Spike. Then we saw the mad Ahab's car already parked, even closer—but on the sidewalk. The car looked like it was brand new. The driver had left the windows open and the radio going at full blast, daring somebody to steal it.

"*Mad!* The man is crazy!" I said.

We went into The Spike and there was all sorts of dancing going on.

You

Are

My world

And the crowd was going at it. And this guy—this blond guy—he was at the center of the room. He'd actually taken off all his clothes except his sunglasses and his boots and this dinky G-string that called your attention to what it was supposed to be hiding. Philippe, I have to tell you, the first thing I noticed was that he had a great ass. Also I could see he had a *big*—

("I know," I said.)

So there he was, dancing, flopping. He's got this blond hair snaking wildly above his head and a smile full of perfectly white teeth gleaming, glinting, turning from side to side, his head back, big chest bulging in the light.

You

Are

My world

Pretty soon there's a couple of guys who just want to dance, but he's not playing any games. There's one big, gentle-looking kid with doe eyes looking at him, fascinated. This crazy blond man looks at him, once, and faster than the blink of an eye, they're both down on the floor, this kid on his ass, the blond monster on top of him, and their mouths locked tight as an airborne refueling nozzle and the gas tank. The kid's white T-shirt is off, gone, you can see all his young muscles rippling. But the kid says, "No, no" and this mad crazy avenging angel of death puts a hurt expression on his face, a hurt expression full of contained fury: "Don't you *like* me? Don't you *want* to do it? Doesn't this *feel good*?" And he's pressing up even closer to him and now he's actually got his hand *inside* this boy's pants and this boy is looking up like he can't believe it's happening all so fast and he doesn't want to stop it. "Feels good, doesn't it?" this madman says, and now he's actually pulling this guy out, and he's got this great big hard-on in this mad red red rotating light, and there's a crowd of people around them, looking on. They just can't believe it. Everyone hears stories like this, but this was for real. I'm staring; my eyes are popping out of my skull; this guy is setting off all sorts of reactions in me; I feel like I'm being twisted around and I like it. "How many do you like to do it with?" The blond guy is hissing. He's got this hysterical, commanding look in his eye, the kind that demands your horrified attention, absolutely draws it out of you. "Do you like two, three? Huh?" He's asking this and the poor kid doesn't know up from down or his mama from a pork basket. Then the blond stranger looks at me. And to my surprise I find I'm standing next to them, closer than anybody. And he says, "C'mere, girl." And I'm on my knees now, and I'm leaning in now, and I'm kissing this guy, and he's kissing me so hard I feel like I'm being sucked inside, my whole being starting with my tongue aspirated into this dark gory hole, and I could see the smooth contours of my shoulder, and blond tufts of hair on his bare chest, and this kid underneath is looking at both of us like a kid at a candy store.

But now *I'm* on my back, and this guy is going at me, and this feels impossibly good, impossibly real, with the cold dance floor to my back, the whirling red red lights turning up above, an angle I've never seen before and there's this demon now, his hair is orange now, his face keeps moving it into my vision moving into my vision. There's a song going through my head and I can't recognize it but I know it expresses exactly what I'm feeling. He lifts me by my waist and no one's ever treated me like that before and by now his huge erection's flapping out of his dinky G-string. He's huge and strong and he literally pulls me over to a corner somewhere, and we're going at it and it's all happening so fast and I'm loving every second of it.

Murphy Stavros was a nonstop fucking machine. He'd been doing it twice a day, three times a day, four times a day, every day. It was as necessary for him to squirt as it was for us to milk those cows. Always with different people, too. He wasn't handsome, but there were very few people who could resist him. He'd been doing it so often he'd come down with every conceivable disease. Hepatitis, every known variety of herpes, crabs in places you wouldn't dream of looking, and of course the big A. "But what the fuck. I'm not dead yet, and I'm gonna go on until I die," he said. He managed to get herpes sores on his rectum which hurt like hell when he used it or got it used.

"How many guys do you think you've done, Murph?"

"I don't know. Go figure. Ten thousand?"

I did go figure it out, and it came to at least that many.

I invited him over for dinner. At that time I was still living in the Brooklyn Heights brownstone. Steve and Ward had made the place look really civilized. The furniture was unpretentious but pleasing; there were framed aquarelles and etchings, everything lined up, symmetrical, nice. And the Devil arrived in the middle of all this.

Ward had gotten more refined since his Grenoble days, refined without being *too* pretentious. I'd invited him—well, I had to, since he lived there, but also I had this queer desire to show this other blond maniac some of the more refined pleasures of life. I had an idea I could turn him around a little. Ward put on Handel.

"Who *is* this guy, Darren? I've never seen you taking so much trouble over someone. Are you *in love*?" Nancy asked me, teasing the word "love" upwards with a laugh. She had a quick, chirpy personality. Nancy had baked a mean chocolate cake—and covered it with jelly bellies. "Cherry is the best flavor," Patti said, popping one in her mouth. Neither she nor Ward nor Nancy had any idea who Murph Stavros was.

"Can we change the music?" I said.

"But you like the *Messiah*," Nancy said. She was a cute brunette with the slightly anguished eyes that came from caring for too many people.

"I know I know," I said.

"Put on some jazz," said Steve. He was easygoing, struck a balance. "Put some Tostoff on." Tostoff was cool and swinging.

Exactly half an hour later Murph materialized at the door. He walked through it as if it wasn't there. He was wearing an extremely elegant European suit that must have cost a couple of thousand dollars. He walked in and his trousers moved like vertical puddles of water. It was all fluidity and cashmere chic.

"Nice place you've got here." He looked around the room. Nancy, he decided, was a fag hag, Ward square and straight, Steve likable but boring, Patti amusing. Riccardo he wasn't sure about.

"Been living here long?" he asked, checking out the house as if he might want to buy it.

"A year," I said. "No—no, two years."

Patti and Nancy looked at each other with I-can't-believe-it expressions. Can Darren be *in love*? they seemed to ask each other. Why is he so *nervous*?

"You guys always listen to this shit?" asked Murph.

"It's Tostoff," I said.

"Yeah, yeah, *History of the World,* lah-de-dah, boring, dull, *dead.* What else have you got? Oh! Hel-lo, Bronski! This'll work."

Instantaneously the song "You Make Me Feel Mighty Real" came on, at three times normal volume. It was deafening. Murph turned it up another quarter notch. He shook his head to the beat.

Nancy looked at him with increasing concern. "Can we turn the music down?" she asked with what she hoped would be quiet authority.

"You, baby," he said, "have got a *great* ass." Nancy looked at him, shocked. Smiling, teeth all white and bright, Murph turned down the volume, but the music was still deafening.

Riccardo decisively stepped over to the stereo, reached across Stavros, and turned down the volume to a murmur. "The speakers aren't quite up to the amp," he said, with a forced smile.

'What's *your* name?" asked Murph. Riccardo was a handsome Italian.

"Riccardo," said Riccardo with strained amiability. Murphy Stavros had slipped a finger into Riccardo's palm and was smiling at him, perfect white teeth on display, unwilling to let go. Riccardo disengaged himself and looked at Murph with mild defiance.

"Murphy Stavros," he said, introducing himself. "Nice shirt, Riccardo. Where'd you get it?" He let his fingertips glide around the collar until they touched Riccardo's neck, and he fingered Riccardo's neck until Riccardo pulled back with a jerk and said, "Your compliment was sufficient." Murphy just smiled at him even more winningly. The rest of us looked on in a kind of fascinated horror. Except for me. I thought Murph was fun.

Oh, he fascinated me. There was a mad energy in him, unstoppable, always a restless foot or hand tapping somewhere—and that was when he was still.

A few weeks later it was Easter, and Nancy and I had planned to go on a vacation, just the two of us. Perhaps she wanted to seduce me—or, what is more likely, she just enjoyed my company. But a day before we were to leave, and after she'd booked the hotel and bought the tickets for both of us, my phone rang at the office. It was Stavros.

"California, man. This weekend. Up for it?"

"I can't, Murph," I said. "I've already got plans to go with Nancy."

"Gotcha. No problem. I'll go without you. I'm going to cruise up and down that strip in L.A. and get me at least six or seven boys every night. I mean *every night*. I got money to burn and I don't care about prices. How about it, man?"

"Uh . . . uh . . . okay. Let me call, Nancy, maybe?" I was giggling. I loved how improvised it all felt. With Murph you felt there were no limits.

"Gotcha. We'll be in LAX tomorrow night, and if I haven't got a couple loads and dinner down my throat within three hours after I land I'll consider myself behind schedule. That goes for you, too. Later." He hung up.

I called Nancy.

"Nancy? Uh . . . hi, it's Darren."

"Oh, Darren, you don't have to tell me who you are. Are you all ready? You all packed up?"

"Uh . . . no. Actually, I'm calling . . . uh . . . to let you know I can't go."

"Can't go? What?"

"I can't go, that's all.'"

"What happened? Nothing serious?"

"No, nothing serious."

"What, then?"

"Uh . . . well, I made plans to go to California."

"California?! Why?"

"I'm going with Murph Stavros."

"Murph Stavros," she echoed. "Murphy Stavros! That goddamn Stavros is the fucking Devil. Well, I hope you guys have a great time in California. I hope you enjoy yourself, without me, Darren. I hope you really *get fucked,* Darren." And she hung up.

And she was right: I really *got fucked* in California. Stavros managed to beat all records by getting his first load in California at the men's bathroom in the airport, before he'd picked up his baggage. I waited for him outside the lavatory for ten minutes. He came out smiling.

"*This* vacation's off to a *good* start," he said, teeth shining brightly. The score was one-zero, with Stavros in the lead, only thirteen minutes after we'd touched down. Murph's handsome suitcase came off baggage-handling broken. "Fix it later, man. No time now. Let's go, let's go!" and we were in back of a cab, chatting up the driver, demanding to know where the good bars were. Murph was leaning between the seats, leaning in towards the driver. "I have this tremendously pressing need, you see. I have to get some loads down my throat, fast. Do you think you could drop us off at a bar and wait while we do our thing?"

"Whatever you want, man," said the cabdriver, amused.

"Fine. Take us to The Done Frontier."

So the driver did. "Come back in fifteen minutes," Stavros said.

When we came out, twenty minutes later, the score was three-zero.

"How was it?" asked the driver.

"Oh, beautiful. Beautiful boys in this town. Yes yes, I like it, I loved it, I do *do* love it. Take us onwards and outwards! Having fun, Darren? Don't miss Nancy, do you? *No* girls out here tonight. This is the *boys'* night out. Hang with me, brother. But you should be more aggressive! Get *in* there, girl! *Work* them!"

I promised myself that I would make Murphy eat those words, and anything else I could shove in his face, before the week was out. Murph was fast, but he was more interested in quantity than quality. I told myself I would do less girls, but of substantially higher quality.

"You wait and see," I said.

"I'm waiting. Hey, can you turn up the volume! I can't hear a thing!"

Murph was happy now. We arrived at the flat; the cab fare was eighty dollars, and Murph charged it. The flat belonged to a friend of Murph's, who had lent it to him for a week. He'd also left us the keys to his car, which he had asked us not to wreck, and some caviar in the fridge which he had asked us not to eat. Murph ate the caviar right away. "We must cut down on the cost of living," he said. "L.A. is sooooooooooooo expensive. C'mon man, let's go, go go!"

We were out on the streets like a mad white rocket, hurtling down Sunset. "Boys!" he called. "Oh no, boys, too stupid to understand *inglés*? *¡¡HOLA, CHICAS!!*" he screamed, and did a wolf call. Immediately a couple of handsome hustlers came over to his rolled-down car window. "How much?" Murph asked.

"Hunnert."

"Forget it. Seventy-five and I'll do both of you." The kids nodded. "Get in." Murph knew where a deserted parking lot was and we had a four-way screw right there. "Okay, you guys are *good*. But let's get one more as a reserve."

And so on. We took three boys to our flat. Murph was about to have a go at one when he turned around.

"No, get a condom, man," he said.

"Aw, c'mon!" Murph roared. "Seventy-five dollars and you take it without."

"No *way*, man. I don't wanna get AIDS."

"I swear I'm negative," said Murph.

"Like *fuck* you are, man," said the boy. He was beefy and looked streetwise and tough. "Get a condom, man, or I'm outta here." The other boys looked at him. They had both already taken it without.

"Fucking AIDS," Murph said. "I haven't *got* a condom," he snarled.

"Well, *I* do," said the boy, and he got one out of his jeans lying in a puddle on the floor. "This'll help," he added, giving Murph a packet of lubricating fluid. Murph stared at both packets and then glared at the boy.

"You're no fun," Murph said.

"Do it, Murph," I said.

Was Murph scrupulous about condoms? He liked condoms as much as Nancy liked Murph. How do you think he got it in the first place? Some other Stavros gave it to him.

So this went on and on. He fucked them all that night, and me twice. I loved it. I mean, I *really* loved it. Stavros was *so* much fun; he infected people left and right, but that was part of the fun.

The next night we zoomed out of the flat at nine o'clock, Looking For *Dick*. Murph had found his friend's stash of mushrooms and smoked them while he was drunk, and he got behind the wheel as if he were driving a race car. "Let's gooooooooooooo!" he yelled, and back we went out to Sunset, burning stoplights, yelling, screaming, and waving, weaving in and out "LOOK OUT, MURPH!" I yelled and *BLAM!!* he plowed straight into the divider. He'd rammed straight into it, he hadn't turned fast enough, he'd knocked out the transmission and dragged it along for a hundred yards, and it lay clinkety-clankety on the street, ticking like a perco-lator. He got out of the car and looked at it.

"Fuck! Is that the *gearbox?* Do you suppose we can keep going?" He got back in the car, succeeded in getting it into first. He got off the divider, positioned himself to reenter traffic. "Well, I've got first gear. What else do we need? Huh? Hey, we better pick that part up, might need it later!" So I picked up the thing that looked like a metal box with a hole in the top and threw it in the backseat. "First gear—that's all we need, man, that's all we need!" He was happy now. We were going twenty miles an hour in first gear, and we stopped at the first bar. Reverse didn't work, so instead of parking Murph just rammed the car into the sidewalk where he could drive it off later. We went inside the bar, and it was full of these wanna-be movie stars each dolled up, just asking to be noticed by a talent scout. They were all watching these videos. No one was looking at anyone; the back room was empty. The score was 6–3; Murph and I didn't count each other. We stared at all the fags, not all of whom were cute, and said, "Right! We can do better than this!" and we got out of there, fast, still Looking For *Dick.*

We came to Sunflower, the big bar in L.A. It was packed. Murph was wearing his tight jeans and his monstrous cowboy boots and looked as sexual as a bitch in heat. He got us in. Inside, it was like the Miss America pageant, for boys. Everywhere you looked was another incredible-looking hunk. Murph just went right up to the center, got up on the bar, took off his shirt, and screamed, "HELLLLLOOOOOOO *GIRLS!!*" and the crowd went wild. A couple of hours later the score was 22–7, Stavros still in the lead, on our third day in L.A.

"No time to waste, no time to lose. Let's go back and do some *more!* Let's do 'em *all!*" So we got back into the car, which had a parking ticket. With automatic hand Murph threw it away. It was his friend's borrowed car, and Murph was going to have to repair the transmission, he thought, but he would do that later. With the stereo on full blast, in first gear, the transmission screaming, we clinkety-clanked over to another bar, with three boys in the back.

"What's the matter with the *car*?" one of them asked. He was a husky Iowan with corn-fed teeth. I heard he later got AIDS, probably from Murph.

"Transmission problems," said Murph, with a serious look on his face. "You never know with these stolen cars. Wanna steal another car?"

They looked at each other, not knowing what to believe. Then one of them said, "*Eeeeeeeee-hah!*" They thought this was great.

So we got to *another* bar. Murph hit the thirties; I hit the teens. Finally we drove four boys back to our flat, and they were already at it when we arrived, in the backseat.

"Last stop, boys, get out and *drop 'em!*"

Then at the end of the night, after having fucked them all without a condom—he'd run out, he said, and these big farmer boys come to the big city didn't think no little virus was going to infect them—he fucked me again. "My doctor told me to avoid reinfection," I protested, weakly. "Aw, it doesn't matter!" Murph said. "We've got the same strain! Whoooooo-eeeh! Thirty-five in three days and three nights. Can we ask for better than this? God my butt hurts." He took some aspirin, smoked a joint, some mushrooms. We all fell asleep in the living room. The next morning one of the boys was gone, with Murph's wallet. Murph got angry.

"Fuck! Shit! Goddamn butt-fucking asshole! Dickhead! Dick-brain! Fuck! Fuck! *FUCK!!*" he said, banging on the tabletop. He called up his charge card services and canceled everything. "And cut his pecker off if you catch him," he said. He asked them to wire two thousand dollars. "That boy won't get away alive," he said to me. "Noooooooooooooo way. I fucked him *good*. I'm going to take them *all* down with me," he hissed. "Darren, how much money you got?"

"A hundred."

"A hundred! That might get us through till lunchtime. How much on your credit cards?"

"Ten thousand."

"Is that your debt or your credit?"

"My debt."

"What's your limit?"

"No limit."

"Well, then *spend it*! In four years you're gonna be *dead*, man.

And then what are they going to do? Go after your parents? I *don't* think so. Can one of you boys make breakfast? Hey, you, don't put your pants back on. I'm not done yet." The boy looked at him slinkily and went off to the kitchen to kill some eggs.

Murph gobbled up those two thousand dollars in the next three days—a lot of it went into a cocaine blasting session that lasted straight through three bars. I wound up paying the transmission repair; it cost three thousand dollars. Murph had caused structural damage to the car.

"It's only a machine," Murph said. "Imagine doing that to people," he said, grinning awfully.

"Murph, don't you *ever* stop?"

"I'll stop when I'm dead," he said, pissing in a car park. "C'mon, let's go. And *work* those girls, Darren!"

And so on.

When I got back from my vacation, I called Nancy in the office.

"Hi, Nancy, it's Darren."

"Hi."

"Did you have a good vacation?"

"Oh, great. It's great being by yourself all the time. Yeah, I had a *great* time. How about you?"

"It was—it was pretty good."

"You guys get fucked a lot?"

"Seventy-two, thirty-one," I said.

"Seventy-two, thirty one? What's that?"

"That was the final score! We kind of lost count near the end. I'm sure we did about that many."

"Jesus Christ."

"How was your vacation?"

"Zero-zero," Nancy said.

"Oh no. Not one? Sorry about leaving you in the lurch like that. But you know me. Mister Compulsive Personality."

"And they used to call you Mister Perfect in school. You're lucky I don't write you off as a friend, Darren."

"I'm sorry, Nancy. Lunch? Please? My treat. Wherever you like."

"Somewhere expensive, it would have to be."

"No problem. I have this revolutionary new method of dealing with credit cards."

"Oh really? What method is that?"

"Oh, with this method you can spend as much as you like and not worry about the future."

"I don't know about this method, Darren."

"Trust me. The Metropole?"

"Save it. Let's go to my office canteen."

Life at the canteen, life with Nancy, life in New York, seemed really slow, tedious, and poor, compared to seven days with Murphy Stavros in L.A. At the last minute we had decided to drive up to San Francisco; he had rented another car, left it in San Francisco, and flew back down, first class; that had been another thousand dollars. But it had been fun, fun, fun.

Lunch with Nancy seemed to go by in slow motion. That afternoon Murph called me at the office.

"How goes it? You getting any?" he asked.

"Murph, you are *non*-stop."

"Let's have dinner," he proposed. "The Metropole?"

At dinner I told him I'd come back to find life in New York slow, tedious, and poor.

"What do you want me to do?" he snapped. "Give you money?"

"I'm just complaining, that's all."

"Don't complain. That's self-pity. *Do* something about it."

"What?"

"Change jobs, get another job."

"Like what? I can't do another paralegal job."

"Nnnoooooooooo! Not a *para*legal. Something *else*." He looked at me. He fondled my thigh under the table. "You've got a nice body. And a nice voice, and a pleasantly servile demeanor. Rich guys like that. So go work for rich guys. You always said you could get them, no problem. Well, *go get them*. Go work as a gigolo."

I looked at him.

"Go *sell* your little cunt," said Murph. "You'll make a lot of money if you do it right. And you'll have *fun*," he said.

I gave the matter twenty-four hours of thought.

I showed up at Ritzy's, the bar where boys working tricks went. There were a lot of young studs lying around, a couple of sad old homos looking for a whore for the night. There was one guy that came in so often and paid so well the boys called him Santa Claus and he looked like a gift giver, his white beard shaggy in the light. He was talking to a few boys at once. He especially liked the nineteen-year-olds.

Half an hour passed and I was beginning to wonder if I was gigolo material. Then suddenly someone tugged me on the arm. I turned around and saw it was a middle-aged man. I swallowed and wondered if this was my first customer.

"What are you here for?" he asked me.

"I'm working," I said.

"You here by yourself?"

"Yes." He looked me over, seemed to like what he saw.

"You're too good to be working here," he said suddenly. "Do you want to work for an agency?"

"Sure."

"Why don't you come with me."

So I did. He took me to his flat uptown, near MoMA. His flat was a spacious, discreetly shining palace with a Brancusi bird lifting off into a corner. The windows were curved and looked out over the city.

"Sit down," he said. "What's your name?"

"Darren Swenson."

"Why do you want to do this?"

"This is a business proposition. The financial angle interests me."

"Any other angles you're interested in?"

"I'm interested in meeting some people. But principally, I look at it as a job."

"Do you work?"

"I work full-time at a legal office."

"How old are you?"

"Twenty-five."

"You ever worked as an escort before?"

"No, not really."

"But you know what it's all about."

"Yeah."

"Okay, Darren, I'd very much like to hire you. But I have to ask you to do one more thing—I'm sorry about this. I have to see what you've got."

"Okay," I said. I showed him what I got.

"Okay!" he said, leaning back into his chair and making a note in his pad. He looked impressed. "When can you start?" he asked.

"Right now."

"Why don't you go home and wait for my call then."

We shook hands and I went home to sit by the phone, the first time I'd been home for a Saturday night all year. The house was empty. At about eleven o'clock the phone rang. It was Dave, my new boss.

"Darren? Got your first job for you. Middle-aged businessman, Plaza, wants a big blond boy for the night. He plays it very safe. We normally charge him six hundred. Is that all right?"

"That's fine."

"We've got his charge card number so you don't even have to collect. Just pop over to the Plaza and go to room 713. Think you can handle that? Know where the Plaza is?"

"Yeahp."

"Great. Give him a good time and that's you for the night. Ciao."

So I went to the Plaza, feeling as mean as a gigolo in demand—which I was about to become. The man in room 713 wasn't too hot, but he had an awesome expense account. He ordered champagne for the both of us, and asked about my days at the fraternity, the hazing and so forth. It really excited him to hear about the hazing, since he had never done it. We talked a lot, he touched my wee-wee, and snogged, and that was the easiest six hundred dollars I ever made.

I moved up the ladder at Star Studs pretty quickly. They gave me a vibrator—I should say, a vibrating beeper. Some of our clients worked downtown and sometimes wanted a lunch break. I'd be working and would feel this thing going off in my pocket.

"Whoa, guys," I would say, "sorry, gotta run. Back in an hour."

"Oh, off again, are we?" asked Nancy.

Off again and again. It was fun, fun, fun. But when people were paying the kind of money we charged, they were no longer inter-ested in just a pretty face. They wanted perversity.

I was with Anastasio, the TV guru. He had a nice flat, with lots of leather couches and fancy glasses. We were going at it when he asked me if he could request a favor.

"What's that?" I asked.

"Can I shave your ass?"

I was a little surprised. But I thought it probably wouldn't hurt. So I said, "Go right ahead. It probably needs it."

So he went to the bathroom, got a safety razor and some lovely white cream and a *blaireau,* and did to my cheeks what a barber does to your face. He was very patient and very slow. It felt quite good when he was done. He asked me to let it grow back so he could shave it again. He paid me twelve hundred dollars.

After that my vibrator started going off all the time. I'd be eating dinner with Nancy, Steve, or Patti when I would get a call.

"Excuse me," I would say, getting up from the table, "but Cinderella has to go to work."

"*Again?* How much money are you making at this, Darren?"

"More than I need," I said.

"I don't know," said Nancy. "You need an awful lot."

Nancy was right, of course. I was spending it as fast as I was making it—faster, even—on dinners, on shows, on vacations with Murphy Stavros.

"I don't know where it all goes," I told him, as we went up a ski lift in Aspen.

"What the hell, Darren. What the hell."

"Murph, do you ever let up? Do you ever stop to smell the flowers?"

"Sure I do, man." He opened the door of the cabin. We were suspended in space, silently, far above the ski run. "Look at those mountains," Murph said. "Look at that sky. Smell the fresh air. The beauty of nature. Just think what we have to thank nature for— mountains, sky, the silver pepper of the stars—and our dearest friend: the AIDS virus." He unzipped his pants and started urinating into space. "Ahh, nature. What a pleasure it is to piss on you, pal."

Pissing on my clients came just a few weeks after that. There was a guy who wanted two boys for a couple of hours. First we had to tie him up—we used electrical cord to tie him to this hotel bed, legs splayed, wrists against the hard bedposts. Then he asked us— no, he *yelled* at us—to kick him, in the legs, in the torso. Then to whip him, leather belts cracking against his leathery skin. Then he wanted boiling water poured on him. "Boil some water, pour it on me, do it, NOW!" He had a terrible voice, and I listened to him as I poured scalding water on him, and he blubbered like a beached whale. "More!" he yelled. "MORE! MORE! Now piss on me! *Piss on me!*" So this other boy and I, shaking our heads, each getting paid two hundred dollars an hour, pissed on this businessman strapped to his bed. Then he wanted us to shit on him. I squatted over him and pushed hard, but nothing came out. "I can't do it!" I said. "*You* have a go at him!" So my partner had a go at him, but he couldn't shit on him either. There were four hours of this.

Then there was the guy who wanted to be hazed like at a fraternity. We had him kneeling with his hands tied behind his back, and we smeared his head and body with mayonnaise, Vaseline, egg whites, peanut butter—anything we could find in this vast apartment that overlooked Central Park. At his request I'd brought an old fraternity paddle I had, and I used it to just beat the shit out of him. Finally, we covered him in chocolate, egg shells, mustard and vinegar, cornflakes and caviar, wiped a piece of salmon into the hair on his chest, and threw him in the shower with his shoes still on. They were expensive shoes; he didn't care. Five hundred dollars for two hours of work—and eight hundred for the paddle which I sold to him.

Then there was the guy who wanted to be beaten and pummeled, to be made to bleed; oh, it was awful, I can tell you. The things that these people wanted done to them, the intensity of emotion they needed to experience to feel satisfied, it was never ending, horrible.

That was my part-time job for a couple of years. Dave died, of AIDS, and for a while his agency fell into my hands. I redirected the phone calls to my house in Brooklyn Heights and would spend my evenings playing matchmaker for millionaires. I'd answer the phone, they'd tell me exactly what they'd want, I'd tell them what was available, and if it was late at night, or the corral was empty, I'd go and do the call myself.

Nancy sometimes watched me while I played the pimp. "Well-hung, blond, and big. I *think* I've got what you're looking for. . . . Passive urban boy? Possibly, let me check. . . . Oh, hello, Mr. Pa——. Pardon me? A Latino boy, nineteen years old. Just give me a moment. . . ."

And so on.

The score at the end of the year, before I left New York, was several hundred quality men. Stavros had racked up another thousand, and I had racked up another ten thousand on my credit cards. Where did it all go? I was really too busy to ask.

Of course, my mom asked. She called from time to time. And our conversations went like this.

"Hello, Darren," she'd say.

"Hello, Mom."

"How are you?"

"Fine."

"Ya eatin' all right?" she asked me.

"Yeahp."

"How's your job?"

"Good. Can't complain. Interesting; I like it."

"Good. Your sister's here, she says hello."

"Good."

"Wail, the big news is, Davey's gettin' married. That's what I'm callin' to tell ya."

"Good. I'm happy for him."

"Okay. You'll get the invitation, I suppose. Susie's takin' care of everythin'."

"Good. Uh-huh."

"Takin' care of yourself?" she asked.

"Oh yeah. No problems."

"Right. Your dad says hi. We all say hi. I love you."

"Good; uh-huh."

That was it. I'd never felt so far from Kansas as when she called me that day. I never felt so far from America, from everything I was born into. My New York situation was going nowhere. I had thirty thousand dollars of debt, a dead-end job—*two* dead-end jobs, actually—and my friends were all off doing their things, and I felt they were going to leave me alone with my illness. I decided I had one more chance to get it right all over again. But to do that I had to cut loose, try to make a fresh start, in another city, another country—in another world.

The Limits of Compassion

Paris happened. There was no other way of describing it. I had been vaguely planning it for years, always thinking and never doing, and one night at one a.m. on overtime in the office, I said, "Screw this. I'm leaving today." So I quit my job and packed my bags and told my friends I was restarting my life, in France. New York was over-drugged, overworked, oversexed, and overhyped. My love affair with the Big Apple was altogether over. So I turned my ass to the west and bought a flight to Charles de Gaulle from JFK, thinking I would never go back—although my ticket was, for economical pur-poses, an open return.

When I arrived in Paris at dawn I felt I'd found the magic land at last—the end of the road. I had at last found myself. But although Paris was Mecca and the Promised Land and the end of the rainbow all rolled into one pancake, I still needed a place to stay. So out came the little black telephone book.

"Hello, Francesco?"

"Is this . . . Darren?!"

"Yes! It's me. Guess where I am!"

"New York?"

"Guess again. *Your* neighborhood."

"Darren, are you in *Paris*?"

"Paris at last. Can I crash at your house?"

That was when I met his fiancée. Marzenna glided into the room with exquisite grace, in bare feet and a white gown. She was holding a rose to her nose when she smiled at me. Her judgment was instantaneous. I was an adorable little boy—well, an adorable little spoiled brat, but Marzenna could forgive me.

My overnight crash became a month-long visit. Quite honestly, I was such a good guest—they really didn't want me to leave. I did cooking and cleaning and shopping. I made my bed. I made their beds. I didn't leave hair in the sink. I shared my joints. What more could you want? But after their place turned into a smoky Amsterdamer Special factory they wondered aloud if I could sort of push off. Into Yolanda, for instance.

Yolanda was a pint-sized Spanish girl always looking for her dream man. I was out of the question, but it was fun to pretend.

"Oh, Darren, I could love you so, if only you weren't—"

"Gay?"

"No—American."

"American? I'm not American."

"Yes you are. You're too straightforward."

"I'm not straightforward. Can I crash at your place?"

"Yes, but only until I go back to Madrid next month. *And* you must bring those cigarettes."

"Oh Yolanda, I love you. You're adorable. But I'm not American."

"Oh yes you are. You're very American."

"I am? Really? Do I have to be? Do I really have to be?"

The soon-to-be Frenchman called Darren turned heads in Paris. I raised hell and whooped it up and tried to make people *live*. Once I got stuck at an intellectual party. Everybody wore eyeglasses that looked like Coke bottles and discussed the awful solipsisms of existence. I jabbered on the phone and in half an hour twelve of my friends arrived. We rocked and roared and these nerds who preferred to be miserable and intellectual were aghast. They didn't invite me back. Damn.

But I was not a Murphy Stavros—I was barely Murph's shadow. I was slowing down. The first signs of the HIV were popping up. I was tired. All the time. I got depressed. It took an effort to keep smiling. The parties helped. And I could still be very dapper and very chipper and very charming. *Charm*—I still had that.

In New York through d'Annunzio and Panofsky I had managed to crash some very chic parties. That was how I met Chet Hyland. We'd chatted quite amicably and he asked me for my phone number, which I took to be a courteous gesture, nothing more. But a week later he called me and asked that I join him at another party. I suddenly realized he was quite serious; he wanted to have me around—a sort of ornament. It was a role that I liked—like being a beautiful girl kept at court because she was so decorative and so charming.

Then in Paris, quite by surprise, a year later, I received an invitation. The pleasure would be entirely his, it said, if I would attend his "little birthday party" that month at his family château. It was signed Chester Hyland, in a majestic hand. That was an easy invitation to accept.

I arrived by car; most other guests had flown in. Chester's helicopter cavorted like a busy dragonfly near the lawn, returning every fifteen minutes; a battalion of blue limousines kept arriving and departing with guests wearing perfect tans and dinner jackets and taffeta dresses that rustled lightly. That afternoon the moat around the château was a still blue, and the green lawns looked as smooth as emeralds. Every row in the garden, every line in the château, shot through the park and seemed focused on the needle in the center of the top lantern.

It was a black-tie occasion; I turned up in a business suit. Everyone was a little embarrassed by my lack of decorum, but I put on the hawr-hawr-hawr goofy farm-boy smile and everything was all right. It's a neat trick, to be a farm boy lost among the lawyers—and make it charming. At the lavish two-hundred-person dinner that night, I was placed next to Chet's handsome estate manager, who also wore a business suit. No doubt Chet had put us together so he could swallow us in one glance and think, my boys in business suits. It was quite a party. Under the dark and ancient hammerbeams, the white-jacketed waiters flitted like moths, pouring wine into goblets chased with gold, laying down silverware nicked over centuries. Giant tapestries woven with silent mottos covered the stone walls. Afterwards Chet gave a funny speech about how the only Frenchmen who could afford to live this way were former Americans. In the games room I watched the heaviest heavyweights banter and play three-rail billiards and other games so refined and ancient most of the guests were too young to know one from the other. There was dancing. The port was eighty years old and ever flowing. Seemingly the corks on all the champagne bottles had burst, and Chet was trying to avoid flooding the cellars by having us drink every drop of his Dom Pérignon. At one point every table in every room was cluttered with the fizzy crystal flutes. One girl, a millionaire heiress, tried to make a champagne glass pyramid on the pool table, and when she crashed down with every-thing, this whole gaggle of models in dinner jackets came over to lift her from the champagne mess. Later I learned who she was: she was Catherine Lancaster, Chet's cousin.

Anyway, at about one-thirty people began slinking off into their quarters; the château was so big that each guest had his own suite.

Not long after all the lights had gone out, a knock came on the door. It was Chet. He leaned his head in just long enough to say, "Darren? Would you come to my room, please?" I followed him, astounded by the château's labyrinthine corridors, the circular stone staircases, the unusual doors. Chet's room had been outfitted with an immense canopied bed and silk sheets and billowing pillows. Cupidons peeped out from every corner of the room. The antiques had gold figures dancing on silver clouds, and the ceiling painting had borrowed the gods from the *Shepherds of Arcadia*.

Chet undressed me. He took me to the canopied bed and cov-ered me in oriental oils. The whole room seemed to breathe luxury, redolence of past monarchs—all of them gone to the great big underground restaurant. But despite it all, and despite my affection for Chet, I couldn't rise to the occasion. He was so posh, so civi-lized, so pale—there was nothing of the sunburnt animal in him. He took his pleasure from me, although I was as excited as a damp dishrag.

But he didn't get mad. Chet was a gentleman. He treated me as well as any other guest. Better, even, considering why I was there. The next day I practiced my charm; one man worth a mere hundred million dollars drove me around in his sports car. I made advances on him, but he wasn't interested. It seemed I'm always running from the people who love me and running towards people who don't, trying to change their minds.

It was the end of the party, at the end of the third day, after the sun had dipped neatly into the axis of the garden—I was sitting on the stone steps, the château behind me, looking towards the parterres, thinking: I don't want to leave, ever; I don't want this to be a three-day stay; I want to live forever. The moon seemed suspended. Then I remembered I was sick, I remembered I actually had much less time than everybody else. I felt doomed, gone, dead. I was in this woebegone mood when suddenly someone said,

"Sorry to ask—but are you waiting for a lift?"

I looked up. It was the champagne-glass pyramid girl, still in her black evening gown, her face washed of makeup, her lines and cheekbones as perfect as on Italian statues. She looked heavenly.

"I look a fright, I know," she said.

"No," I said, "not at all." I thought she was the most beautiful girl I had ever seen.

"I say, *are* you waiting for a lift?"

I didn't know what to answer, and I didn't want to appear like a Kansan numbskull without a chauffeur. "Yes," I said, "I'm waiting. But I'm not sure I can get one."

"You don't mean they've stopped, do you?"

"I haven't seen one come or go. Not for a while."

"Oh, no. Not really. Oh . . . shit," she said, staring with dismay into the distance. "And I've got to be in London. Do you mind if I sit down for a minute? I'm absolutely shagged. And I don't know what to do."

She sat down next to me and then suddenly lay on her back. I watched the black folds of her gown drape between her legs, the fabric cascading between her thighs. I looked at them, stupidly, while she stared at the sky crowded with stars.

She said, "So now, Chet is gone, Westy's gone, Paul is gone with my luggage, thanks Paul, and now there are no rides. Fantastic."

"Are you certain Chet is gone?" I asked her.

"Well. I haven't seen him all day. No one else has. You wouldn't know where he is, would you?"

"He's not in his room?"

"No one knows where his room is."

I thought a bit. "*I* know where his room is."

Hearing that, she smoothly hoisted herself to a sitting position.

Now I was looking at her round and white breasts, nested in a silk facing, and then I lifted my face up to hers.

"How do *you* know where his room is?" she asked me. She looked at me as if for the first time, studied my clothes, and then looked up at me, remembering my face. "Ohhhh! Well!" She nudged me playfully with her elbow. "My, my! Mmmmmmm! You too, huh? How was it?"

"What do you mean, me *too*? Don't tell me you . . . were here for. . . ?"

"Oh no, no. Chet and I stopped bonking a long time ago, when I was about fourteen. Well, no, a bit later. But I was his first, back when he liked girls. We liked each other, back in the good old days. Newport, you know. Ah, well. How is he?"

"Hasn't changed, I suppose."

"Really? You know, we used to call him 'cuey.' Like a cue ball? Pale, smooth, round?"

"And hard?" I said.

"Well, maybe 'gooey' would have been more appropriate."

We looked at each other. All of a sudden, she seemed very, very interested by my eyes. I was looking into these pale green fires.

"What's your name?" she asked.

"Darren."

"I'm Catherine."

I raised my arm to shake her hand, but instead of grabbing my hand, she grabbed my biceps, and then my shoulder, and then pulled me towards her, towards her face, and suddenly she was kissing me! She was pushing down on me! I was on my back, her on top!

But I said, "No!" and wrenched my lips away from hers. "Stop. You have to stop. It's not right."

"Why? Isn't this *fun*? Don't tell me you don't like girls." She felt light on top of me, and I could see the bare white skin at the base of the neck.

"I don't like girls."

"Oh, rubbish," she said, and tried to start kissing me again.

Then—I did the gentlest thing I ever did—I put one finger lightly on her lip, and exerted a tiny pressure until she lifted her whole face away from me, and I could speak to her.

"I'm sorry. I—I have AIDS," I said.

"Oh! You don't!"

"I do."

"Oh no!"

"I was infected in 1988."

"Oh, Darren." She tightened her lips. "You don't. Not really." She looked me in the eyes, tried to extract some irony, or a joke, or an exaggeration. But I looked sadly on. She looked around. "Should I get off?"

"Well, only if it doesn't bother you."

"No, I'm not bothered." But after her silk glided off my wool and she had sat down, she hugged her knees, and brought them up to her face.

"But—you look like such a nice boy."

"I've done some pretty awful things."

"Oh, yes, and I haven't, of course." She smirked bitterly. "Luck, Darren. How unfair. Oh! Don't tell me you liked to feel skin against skin?"

"Yeahp."

"Thought you would live forever, huh?"

"I was young, dumb, and full of cum."

"Oh, dear. Where are you from?"

"The States."

"Yes, I know that. But from where in the States?"

"New York."

She laughed. "Oh no, no. You're no more from New York than I am from Kansas. Where are you from, originally?"

"Immaculatum, Kansas."

"You're not."

"I am."

She looked at my face as if it were a receipt and would indicate where I had been bought. "From *Kansas*?"

"I haven't lied so far, have I?" I said.

Her eyes flashed from side to side in their sockets, and then her mouth drooped in dismay. "No. I guess not. From Kansas? Is that why you look so strong?"

"Well, technically speaking, my T-cell count is quite high. So there's still time."

"Time for what?"

"To find a cure."

Quite slowly, she turned her head, and her eyes met mine. She looked at me hard, then she turned away. Her tongue wet her lips, and she shook her head in disbelief.

"A girl I knew from school died last year. Of *it*."

"I'm sorry."

"Don't be sorry. You didn't know her," she said.

"But I know you."

We were silent a long while.

"Darren, how can you be sure? Have you got any symptoms?"

I rolled up my sleeve and showed her a symptom. She touched it gently. She drew back her hand and tightened her lips.

"Ooch. That's the biz." She sighed. "You know, apparently, smoking marijuana makes those things go away."

"Really?"

"Helps, anyway. Well—that's what my friend told me. She didn't have any. She kept smoking right up until—"

She stood up quickly and said, "Come on, Darren, get up. We're going to find Chet. We need a ride out of this dungeon." She shook her dress and slapped her thighs. "I say. Not very clean, is it? Chet will have to get better gardeners."

We walked up the steps, where an army of servants were repairing the ravages of the night before. Gaudy colored paper was strewn all over the floor. "That bunting was really tatty," she said. "I'm beginning to wonder if Chet isn't slipping at bit. Darren, are you really from Kansas?"

"Yes."

"Kansas. Well. Then I must tell you our dirty family secret. It's quite juicy. Prepare for shocking news."

"I cannot be shocked. I've seen it all."

"But this is quite beyond the Hyland pale. Well, Darren, my own blood grandmother was a middle-class housewife from Abilene. From Abilene, *Kansas*. Now isn't that shocking news?"

I put on my best snob accent. "Oh, deahr!" I said. "Isn't that just the dirtiest thing I've ever heard!"

"Isn't it, though?"

"Deahr oh deahr! One can never live things like that down. But surely one can do something about it?" I asked.

"Oh no. It's too late. They've bloody put it in the family history and everything. We're fucked now. Officially middle-class, now and forever."

"But you know—one learns to live with these things, terrible though they are."

"Yes. One does. One does learn."

"Promise me, Catherine, you won't hang your head in deepest shame, shame, shame?"

"I won't. Now Darren, will you promise me something?"

"Of course."

"Will you promise me you won't infect my cousin?"

I was shocked. She was so direct!

"Catherine—nothing happened."

"No. *Promise* you won't hurt him, ever. We'll be friends, Darren, but not if you're a bitch."

"Catherine, I solemnly promise I will not spread my disease."

"Good. Now be a good lad and take me to my cousin's room."

"*Immédiatement!*" I cried. "Let's go running!"

"Let me take off my shoes first."

And we ran through the rooms, up the staircases and down the halls, past patrician Frenchmen scowling from their paintings, sprinting over marble suns in reds and grays and greens, over colorful rectangles and circles, finding passages leading to passages leading to more passages. Finally we came to a part of the château I recognized, and after a while we came to a door I knew. It was a massive oaken door flanked by two tapestries. There were torches in iron holders burning between the tapestries and the door.

"You're sure this is it?" Catherine asked.

"I'm . . . sure," I said, panting from all the running.

"Okay," Catherine said, bending down to put her high-heeled shoes back on. They were exquisite; the strap and its white jewels looked fine enough to wear around a neck. There was no jewelry around her collar.

"Don't you . . . wear jewelry . . . round your neck?" I asked.

"Did, once, but I always wound up leaving the rubies in bathrooms. Damned embarrassing after a while. Darren, you're not getting shagged that much if you're so out of breath. Hired boys always have amazing stamina."

"But . . . I'm not . . . hired boy."

"Chet didn't hire you?"

"No, we're just . . . old friends, with the occasional tryst."

"Really? How rare. That's amazing. Sex these days is so impulsive and pointless."

"Tell me about it."

She knocked on the door. "Chet?" Knock-knock-knock. "Chet?" She knocked harder, knock! knock! "Is this the right door?" she asked me. There was no handle. She tried looking through the keyhole. It was dark. "Keeping the tabloids out, I see."

"I *think* it's the right door," I said.

"Chet?" She knocked again.

"Oh, wait!" I said. I remembered. I grabbed the left torch and pulled down. With a creak and an appalling groan, the door swung open. Inside was a dark hallway with torches all along its length. Catherine stood there and blinked her eyes.

"Good God," she said. "Chet," she said to the darkness. "Your mental age is fourteen. If you ever grow up, I swear I will get my virginity back. Is it through here? Darren, why don't you lead the way; I'm sure he's bred spiders just to scare the females who might enter his lair. I really can't believe this. Why can't he just have a *lock*?" she said, grimacing at a cobweb.

"Hey, if it gives you that much pleasure, do it, that's my motto."

"Oh, that's a good motto to live and die by." We were in front of the oak door embossed with a dragon. Catherine knocked with all her might.

"CHET! It's CATHERINE!"

"Cthrn?" a voice behind the door said.

"Yes, it's ME. And DARREN. Open the DOOR!"

"Cthrn, m nkd."

"WHAT?"

"m nkd!"

"You're NAKED? Well, what do you think WE are? Why do you think we're HERE? We're STARK NAKED!"

The door groaned open. There was Chet, telephone pressed against one ear, dressed in a three-piece suit. He glanced at us and smiled.

"Cats, you're not naked."

"Oh really?"

"Mr. Panofsky?" he said into the phone. "Sorry, can I call you back?" He pressed a button and smiled. "So, Cats, did you like the party?"

"Oh, it was frightfully interesting."

"Fwightfully intewesting." He stuck his tongue out at her. "Darren, did *you* like the party?"

"It was the best party of my life."

"There, Cats, that is how a *gentleman* answers."

"You're right. Darren *is* lovely."

"Although his loyalty is questionable. Did you lead her here, Darren?"

"I thought it would be all right."

"Well, besides moving bedrooms *again,* I suppose it's all right." Catherine's face radiated pure innocence. Chet looked at her and tried to let his face fall flat mockingly. "Let me guess. Catherine needs a lift?"

"Please, Chet."

Chet groaned and mumbled and dug through his pockets. Finally he handed her some car keys dangling on a Mickey Mouse key chain.

"Which car is it for?" Catherine asked.

"I don't know. Figure it out for yourself. Now go away."

"Chet! I'm not going to go through thirty cars only to find I'm to drive to Paris in some malfunctioning antiquity."

"Beggars can't be choosers, I'm afraid. Now—"

"Chet! I'll keep my mouth shut about your terrible *secret* bedroom if you give us a lift."

"A lift?"

"Yes—a *real* lift."

"Catherine—it's so expensive."

"Pleeease?"

Chet rolled his eyes and dialed a number.

Well—that helicopter night ride to Paris was the most incredible experience of my life. Imagine the sky at night in Kansas, but turned upside down; imagine looking down at a universe of lights, the grand avenues racing to the corners of the city, the monuments lit in dazzling white, the little red lights of cars that flowed along like fireflies up and down the streets.

Catherine and I talked the whole way. I was fascinated by her dramatic, forceful eyes.

"What did you think of him?" she asked me.

"Of who? Of Chet? Great guy."

"No, I mean in bed."

"Umm—well. Not too exciting."

"I know, isn't he terrible?" she said. "I had to practically fake it."

"I know, I faked it too," I said.

"You faked it? But—how can a man fake an orgasm?"

"Oh, you just swivel your hips and shout a lot. Do it under the sheets. Insist on cleaning up yourself."

"Ave Maria. Where did you learn that?"

"Working for Star Studs, in New York."

"I wasn't aware they had vocational training."

"I was one of the main trainers," I said.

"Were you really?"

"Yes, I really was."

"Darren, why'd you come to Europe?"

"Isn't it obvious?"

We were passing almost directly over the Sacré-Coeur, its Byzantine cupolas like eggs in egg cups, white against the backdrop of the thousand holy steps.

"And you plan to stay?"

"I plan to try. It may be tricky."

"How so?"

"I haven't got any papers."

"Oh, that's easy. Marry a frog."

"Get *married*? *Me?*"

"My dear, everybody wants to marry an American. Green card, you know. Every Eurotrash bimbo wants to meet some American billionaire who keeps his cocaine in the flour jar."

"Get married?" I repeated.

"Just ask your friends. Ask everybody you know. Or if worst comes to worst, put out an advert. On the Minitel, for instance."

The helicopter touched down: I had arrived.

Beneath the whipping rotors, the helicopter hovering over the ground, Catherine leaned out of the hatch and said, "Don't hesitate,

Darren. Live while you have time. Must run, now. London awaits."

"Good-bye, Catherine."

"Good-bye, Darren. Don't think we've seen the last of each other."

"Good-bye again." I blew a kiss at her, and she smiled. Then she closed the door tight, and with a whirr of turbines her helicopter ascended into the stars and twinkled out of sight. If people like this were in Europe, I decided, then Europe was where I wanted to be.

I was married in June. Wedding bells rang that day. All Choisy-le-Roi seemed captured in a yellow haze. The chapel was a neoclassical temple with thick columns in front. My pathetic Minitel bride had bought herself a smart little outfit and a sash of lilies. I turned up in a blue blazer and slacks. We were both very happy that day. She was getting married and I was getting French papers. It was the fulfillment of her little-girl dreams, to be married to a big handsome groom in a big handsome chapel like a Choisy-le-Roi. It was the fulfillment of my dreams, too: I became French. Sort of.

During the wedding, I acted the tall broad-shouldered American. I greeted all my gay friends, most of whom I'd slept with, with grave seriousness; I inquired after their health and families, thanked them for coming, and was very officious about uncorking the champagne and being the one to serve all the guests and not letting Madame Dumpling get up. It was an outrageous put-on, of course. I should have turned up in a skirt and high heels and sworn everlasting love to Christopher Street. But something stopped me—a fundamental sense of decency, I suppose.

That night, I drove the bride home, dropped her off at her cruddy suburban flat on a grimy, sad street, and walked her to her doorstep. I had told her, at our very first meeting, that I was gay and ours would be a *mariage blanc*. Nonetheless, on the doorstep, she turned towards me. Her eyes were full of questions.

"But . . . Darren . . . you do not come upstairs?"

It was a pretty appalling moment. I was ready to give her a lot of things, but not that. So I shook my head sadly and said, *"Non . . . non . . .* I don't think so."

And I turned away. There were just twelve steps from her porch to the car and for every one of those steps I felt her eyes burning into my back, unforgiving. . . .

I tried not to care. I drove straight to The Trap that night and did five other guys, I can't remember who. And so on.

Then six months later, in Prague, another marriage—Marzenna and Francesco. Wedding bells rang that day. On a glorious winter morning, the air as sharp as freshly cut grass, Marzenna arrived at the cathedral. In her very simple and beautiful dress, carrying a spray of orchids, she glided along the aisle like an apparition. Over her on the highest walls cherubim played in the dark golden light and the air was still.

Francesco received her before the altar and, before a God in which he at that moment believed most fervently, swore he would always love and cherish Marzenna. And she, no less truly, swore she would always love and cherish Francesco. Then they kissed.

I was moved to tears when I saw that—two human beings entering the greatest commitment of their lives, and meaning every syllable of the words they uttered. As I watched them, in the December chill, while the dust lit by a shaft of light hung in the air like a supernatural cloud above them—I wondered if I ever, ever, could muster the courage to say such a thing to any person.

Of course not, I thought. My love life consisted of never-ending cruising, restlessness, ducking into bars, clubs, parties, drugs. Other nights I woke up panting, my body covered in sweat, and when I looked in a mirror I saw the disgusting white thrush all over my tongue and down my throat. I dreamed of awful black patterns and green shapes with dangling eyeballs.

When your body starts to give up, you can't get death out of your mind. If there's a black spot on the horizon, death is there. If there's a pause in the conversation, death is there. If there's a sudden absence of someone, it's because you're dying and they don't want to see you. The pendulum ticks: death is there, between each tick. And then there's the final horror, the ultimate punishment: you are alone in dying; nothing else is going with you. Everything, everyone else will continue, and everything, everyone else seems so much more living, so much more full of promise than you.

Everything seems worth cherishing. The flowers seem priceless; the children, treasures; everyone you don't know seems exciting and worth knowing—all because you're dying, and they're not. You want to bring the whole world to your chest, hug it all, before you lose it.

But the whole world was not enough. Europe wasn't enough. No place was enough, for me. Prairies looked to cities, Kansas to New York, New York to Paris, Paris to . . . and then. . . . Everywhere I went was nothing, nothing except good times, bad times, and a sign telling me I had further to go. So I endlessly repacked my bags and always took off at full speed towards the next place, in the direction of the arrow.

Because I was on a holy quest, ridiculous as it may sound. A crazy, strange, pure, inexplicable quest. It justified everything. Deep down, no matter what I did, I knew I was good, because of what I was looking for. Deep down I never hurt anyone, except myself maybe . . . or let me say, I didn't hurt too many people. I hope.

Growing up in the Midwest had made me feel pure. It was part of those childish assumptions, made under cold and winking stars. We boys all felt invincible: neither nature, with its seasons, back-breaking labor, and the invasive pains of age; nor our enemies, with their lying, conniving, stealing, treacherous, plastic double-crossing two-faced wickedness, would stop the least of us. No sir: we big-hearted Midwesterners pissed fire and shat lava and slept comfortably on a barbed wire fence. Nothing could hurt us. Especially not me—the little prince of Immaculatum, Kansas, United States of America . . . nothing could happen to me.

Is there any time left on this tape? I guess not. I better finish quickly. The story of how I got here. When I broke off for Europe, I left behind the thirty-thousand-dollar debt, but Mom called and said: "We've got the credit card people here, Darren. They say you owe them thirty thousand dollars? Can that be *true*?" And I said: "Mom, tell them to go away; tell them I'm out of the United States *for good*"—because I thought it would be better to start again at zero—

The tape stopped with a clunk.

CHAPTER 13

Writing the long monologue for Darren, I became aware of an emotion within me, unnamed till then, unspeakable at that time. I had felt it strengthening since my tirade at Café Marly; it was extremely strong when I had to stop eating in Darren's presence; it was with me at the Place de Furstemberg when I fell. At first, I had blamed Darren's disease, not Darren himself.

Frustration at seeing a human being laid waste, rage that it could happen, fear that it could happen to anyone: these I first blamed for the intense discomfort I began to feel when around him. And it would have been almost one hundred percent honest to say that was all that was the matter with me. But like Darren, I was an obsessive perfectionist, and it was vital in the novel that I should capture every aspect of his character dealing with his illness: not just bravery and strength, but also cowardice and selfishness. Darren, in harsh circumstances, was courageous and strong. He was also selfish and manipulative. When he joked about his death and showed courage, I admired him. But when he became cowardly, or when his demands exceeded my sympathy, or when he extorted compassion, I became resentful.

He was ill, true, but he used his illness like a charm. Initially I forgave him for the way he played me. But then the charm began to fade. Gradually I saw he was not so much playing me as stepping on me. His was a restless nature; he had to step on the pedal to see how fast the car would go—in any car, with any person. I did not consider myself weak, and in other circumstances I would have tried to match his pace or have left his company. But—there were no other circumstances. I had to take him as he was, sick, and requesting my help. He demanded little, at first. In fact, he provided me with a rare opportunity: he had given himself as a character in a novel. But as he began asking for more and more, I felt resentment build. Before such a demanding man, was I to give everything I had? A saint would have, I suppose; sometimes I thought Darren expected me to act like a saint.

Darren himself was not a saint, and said so. But secretly, in a cherished part of himself, he nursed the belief that despite his enormous sins, perhaps even because of them, he was destined for sainthood. I became aware of this impossible ambition very soon after I met him. It was endearing to find a man believing so boyishly in his ultimate saintliness. And that was what undid me. For, as a true saint loves God, so a would-be saint loves his would-be destiny. He was only being overwhelmingly self-absorbed, of course. That mad ambition for saintliness had given meaning to his life; it had refocused any love he might have had for others back on himself. It was Darren's deepest secret, and he would not abandon it, not now, especially not now—so close to death. . . .

Note from the publishers

The manuscript breaks off here. What follows is a reconstruction of the remainder of the novel, based on drafts found in Philippe Tapon's notebooks [B.N. Fol. 8° 2011615, vols. 1–4].

Tapon's tragic and unnecessary death, with barely half his first novel finished, leaves us anguished at such a premature loss. Philippe Tapon frequently read his notebooks in the street while taking walks outside his deux-pièces in Saint-Germain-des-Prés. Quite oblivious to traffic, he stepped in front of a bus and was instantly killed. The loss in terms of what Tapon might have written is immeasurable.

The publishers wish to extend their condolences to the family of Philippe Tapon.

Note from Darren Swenson

It would be impossible for me to express the emotions I felt upon learning of Philippe's untimely death. I had always thought I would be the first to go. But Philippe had always insisted that death might come at any moment, and truth to tell I had trouble believing him. He was proven right. The lesson learned, if there is one, is this: cherish life. It is altogether too brief.

Note from the investigating officer

The undersigned having by these presents determined sub-
sequent to a complete and thorough investigation of the evidence surrounding the circumstances of death of
Philippe-Gérard Silva TAPON [U.S. S.S. N° 545-47-4545]
having contacted an autobus in the vicinity of rue des
Saints-Pères (quartier Saint-Germain-des-Prés), have determined that the aforementioned individual was guilty of neg-
ligent and unauthorized street crossing. In flagrant
infraction of the Paris code of pedestrian conduct, the aforementioned party stepped into the aforementioned street
and contacted the aforementioned bus. The inquest officers
have determined that at the time of the incident Philippe
TAPON was reading in a notebook without according attention to prevailing traffic conditions. . . .

[signed] DUCLOS

Note from the psychiatric officer in charge of deter-
mining motive of accident

It appears that Mr. TAPON had a habit of walking into
streets without looking; he was careless, it seems, of surrounding traffic; friends said this was not the first time he
would have crossed the rue des Saints-Pères in the manner
described. . . . I am very sorry for the family of Mr. TAPON,
but must sternly add, as it is my duty, that he brought this
evil upon himself and entirely by himself.

[signed] DEHEE

No I didn't.

Darren was in Mont-Louis, I was in Saint-Germain-des-Prés, and exactly that much was right with the world.

In Paris Jean-Baptiste had come back from Australia.

I had found a part-time job working for a bank.

And I had reached the midpoint of the novel I was writing. I knew midpoints were supposed to coincide with crucial turning points, or at least with highly significant passages, but I could think of no element of plot that turned, no character entry, no development around which I could turn the Darren Swenson novel. I became *blawked*. I stopped writing, waiting for a phone call that never came. I imagined I had become complacent and repeated my old rugby coach's formula. I even wrote this mocking paragraph, hoping it would encourage me to continue:

> The extraordinarily engaging story-within-a-story of the friendship between a disaffected world-weary AIDS patient searching for a book to redeem his life, and the sensitive, poetic young man who agrees to write it. An emotion-packed meditation on the limits of compassion and the ills of a generation by one of today's most acclaimed young writers.

But it was no use; nothing came. There was zero new writing.

In my desperation to get material for the novel I began trying to remember things that happened. My imagination, I felt, was failing, and one recourse of a writer with zero imagination is memory. I also complained to friends. Since Jean-Baptiste lived only a few blocks away, on the Quai Malaquais, it was easy to go complain to him. I did not really complain: I just went to see him. In fact, he would come to see me. In fact, he began calling me quite frequently.

Darren had left for Mont-Louis, in the southernmost extremity of France, shortly after Jean-Baptiste returned from Australia. The sojourn Down Under had done him good; he looked relaxed and tanned in his little studio on the Quai Malaquais. He had acquired yet another photograph album—pictures from Australia.

"Here's E——," he said, showing me a man with an interesting hairdo.

"My goodness. It really *was* orange."

"It really was. And this is M——," showing me a narcissistic-looking Englishman.

"He looks narcissistic," I said.

"He was a *great* guy," said Jean-Baptiste.

"Oh," I said. "That makes him harder to judge."

"Oh, of course. If he were just a narcissist then it'd be easy. It's when someone's narcissistic and great at the same time that it becomes hard. Look at this woman."

It was a photograph of a lovely woman, her skin drawn attractively tight. "She was so sweet to me. She said she would have liked to have me as her son."

"My goodness!"

There were more pictures: Jean-Baptiste in front of a snowscape, Jean-Baptiste in front of a koala, Jean-Baptiste in what looked like the Australian bush.

"Where's E——?"

"He's taking all the photographs."

"Must have been nice for you to have been in front of the camera all the time."

"Philippe, he *liked* taking pictures of me."

"I'll bet he did!"

"Shut your dirty mouth," Jean-Baptiste said, laughing.

He was a good-looking boy and I admired his boldness. He'd set off to Australia with the intention of possibly settling in for life with an Australian man he'd met at another sordid nightclub. He'd taken his entire collection of chic socks, chic underwear, and lovely shirts and trousers—and all his experience. Enough, anyway, to begin his life again, to make a fresh start in the antipodes. He was twenty-two when he left.

But things hadn't worked out. *What* had not worked out was hard to say. The older man housed and fed him and introduced him to the Sydney literati, but although Jean-Baptiste felt more liberated in the vast spaces of Australia, and comfortably drunk amongst his new substitute family, he decided he now belonged in Paris.

"At least for now," he said. "I'm going to start my studies again, finish my degree. Then, after, I'll go back."

It seemed odd to watch Jean-Baptiste setting out on his studies just as I had finished mine. He was twenty-two, I was twenty-seven, but while I had been trying to understand how self-referent, allusive novels about life and death worked, he had been chasing true love: principally Darren, as far as Kansas.

I never tired of hearing him describe how things happened the moment he arrived.

"Darren's father said, 'What the HAIL is John-Batiste doin' HERE?' " Jean-Baptiste said, again. I never tired of hearing him say it.

"He sounds as if he didn't have much sympathy."

"He had great sympathy. It was his mom who was monstrous."

"Monstrous?"

"Just awful."

To what extent, I asked myself, could a mother be monstrous to her child? Even involuntarily monstrous? Plenty, was the answer.

"After we left, she sent Darren a bill for our stay."

"A *what?*"

"An itemized bill. She charged us as if we had stayed at a hotel. Room and board; three meals a day at three ninety-nine each, or something like that."

"I don't believe it."

"You don't believe it? I'll show you the letter." And he dug it up out of his drawer. "Here."

There it was: room and board for two months at the Swensons' Yew Tree Farms, charged to Darren Swenson by Lilian Swenson for his stay and the stay of Jean-Baptiste Duvet. Breakfast at 99 cents, lunch at $1.99, dinner at $2.99—itemized.

"Jesus Christ," I said. "I don't know how I'm going to work that into the novel."

"Just say she did it and let the reader decide for himself."

I frowned. "That's going to be hard to do," I said.

"Why?"

"I try not to let the reader judge anything without my permission."

" 'Literature is perfect control,' " Jean-Baptiste said, mischievously. I had taught him that.

"How right you are. Who taught you that?" I asked, and we both laughed.

Jean-Baptiste then dug up another letter out of his desk and said, "And here's the letter Darren wrote to me."

It was an affectionate, serious letter. I remembered Darren had told me about the itemized bill. I had not believed it. Here it was again, in the letter. My eyes picked out one sentence. *My mother is crazy*, Darren wrote.

They both are, I thought. I don't know. They resembled each other so much, I thought. In the letter was a paragraph of Darren explaining how he could afford to purchase a CD player despite having canyons of debt.

"But she just wouldn't hear of it," Jean-Baptiste said. "She thought he was crazy to *not* be working himself out of his debt, instead of just running away from it. They were always arguing about something. Usually the smallest, stupidest little things. The CD player probably cost a hundred dollars. Then he thought *she* was crazy. All he wanted was a stupid CD player. He was going to die and all his debt would disappear. But his mother wanted him to remain sober and serious until the end. Whereas he just wanted to get as much out of life as he could.

"You know, that's one thing that you haven't really brought out in the novel. Darren's *joie de vivre*. He may not have it that much now, but he did, once—much more."

"I talked about it in New York."

"But that's just one part of it. There were other dimensions to him, too. He was generous with everybody. That's one of the reasons he got into so much debt. He kept inviting people out."

"To show off."

"You accepted his money."

"Correct." It was not possible to write objectively, I decided.

"You haven't once described his laugh—you know, that great laugh of his, when he compresses his lips together and goes 'hee-hee-hee-hee' and makes it sound like it's coming from far away."

"His lips look like his mother's lips when he laughs," I said.

"So? *Most* of what's good about him came from his mother. Most of what's bad, too," he said.

"Who's writing this book anyway?" I asked.

" 'It's writing itself!' " Jean–Baptiste quoted.

"You *are* clever." And he was, too.

"Who else have you given the manuscript to?" he asked.

"Yannick."

"Why *Yannick?*"

"He's my friend."

Jean–Baptiste rolled his eyes. "You have *too* much sympathy for people."

The phone rang. It was Darren, calling from Mont-Louis. I waved my finger at Jean–Baptiste, asking him to be quiet.

"Philippe?" Darren asked. He sounded tragic.

"Yes?"

"What are you doing in Jean–Baptiste's flat?"

"We're talking."

"You're *talking*," repeated Darren skeptically.

"Yes. We're talking about you. Why?" It took me a minute to understand what he was implying. It was ugly when I did.

"Why, *yes*, Darren, Jean–Baptiste and I really *are* fucking. We're fucking and fucking. The whole neighborhood is watching," I said. I rolled my eyes. "Just a second. Let me disengage from him. Here's Jean–Baptiste." I passed him the phone and tapped my temple.

"Darren?"

Jean–Baptiste whispered to me: "I think he's drunk."

I whispered back: "Tell him I'll say he's a suspicious drunkard in the novel."

"Darren?" Jean–Baptiste said. "Philippe said he'll say you're a suspicious drunkard in the novel if you keep acting like this. . . ." He listened to Darren, and smiled.

"What'd he say?" I asked.

"He says he doesn't give a shit what you put in the novel," Jean–Baptiste said.

"Oh!" I said. "Tell him I'll put *that* in the novel, too."

"Darren? He says he'll put *that* in the novel, too." He listened again, and turned to me. "He says he doesn't give a shit about that either."

"Oh, great," I said. "Tell him I'm putting it in anyway. Tell him it's as good as done."

"It's as good as done, Darren," Jean-Baptiste said, then, "No, Darren, we are not *even* sleeping together."

I scowled at Jean-Baptiste and gave him the finger. Jean-Baptiste smiled. He whispered to me: "I think he's totally high." Then to Darren: "*No*, Darren, you don't understand him. Here he is. Here's Philippe." He passed me the phone.

"Philippe?"

"Yes, Darren." I expected more jealous vituperation.

"I'm sorry," Darren said, abruptly. "I'm sorry. I thought that . . . I thought that . . ."

"Relax, Darren," I said.

Then I listened to him apologize and apologize. It all seemed like a bad play.

I began to realize that Darren was abusive. Abusive of himself most of all: but also of others. Murphy Stavros abused everything around him, objects and people, and Darren was to some degree Murphy Stavro's disciple. He thought that "living a little" and "raising a little hell" always cost nothing—or that the cost was negligible, compared to what was waiting for us, in the end.

But it was not so simple as that, either. Darren had been trying to convince himself that since, in the end, we all died, nothing really mattered; but at the same time, he didn't believe that. The proof was that he wanted a book written. Not a picture taken, although there were plenty of those; not a portrait painted, or a sculpture sculpted, but a *book written*. Only through a book did he feel his life would be redeemed, and to some extent immortalized. He had never read a novel, but he knew, by word of mouth, that that was how things were done. In this he was different from the Devil, who seemed to never, ever, feel the need to abandon the surface, surface, surface in which he lived his life.

Would I have considered Darren diabolical? *Would* I have written the novel, *would* he have asked for the novel if he had not begun dying so soon? *Would* he have asked for the novel if he had been happily married with a Kansan wife and had a beautiful blue suit and a huge state-wide dairy farm and four wonderful children?

Could-have-beens and would-have-beens. The present was

all I had: neither the choices made in the past, nor the choices of the future, excused me from the present.

Yannick listened attentively when, during the course of writing the opening chapters of the novel, I explained to him the conflicts and formal antagonisms that existed in it. He listened patiently for a quarter of an hour while I described the conflict between Europe and America, city and country, fathers and sons, life and death.

"That is all very well," he said. "But it does seem to me you are avoiding mentioning the central conflict: you and Darren."

I looked at him.

"You and Darren are fighting for control of this book," Yannick said. "Darren wants it written *his* way. You want it written *your* way. You keep trying to give him chapters that are sympathetic to him, even though you don't condemn the characters he wants to have condemned."

"I condemned the fraternity."

"That's not the person I was thinking of," he said. "And— you and Darren are fighting for control of *your* life. Darren's belief in the superiority of his position—his mystical mumbo jumbo and all that—allows him to look down upon you. And your compassion means that you are something he can clutch onto as he goes down. You want to be clutched onto and be able to resist; it makes you feel worthwhile. But lately you felt as if you were beginning to get sucked down into the hole with him. So you come to me. But I'm not going to get any more involved with this. I have sympathy for Darren—but not so much that I'll go visit him in the hospital or write a book about him. Why should I? He's no friend of mine. I'd only be visiting him because he has AIDS and because I feel sorry for him. I never knew him; he's no friend of my youth, nor family of mine; why should I visit him? Why not visit everyone in the ward? Why not try to save the world?"

"I'm not trying to save the world," I said. "I'm just trying to give Darren the one thing he's asked of me."

"What gave him the right to ask?"

"Himself."

"He didn't ask you to destroy yourself."

I thought about that. "No, he didn't. But it gives him pleasure to see other people going down because of his bad fortune. Like the emperor getting incinerated with all his slaves and wives and domestic animals."

"And his scribes, too, I suppose?" Yannick asked.

"Yes."

"*Why* did you decide this man deserves so much of your compassion?"

"You know how literature works. Tragedy makes for good literature. I'll go even further, I'll even say the monstrous thing: tragedy sells. You know it's true."

"I think it's better to say sometimes it's true."

"Anyway, Darren's providing me with the literary break of my career."

"He's not providing you with anything except a sense of urgency, which is the one thing you never imposed on yourself. You're being forced to keep writing quickly, with an end in mind. That end is being imposed by Darren."

"But that's not entirely true, either," I said. "*I'm* imposing the deadline upon myself. He doesn't want me torn to shreds; that's just the way I react. *I* do it to myself. I'm a big romantic, you know. And—Darren, in his own way, knows what people want. Café Marly, the Murphy Stavros Chapter, all the stupid setting descriptions of Paris, all the damn references to Saint-Germain-des-Prés—"

"It does get tiring to keep hearing about your 'deux-pièces in Saint-Germain-des-Prés.' "

"I know, but that's just what people *want* to read about. Saint-Germain-des-Prés is supposed to be a romantic writer's paradise. You and I both know that I actually live in the Quartier de la Monnaie."

"That's true."

It was, actually.

"So Darren knows all these things, instinctively. I'm grateful for that."

"Without Darren, you never would have descended to that level."

"Oh God *damn* it, Yannick, what the hell are you trying to say?"

He looked at me with a calm face that I knew from past experience was at once stern and fond and smug. "Finish this novel, on schedule, as you planned. Get copies out to a pub-lisher. And then get out of Paris. Get away from everything. You see, the real battle for you is whether you'll be able to write this novel about Darren and then walk away from him. This is the battle everyone else is fighting, in their own way. Jean-Baptiste fought it, and lost; he couldn't walk away from Darren; that was what Australia was about. Darren's mother fought it, and everyone except Darren can see she was completely defeated. His father was defeated also, but more graciously. Now it's your turn. That will represent the real victory for you in the book: to write the book about him, to do him the favor, and not get pulled down yourself. Hating him will not be a victory. And if you love him you will have to mourn him. Your solution has to be indifference."

"That's monstrous."

"It's not monstrous. You have no other way out. Darren wants everyone to think he's God. He wants all America to mourn him, to feel crushed by his loss. You're helping him do that, by writing this book. But don't think that someone in front of death is going to show moderation. He will ask for everything you have.

"If you're not indifferent, then you'll suffer for his sake. And that's exactly what he wants. Nothing would make him happier, except another chance."

CHAPTER 14

Zero-zero, I said to myself as I began the fourteenth chapter. Except of course that it couldn't be zero-zero, anymore. It could never be zero-zero, after the first sentence had been written. That was only a formula to avoid complacency. As in the rugby game, it was something you told yourself so that you would play with all the intensity of the opening minutes. But it was a trick: at a deeper level you always knew what the score was. The trick was to hold contradictory beliefs while confronting your opponent. I am attached to Darren, I am detached from Darren, I am indifferent. Indifference had been easy, at the beginning of the game.

Darren used to love those Grenoble rugby games because he was a prop, and he loved the sensation of being held tightly by other big, burly men (he was twenty at the time), and of shoving and straining together; to him it seemed they were all straining together. The male camaraderie is the greatest reward of rugby, I thought, but like all good things—I thought—it had to be worked for. And like all things that are worked for, sometimes it didn't pay.

On the pitch, Darren worked and worked; he pushed, he

shoved, he ran like the wind and surrendered the ball only to his teammates; he rose unfazed even when he'd been at the bottom of a bloody ruck; he bore all of the game's aches and pains smilingly. And yet despite all the intense male closeness, Darren felt unsatisfied; he wanted something *else*. I thought that if perhaps one of the big burly ruggers had held him tightly in his arms and said, "Darren, this is as good as it ever gets," he might not have gone to New York and done everything else he did.

"But someone *did* say that to me," Darren said. "Benjamin was not only a big burly rugger but the son of an earl. He held me in his arms and said, 'Darren, this is as good as it ever gets, and I love you.' "

"But that was much later," I protested. "You only met Benjamin after you were through with New York."

"That's true," said Darren. He thought about it for a moment. "And chances are, I probably still would have gone to New York. It was destiny."

Destiny was a word that came up more and more frequently in Darren's conversation. *Destiny* had decreed he would die in this way; it was a fate he had known to be reserved for him all along, but had been forced to keep secret. *Destiny* had decreed that he and Jean-Baptiste should meet. *Destiny* had decreed our own meeting in Paris. *Destiny* had decreed the unexpected move to Mont-Louis, a tiny village that Jean-Baptiste called "a French version of Immaculatum." He was the only one who dared point out to Darren that he was stupidly returning to exactly the kind of thing he'd been fleeing his whole life. But Darren resisted even Jean-Baptiste's cajoling. He *had* to go back to the countryside; it was *destiny*, he said.

I agreed, somewhat. I certainly thought Darren's life had been all but settled when Grandpa Anderson had taken the boy to Washington, D.C., and kindled his ambition.

"See that big house over there?" Grandpa Anderson said, one old hand on the boy's shoulder, the other pointing at the White House. "That's where the President lives." Darren smiled in recognition. "And now, maybe—*maybe*"—Grandpa Anderson had a gleam in his eye—"you might live there someday." The old man lowered his voice. "God willing," he said. Later Grandpa Anderson thought he would help God along, and provided a trust fund for Darren which took effect when he was thirty. It wouldn't get Darren to the White House, but it did get him to Café Marly.

God was the Midwestern destiny. God saw everything; God foretold everything; God decreed everything. The experts in Paris had long since begun using other names—some of which, I gathered, were "rationality," "cause and effect," and "free will"—pompous words that paraphrased "God," a provincial word that offended the Parisian metaphysical experts.

"It's very unfashionable to believe in God in Paris," Jean-Baptiste once told me. "Especially not a Catholic God. It's perfectly all right to *behave* like a Catholic, but not for Catholic reasons."

"Is that why you refuse to have sex before marriage?" I teased him.

"I don't know why I'm that way," Jean-Baptiste told me, in the secluded quiet of my deux-pièces. Darren was far away in Mont-Louis. I was intermittently working on my novel, past the halfway point, and working part-time at the bank. Jean-Baptiste had started classes; I had started saving money to pay back Darren's loan. Aside from these things everything for me was exactly as it was before Darren had arrived—except that everything was completely different.

I looked at Jean-Baptiste as he lay on the bed, his tie precisely knotted, his hands behind his head. He stared at the blank ceiling. He was really very handsome. His glasses lent his face a sophisticated air. And he had long, sprightly, animated fingertips—slender fingers that seemed as delicate as spider's legs. I never saw him with a hair out of place or heard a very loud laugh. He kept even his expressions of pleasure checked within the limits of a classy urbanity.

And yet this boy who was a Parisian to his fingertips fell in love with a man who was Kansan to the core. It would be silly, I later realized, to take too seriously the title Darren had chosen for himself: a Parisian from Kansas. Certainly this native of Immaculatum had lived in Paris, but he had moved four times, never bought a flat, never learned the language faultlessly. He merely liked calling himself a Parisian. It was a little like calling a raccoon by a name. He thought it was distinguished.

Jean-Baptiste, though, really was a Parisian—born, and to some extent, bred. His parents owned a gilded antiquity shop on the Quai Malaquais, but the shop was boring for Jean-Baptiste. Paris was boring for Jean-Baptiste. At age twenty-one he gave up a boring English-language course and followed Darren to Kansas.

He did not love Kansas: and he did not love New York: and he thought Immaculatum was also boring. But he loved Darren: and Darren was born and bred a Kansan. It was almost as if the Parisian from Kansas were really *Jean-Baptiste*—a Parisian on the outside who was a Kansan inside, or at least Kansan enough to fall in love with one. Darren's Kansan nature was as undetachable from his self as a writer's style is from his writing.

"You can take the boy out of the country, but you can't take the country out of the boy," he would say.

So he became European in a Kansan way. With typical Kansan bigness he decided he only wanted the best. For him, that meant Café Marly. There he had thrown his parties: not sophisticated Parisan parties, with people lightly coughing into curled knuckles, but hoedowns with every single one of Darren's friends invited—a bit like a Kansan homecomin', whar there's food an' drink from 'bout five o'clock till we *all* keel over.

And, for someone who professed absolute detachment from his place of origin, his sentimental attachment to relics of the past was almost beyond belief. At age thirty he still clung to his old schoolboy knapsack, a blue nylon rag with split seams. His French was outstanding for someone who had started studying the language at age nineteen, but it was execrable for someone who wished to pass himself off as a Parisian.

And he *did* want to pass himself off as a Parisian. That had been the point of the title he himself chose for the book. He wanted to be considered a Kansan who by heroic force of will had penetrated Paris. In this he demonstrated to me that he had a farmer's understanding, at least, of the force of the written word. Because if a *book* called him a Parisian, then by God he was one, wasn't he?

But when he no longer felt the urge to be exotically different, or when his emotions carried him off, he became truly Kansan. And this truly angered him; it made him think that he had not left Kansas at all, but that it had followed him, the way the rails follow a train. They would never leave him, he thought, and his life would be overturned the moment he tried traveling without them.

And yet he tried; he made many primitive experiments in obliterating his self. He sought disguises and poses in increasingly wide sweeps. What Immaculatum had failed to provide he sought at K.U. What K.U. had failed to provide he sought in Grenoble, and then New York and then Paris, and now he was seeking it in the novel, which stood before him like a still point on the receding horizon—the most recent location of the end of the rainbow. Darren had decided his destiny was to touch millions of people—and earn billions of dollars. And yet this banal Kansan dream was still dissatisfactory to him, as if money and fame and prestige were not enough to nourish his great heart.

We were happy for that. We—I mean those of us who had known him, who had approached him first in person, not through a book—we loved that boundless heart of his. We were moved by his capacity for wonder, by his electrifying faith.

Somehow I feel I have not brought out this part of him. Darren never lost hope that one day all would be well, and all manner of things would be well, for him, for us, and for the world. Even while he sat in Café Marly, his body wasted away, his life mostly behind him—even then, he had not lost faith. He was arrogant and impetuous about the impossible. Only my fascination with this brand of mysticism, and my own ambition to write the book, kept me from leaving in disgust when he fervently told me what only *he* could know.

The other side of the fervor was a childlike naïveté, which bordered, even trespassed into, an insolent disregard for convention, for rules, for "common sense" and for tradition—and which actually drove all his incredible sinning. Murphy Stavros and his ten thousand men—the thrown-together marriage—the massive debt shrugged off like an old coat—all these things in Darren's mind were but trifles, tiny amusements, distractions, almost, from the quest for whatever he was seeking. In this he was truly mystical, or what is perhaps more accurate, romantic— as if he were God's chosen, miserable, and long-suffering favorite.

Unfortunately, Darren's beatific state gave him tremendous airs of self-importance; in his mind sometimes he had joined heaven and earth, or was about to, and the rest of the world was an audience, which in his estimation could only stare and listen in awe, as if at a pianist who could play in the dark. His "mystical mumbo jumbo," in Yannick's phrase, and his egotism were joined in a sad, overwhelming self-absorption.

Even Jean-Baptiste tired of it, occasionally.

"When I first knew Darren"——

(said Jean-Baptiste, lying on his back looking meditatively at the ceiling while the concierge blabbered just outside his window)

"—he was just as snobby, just as mystical, but there was a lightness to him which he's since lost. Now he takes it all very seriously."

"Because of the illness?" I asked.

"Of course. What else would it be? He's trying to give his life some meaning, and the snobbiness and the mysticism are his way of doing that."

"A mystic is the only person who can look down on *everybody*."

"Exactly."

"I get tired of his looking down at all of us."

"He doesn't look down on *you*, Philippe."

"Oh no?" I would have bet that Darren thought of us, Jean-Baptiste included, as side attractions in a universal fair of which he was the star. But something in Jean-Baptiste's tone stopped me from saying this.

"He really cares for you, Philippe," said Jean-Baptiste. "He cares for a lot of people."

But most of all for himself, I thought.

Jean-Baptiste seemed to read my mind, and said: "He can be an egotist and still care for other people. He loves people who put him on a pedestal. He is really grateful to them for it. He loves and admires himself, true, but he loves people who love him, because he's aware that it's because of them he can reach the other thing."

"What 'other thing'?"

"The feeling that he really is at the center of everything."

"He's not at the center of anything."

"He's at the center of your book."

"Oh, fuck you, Jean-Baptiste." But he was right, of course. Darren was at the center of my novel. It could not be otherwise;

the novel was structured around him. But what I had neglected
to take into account was that by putting Darren at the center of
my novel I had put him at the center of my life.

"He doesn't understand what it's like to write. When I'm
writing, the events feel as if they're really happening. Sometimes
I can't separate what's happening in the book from what's happening in reality. So when I spend four hours writing about
Darren, then spend four hours with Darren, it's like spending
the whole day with Darren. And now, as if that weren't bad
enough, I'm blocked. I can't even write. And he hassles me for
more writing, and I hate it!"

"I know. He doesn't understand what you feel. But," Jean-
Baptiste said, "you should make him understand. In writing."

While I was working on the novel, Jean-Baptiste frequently
telephoned. Frequently, for me, was once a day. He tried to
cheer me up and to see that I was well fed; he had a store of
sympathy for me and for what I was trying to do. However, I
did not want to accept his sympathy: I felt accepting it would
put me in his debt, and I had enough debts. I did not understand
sympathy then, because I tried very hard to be hard-boiled
about everything. Perhaps if, during the time I was writing the
chapters concerning the limits of compassion, I had accepted
Jean-Baptiste's sympathy, and agreed to talk and drink and laugh
and go to movies, then those chapters might have been less tortured. But at that time, I had wanted them to be tortured. Tortured people make good art, I had told myself. I was being
excessively romantic, of course. But even months later I did not
want Jean-Baptiste's sympathy. It was lousy not to want it, but I
felt lousy, writing the novel about Darren.

In my deux-pièces, brooding over nothing—over my blank
page—I tried drawing squiggly doodles; when those failed to
invoke words, I drafted sharp, lacerating angles; when still no
words came, I drew horrible clouds and black figures, until
finally the pen point tore the page and ink sprayed over my
hand. Cursing Darren, cursing writer's block, cursing everything, I went to the bathroom to wash up, and just then the
phone rang. It rang and rang. I ran back into the room and
picked up the receiver with my left hand.

"Yes!" I shouted into the receiver.

"Philippe?" It was Mom. "What's the matter?"

"I'm busy!"

"Don't be upset."

"I'm busy, I said!"

She took a long breath. "Well . . . I'm sorry to interrupt. Can I call back?"

"No! Wait." I dashed to the bathroom, where the rest of the ink came off easily. I went back to the phone, my hands still wet. "Yes, Mom, what is it?"

"Ah well—what I was calling about was—are you all right?"

"Yes yes; I'm fine."

"You're fine? You are?"

"Yes, I said!"

"How's Darren?"

"Darren? I don't know."

She thought about that. "Well—it's just a little idea I have—but last week I sent you a magazine article. You might want to read it. I think it might be helpful."

"Oh, boy, Mom. Let me guess. A magazine article about AIDS? Do you realize how fucked off I've gotten, reading your deluge of magazine articles about AIDS?"

"Philippe, this article has nothing to do with AIDS."

"Then why the fuck should I read it?"

"It will interest you. And please, watch your language, son."

"Oh, yes, Mom."

"Philippe, please call me when you feel better."

"Fine. Whatever. Bye, Mom."

"Take care, Philippe! We love you!"

I hung up. Still angry, I dried my hands and replaced the cartridge in the ink pen. Why did being blocked make me so upset? I forced myself to breathe very slowly. What could I write about? Nothing. I sat down. Then it hit me—write about nothing! I ripped out the torn page, got the ink flowing in the fountain pen, and started to form words: *Zero-zero, I said to myself as I began,* I wrote. I described how upset, how empty, how worried I had felt until, slowly, the page filled with the vital scrawl of real writing. This is so easy, I thought. Just be sincere: that was such good advice to follow. Sort of.

A few days later the helpful article Mom had sent arrived—an interview with William Abrahams, a senior editor of Gerontion, the New York publishing house, and who seemed to be living in northern California. The article began: "It is impossible, meeting him, not to fall for William Abrahams. A legend in the literary world, he is every serious writer's dream editor, brilliant and funny and kind."

Mom, I thought, you can't be serious. You can't be suggesting I write to this guy? This is absolute lunacy! But then I thought, why not? What could I lose, besides the postage? Mom, I thought, you are brilliant! And funny and kind! An editor, in northern California, my home ground! I felt ecstatic. But I also felt a little sorry. I was, after all, my mother's son. I called her.

"I'm sorry," I said.

"That's all right. Did you get the article?"

"Yes, Mom, I did. Exceedingly interesting."

"Don't you think he can help you?"

"But there's no address, Mom."

She was prepared. "I already have the address of *a* W. Abrahams who lives in our neighborhood. I also have his telephone number. I looked it up."

I thought of the damage we could do with that telephone number. Give it to Darren, I thought; we'll see if Mr. Abrahams gets any sleep at night.

"But I'm not sure it's the right number," she said. "I know. I'll call and see if someone answers. I'll do it right now. I'll call you right back."

"All right."

We hung up and I waited. After a moment the telephone rang again.

"Well, I called the number," she reported. "Someone with a strange voice said 'Hello?' I think it might have been the William Abrahams of the article."

"Did you talk to him?"

"No. I hung up right away."

"You hung up!"

"Yes. But I think it's him."

"You *think* it's him?" I asked.

"Philippe, after all, it's *your* book. *I* had nothing to say to him."

"Mom, *I'll* call him."

"And I didn't want to get involved," she said.

"Mom, this is where I'm much better than you."

"You were never better at talking. At writing, certainly."

"Mom, I'll show you. Give me the number."

She did and we hung up.

I dialed the number, and it began ringing. What would I say? "Hello, are you William Abrahams? . . ." Or would I say, "My mother saw you in an article. Oh, is this not W. Abrahams? The wrong W. Abrahams?" Oh, fuck! What would I say? "I've just written a self-living novel about reference and death." What? I couldn't even think straight!

"Hello?" someone said.

I tried to say something, and couldn't. I stammered—and yammered—then hung up. My mother's son, after all.

The next day, I went to see Jean-Baptiste. Outside his window the concierge was still blabbering. I had a strong sense of déjà vu.

"Hello!" he said.

"Hello!"

"Back in the world again?" he asked.

"Yes."

"Tired of hiding in your flat? What happened? Earthquake? Tornado? Death?"

"No. I managed to start writing again."

"Well! That's something. What got you started?" he asked, showing me in.

"I started writing—about my writing. Self-referential novels are *so* great, you understand. How else could I make writer's block the main plot?"

"So it's coming along?" he asked.

"Oh, it's coming along grandly. Swimmingly. I'm almost there."

"Almost where?"

"Almost at the end."

"Gosh. And then what?" he asked.

"Then I sell it. I become fat and complacent."

"Sounds grand to me. But—who will buy it?" he asked.

"Well—I'm not really sure. My mother—"

"Your mother wants to buy it?"

"No, you twit. But she sent me a magazine article. An article about an editor in California."

"This editor wants to buy it?"

"He might. I sent him a letter."

"Your mom thinks you can just write to him, without an introduction?"

"Well, to be honest, my mom thinks he looks like an angel."

Jean-Baptiste burst into laughter. "Your mom. She is something."

"I know," I said. "But it's California, you know. Anything can happen."

"Why don't you call him? Why not use a telephone?"

"Ah—well. That's not the way things are done, I think."

"Oh really, Philippe?"

"Well, it is *literature*, you know. I think. They want to see your actual writing."

"When did you send the letter?"

"Today."

"What did you write?"

"I wrote—wait." I had a copy of the letter in my pocket. I unfolded it and read it to Jean-Baptiste, translating as I went along:

> Dear Mr. Abrahams,
>
> My mother sent me an article describing your career and interests as an editor. I am not sure you read unsolicited submissions.
>
> I am sending you three chapters of a novel called *A Parisian from Kansas*. I am sending them to you because I think you will like them. I will let the writing speak for itself (or not speak for itself). The novel is twenty-two chapters long; I am sending you the three best ones.
>
> A synopsis of the novel is as follows. An ambitious young writer living in Paris meets a seropositive Kansan with little literary ability but an intense story to tell. They strike a deal: the writer will use the Kansan's life as the subject of the novel; the Kansan will accept self-referent form as the novel's medium.
>
> The completed manuscript is accepted by a Californian editor who allows himself to be written into the

book. The book is published and the Kansan dies, leaving his friend to carry on.

If you do not like the writing, could I ask you to send the manuscript back to my parents? They live in your neighborhood, etc.

I look forward to your reply, and remain,

Yours sincerely,

[signed] Philippe Tapon

"Who is he, this William Abrahams?" Jean-Baptiste asked.

"Some editor in California. I think he's retired."

"Retired! You might as well drop your letter into a whirlpool bath."

"Goodness, Jean-Baptiste, you are cynical."

"You don't really think he'll read your letter?"

"He might."

"What three chapters did you send him?"

"Chapter one. And the Murphy Stavros Chapter. And—"

"Not *Murphy Stavros*! Not the *Devil*! You didn't! You *can't* expect him to want *more* after that?"

"Well, it *is* good. It *will* sell."

"What! I don't understand. How can anyone be interested by that? It's disgusting."

"It's *true*," I said.

"The true story of how I met Darren?" Jean-Baptiste sighed. "Do you really want to hear this again?"

"Very much," I said.

"I'd been brought to The Trap by some guy I'd just met on the quais. When I stepped into the bar I saw this big blond stranger wearing glasses, at the other end of the room, with a glass of wine in his hand, leaning against the bar and looking at everybody cynically. I was consumed with—I should say, I was *thick* with attraction. But I also wanted him to like *me*. And yet there was more to it than that, too.

"I approached him through the swirling lights at The Trap. I approached him the way a stray animal approaches a stranger. I desperately wanted him to like *me*; I was twenty-one; and I felt younger, gawky, awkward, tender.

"As I approached him, I was acutely conscious of the way

the blond hairs on his fingers crisscrossed each other, and of the way he leaned against the bar, maybe not noticing me, maybe watching me intently. . . . I kept moving closer to him; he stayed in place. I was nearly close enough to Darren to touch him. I thought time had stopped."

"You felt this?" I asked.

"Yes."

"Yet you never slept with him."

"I *only* slept with him," Jean-Baptiste said.

"Could that be lust? What *is* lust?" I asked no one in particular.

"When sex takes over?" he asked.

"I don't fucking know," I said.

This answer seemed to satisfy him, so he went on with his story.

"I was close enough to touch him, and he raised his eyes and looked at me. Just once: and he held my gaze, looking at me through his tortoise-shell New York glasses. I felt pinned by his gaze, vulnerable, stupid. I felt he had me at his mercy. Then he spoke, as if to formally begin the friendship.

" 'Bonsoir,' he said.

"I cleared my throat. I was sure now he would at least talk to me. 'Bonsoir,' I said, and my throat felt very dry, as if it had never been used before. But I couldn't say anything. I just wanted to hug him, immensely. He looked big, and massive, with a sweater underneath a big coat. But he just looked at me as if he found me amusing.

" 'Would it save a lot of time if I used a standard pickup line?' he said. 'Do you come here often?'

"I was too nervous to laugh, but I did smile and sort of snort.

" 'Haven't I seen you before?' Darren said, going on with his collection of pickup lines. 'You look a lot like someone I know. Can I buy you a drink? What's your name? My name's Darren Swenson.' He extended his hand and that was when I felt his long, bony fingers; strong fingers, I thought.

" 'Enchanté,' I said.

" 'How do you call yourself?' asked Darren. I had not offered my name. In the back of my mind I imagined he would know it, and everything else about me, automatically.

" 'Jean-Baptiste,' I said.

" '*Enchanté,*' he said, delivering the formula with an amused air.

"The nightclub was full of young, smooth men with wavy hair, bouncing up and down, dancing by themselves or with each other, but I didn't see a thing. He was before me, straight out of my dreams.

" 'Are you all right?' he asked. He had noticed I was trembling. 'You look like you need a hug,' he said. He put down his glass, and in a movement that seemed too unbelievably good, he warmly wrapped his arms around me and pressed me to his chest. I felt my arms move almost of their own accord around him and that was when I noticed he was much thinner than he appeared underneath his clothing. But I didn't care; I was too excited by the sudden warmth to mind. He hugged me warmly, tightly, for what seemed like a very long time and I was too embarrassed, too grateful, to speak. When he finally let me go, he smiled at me, as if I'd just passed some kind of test.

" 'I'd say you really needed that,' he said.

"I kind of mumbled a response.

" 'Come here often? Haven't I seen you before?' he asked, sneering a little.

"I kind of said yes. Oh, I was on the point of crying, I can tell you."

For him, meeting Darren must have been heaven, I thought. Jean-Baptiste paused in his story. Underneath all his elaborate Parisian clothing, he suddenly seemed very simple, very sentimental, in a candid provincial way. Then he rearranged his delicate glasses and continued.

"Darren said, 'Let's get out of here before someone ruins this moment.'

"I had completely forgotten about the guy I'd come to The Trap with. He was off somewhere, I thought, maybe in the back room, and I thought Darren and I could slip off unnoticed. No use, though—he saw us before we got to the door.

" '*Hé-oh!*' he said. 'Where do you think you're going?'

"Darren answered for me. 'He's leaving with me.' And he smiled, as if to say, 'Tough shit.'

"The other guy got angry with me. 'So that's it, eh? I take you here, pay your way in, and you run off with this asshole?'

" 'That will be *quite* enough,' Darren said, raising his voice and drawing a few stares. 'He owes you nothing, and you're in our way, if you don't mind.'

"The other guy glared at both of us. Then he said, *'Salut, connard,'* and finally stepped out of the way.

"But Darren wouldn't let him have the last word. He shouted after him, 'Thou art *charming!*' and when this guy turned around, Darren said, laughing, 'Let's get out of here before he tries violence.'

"So we left. It was a real adventure for me, Philippe. I'd never been fought over like that, and Darren seemed so at ease with the idea of fighting over me. He seemed so at ease with himself. Next to him I was just a Parisian boy, full of Parisian hang-ups and internal brakes and anxieties. Darren broke through all those things.

"We stepped outside and automatically walked in the direction of the river. It was a cold, wintry night, but the air was crisp, and you could see the very white moon clearly in the dark. We were near the river and I asked him if he liked it at night.

" *'Bien sûr,'* he said. 'It is the most beautiful thing in Paris, at night.'

"The river was smooth as glass. Not absolutely flat, but smooth. The undulations were not ripples or even waves, but vast sub-bodies of water that moved silently under the surface. You could see the moon suspended like a disk in the water, and the glowing yellow strips created by the streetlights. And the water reflected the bridges, and the buildings, and the dark sky. It was quiet.

"Time seemed suspended. We hadn't talked since we'd left The Trap. I gathered the nerve to ask him a few questions.

" 'Where are you from?' I asked him.

" 'Guess.'

" 'America?'

" 'But which part?'

" 'New York?'

" 'No,' said Darren, amused. 'From Kansas.' He pronounced it the way the French do, kon-*SAS*." Jean-Baptiste giggled merrily at this, remembering. I laughed, too.

" *'D'u-ne fer-me,'* " said Jean-Baptiste. " *'Avec des va-ches, et*

des co-chons et avec ma mè-re.' " From a farm, with cows and sows
and mommie.

"He always manages to bring up his mother," I said.

"Always. He's obsessed by her, you know."

"I know."

I had my own theories about that, but Jean-Baptiste didn't
know what they were, because he had hardly read the novel—
although he liked what he had read.

"It's brilliant, the way it jumps around and everything," he
had once said. Jean-Baptiste had been one of my strongest pro-
ponents. Alone among those who had read portions of the
novel, he had no changes to make, no corrections to propose—
not even to his own character. I decided on the spot I had been
too harsh with him in the novel's opening.

"Do what you like," Jean-Baptiste had said. "Write it the
way you see it."

"I am sorry I'm so harsh with you, in chapter one," I had
told him. "But I thought you were a bit stuck-up then."

"And now?"

"Less so."

"Philippe, do you know something about yourself? You're
too hard."

"I have to seem hard. I don't want people thinking I'm some
nice, pansy, all-forgiving faggot."

Jean-Baptiste snorted with laughter. "As if faggots are always
nice."

"Oh, always."

"Always full of sympathy and always nice to their mothers."

"Oh, always full of sympathy and always nice to their poor
mothers," I said. "When I was writing chapter one, I thought I
should be hard with homosexuals so that people who don't like
homosexuals can get into the book."

Jean-Baptiste looked at me with surprise. "People who don't
like homosexuals are not going to get past chapter one." He was
right, again.

I looked at him. "Fuck you. Why don't *you* write the damn
book?"

"I'm not a writer. That's your bad luck."

CHAPTER 15

I had been wondering what names I should choose to give all the characters in the novel about Darren. They were all real characters; everything that happened in the novel was *true*. Darren would want his own name going into the novel. He had written to everyone he knew—his mailing list was six pages of tightly printed characters—sending them all postcards of Café Marly on which he had written that he was busy on a novel and would anyone mind being mentioned by their real name? Some people were surprised they were even *in* the novel, like the Websters, who had driven Darren and Jean-Baptiste from the airport to the waiting porch of the Swenson family home. But they had no objections, it seems, to being mentioned. Nor did any of Darren's friends, lovers or not, object in the least. Chester Hyland, ensconced high and mightily in his Fifth Avenue apartment, hadn't deigned to reply; Darren took his silence to mean a tacit *yes*.

I was not so sure.

"People are always confusing art with life. We had better make sure that everyone realizes that this is *only* a novel," I told him on the telephone.

"But it's not a novel. I'm not ashamed of anything I've done and I'm willing to stand up for anything I've said I've done."

"Still, it would be better not to take chances."

"You really think so?"

"Think about it, Darren. Think about the Hyland lawyers."

He thought about them. "I see what you mean."

"Here—I'll send you a text I wrote, something we can put on the inside cover."

It was a text designed to protect the identities and the reputations of the persons I mentioned in the novel about Darren.

This is a work of fiction. Names, characters, places and incidents either are the product of the author's imagination or are used fictitiously.

"I like that," Darren said. "It makes us sound like we're lawyers."

"We'd *better* be protected by lawyers," I said. "We'd better have the law on our side. I don't even want to think about what things will be like with Chester Hyland coming after us."

"He *won't*," said Darren. "He's too much of a gentleman."

"Oh, of course he is."

"And *I* have the pictures in case he does."

That was true; Darren did have the pictures. I had seen them. They weren't anything for which to pillory Chester Hyland, but the other guests could well have wondered what on earth Darren J. Swenson was doing at the Hyland birthday party. It was a strange way to socialize with other than the best of friends. And that Chet had *sent* the photos to Darren was even stranger.

"Let Chet explain that one."

"Why should he bother? It's just a novel," I said.

"Exactly. It's just a novel." He seemed delighted by the idea.

But actually, things had not been going too well between Darren and me when I began work on the second half of the novel. I was imagining more and more of the conversations, transcribing them less and less. We had exasperated each other almost to the point of no longer speaking. This was at least partially my fault. In my desire to funnel all my thoughts and feelings about Darren into my writing, I had deliberately refused to vent any of my frustration and anger, except in writing. And when what I thought and felt became unfit to be written, I grew irascible and explosive, in life and in literature, and wrote a chapter that was almost entirely self-pitying anger. Luckily I recovered some control and cut it from the manuscript and destroyed it. It was very poor writing, although I was sure there would be some malicious people who would have wanted to read it anyway. I was also sure many people would not be able to accept that the novel about Darren was, after all, just a novel.

At about this time, as I was working my way towards the end of the first draft, and when the words had all but blocked me, I decided to show the manuscript to Yannick. He had vigorously requested that I show him what I was doing, and I had thus far resisted his requests. I did not want to get him involved. The act of observing the book's creation would impel me to include him in it—for it was supposed to be a self-referent novel. And I did not want Yannick to meet Darren, either in life or in literature. But now, with my writing blocked once more, and Yannick more insistent than ever, I relented, and showed him what I'd done.

Yannick had told me he enjoyed editing manuscripts. I had once given Yannick my play to edit, and he had breezily suggested changing one character from a homosexual into a heterosexual, so I suspected him of not having much sympathy for homosexuals.

"But he really *was* homosexual," I said, speaking of this character, who was based on a person in real life. I meant that the play felt less true if the fictional character was not traced exactly around the character in reality.

"Perhaps," said Yannick, "but as it is, the entire play is too faggoty."

"Too faggoty," I repeated, numbly, the way I had repeated "It's too gay" to Darren at Café Marly.

"Yes, it's too faggoty," Yannick insisted.

Oh, boy, I thought. Yannick certainly withheld his sympathy from faggoty fags. And, oh, boy, I thought, when I handed him the manuscript of *A Parisian from Kansas*. It was the first time I'd actually shown anybody the whole thing—not even Darren had seen anything after chapter four, which I judged to be too harsh for someone at the Institut Pasteur. Darren would eventually see it all, of course, but only later.

So I gave Yannick the manuscript and held my breath for a week while he read it. After a silence of a week, then two weeks, then three, I was sure he detested it, or at the very least found it too faggoty. After three and a half weeks he called me up to have lunch at his deux-pièces in Val-de-Grâce. In all that time I hardly wrote anything. On the appointed day, and with a heavy heart, I ascended the five stories to his flat in the Fifth, with about five different tirades ready in case he didn't like it.

"*Bonjour,*" he said, opening the door. Yannick was a mild-mannered man living in a mild apartment painted in a light mild green.

"*Bonjour,*" I said. He and I had been classmates in our course in Paris. We had become fast friends when we had simultaneously discovered that I wanted to write and he wanted to edit. This would not be our first meeting imitating our professional counterparts, but because *A Parisian from Kansas*, as Darren and I had decided to call it, was my biggest effort so far, it was perhaps the biggest meeting between Yannick as editor and me as writer—even though we were only imitating our professional counterparts.

At first our conversation danced around every other possible topic. How is so-and-so? He is fine. Any word from so-and-so about such-and-such? No word yet. How is the job with the bank? Humble work for a small salary. But it paid my debts. One debt in particular. My debt to Darren. That was how I slipped it into the conversation; I desperately wanted to talk about the novel. Yannick finally obliged.

"I liked it very much," he said.

I breathed a sigh of relief.

"I have only a few comments to make," he said. "Very minor comments." He conscientiously pulled out a little notebook. I sat cringing at his list of bullet points and sought to defuse what I thought would be his bomb-like criticisms.

I said, "I know it skips around a lot. But beneath the chaos is a lot of organization."

"I know," said Yannick.

This genuinely surprised me; I was unprepared for this amount of comprehension and sympathy.

"I'm sure you don't like the subject," I said. I restrained myself from adding, "Not *too* faggoty, is it?" which I thought would be unsympathetic towards Yannick.

"No, I like it; it's good."

This again surprised me. Then I thought: *You must think I'm going to put every bit of the conversation we're having in the novel. So you're only going to say sweet, sensitive things.* At this stage in the writing of my self-referent novel, particularly with my writer's block, having a conversation with me was the easiest way to become a character in the novel. I realized this, and Yannick realized this, I thought, and, I thought he saw an opportunity to get into my novel doing nothing more than what he normally did as my friend and make-believe editor. Of course, it could be that, out of fear I would describe him unfavorably, he was only saying nice things; or perhaps he no more wanted to be included in Darren's faggoty novel than in the rest of Darren's faggoty life. Or perhaps he was angling for a mild dialogue with me about the novel, in the novel. . . . It was all very ambiguous.

"I just have a couple of comments to make," he said.

"Go ahead."

"First, about the self-reference. It's very American, the way you explicitly point out every moment of self-reference. It's very obvious when you change levels."

He really did say that. And I really did write it down; *am* writing it down. *That* was what he found so American.

"Perhaps it's just a matter of sensibility," he continued, "or of very personal aesthetics, but in the European sensibility, I think, it's more attractive to put a coat of paint over everything, making it smooth."

My ink ran dry at this point; I remember changing pens.

"It *is* attractive," he continued, "but you point out too often *why* it's attractive. Think of it as being attractive to a girl. It's better if a girl is attracted to you without really understanding why."

He really did say that—sort of. In the world according to Yannick, being attractive to a girl was very important. I wondered if being attractive to a girl would have any place in the

world according to Darren. My answer to Yannick's criticism
was ready, anyway.

"At Beaubourg, all the structure is on the outside, clearly
visible. There's no effort to smooth it over, and I like it that
way. And it's in Europe."

"All right," he said, slightly more kindly, for he saw I was
combative. "But what about the constant insistence on your
deux-pièces in Saint-Germain-des-Prés? I thought you were
going to demolish that."

"I *did* demolish it." I had, actually, but in a chapter still
under way. "And besides, you're just jealous of my address."
And he was, I was sure.

"So I am," he said. Well—not quite. That was what he
would have said, *if* I had told him he was jealous. But in reality I
had said no such thing. Wouldn't it have been great if I had?

What I really said was, "Well, I kept insisting on the deux-
pièces in Saint-Germain-des-Prés because in such a confusing
novel I thought I would give the reader certain things to hang
on to. But I will demolish it, later."

That was true: I would. I actually lived on the rue Saint-
Dominique, in the Seventh, but I was saving that revelation for
later in the novel.

"Next point," I said. I was eager for more arguing.

"There are some things that are difficult to believe."

I stiffened. "You *must* tell me about that. Anything that
doesn't sound true needs work."

"How much of the story did you make up?" he asked.

"All of it," I answered.

He smiled mildly. "Well, I have difficulty believing that
Jean-Baptiste *only* sleeps with people."

"Gotcha!" I exclaimed. "That part is true."

"That part is true?"

"It's factually true."

"You know this for sure?"

"I didn't make it up."

"What about Murphy Stavros having sex thirteen minutes
after he lands?"

"You have trouble believing that?"

"Yes."

"I thought it was the most believable part of the story," I said.

"Is it true?"

"No," I admitted.

"Aha. *But*—I like the conversation with your parents."

"*That* I made up."

"You made that up?"

"Entirely."

"So I suppose you didn't make up the visit to the fortune-teller, because I thought you did."

"I didn't."

"God."

"Three out of four," I said, gleefully. I was keeping score of what he had thought was true and what he had thought I'd made up. As long as he was completely confused about what was real and what was imagined, I was in the lead.

"The next point," said Yannick, recovering some of his dignity, "is about the allusions. It's very, very raw. I mean, it's good, but it's much too raw."

"It's indirect most of the time."

"I can't see it."

"Then you would say it's not direct enough. I can't do both. And please stop talking like John Wolf. Next point."

He laughed. "Okay, third point. The self-reference. As long as you're following *The World According to Garp*—why don't you speculate on what will happen if the novel is published?"

"Keep reading," I said. "I'm following *Garp* so closely people are going to accuse me of plagiarism."

"Plagiarism sells. Fourth point. The names. Chester Hyland is going to file a lawsuit against you, you know that."

"I expect he will. But that'll be the beginning of literary immortality. Nothing better than a lawsuit to get a writer's career started. Almost as good as a suicide."

"Even so, I think you should be careful."

"How can I? I don't want to change his name."

"Well, Philippe, you probably shouldn't print it as fact."

"I won't. I'll put a disclaimer on the jacket. And another one in the book, to keep people guessing." And I smiled at him. "Trust me."

But Yannick did *not* trust me. He was afraid I would take

whatever conversation we did have and twist it around until it fitted my novel. I must confess I did nothing to allay his fear.

And now, suddenly, he had no more to say. I had expected him to come up with five different criticisms to go along with the five stories to his flat or the Fifth Arrondissement or the five counterarguments I had prepared. But nothing of the sort happened. Life, after all, was not structured like a good old-fashioned novel.

Much later, after he read some of this chapter, Yannick called me up.

"Bastard!" he said. "Asshole!"

"That's not a very mild thing to say," I said.

"Fucker! What is this shit about mild-mannered Yannick?"

"You *are* mild-mannered, when you're not pissed off."

"Well, I *am* pissed off. I can't believe you wrote up our conversation about allusions and *Garp* like *this*."

"Hey, tough shit!"

"I'm not reading any more of your fucking novel!" he said.

"Aw, that's too bad. Your character gets a lot of exposure, later."

"Oh, no. Get me out of this! I want out!"

"Relax. You haven't got long."

"Get me out, now!"

"Okay, okay. Good-bye—talk to you later."

I smiled as I put the phone down. So much for criticism number five. I was beginning to become pleased with the way things were going; life was beginning to imitate a good old-fashioned novel. I took the master list of characters, found Yannick (character number 161) and, inwardly, agreed to let him go—but not before one last appearance, at the party where I hoped to reunite the entire Parisian cast of characters.

CHAPTER 16

I was awakened from a deep sleep by the sound of the telephone ringing. It was Jean-Baptiste.

"Philippe?" he asked.

"Yes."

"I'm sorry to call you this early. But—I thought you should know right away. Darren is dead. He died this morning."

I sat up. "Jesus," I said.

"I thought I should tell you."

Instantly my head was filled with Darren.

"His landlady found him this morning, and she called me."

I breathed into the mouthpiece; my eyes were shut tight. I had expected relief, in some way; instead I felt a sudden, overpowering guilt for not having done more while it would have mattered. I had finished the first draft only the night before. It was still lying on my desk. It was still—

The telephone was still ringing. What? I picked it up, and it was not Jean-Baptiste. It was my boss, at work.

"Philippe?" he asked.

"Yes?" I said, trying to sound awake.

"What are you doing?"

"I'm . . . I'm sorry, I'm feeling a bit ill."

"What is going on? This is the second time this week."

"I . . . have a nervous problem, I think."

"Nervous problem? Your next boss better believe in nervous problems, is that clear? Next time, you're fired. Be here in half an hour, or I'll fire you anyway."

"Yes," I said.

He hung up. He was right to be angry; I had broken our arrangement. I put down the phone and ground my fists into tight balls and shut my eyes so hard it almost hurt. That job was my only rent and food money, and I was purposely sabotaging it. Did I *want* to destroy myself? Did I? Now Darren came back—I saw his huge face over the plains—big as the sun. I curled up in a ball, my arms crossed, my legs crossed, my eyes tightly shut, but it was no use; I saw him more intensely.

Walking quickly to work, I thought, it's the novel that's doing this to me. Christ! Somehow I had to get it out of my mind, or else become so at one with the writing that everything I felt and thought naturally organized itself on the page and the rest was forgotten in indifference. Zero-zero? I thought. But that was a ridiculous notion. I was too far along; too much was already in place; what was demanded now was not the energy of the opening minutes, but resolution, coherence, strategy, clever closing of boxes opened up in previous chapters. I could not get complacent: and yet I could not ignore what had been done. I had to build and finish what I had—that was the only way out. And afterwards, I told myself, I could have the satisfaction of feeling indifferent about the whole thing.

To Yannick, indifference meant victory. But I preferred losing to not feeling. Feeling for Darren had led me to write a novel of his life. It seemed wrong to let him pass without trying to fulfill his simple request. Of course, if I had known how the request would dominate my life—I might not have tried. I would have agreed that indifference was the wise middle course between a life of my own and Darren's approaching death.

There were times, writing the novel, when I was sure I hated Darren. I did not hate him, of course, but my feelings were sometimes hard and bitter. Darren enjoyed watching me wrestle with my feelings: for him, it was evidence he was affecting me. And with him, everything reached epic proportions. My role, as he saw it, was to chronicle the extraordinary life of an ordinary man (as he would have said) and to create a masterpiece (as he also would have said, though with no clear notion of what a masterpiece was). My role, as I saw it, was to patiently watch him die. He was watching my writing, of course, but I was progressing to an end much slower. That was the gulf that separated us, more than any "fine philosophy" about life, death, and values.

The extraordinary life of an ordinary man. I had a hard time not gagging when he said that—and he really did say it. It sounded like he'd been flipping through a dozen New Age magazines. I didn't gag when he said that I was writing a masterpiece, though perhaps I should have; to believe it signaled the onset of complacency. But I was relatively innocent, at the beginning of the project; I was a young writer trying to never break anybody else's illusions. Now I realized things had changed. It was not possible to write a "masterpiece" about Darren to his specifications, and not break his illusions about himself. In the book, I revealed him as I saw him, and I realized that the development of myself as the narrator was the breaking of my one small virtue. I wanted to put that break at the center of the book—right before chapter thirteen.

And then—I sent Darren the entire first draft.

I really did.

Much later, Darren wrote back from Mont-Louis. I held the unopened letter nervously, figuring he would send me to hell; that would have destroyed my nerve, and the book, for good. The envelope snapped like bones when I finally opened it. I expected hatred. But instead I saw these words. "This is extraordinary. . . . You are writing a masterpiece." There were other, very flattering things. There was evidence that he'd read and approved of my criticisms of him. Not that he expected to change: you can't teach an old dog new tricks, as he liked to say. But he saw that despite all the dreadful things I had said about him, I still had sympathy for him—not bottomless sympathy, but a decent, human-sized reservoir which he could be expected to drink at from time to time.

I was quite moved by his response. He was sincere in his praise (I think); and it was the least he could do; but I was the sort of person who constantly expected less than the least from people. I gave, as much as I could, but in Darren I had found someone with an insatiable appetite for my sympathy. I could never have satisfied Darren; I would have had to sacrifice my sense of right and wrong, I thought—as if I could ever write objectively.

With a first draft finished, decisions and revisions could be made and then reversed. It was in the spirit of finishing the book once and for all that I bravely deposited it at the Village Voice bookshop, on the rue Princesse (in Saint-Germain-des-Prés) for the attention of Edward Gray.

Of course I'd heard of Edward Gray. His face had peered out at me from a long series of books and periodicals—mustachioed, sometimes, young at first, then progressively older and older. He had written the most successful coming-out novel I'd ever heard of, he had written a mammoth literary biography, instantly translated into French and winning widespread acclaim, and he'd written enough essays to fill a whole book about art and politics and sexuality. In his own way, he presided over an entire facet of literature, and it was with no little trepidation that I bundled two-thirds of my book (the rest I kept revising) into a manila envelope and waited for him to read it. I left a little note on the manuscript:

> Dear Mr. Gray,
>
> *During the course of writing this, my first novel, in which I am collaborating with a friend, we thought we would ask for your assistance and advice regarding how to publish it.*
>
> *We decided to place in your hands a copy of the manuscript, asking you to read as much, or as little, as you please. We would be quite grateful if you would be kind enough to make a few comments and possibly suggest some way of getting it into print.*
>
> *Yours sincerely,*
> *Philippe Tapon*

But I was not sincere. I was not interested in Mr. Gray's comments; I only wanted a publisher. Mr. Gray, in my opinion,

could not improve my novel. In fact, I felt I was competing with
him for shelf space—in the future, if not right away. I was a
young writer, and I had a young writer's killer instinct.

A letter arrived a few days after that. But the letter was not
from Edward Gray; it was from William Abrahams, the editor in
California. He had not been in a whirlpool bath after all.

> Dear Philippe Tapon,
>
> I have read with admiration and uncertainty the three
> chapters you sent me from your novel, *A Parisian from
> Kansas*. Admiration because these chapters show an
> authentic talent; uncertainty because three chapters
> selected from 22 don't really give me enough to judge
> the novel as a whole. Since the novel is indeed complete,
> I would welcome the opportunity to read it, and even, if
> it turned out that I could not make an offer of publica-
> tion, I would not hesitate to recommend it to a literary
> agent in New York who might find a congenial home
> for it.
>
> I am keeping the three chapters you sent and look for-
> ward to the full manuscript.
>
> With all good wishes,
>
> William Abrahams

So I packaged a copy of the full manuscript and sent it to
him. This should be fun, I thought. Put Abrahams and Gray in a
race. See who likes it first.

A few days later, the phone rang.

"Philippe?" said the voice.

"Yes."

"This is Edward Gray."

"How are you?"

"Fine, how are *you*?"

"Well, thanks."

"I received your manuscript, and I have read it, and I like it.
I wonder—"

"Thanks."

He smiled audibly on the other end of the line.

"I wonder if you'd like to have coffee together. Or dinner—whatever you like."

"Certainly. I'd like to very much."

"Where would you like to go?" he asked me.

I could only give one answer, of course. "Café Marly."

"Of course."

We agreed to meet the following night. I had only met published novelists twice in my life; I held them in considerable respect. So I arrived early. It was cold. At night, the pyramid was illuminated from within like a ghostly transparent skeleton, and the frothy, white fountains showered watery clouds. The palace itself was delicately illuminated, and I noticed that the statues lining the rooftops were mostly of the men who had done the most to undermine the régime whose symbol the palace was. Reflecting on this irony, I entered the café and, as usual, was coldly received by Madame Doorkeeper. Her occupation was to guess how much money I was likely to spend and she obviously thought I had a cheap look. I ignored her smilingly and walked straight into the first room, where I sat down and rearranged the yellow rose I had placed in my buttonhole so that Mr. Gray could recognize me. I looked around. I noticed, for the first time, their chandelier—a bulbous blue and red plastic octopus that hung from the middle of the ceiling—and found it repulsive. I thought it so repulsive that I felt a bout of superiority to the snotty place; it was in this mood that I began waiting for Edward Gray.

I knew what he looked like from the countless photographs I'd seen of him—munching a croissant on the Left Bank, in front of Notre-Dame; smiling from the back cover of an essay describing humor in France and England; looking at me sternly, in a thin-lipped, patrician way, from the cover of a book placed high on the racks of the Village Voice. I had read his books and his essays, and my admiration for his prophetic gifts and the courage of his stance was mixed with mild scorn for the actual powers of his writing. He was widely reputed to be a good writer; I preferred to think he was a good man, true to his convictions.

But of course I didn't tell him any of this, and I had left it out of the manuscript I'd given him to read. He didn't learn my real opinion of his writing until long after the chat I am about to imagine, in the Café Marly, with the roaring fountains silently flowing behind the thick glass panes.

I recognized him as soon as he came in. Because he had been living in Paris even while I was a high school student, which was years and years ago, I had assumed he would have assimilated all the Parisian ways, so I was rather surprised to see a very American-looking gentleman stride in, look around the room intently, greet me and my yellow rose with a sudden smile, and stride to my table. I got halfway out of my seat and shook his hand.

"Good evening," I said.

"Good evening," he said, and sat down.

"Have you been here before?" I asked.

"Oh yes," he said, rubbing one of his eyes. "This is one of my favorite cafés."

We were both accustomed to French service and did not gesture for a waiter. I looked across the table at what I might one day become: the expatriate American writer enjoying a sizable reputation in Paris, living mildly and elegantly on the Left Bank, writing distinguished scholarly books and essays about literary Frenchmen and America.

And I am sure he looked me over, too. Was I the him of the past? Was I one of the things he could have been? I thought he considered me a promising young writer; he would not have assented to a café meeting if he had not thought so. Was I as promising as he had been at my age? And if I was, could I be expected to show the same sort of courage? There was a battle being fought between the him of his past and the me of my future. I was trying to see who would have been the outright winner in a hypothetical literary competition. It was not hypothetical, in a way—it would start in earnest once we were both dead. Till then I felt a terribly competitive, murderous urge. That urge probably awakened a lot of my writing—and ruined a lot of it as well.

"Have you been in Paris long?" I asked. I knew that he had lived in France for years, but *I* was half French, so I thought that despite all his adult efforts, I had probably mastered the language better than he. I was thinking nastily.

"Ten years," he said, matter-of-factly. "But I began visiting long before that."

He appeared to want me to give him credit for the months he had visited—probably as a wide-eyed student spellcast by Paris, as Darren had been by Grenoble.

I have your youth in my novel, I thought. I've recorded your experience.

What he could have said, had he read my mind, was, "And I have recorded yours, in mine." But I was very good at hiding my killer instinct and I let him think I was admiring his deep experience of the French.

"I remember you wrote that in England you must make jokes at the expense of yourself, and in France you must make jokes at the expense of others."

"Yes." He smiled a little. I was consciously flattering him; I had thought his essay perfectly readable but banal.

"Which do you enjoy writing more, essays or fiction?" I asked.

He stopped to think. "Essays about fiction," he said.

I laughed. That was a good answer. He disarmed me a little with his wit; he had perfectly understood what I was getting at.

"When you write objectively about fiction, you're treading solidly on a cloud," he said.

"You like that?" I asked. But I had winced, inwardly, at the word "objectively."

"Oh yes," he said, "it's a perfect blend of literature and life."

I smiled. He really did say that. "Two worlds—" I began.

"—become much like each other. Where does one start and the other begin?" he asked. "This is the point of the book you've written about Darren, isn't it?"

"Am *writing* about Darren," I said. "I'm still revising it, right this moment in fact."

"I suppose I'm going to be a part of it," he said. "When will it stop?"

"It'll never stop. Even after it's published."

"You may find that difficult."

"I'll find a way. I'm a relentless perfectionist."

"Oh. You unlucky boy." He looked at me—paternally, soulfully.

"Now," I asked, "can I ask you *how* I get published?"

"You told me others are interested," he remarked.

"Sort of."

"Well, send out manuscripts and call people once a week. If you're not getting at least a phone call a month someone's not doing their job. It shouldn't be that hard to sell, your book. Your timing is good. AIDS is news again."

"It's an AIDS book, isn't it?"

"Oh yes. You and I know it's more than that, but that's what it'll be labeled as. You wait and see. No one likes labels as much as the literary establishment."

"I can't wait." My feelings for Mr. Gray—inside, I called him Mr. Gray—were changing. He was genuinely paternalistic now, and I was genuinely grateful for his advice.

The waiter arrived. I felt whimsical.

"A tea, please. Mint, if possible."

"A gin rickey, please," Edward asked. It was winter, but he obviously wanted something refreshing. The waiter left, his nose high in the air.

"*Now*—I have a question for you," he said, looking at me affectionately but sternly. "A question about the names. What kind of row are you trying to cause, anyhow? You know you're asking for trouble."

"I know."

"You must be careful. If the book is at all popular, there *will* be lawsuits. No one will bother if it doesn't make any money. And not just Chet Hyland. Think of what you're doing to Murphy Stavros."

"And if I change the names. . . ?" I asked, speculatively.

"The book loses nothing."

"Yes it does."

"Very little," he said. "Why do the names *have* to be real?"

"So the line between life and literature is completely blurred. I don't want a critical essay stapled on top of the book to explain who was who."

"You have to do it that way," Edward said, "to avoid libel."

"But I *don't* want the reader to have to rely on a critical essay, however good it is. Ann Charters wrote a good introduction to *On the Road*, but if Kerouac had had his way she wouldn't have needed to. Everybody would have known that Dean was Neal and Sal was Jack and so on."

"Ah, but then it wouldn't be fiction, would it?"

"It's always fiction!" I exclaimed, loudly, and a well-heeled businessman eating out of a smooth plate turned to look at me. I shot a glance at him and turned back to Edward. He was clearly a little amused by my outburst. "If I *call* it a novel, it *is* a novel," I said.

The tea and gin rickey arrived.

"Is that what it was like when you lost your temper with Darren?" he asked, just a little sarcastically.

"No," I said. "It was much worse."

"I can't imagine."

"I wished I *had* imagined it."

"Did that really happen the way you described it?"

"Sort of."

"What did you change?"

I tried to remember. "After I lost my temper, Darren immediately asked me to have dinner with him at Matsuya's. It was tremendously gracious of him—a very gentlemanly thing to do."

"Why did you leave that out of the novel?"

"I was angry with him."

"Are you going to revise it?"

"No."

"Are you just going to leave it that way?"

"Yes."

"How will people know that Darren invited you to dinner right after?"

"I don't know." I sort of snorted. "They'll read about it in the critical essays, later," I said.

"Or elsewhere in the book," he said. He smiled. "What else did you leave out?"

"I didn't mention that I paid for those damn Monacos."

"Money, money, money."

"I live in a limited world," I said. "I can't give it away endlessly."

"Money or sympathy?" he asked.

"Both," I said.

We had arrived at the main topic. "How is Darren?" Edward asked.

"I don't know."

"Really."

"I don't know. He left for Mont-Louis and I asked him not to call me. He could be dead for all I know."

Edward looked at his gin rickey. Then he looked at me, eyes tender and waiting.

I guessed what he was thinking. "Did you expect me to accompany him all the way to his grave?"

"That's your business."

"You do," I said, a little anger in my voice. "You really do. He's half saint, and half con man. He's a nice guy and an asshole."

"He's being human. Put yourself in his place."

"I *am* putting myself in his place. That seems to be the problem."

"Don't get upset," he said, reclining in his chair, in a counterfeit display of perfect ease, even of boredom. "You know, I think it's this *café* that makes you upset."

"Yes." That was true; I hated Café Marly, with its snotty, stuck-up waiters and pretentious décor. I hated most Parisian cafés, because I hated spending money on snotty, stuck-up waiters, and I thought doing so would eventually make me snotty and stuck-up and complacent. I was merely being snobby and stuck-up and complacent in my own, much higher way, but I liked to think of it as virtuous economy. I had found my yellow rose in the street, shorn and abandoned, and I had felt sympathy for the wasted pretty flower; so I had put it in my buttonhole and decided to give it a tour of Paris before it definitely died. I had found it only a few hours before Edward called me.

"Perhaps if you avoided this café you would be less angry," Edward said, half in jest.

"Perhaps if I avoided *Darren* I would be less angry," I said.

"You're not angry. You're angry at him for dying, because you care for him."

I glared at him. I did not like having this said.

"You do. I've seen this before. And it is *such* an awful death, Philippe. It's such a horrible way to go."

"There are millions who go just as horribly."

"Yes, but you don't *know* them. You know Darren. He wanted you to know him so you could memorialize him for everybody who didn't know him in person. He knows that it's his last chance." He looked at me. I was sullen. "There's no shame in caring for him."

"He's an asshole."

"So are we all, under duress."

"Him especially."

"He's dying especially."

"That's no excuse."

"I know you think what's *right*. But you must think about what's human. Darren isn't a Dean Moriarty. He's not a con man. He's never hurt you voluntarily."

"Do you know what he said, once?" I said. I was angry now. "I came to this café once, completely wrecked after living with him and writing about him for three weeks, and he saw this, and he said, 'I'm glad to see you're stressed. Good.' He *really* said that. That *really* happened." I had closed my eyes and was fighting back emotions.

"Easy," Edward said; he touched my hand.

"Don't—touch me," I said.

"Fine."

You old fag, I thought, but I didn't say this. "Excuse me," I said, sighing heavily.

"No problem. Have some more tea." He ordered some more tea; with my eyes closed tightly, I could hear him ordering; he had a perfectly satisfactory French.

"You know," said Edward, "your character in the novel is not going to get much sympathy if he keeps losing his temper. Right now, 'Darren' is a lot more sympathetic than 'Philippe.'"

"I built it that way. I made it that way, on purpose. I left out Darren's worst defects, the actions I consider to be criminal."

"What actions are those?" he asked.

I smiled thinly but with my eyes shut tight. "You'll have to read the critical essays," I said, and then I heard my second cup of tea arrive.

And I wondered what a surprise Edward Gray would have when he found the conversation I imagined in the novel about Darren.

Edward Gray, I thought, might have won the race to my telephone, but I had gotten nothing from him except a dialogue and a mint tea. So I decided to call William Abrahams. Six weeks had passed since I had last called. This time, I steeled my nerve and resolved that I would at least introduce myself. I dialed the number and waited.

"Hello?" someone said.

Now or never, I thought. "Good afternoon," I said, in a fragrant, soft voice. "May I speak to William Abrahams?"

"That's me."

"This is Philippe Tapon, calling from Paris. I—er—"

"Oh! I'm so glad you called! I'm just about to type out a short letter—"

A *short* letter? That clearly meant, *No thanks, please go away.*

"—to tell you I'm sending the manuscript to John Hawk, an agent in New York whom I know and respect. Even if I should decide to do your book I would want you to have an agent—it simplifies things."

"Oh! Does it?"

"Unless you've sent it to someone else already. Have you?"

"No." That was a lie. Halfway through I'd sent it to an agent in London, and I'd been turned down. But I would change that in the book. So far as the legendary Mr. Abrahams knew, no one else had seen it.

"Good!" he exclaimed. "Your novel is very, very good," he said.

"It is?"

"Oh, yes. But I would think about cutting the final chapters."

"Cutting!" I said.

"Or at least revising them. Is that troublesome?" he asked.

"Cutting! It's just difficult."

"Yes, well—many things about this novel are going to be 'difficult,' as you say."

"But *what* can I do with those chapters?" I asked, helplessly.

"Oh, many things, I think. Cut them. Or present new material. If you have it; if you can imagine it."

"Er—I guess so."

He caught my hesitation. "May I ask you a few questions? Which you needn't answer."

"Yes, yes," I answered precipitously. "I know what you're going to ask. Most of the novel is *true*," I said.

"No, no, it's not about that. What I wanted to ask you is, why Café Marly? When I went there, I didn't think it was so great."

Good Lord, he'd been there. This was a *serious* reader.

"Well, Darren thought it was a good place to drink."

"Hmm," he said.

"Well, I didn't agree with him," I said. "And I hated the snotty, stuck-up waiters."

"So Darren is his real name."

"Yes."

"Hmm. Still, Café Marly was a good place for you to seek advice from 'Edward Gray.' "

"Yes, it was."

" 'Edward Gray.' Hmm. I believe I know who you're talking about; in fact, it would be difficult *not* to know who you're talking about. He gave you some very good advice. You should think about what he said."

"Mr. Abrahams, I am so sorry. That conversation was made up. It never happened," I said, slowly savoring this major victory over my *serious* reader. "That's one point for me, I'm afraid." The old killer instinct.

"You made it up?"

"Entirely."

"Well then—you—you—gave *yourself* some good advice." He pondered. "Did you really make it up?"

"Yes."

"It sounds so much like him. Well. But perhaps you should change his name one degree further, move it a bit further along the spectrum."

"How?"

"Perhaps Edward *Pink*?"

My face blasted into laughter.

"Ahem," he said. "We haven't had that part of the conversation."

"What conversation?" I said, still tittering.

"That's what I said."

"Do you really like the novel?"

"Do I like it? Let me tell you what I plan to do. I will recommend that Gerontion make a bid for the novel. So I may be your editor—that's if we can work together. We shall see."

"I see."

"You will hear from John Hawk in four weeks. He will tell you what future is in store for the book."

"Time future," I said.

"Time future and time past. Oh, I'm so glad you like Eliot. We at least have one point in common."

"At the still point of the turning world."

"The still point! Goodness! Well, think about time present. Right now you must cut, revise, improve."

Immediately after that I wrote a letter to Andrew. Andrew had returned to Denver and had written to me, asking how the novel was going, and so forth. I had delayed a response but now could wait no longer.

Dear Andrew,

I received your letter (the one you sent on green paper). Thanks very much, again, for all the goodies you left on my doorstep the morning you left. The anthology has been especially amazing; I have been using it to make all sorts of discoveries about allusions. Here is The Waste Land*:*

> *At the violet hour, when the eyes and back*
> *Turn upward from the desk, when the human engine waits*
> *Like a taxi throbbing waiting . . .*

And here is Gatsby*:*

> *Again at eight o'clock when the dark lanes of the Forties were five deep with throbbing taxicabs . . .*

Again, Eliot in Prufrock*:*

> *Shall I say, I have gone at dusk through narrow streets*
> *And watched the smoke that rises from the pipes*
> *Of lonely men in shirt-sleeves, leaning out of windows?*

Fitzgerald:

> *At the enchanted metropolitan twilight I felt a haunting loneliness sometimes, and felt it in others—poor young clerks who loitered in front of windows . . .*

Allusions? Or coincidence? I suppose I'll have to read the "critical heritage" to find out.

I am debating with myself about the relative value of using explicit allusions or of cloaking them. Somehow a disguised, restrained allusion seems more refined, more ambiguous, and more susceptible to multiple interpretations—hence, more artistic. On the other hand a direct quote is quicker to the point, stronger perhaps, and hence—more artistic? I don't know.

The novel is done. I have an editor who says he is interested—we shall see. I am winding down a little. I keep working part-time in a bank, which is not as bad as it sounds, because I don't have to wear a tie and I can walk to work, though occasionally I take the bus, which is direct and uncrowded. The bus goes along the quais from the Sixth to the Seventh, right past your old house. For doing graphs and translating brochures I earn 40F an hour, which sucks, but is better than nothing.

Towards the end the novel got very difficult. Partly due to time (it seemed I was always revising, working, teaching, eating, or cleaning up my room) but also due to feeling (I was having difficulty expressing feelings about Darren I didn't dare express earlier—more intense feelings, both of love and hatred). It seemed ridiculous to get stuck right at the end; the last pages were the most difficult. I thought I would have a nervous breakdown the morning after I finished the first draft. Darren doesn't yet know it's finished. I am afraid that as soon as I tell him he will try to take the manuscript and run. I will tell him, of course, but only once I am sure he will acknowledge I wrote it alone, sort of. I scrupulously wrote up the conversation you and I had, and that is that. I refuse to revise any longer. (Do you object to going in the novel as "Andrew"?)

In order to avoid the temptation to endlessly rewrite, I do a lot of fucking around in the garden, so to speak. I began wrestling again, with a club not far from the Louvre; wrestling is an excellent excuse not to write. Besides, the wrestling is great; all the guys (and the 2 girls) are really nice and the coach is demanding but kind—the best kind of coach. I wrestle twice a week, for 2 hours at a time; it's great.

Darren is in Mont-Louis now, about an hour's train ride from Barcelona. By a tacit agreement there is no communication whatsoever between us. Tacit—he called me four or five times before I finally got the nerve to say that talking to him was oppressive. You know, I think I really care for him, but at the same time I think he's a bit of an asshole. I always keep wondering if we would have been friends if not for the novel. Of course, that's a useless, speculative question—but I can't help asking it anyway. I want this whole Darren project to end. I've gotten tired of it. Strange: having finished the writing, I am beginning to feel more pent-up than ever, because anxieties about this project can no longer be released in writing. I have promised myself to sit tight, revise nothing, relax, and wait for publishers to write to me.

This morning in the metro I saw the child with Down's syndrome again. He looked awfully needy, his palm turned upwards at me, and when he fixed me with his eyes I could almost hear them beg. He passed down the aisle. Then, before he had gone, a man came in to sell loops of red ribbons. He said he was an HIV-positive person. The ribbon he was selling cost ten francs of which six went to AIDS research and four went to him. I could not imagine what four francs could buy him, in Paris. He was wearing an Irish hat. He looked very tired and gaunt. Then I noticed he looked like Darren; his hair was a dull blond color. When I realized this I turned my face to the door of the metro so no one could see my expression. I felt very moved. Then all of a sudden I started to cry. I did not want anybody in the metro to see me crying, so I raised a hand to the side of my face and held on to the metro banister with my other hand. I was counting the moments up to my station. Finally my station came up and I walked out quickly on the metro platform, shielding my face from the looks of passersby with a flat hand. I did not stop crying for a while; even after I was out in the open, I felt badly. I got to work feeling worn-out and clean in the way crying makes you feel. I could not work; I had to write out what had just happened, what I have just recopied.

I was no longer writing a letter; I was writing my novel. I had started the letter to Andrew as a letter, on letter paper, but had finished by revising it into the manuscript. I finished off as lightly as I could.

Take care and good luck. Regards to everybody.

Yours from the frying pan,

Philippe

The incident in the metro really did happen.

That was the last month before John Hawk called—telling me what the novel was destined for, in time future.

CHAPTER 17

A year later, my novel about Darren would be published. All sorts of things happened before that and after that. The immediate result was that I came into some money from Gerontion, as an advance, and was able to repay Darren the loan I'd owed him while writing the book.

When he had been in the monastery in Sénanque, he had written me a postcard, saying the food was good, the weather was fine, he had talked to God, and so forth; I had placed the card on my desk, where it lay like a window to a silent landscape for several weeks. Then the phone rang in my deux-pièces.

"Philippe? It's Darren."

"I know. I can tell. Hello."

"How are you, Philippe?"

"I'm fine. Better than ever."

"Good—very good. Because I'm back in Paris!"

"Paris?"

"And—I have lots more material for you."

"More material? Hmm," I said. I had taken up my hmm from William Abrahams, about whom Darren had heard nothing, yet.

"Yes," he said, *"more* writing for the book. More material. Oh, Philippe—I just never stop generating material. My life— it's so—"

"Let me guess, Darren: extraordinary?"

"Oh, *yes*, Philippe, that expresses it perfectly! So many things have happened. Mystical things. And—Philippe—something else. For the first time since 1988, there is hope. There is hope, Philippe, there is hope!"

"Hope for what?" I asked.

"You'll see. Your next chapter's going to be about hope!"

I debated whether to say right away that there were going to be no more chapters. The book was done, I wanted to say. But Darren in his ecstasy rode over my objections.

"Oh—I've got so many, many things to tell you, Philippe. How can I even begin? How? Lunch?" he offered. "At the Marly?"

So we agreed to meet at the Marly.

When I arrived, Darren was at his usual place. It was a crisp spring day; the sunlight was falling in slanted beams into the arcades. I was carrying my completed manuscript in my leather satchel. That satchel had once held Darren's imaginary leg; now it was holding his entire imaginary life. I had resolved that no matter what Darren told me, the book was done, and I would not revise it anymore.

"Hello, Darren."

"Hi!"

"You look well, Darren."

"Oh, I feel so great. So many things have happened. Did you bring your notebook? I hope so. Because you have a lot of notes to take."

I sat down heavily and put the satchel carrying my copy of *A Parisian from Kansas* next to me. I crossed my hands on my lap and looked at Darren.

"No," I said. "I don't have my notebook."

"What's in your satchel?" he asked.

"First tell me all about where you spent your winter," I said.

"Philippe: I was in Sénanque. It was incredible."

Sénanque was in the mountains—and I imagined that in winter, with the birds gone, the cold monastery was enclosed in complete silence.

"I suppose you could listen to yourself out there," I said.

"Not just to yourself, Philippe. To nature. To the voice of God."

I did not let my expression change. I knew this mood of his, and I had to wait patiently while he got himself out of it—the scarred prophet coming down from the mountaintop.

"I know God, Philippe. I know Him. He has spoken to me. And He has given me his revelation."

I crossed my arms.

"And He has told me—there is a cure."

"Oh, really."

"There is a cure. Yes. A cure. I saw a newspaper at the monastery—in the library. It was next to the holy illuminated Bible, open to a page that said: 'You shall live forever.' And Philippe: there is a doctor—in Amsterdam—who has discovered the cure."

"That's very good news, Darren."

"So I'm going to Amsterdam. Philippe—I'm not going to die. Because—there is this doctor in Amsterdam, who has found the cure."

"What is the doctor's name?" I asked.

"I wrote it down," Darren said. "I've got his name and his address. I've got everything. I'm leaving for Amsterdam on a train, first class, tomorrow morning." He looked at me. I lowered my eyes.

"That's quite a piece of news," I said.

"That, Philippe, should be the ending of the book. The new ending. Now, do you want to come with me, and watch this cure take place?"

"I would like to, Darren, truly. But I have my job here."

"I can pay your way, and you can take time off. Philippe, this is going to be one of the most important events in history."

I looked away, my lips tight.

"I have other responsibilities—Darren. English lessons," I said. "Wrestling," I said.

"You're wrestling?" he asked. "In Paris?"

"Twice a week."

"Well, Philippe, good for you."

"Yeah, good for me." I cleared my throat. "But I'm sorry. I

cannot go to Amsterdam with you. I'll write about you, when you get back. Will you come back? After you're cured?"

"Oh, of course, of course! After I'm cured, I want to do it all. People, parties, places—traveling. Philippe—when I'm cured, I want the most *gigantic* party for me in Paris!"

"Plan on it, Darren. Plan on it. What else happened at Sénanque? In the way of . . ."

"Miracles? There was one other miracle," Darren said. "But more gross. I managed to masturbate. First time in two years."

"Fantastic."

"The color was a bit off," he said, "but at least there was something."

"There's still hope, Darren."

"Oh, there's more than hope, Philippe. The sun has risen. My long night has finally ended."

I leaned into my chair and crossed my legs and arms.

"Now you see, Philippe, why I wanted you to take notes."

"Yes, Darren, I see."

"So. Tell me what you've been doing—I want to see your manuscript."

"You'll see it."

"Good! When is it going to be finished?"

I cleared my throat. "Well, actually, it's finished already."

"It's finished! Congratulations! Wow!"

I nodded.

"Have you told anybody?" he asked.

"A few persons," I said.

"Who?" he asked.

"Andrew," I said.

"Great! Who else?"

"A few other persons."

"Does Jean-Baptiste know?"

"No. Not really."

"Well! Wait till I tell him. Incredible! I'm sure it's a master-piece, Philippe."

"Thanks. Really."

"Philippe, I do so want to start editing it. Philippe, you can't imagine how enthusiastic I am about editing it."

"Er, yes, Darren. Actually—"

"You want another editor? Jean-Baptiste maybe?"

"Er—no, Darren. Not Jean-Baptiste. But—I think I already have an editor."

"Another editor? Andrew?" he asked.

"No, not Andrew," I said. "William Abrahams."

"Who's he?"

"He's an editor."

"Well, that still means you have to sell the book. This is where I come in. I can sell the book, act as your agent."

"Er—actually, I already have an agent."

"You already have an agent," he repeated.

"John Hawk. In New York. I gave him the manuscript."

"You *gave* him the manuscript!"

"Yes. I did. But I have a copy here, in case you want to see it." And I put the fat manuscript on the table where the sunbeams lit up the title: A PARISIAN FROM KANSAS, in capital letters.

Darren stared at the rectangular white apparition.

"Fantastic," he said.

Darren looked at it, thumbed the pages in disbelief. He was thinking of how to congratulate me.

"You *bitch*," he said finally, affectionately and yet with some anger. "You might have *told* me you'd gone to a literary agent."

"I did tell you," I said. That was true; I'd told him once, in the manuscript, but he thought I had made it up.

We parted, after some chitchat about the trains to Amsterdam; and I did not expect to see Darren for a few months at least. But three days later, I got a phone call.

"Philippe?"

"Darren! Where are you?"

"Back in Paris."

"Paris! Did you not go to Amsterdam?"

"I did."

"And . . . ?"

Darren hesitated. "It was a hoax. A fucking hoax for stupid HIV idiots grabbing at anything. Oh, Philippe. It was awful. He wanted me to sign away my checking accounts—this ugly man with a glass eye. He wouldn't show me the least piece of paper until I had handed over my credit cards. Not a hospital—not a doctor—just some . . . *quack!*"

He breathed into the mouthpiece for a long while. I thought he had been crying.

"Where are you now?" I asked.

"I'm back at Pasteur. That's what I'm calling you about," he said. "Looks like the arm's gonna come off."

"I'll be right there."

"Oh, and Philippe—"

"Yes?"

"The trip was not a complete waste. I tanked up on enough Amsterdamer Specials to last me until the cows come home. So now, come what may, I'm in a *good mood.*"

That afternoon I was back in the Institut Pasteur. So were Marzenna and Francesco. It was warm; the wide windows were open; the smell of the gardens below was drifting up, lazily, and clouds moved slowly between the red brick towers of the hospital. Darren was hospitalized for an infection inside his elbow. This time the rumor was that his whole arm would have to come off.

"If they do take it off," I said, "I'd like to keep it. As a form of souvenir."

Darren howled at that. "Put it on your wall!"

"People will say, 'Gee, that looks like an arm on the wall, Philippe.' 'Well, it is an arm,' I'll say. 'It belonged to Darren. Yes—*the* Darren Swenson.' " Both Darren and I closed our eyes because we were laughing so hard. "Let's not be conventional like other people. You see, other people would want a lock of your hair or your jockstrap. But me, I want your arm. Any other parts of your body you want to give up?"

"You can have it all!" Darren roared.

"No, no, not for me. Not that part. Save it for Chet."

"Oh, God!" Darren howled.

We both took long, deep breaths and tried to recover some dignity. Marzenna and Francesco raised their eyebrows and shook their heads. Darren and I were incomprehensible with our cruel jokes and violent possible futures.

"*The* Darren Swenson" had become a new kind of pep-talk phrase between us. We didn't use "*Dead* John" so much anymore, because Darren seemed nearly dead himself sometimes. I was again reduced to a kind of pep-talk, cheerleading

position—but that didn't annoy me now. I had finished my
novel. Darren had read and liked it. He was sort of forced to like
it, because barring a medical miracle, he was going to die, in a
matter of months, or weeks. So I became intent on making his
last moments as endurable, even as *fun*, as I could. Accordingly
his room was filled with redolent orchids and the beat, beat, beat
of Bronski Beat. Some of the nurses thought the music was great
for dancing. They continued bringing Darren six meals a day,
which he ate hungrily, though without gaining any weight. And
every day, together, we read the papers.

I normally did not read the papers; I was always, as a rule,
more interested in my make-believe world than in what was
going on outside. But now, suddenly, *I* was "going on"; more
precisely, *Darren* was "going on"; still more precisely, the book
about Darren was on its way to being published.

I had learned this the first time I spoke to John Hawk, who
called me exactly when William Abrahams had said he would:
four weeks later. The telephone had rung in my deux-pièces.

"*Allô?*" I had said.

"*Allô, puis-je parler à Philippe Tapon?*"

"*Oui monsieur, c'est moi.*"

"Philippe, this is John Hawk—literary agent in New York?
I'm representing your book. Billy has told you, I suppose?"

"Oh! Yes, yes. He has."

"How are you?" he asked. "Everyone's been wondering
how you are, who you are, where you are—well, I suppose we
know where you are. You're in a—let me get this right: a
'deux-pièces in Saint-Germain-des-Prés'?"

"Yes, I am. Truly."

"And are you truly Philippe Tapon? Is that your real name?"

"Yes."

"No 'sort of'? No 'fiction meets reality,' no . . . ?"

"That's my real name—my own name."

"Good! Now then—your novel. Well. I read it. This
weekend. I loved it. I mean, I really, really loved it, Philippe.
Have you been writing long?"

"Er . . . no. This is my first novel."

"Ah—this is your first novel, you said? Did I get that right?"

"Er . . . yes."

"How old are you, may I ask?"

"Twenty-seven."

"I see." He paused. "How did you hear about Billy Abrahams?"

"I read an article about him, which my mother sent to me."

"Do you know who he is?"

"Er . . . well, he's William Abrahams, the editor."

"Yes, but do you know what that means? His wanting to edit your first novel?"

"No."

He chuckled a little maliciously. "Well," he said. "You *will* know, someday. Billy wants—*your*—*novel*. And what Billy wants, Billy gets. Interesting man to work with, as you'll find out. I once heard an *à propos* crack about him. In fiction, he likes the omniscient narrator, because in reality he is the omniscient editor of the book business. Truly. Now, Philippe, the point of this call—besides actually speaking to you—by the way, Philippe, I'm so *curious* to meet you! You can't imagine the debates you've sparked around the office! Is he real? Is he fake? Is Philippe Darren? Is Darren Philippe? And so on, every possible permutation. Well—okay. The point. Philippe, I have here a letter from—Gerontion! Congratulations! They've offered to buy your work."

I could not speak.

"Conditionally," he said. He chuckled softly. "Ah yes. Conditionally. The condition is not in the contract, but I know what it is. Yes indeedy. You must change all references to Chester Hyland. Hyland just happens to own one-half of American publishing. Otherwise, no deal. So what say you, Philippe? Will you do it?"

John Hawk, as I later learned, was something of a marketing shark. He had come to the belief that writers were like commodities that had to be hawked at bazaars, and it was better for them to be visible, attention-getting, and for their books to be valuable but approachable, exciting yet traditional, intellectual yet accessible—in short, all things to all people. Thus, in his letter to his friend and business associate Ms. A——, he had written:

A Parisian from Kansas is an AIDS novel—the central
character's struggle with the illness at the end of his short
life is at once the departure and arrival of the story. But
it is not just an AIDS novel. *A Parisian from Kansas*
positively teems with literary references—questioning,
exploring, confronting, philosophical, literary, and metaphysical ideas, with humor, intelligence, and grace.

John Hawk was well named, I thought. Mister Hawk! It was
destiny.

. . . I cannot even begin to tell you how passionately
it alludes to such American classics as *The Great Gatsby* or
The Sun Also Rises or *On the Road*. Nor can I relate to
you how it draws upon the poetry of T. S. Eliot. . . .
Tapon's wit and imagination, his own brand of magi-
cal realism, in which the dead speak, in which characters
travel through time and space, and in which the impossible becomes possible, is the best advertisement for this
novel.
I think the novel will sell, not just because it has
genuine literary merit, but because it is an AIDS novel,
and suddenly AIDS is fashionable again. The novel certainly deserves your closest attention. There may even be
a movie in it.
Yours,
John

I would have preferred to write:

A novel about a novel written about, and for, a
Kansan living in Paris who is dying very young.

Of course that was not what Ms. A—— would want to hear.
And John's marketing copy seemed as poetic as a Homeric
simile compared to what Ms. A—— sent her colleagues.
APFK:
    –readable, meaty
    –PC but not overwhelmingly so (AIDS gay etc)
    –publishable: 1000 pp (can be cut)

–possible movie interest among young experimental directors

But the nadir of reductionism was probably reached in the boardroom, where an executive said, very simply, "This novel is a *buy*." So was that month's diet book.

However, the company lawyers had hesitated.

"What about the name? Not just any name: *Hyland*."

Their objections got back to John.

"You must change all references to Chester Hyland," they told him.

"You must change all references to Chester Hyland," he told me. "Otherwise, no deal. So what say you, Philippe? Will you do it?"

"Yes," I said. "In fact, nothing could be easier."

"Darren," I said, "Panic! Chet Hyland has got to be *removed* from the book!"

"Removed? Why?!" Darren demanded. "What about our disclaimer? Isn't that good enough?"

"It isn't," I said. "We're stuffed. Unless Chet personally guarantees that he won't come after us."

"Well, in that case," said Darren, "*I* can talk to him."

"Oh, boy," I said.

"No, really. I can talk to him."

"Jesus, Darren. What is this? Are you going to get a gentleman's agreement out of him?"

"Just let me talk to him."

"Darren, you can *sleep* with him for all I care. It's not *me* you have to convince. It's not even him, really. It's the publishers that have to be convinced."

"Well, I'll call him."

"Oh, boy," I said. "Excuse me while I hold my breath."

"Hold your breath, then. I'll call you back."

I held my breath a week and had died a thousand times before he called me back.

"Too late," I said. "The book's already been published; I've already been sued and imprisoned. But it's touching, and a little surprising, to see that you still *care*."

"Chester Hyland," Darren answered solemnly, "wants to meet you."

"What?!" I said. I had expected every reaction except that one. "Why should he want to meet *me*? Tell him I'm not available," I said.

"He'll be in Paris next Thursday and he wants to take us out to dinner."

"At the Tour d'Argent?"

"Maybe." The Tour d'Argent was one of the super-snobby restaurants Darren enjoyed criticizing. He thought their presentation of a card commemorating each service of a Canard de Cent Ans was incredibly gauche. I remembered, with a pang of regret, that he had wanted me to mention that in the novel, and I had not.

"Café Marly?" I suggested.

"The food there's not that great," Darren said. He was in his element now. Nothing pleased him more than making snobby distinctions between super-snobby restaurants.

"Arpège?" I asked. I was smiling. I had never had dinner at any of these places, and actually feared that regularly dining there would lull me into fat complacency.

"Not bad, and close to where you live."

"Maxim's?"

"Ugh! Too full of tourists. Too full of Americans."

Obviously we had better steer clear of the Americans.

"Matsuya's?" I asked.

"Now there's a thought."

"Unpretentious. And refined."

"We'll let Chet decide."

"If I have to pay, though, it'll be cold cuts at my flat."

"Oh, he'll pay, don't worry about that. You remember, he gave me two thousand dollars, when I was in New York with Jean-Baptiste, to make sure we had a great time."

"Oh, yeah." That was another incident I'd forgotten to put in the novel. There seemed to be thousands of them.

"So he'll take care of everything."

"*Why* does he want to meet me?"

"Well, because you're brilliant and because you're holding his life in your hands."

Oh, great. This was the road to complacency, no doubt about it.

"Brilliant," I repeated.

"Brilliant you are, Philippe. The novel is incredible."

"It's not even published yet!"

"It doesn't have to be published to be brilliant. And that's what Chet wants to talk to you about."

"He wants his name changed, doesn't he?"

I caught the pause in the conversation. Darren never lied, but he omitted things, and I knew when. "Aha," I said.

"Weeelll—" Darren said, "he didn't *say* anything about that."

"But he would rather we not."

"That's the impression I got."

"Well. The truth is, if I'm going to undress him in the book, I'm going to have to undress myself, and in just the same way. But I know I wouldn't want that. Fair is fair. The Golden Rule."

"But you do undress in the book."

"Not the way I undress Chet. No—I think what he's asking for is fair. Ultimately, of course"—I felt important saying this—"the name will be changed to what it was in reality. The book doesn't really work as an aesthetic object unless the name is the name in real life."

"Philippe, if changing the name takes away the *slightest* aesthetic consideration—"

"No no no no no no no. No consideration to be speaking of. And it can wait until we're all dead. The book will stand up even if we change the name."

"Fine. *Now* will you dine with Chet Hyland?"

"Jesus Christ, why shouldn't I? Tell him to arrive in one of those cars."

"The dinner might be black tie."

"Oh, well then, forget it. I never dine in anything but tails."

"But it'll probably be more casual."

"It'd better be; I can hardly fit in my dinner jacket."

Since I had taken up wrestling again, my shoulders were back to their college proportions.

"Shall I tell Chet you accept? Dinner will be next Thursday at eight o'clock. We'll meet at Jean-Baptiste's flat."

"Tour d'Argent, next Thursday, eight o'clock. Fine. I'll be there. Tell him I want to meet his wife."

"Philippe, you're such a bitch, I swear!"

"I'm not writing anymore, remember? I have no more sympathy for anybody. I can say whatever I want. Tell that nouveau riche shlomo fag that I don't drink *young* Dom Pérignon."

"Yes," he said, and we said good-bye and hung up. I smiled. I was not often summoned to the tables of the mighty and it felt both good and nerve-wracking. I assumed this was the beginning of complacency, the end of literary struggle, the beginning of a career in letters, and of course the beginning of my artistic decline. Nothing ruined young artists faster than the rich. No— perhaps success ruined artists. Or perhaps women ruined artists, or perhaps lack of women, or lack of success. Perhaps artists only ruined themselves. Or perhaps they had no control over it; producing good art was not something you chose. It either happened to you, or it didn't. Perhaps it had happened to me with the novel about Darren, and I thought, why not reap the rewards? It was quite beyond my control whether I could ever write well again. Maybe in the future I would be able to get some good complacent writing out of my future complacency. I knew that if things went wrong, I would turn to the first of virtues, both of life and of literature: humility. Humility was the only wisdom I knew.

Endlessly my thoughts about the novel fermented at night, when I couldn't sleep, because the evening wrestling practices excited me preposterously and made me want marathon bouts of reading, writing, and prowling about, when I should have been resting. I *should* have been resting after finishing my novel about Darren, and instead I found myself revising and revising.

Can't teach an old dog new tricks, I wrote.

But I tried to ignore small mistakes. Darren's sickness had forced me to get the manuscript out in the fastest way possible, and I was ready to accept name changes, imperfections—typographical errors, even. If *Four Quartets* in its English edition had misspelled "Every" as "Evey," and if *Garp* had dozens of typos, I would have to accept a few. Evey book has its problems.

Omniscient William Abrahams called me virtually every day, once the editing began. On the first day, I said into the phone, "Mr. Abrahams?"

"None of this last-name formality. Not anymore. You will call me Billy."

"Yes Billy," I said.

My omniscient editor suggested *lots* of changes, and we haggled about them, one by one, in each day's phone call.

"And what about *this* dialogue? What's happening *here*?" he asked.

"Not much happens, I agree."

"Well, you know what to do. Cut, revise, improve. Cut."

So day by day, I felt I was putting more and more of my book and my life in his hands. But finally, quickly, the editing was done, and Billy said, "You've done a marvelous job, Philippe. Ann Marlowe, the copy editor, says the manuscrapt is very clean. I wish you could see some of the horrors we've had to work with. Now, have you thought about the Chet Hyland name change?"

"The personality change," I corrected.

"The address change," said Darren.

"Yes, I have. I have a new name. Here it is."

I said it.

"That's a good name," Darren said.

"That's a perfect name," said Billy.

"That's a marvelous name," said John.

Thus did Chet Hyland disappear from the fictional work, *A Parisian from Kansas*. But, in real life, we accepted his dinner invitation, and in turn invited him to the big, big party we planned for Darren. Everyone was invited; we were determined everyone would have a great time.

"This is *great* stuff," John Hawk said. "You're almost done with this revision. Now, I'm assuming it's all fiction, as Billy told me."

"Sort of. Most of what I said he said is *true*."

"Are you sure about that?"

"Truth and fiction are relative notions, John."

"Oh, boy," said John. "Let me tell you what. I'll call Billy, right now, and he'll call you. We need to get this fiction-reality stuff worked out before we go ahead. Fair?"

"Fair."

Five minutes later, Billy called.

"John Hawk is fairly off his head because of the 'fiction-reality stuff,' as he elegantly termed it. Now, Philippe, I am going to ask you a question, which I've not dared ask before. I want your answer to be absolutely honest. How much of this novel is true?"

"All of it," I said.

"Hmm."

"Well, sort of," I added.

"Hmm. Is that your best answer?"

"Yes."

"Then that'll have to do, I'm afraid. It will do, actually. Do you know how you got me, Philippe? It was your description of my friend 'Edward Gray.' I can't get over it. I asked myself, can he really have imagined him? Tell me, Philippe—between ourselves—*did* you imagine that conversation?"

"Well—Café Marly exists. I had lunch there, many times. With Darren."

"Does Darren exist?"

"Sort of."

"Oh, let me tell that to your agent. That should make him shriek. As for me, I haven't heard a word. As far as I'm concerned, this is a work of pure fiction."

"If you say so, Billy."

He hung up and John Hawk called me back.

"John, it's a work of pure fiction," I said.

"If you say so, Philippe." I heard him smiling on the phone. "If you say so. That will have to do. It will do. But you know, Philippe, Billy says he has never ever published a book like this."

"What, on the phone?"

"No, a self-referential novel with *him* in it. Or with *me* in it."

"It's my first time, too. There is a time for everything."

"Are you going to throw your big party now? I would like to meet you and Darren in person."

"Oh, of course! We'll invite you and Billy," I said, expansively. "We're going to bring a big boom box and dance along the quais. Everyone in the novel that can come will be there."

"You will do this as soon as it's published?"

"Maybe even before. As soon as possible, really. With Darren's health and all, we can't have a party soon enough. Each party may be his last, he keeps telling me. So come on over to Paris. Is the novel now going to be published?"

"Yes."

"Hurray!"

"You know, Philippe—you seem rather different over the phone than you did in the novel. I inferred you were a quiet listener, indecisive and thoughtful. Instead I find you're dynamic and thrusting and—"

I laughed.

"It's *true*," he added, nicely.

"I'm completely unlike myself in the whole novel. It is just a novel, remember?" I said that as if it were an advertising jingle. "The me of the first part, before the novel pivots, is different from the me of the second—that much is true."

"I particularly liked the way it pivots."

"The pivot point was taken straight out of *Garp*: 'Bensenhaver.' John Irving gets all the credit."

"Maybe you'll get to meet him, once he knows you exist."

"I could agree to meet him in the wrestling room." Although even there, I knew, he would make me struggle for every point.

John Irving was the only living writer I wanted to meet. But I had been too shy to send him a manuscript or even to try to imagine a conversation with him. I was afraid that if we did speak it would go something like this:

"You been writing long?" he would ask.

I would clear my throat. "A few years, now."

I would clear my throat, again, and wait for the uncomfortable silence to gather. After all, he was the old weather-beaten published and republished and re-republished and made-for-movie novelist; why should I do any of the talking?

I could imagine myself asking, "Do you like Conrad?" and then wincing at what a stupid, awful question that would be—and be quite glad I didn't ask it.

He would be thinking, If we were to *wrestle*, would he find it easier to speak to me? And then he asked (in my imagination), "You been wrestling long?"

"A few years," I would say. "But I'm no good," I would add, hastily, in case he should challenge me to a duel on the mat. I had no doubt he would trounce me and I imagined spending a nasty five minutes while he "played" with me, my shoulder sliding around on the mat, back arched furiously and sore for several days afterward. He would play with me awhile and then pin me utterly.

"You've got good technique," I could hear him saying. "You just need more training. Endurance."

You need a lot of endurance to be a novelist, I would think, and I was learning you could not have too much endurance for a self-referent novel that just went on and on and on.

"Thanks."

"It's not a compliment. You need to get in shape."

"All right."

He looked down at me.

"Can I ask you . . . what you think of my writing?" I asked. I had taken a knee on the soft, spongy wrestling mat.

"Not bad. Not bad at all. Quite acceptable, really, given your lamentable physical condition."

I was still wheezing; the "playing around" had completely cut my wind.

"It's awful," I said; I meant my physical conditioning.

"It's not bad," he said; he meant my writing.

"You know—" I said, between gasping, short breaths, "I went over the manuscript—looking for any good old semicolons I could use."

"Good old semicolons," said John Irving.

"I have sympathy for them. There are so many semicolons desperately wanting to be used. I will always try to remember them," I said.

John Irving sat next to me on the mat; a single drop of sweat fell from his big fat head of hair. With a terrific deadpan he spoke the last line he spoke in my novel.

"You will *always* have memory."

CHAPTER 18

The dinner with Chet Hyland at the Tour d'Argent was at first supposed to be black-tie, and then demoted to business suit, then finally to blazer and tie. Darren was now thinking he would dispense with the tie altogether.

"I look ridiculous with this collar fastened. Look at me. You can see this vast gap where my *neck* used to be." He threw the tie down in disgust on Jean-Baptiste's floor. He did not exactly live in Jean-Baptiste's flat, but he more or less lived out of it. The flat was on the ground floor, which was good for wheelchairs. Also, Jean-Baptiste still had compassion for Darren.

The hour before we left was a nightmare of Darren telling Jean-Baptiste what to do, what to wear, to get this, to get that, to stop being stupid, to stop snapping at him; telling him to shave the hairs off the back of his neck; chiding him for the eleven-thousand-franc phone bill he had never paid back, faithlessness, jealousy, and various other things. It was a grim performance, and I hoped Darren's anxiety would ease off once we were there. I remember Jean-Baptiste, pressured and silent after weeks of ministering to Darren, trying to persuade him to take care of himself, to not smoke so much, to not eat so much, as it complicated his bowels, but Darren would not listen, and almost took a perverse joy in watching Jean-Baptiste grunt and sweat around him. For Darren, it was proof of his existence, and more: proof that Jean-Baptiste still loved him.

But we left on time, piling complicatedly into a taxi, with the wheelchair in the trunk, Jean-Baptiste and me in business suits, Darren in a rumpled polo shirt and well-worn blazer. Traffic was clear and we arrived ahead of schedule. We went up in the lift, and were unprepared to find Chet already at our table, nursing a martini with an olive in it.

"Hello!" he exclaimed.

Darren smiled hugely. It was still, after all, Chet Hyland, and, despite the tacky cards given out with the Canard de Cent Ans, it was still the Tour d'Argent, a silk-smooth, gold-brocaded restaurant. The silverware looked bright enough to blind, and unsmiling waiters, their hands by their sides, carrying no pads, no pens, nothing so vulgar as an *addition*, moved around like slow clockwork on either side of us.

Darren, I could see, was in his element. Practically the entire restaurant had glanced at what was obviously an eccentric billionaire being pushed around in a wheelchair by a handsome steward, accompanied by someone who looked like his bright accountant. And everyone knew who his host was. Nothing could have pleased Darren more; minute by minute, I could see, he was reaching the pinnacle of his existence.

"Hi, Chet."

"Hello, Darren." They shook hands. "What would you like to drink? Hello, Jean-Baptiste."

"Hello, Chet." They shook hands. "How are you?"

"Fine. And you?"

"Fine. Just water, please."

"I'll have an orange juice," Darren said. "I can't drink too much alcohol or my liver will give up entirely."

"Don't worry. We're not here to get drunk." He turned to me. "What would *you* like? I'm assuming that you are Philippe."

"Yes," I said. We shook hands. "How do you do."

"How do you do."

"Malt whisky, please."

"See, Darren, here's a man who *wants* to get drunk."

"Oh, Philippe, don't get drunk and have an attack *here!*"

"Oh no, you *must*," said Chet. "It would be hilarious. I'd like to see what the restaurant would do."

It *would* be hilarious, I thought, but it would go unrecorded; the book was done. I would have to exercise some self-control.

"I liked your breakdowns in the novel," said Chet, to whom we had sent a manuscript.

"Weren't they *great*?" asked Darren.

"It's the only part of the novel that's really real," said Jean-Baptiste, speaking English. "The rest was faked. He made up all the details."

"I'm not sure about *that*," said Chet, smiling at the past, reflected and distorted by a silver spoon. The three drinks had appeared at our table as if by enchantment. Such was the service at the Tour d'Argent.

We lifted the glasses. "Here's to your continued success," Chet said. He was sleek and handsome in his dark suit. His silk waistcoat hinted of a delicious eccentricity, but it was barely visible beneath his high-buttoned jacket. He looked at Darren's open collar.

"Darren, do you *always* dress so formally?" he asked, and Darren laughed. "I don't think I've ever invited this man anywhere," Chet said to Jean-Baptiste and me, smiling, "without him turning up in something calculated to *shock*."

"What a queen I am!" said Darren, his head tilting up; he was laughing, in that silent hysterical way of his, so that it seemed to come from far away.

"What a *size* queen," Chet corrected.

I let out one laugh. He glanced at me and then returned his eyes, full of tenderness, to Darren. "You *had* to tell *all*, I suppose."

"Yes."

"*But* you changed my name. Thank you very much."

"We did."

"I liked the way you did it, too. Very clever, very subtle, almost imperceptible, the way it's done."

"You liked it?" I asked.

"I do. Three-quarters of the way through the book, you realize Chet Hyland is *still* a character in the book. And you think, but isn't his name about to be changed? But you're too late. It already has been changed."

"Chet, you're my dream reader."

"Aren't I, though? But that's a comedown for me. After all, I was nearly Darren's dream *man*."

Our table looked out over the Seine at Notre-Dame bathed in light. All the black-jacketed waiters were moving about the paneled room, silently, thoroughly, moving towards each table, glancing at it for a second, seemingly unseeing, then moving quietly on. Some might have seemed like handsome, brooding adolescents, until anyone with a single raised forefinger indicated a tiny wish. Then they smoothly stepped forward to listen. Ordinary wishes, like water out of silver decanters, or refills of the wine, or refills of the golden bread baskets laden with warm rolls nestled in red cloth, had been anticipated; more unusual wishes, as for gold cigar cutters, or for ancient liqueurs, or to make way for a wheelchair, were granted with a grave nod, or a silent smile on a lean, smooth face, with the corners of the mouth of the waiter turned up in little elegant wrinkles. We were in the high life, I knew, and I looked out the window, and reminded myself that down below was a boy who had to earn a living by faking he had Down's syndrome. But I was sure the boy was ill in some other way. The way his eyes looked at me had been too poignant to forget.

"It hasn't changed," said Darren. He had dined there before, which was why I had wanted to include a Tour d'Argent scene in the novel I wrote about him. I started explaining to Chet how an allusive, self-referent novel about life and death worked, and Darren listened, but without interest. While I spoke, Chet looked at Darren, as if at an old, well-loved but mischievous and incontinent dog that simply refused to give up its bad habits. Jean-Baptiste looked at them both; I looked at Jean-Baptiste. He was the only one who seemed in place—a Parisian in Paris. I felt like a California lumberjack; Chet looked like an English lord.

But Darren—Darren looked skeletal, although surgery had saved his arm, and his voice had not changed. He talked as he had always talked, with intense brilliance, but now his words seemed too big for him, like heavy words thrown by a shadow; and when he looked at me, he focused on me with the roaring, fiery eyes of a prophet.

"This old place still hasn't changed," he repeated. "There's the Seine down there . . . and here are the farm animals," he said, looking at the menu. "Chet, I would rather have *pork* than that damn Canard de Cent Ans."

"Oh, come on, Darren, be a sport. I love watching those ducks getting crushed. Let's *all* order one."

"Yes, let's! That way, we could *all* have a tacky card to take home," Jean-Baptiste said.

"But let's have them bring the cards in numerical order," said Darren. "*You* can have ten thousand and one. *I* can have ten thousand and two. *He* can have ten thousand and three—how appalling."

"Have the caviar for starters," said Chet.

"No, I like *saumon fumé*."

"But smoked salmon is so boring."

"We simply *must* have a decent wine."

"Oh, we will have a decent wine. It may be the only thing we have, but we *will* have it. Do you know," he asked us, "how I soften the trials of aging?"

"No," we said.

"Every year I drink a Château d'Yquem that is as old as I am."

"And how old is that?" asked Darren, smiling.

"Shut your face."

The conversation went on like this. Jean-Baptiste looked from one to the other, grinning, his eyeglasses flashing from side to side. But I felt dark and brooding and silent. I was thinking about the book, and about time future. Although I publicly declared myself completely indifferent about book reviews, secretly I hated and feared them, and I knew my book had all sorts of imperfections.

"What's the matter, Philippe?" Darren said. He was genuinely cheerful. The Tour d'Argent, with Jean-Baptiste, Chet Hyland, and his ghost writer—what could be better? Except another chance, but only I thought that.

I let out a deep breath. "Slightly worried," I said, like a taciturn Westerner.

"Feeling depressed now that's it's done?" asked Chet. "After a big project, everything always seems like a letdown."

"I'm not worried . . . about what's happened. I'm worried about what's . . . to come." I had resisted several times the temptation to recall the manuscript to revise it yet again.

Darren's deteriorating health was pushing me to publish; otherwise the book might have loitered in my flat for years.

"What do you mean, 'what's to come'?" asked Jean-Baptiste.

Our waiter approached. We placed our orders and they
were self-indulgent and luxurious. The wine was going to be
potent.

"Some people will find out what I really think of them,"
I said.

"Like *who*?" said Darren. "I don't care what you've written
about *me*. Everything you said about me was true. I am an egotist and I am obsessed with my mother and I accept that. You
were right to say it."

I admired Darren's capacity to face his defects with so much
candor (something else I had not insisted upon enough).

"And I loved those *great* sex scenes," added Chet. We all
smiled and laughed. "I even like the way *I* come off. Not too
exciting in bed, but you can't have everything."

"Aww!" said Darren, and put his arm around Chet's
shoulder.

Chet pretended to be shocked, but really he was very
pleased. "Heavens, sir! Not before the hors d'oeuvres!"

"But sir, you *are* the hors d'oeuvres."

"Young man, I must ask you not to insist!" said Chet.

"I wish I *had* insisted, when it might have mattered." Darren
sighed. "I know. Not in public," he said, withdrawing himself.

"Oh no, sir. I have my reputation to protect," said Chet,
smoothing imaginary wrinkles out of his lapel. His eyes flashed
around the room and he pretended to be very conscious of
others, but really he was only interested in us and in Darren. He
looked at him, then at me.

"Who is angry at the book?" he asked.

"Who *will* be angry at the book," I corrected.

"All right, who *will* be?"

"I don't know. People."

Chet rolled his eyes and said to Darren, "He is *so* neurotic."
Darren laughed. "I know. But he's a good writer."

"Philippe," Chet said, "someone will always hate you, no
matter what you do. You've written a good book, now forget
about it. It's done. Enjoy life."

"It's hard," I said. My mind was invaded by recriminations. "All the people who will say—"

"What?" asked Jean-Baptiste. "*What* will they say? *Who* will say? *Who?*"

"Critics," I said weakly.

"Oh, God," Chet groaned. "To hell with critics. Fault-finders, that's all they are. Next thing you know, they'll whine about your Tour d'Argent details. Forget about them. Are *you* pleased with the book?"

"Yes," I admitted.

"Were you fair with everybody?"

"As much as I could be."

"Well then, what are you worried about? Darren commissioned it, and Darren is happy."

"I am, Philippe."

"So you see?" Chet said. "No worries. And I had my name changed. So: no—worries. Ah! the wine." He sniffed at it, and smiled. The wine was poured into all our glasses.

"Shall we toast?" asked Jean-Baptiste.

"No, this wine is too good for toasting. You don't want to mix emotion with a wine like this."

It was an overpoweringly fine, pungent wine.

"I say," I said.

"Not bad," said Chet.

Jean-Baptiste put on a Parisian impressed face, which broke into a smile when he saw Darren with his eyes closed, head tipped back, mystically tasting and feeling the texture.

"Darren, you are *such* a queen," Chet said, and Darren laughed so suddenly he nearly drew the wine into his nose. The rest of the restaurant was giving us offended looks. We didn't care. We had our values straight: this was to be Darren's night, and a lot of fun.

"Now," said Chet, "you can tell me all about the behind-the-scenes stuff. What *really* happened between you two? *What* did you leave out?"

"Oh, dear," Darren said.

"Oh, shit," I said.

Chet looked at both of us, tilted casually in his chair, effortlessly regal, deeply interested. The waiters were all far away.

"Well," I said, "I left out all the scenes where Darren fucked me."

"Without a condom," Darren added.

"And I left out all the shared syringes."

"And the shared lovers."

Jean-Baptiste laughed.

"I recorded most of the arguments," I said, "along with who said what. I mentioned all of Darren's friends."

"The good ones, anyway."

"Yes, yes. But what did you leave *out*," said Chet, insistently. "That's the only thing that interests me. I know what you put in."

"The rest doesn't matter," I said, brightly.

Chet looked at me with slit eyes that said: you big liar.

But I was saved by the fish. Huge plates floated towards us, where rosy salmon nestled in crisscrossed leaves.

"Yum, *yum*," Darren said, loudly, and drew every Parisian eye, outraged, towards him. Suddenly the restaurant fell silent. Turning his head, Darren made fierce eye contact with everyone in the room, turned back to us, and said loudly, "We should have ordered *frog*."

We ate and ate. Darren loved eating and he ate most of the bread in the baskets that were ceremoniously lowered onto the table. He ate his salmon with gusto, spreading lemon juice over all of it; he ate the sorbet in dainty spoonfuls, politely turning the spoon away from his mouth, as his mother had taught him; he attacked the gigot with energy, piled on it tiny potatoes and little baby carrots that seemed as slim as wheat grains; he wiped away the sauce with bread; he spread cheese after cheese, pungent, aromatic and creamy, onto thin biscuits; he ate the Grill-parzertorte while Jean-Baptiste and I, who had been defeated by the rack of lamb, and powerless before the dessert, watched him.

"My God! what a meal you've eaten," said Chet.

"The wine helps it go down," Darren answered.

Chet ordered yet another bottle. None of us objected.

"Watching you eat," said Jean-Baptiste, "I wouldn't say you were sick at all."

He eats like his mother eats, I thought.

"How is the sickness, Darren?" asked Chet. We had avoided

the topic during the dinner, but now we were pleasantly drunk and it seemed perfectly natural to ask.

"Oh, not too bad. I have my fit of crying once every month and then the rest of the month I'm fine. The Prozac helps. I utilize these Amsterdamer Specials to keep me in a good mood."

"Here," said Chet, "utilize a little of this." He poured him another glass. The wine seemed dark and fascinating. Darren stared at it.

"I am *so* drunk," he said.

"Good," I said. "Wine does you good. Wine puts a man on her horse and a woman in his grave."

They looked at me.

"Sorry." I swallowed to stifle a burp. "Straight out of Hemingway, that was."

"Philippe gets very literary when he's drunk," Darren said.

"He's very literary when he's sober," said Chet. "Were you sober when you wrote the book? More wine?"

"All the time; yes please." We were the last ones in the restaurant, but the waiters did not seem anxious for us to leave. No one was standing by the door. Outside the windows, Paris glowed by night, and the firmament twinkled.

"We can't go yet," said Chet. "We haven't had our *digestifs*."

Jean-Baptiste blew up his cheeks and let out a puff of air through his lips. He loosened his belt a notch. I slouched expansively in my chair. "I'm not sure I can eat any more," said Jean-Baptiste.

"Good," said Chet. He looked at Darren. "Darren, is this the best meal you've ever had in your life?"

Darren considered. But it was doubtful that anything he had ever eaten—even as a boy, when mommy was the best cook, the most learned person, the most sophisticated conversationalist in his entire experience—it was doubtful that he had ever eaten so well as he had at the Tour d'Argent that night.

"Chet," he said. "This was the best meal I've ever had. I'll remember it as long as I live."

There was a burst of laughter from the three of us. I looked at Darren. He was really very brave.

Dinner finally ended several hours later. After Chet had ostentatiously ordered a bottle of the oldest brandy in the house,

we said good night to all the waiters and especially to the som-
melier—who, we thought, had been really efficient about filling
up our glasses—and pushed our sleek full bellies through the
restaurant, down the lift, and along the Quai Montebello,
moving gradually into the Sixth Arrondissement, where Jean-
Baptiste lived. We were happily inebriated, pleasantly tight, and
the night was cool and very fine. We walked along the quais,
and Darren in his wheelchair seemed in such high spirits that I
had the sensation that he was walking beside us—young and
strong, happily drunk, as if on a Kansan joyride. Chet was bent
over from laughter, his tie loosened, a shirttail hanging loose; my
own necktie had completely come off, or was hanging around
my shoulder, I wasn't sure; Jean-Baptiste, doubled over with
laughter, pushed Darren forward by spurts and starts; Darren
cradled the bottle of brandy as if it were a baby.

"*Tomorrow . . . tomorrow . . . there's always . . . tomorrow,*" he
sang. I was staggering from side to side, zigzagging in the street.
If my mother could see me now, I thought; but she couldn't.

Finally we got to Jean-Baptiste's flat and I had the pleasure of
seeing Chester Hyland, multimillionaire heir, lie on the bed, as
still as a centerpiece, jacket sprawled everywhere.

"Get some glasses," he suggested suddenly.

The three of us erupted in assorted forms of laughter.

"I can*not* drink anymore," said Jean-Baptiste.

"Nor can I," said Chet. "I just wanted *empty* glasses. To
look at."

I took my eyeglasses off my face and put them on his
stomach.

"Poor," he said. "Very poor. You have to do better than
that. And you're supposed to be a writer, for Christ's sake.
You're not a writer."

"I'm an expatriate," I corrected, sitting down on the floor.

"That's it. You've lost . . . touch with the soil. You get . . .
fake European standards—how does it go?"

" 'Fake European standards have ruined you,' " I said.

"God, you can't be that drunk if you remembered that. Give
him more brandy."

"Yea," said Darren.

"You get precious," said Chet.

"I *am* precious," I said in a single wine-sodden breath.

"No, *I'm* precious. I'm valuable."

"Like hell you are," said Darren. "I'm worth just as much as you." Darren sort of pushed himself onto the bed where Chet lay and tried to tussle with him. Chet fought back as actively as a damp dishrag. Darren rolled onto the floor, laughing.

"Jesus," said Chet. "For a dying man you sure have a lot of *energy* left."

"You should see him without the Lexomil," said Jean-Baptiste.

You should have seen him before he got AIDS, I thought.

"Compassion," said Chet, looking fixedly at the ceiling. "Compassion. Is that the message of your book, Philippe?"

"That's what goes on the jacket."

"Can't you get some more *meaningful* message? 'How to be a real man and still not take it up the ass,' for instance?"

Darren roared with laughter. Jean-Baptiste shook his head as though dazed. I felt the room was spinning around.

"Compassion," said Chet again. "Compassion?" His voice grew firmer. "*You're* not compassionate. You're an ambitious bastard, that's what you are. You're an ambitious bastard. The whole novel is about making the reader believe one thing and then pulling the carpet out from under his feet. Well, that's the last carpet, isn't it? You're not compassionate, you're ambitious. You wrote the novel to get even with Darren."

"I think you're drunk," I said.

"You're ambitious," he said.

I lowered my chin into my chest. I thought I should say something to defend myself, and didn't know how.

"Ambitious people fuck up the world," Chet said.

"Fuck," said Darren, looking beat.

"I am ambitious," I said.

"Yes," said Chet. "But that's all right. So's Darren."

" 'No one is pure,' " said Jean-Baptiste.

"Not me!" said Darren.

"No, not Darren," said Chet. He looked at him. "Darren. Why did you have to get AIDS? We could have had such a good time together."

CHAPTER 19

A week later, a tremendously hot night towards the end of
July. I was walking on the Pont des Arts, on my way to
the quai party, carrying a lumpy envelope.

I crossed the bridge and turned left into the stairs that led
down to the quais at the Louvre, where despite Darren's fevers,
we had decided to hold our party. Not a party—more of a
picnic, at night.

On the quais, the first guest:

"Salut, Yannick!"

"Maestro!"

He pumped my hand, which surprised me.

"You—you—liked it?"

"Oh yes. I liked it. Masterly. Except for what happens to me
in chapter nineteen, but you can't have it all." He smiled. "You
know, Philippe, now that you've proven you can write, you
may as well learn how to dress."

"I will," I said.

I was again wearing shorts and sneakers without socks. Yannick, despite the heavy heat, wore an elegant blazer with a
cotton shirt.

"Now, where are these characters?" he asked.

"Here's one," I said, and turned to welcome the second guest. "Salut, Jean-Baptiste." We shook hands energetically.

"Salut, Philippe."

"Jean-Baptiste, this is Yannick."

"Who? Oh! *That* Yannick. Well! I know all about you, Monsieur Yannick." They shook hands gravely.

Jean-Baptiste was dressed in gray slacks and a very fine, very ironed shirt. He looked around. "Is this the place?" he asked.

"Yup," I said. "Where desire meets memory. Did you bring something to eat?"

"*Mais bien sûr! Fromage.* Very French. You know, I can't believe we're doing this, Philippe. Picnic on the quais! Why?"

"Well," I said, "we need a party on the quais to echo the one in the book."

Jean-Baptiste shook his head. Then he clasped my hand, solemnly, and said, "Congratulations, Monsieur Novelist. Pity your clothing is not as elegant as your prose. Will you get any money soon?"

"A little money."

"Great. Next, we'll take you shopping. And what have you brought for our party?" he asked.

"Book reviews."

"Splendid. Do you want them with a grain of salt or au naturel?"

"Very funny."

"What about you, Yannick?"

Yannick lifted two bottles of Château Margaux.

"Oh, bra-*vo!*" I said.

"Yes, bravo, Yannick. And for us?"

Yannick gave him the finger.

"Don't be rude," I said.

"Oh, Philippe, please," said Jean-Baptiste. "Rude? *Me?* Don't be ridiculous." He squinted eastwards. "Down there. Could that be . . . ? Yes, I think it is. It's . . . Mar-ZEN-na! And Fran-CES-co!" He was shouting like a Napoli-TAN-o, and flew in their direction.

From down the quais we heard Darren's friends shouting greetings to each other with open arms. Francesco cried, "Jean-Baptiste! You look so *well!* So fine, so—*ready!*"

"Oh, shut up!" Jean-Baptiste said, but Francesco only roared with laughter. "Or I'll take your wife. Salut, Marzenna."

"Salut, Jean-Baptiste." They kissed twice. "Where is Darren?" she asked.

"Not here, yet."

They walked over to us, with kisses and congratulations for me.

"Ahem, ahem. This odd-looking person," Jean-Baptiste said, "is Yannick, a friend of Philippe's, and a great friend of Darren's—apparently."

"Enchantée. How do you know Darren?" Marzenna asked.

"I don't," said Yannick. "I've read about him."

"But Jean-Baptiste—"

"Jean-Baptiste is being very *witty* tonight," I said.

Marzenna looked at all of us uncertainly, and turned to Yannick. "Well, tonight you'll meet the real man. I hope. Jean-Baptiste," she said, "how is Darren?"

"Drunk. Actually, I haven't seen him for a week," said Jean-Baptiste. "He says he wants to be alone. Liver poisoning."

"From the Tour d'Argent?" she asked, and I nodded.

Francesco said, "I hope you didn't go to the Tour d'Argent dressed like that, Philippe."

"No, I wore a tie with my shorts."

"And did you get very drunk?"

Jean-Baptiste and I looked at each other.

"We *all* got very drunk."

"Well, tonight won't be that kind of party, I hope," said Marzenna. She had brought a basket, and inside were some egg hors d'oeuvres, nicely garnished with red splotches of tomatoes, some cold cuts, a pasta salad made with slices of mozzarella, and a picnic blanket for us to sit down on.

"Pasta salad is Darren's favorite," she said. We unpacked the food and spread the blanket flat next to the nearest concrete bench. A few tourists strolling up and down the Seine gazed at us admiringly.

"This is the strangest party I have ever been at," said Yannick. "A night picnic, in one of the most sordid sites in Paris."

"If you want sordid," said Jean-Baptiste, "try that tunnel." He pointed.

"What's in there?" asked Marzenna.

"The past," I said.

"Actually, Yannick," Marzenna said, "I find the quais quite *romantic*."

Across the river you could see the blazing colonnade of the Hôtel des Monnaies, and the bridges with their dark arches, and the Eiffel Tower spotlighted, rising like a modern, benevolent spire.

Jean-Baptiste nibbled at his cheese. "Poor Yannick doesn't like it here because *men* try to punch his ticket."

"I beg your pardon," he said, helping himself to an egg, "one man tried to buy my season pass."

Francesco laughed. He was uncorking a bottle. "Tell us," he said.

"Well, I was doing everything to show I was not interested—but this guy kept trying to talk to me. "So I told him, 'Listen, I'm not gay. You're wasting your time. Go away.' "

"Did he?" asked Francesco.

"Yes."

"Was his name Laurent?" asked Jean-Baptiste.

"Yes!" said Yannick. "How—"

"That Laurent is *such* a whore," Jean-Baptiste said. "I've seen him around."

Yannick shook his head. "What a fag he was. What a pathetic fag." Jean-Baptiste shot him a venomous stare, which Yannick missed.

"Now," said Marzenna, smoothing her comfortable lap, "Philippe, tell us about your book."

"Sorry?"

"Philippe, are you all right? You looked lost, there."

"I'm fine. I'm fine. What was the question?"

"About the book?"

"I corrected the proofs last month. I sent them to New York. Critics got them. Now I'm just waiting."

"Didn't Darren get to see the proofs?" Marzenna asked.

"But there wasn't any time! Darren was in Sénanque—communicating with God, and I had an impossible deadline! Besides, the book will be arriving any day, and that's what Darren wants to see."

"And the reviews?"

"Later," I said, patting the lumpy envelope.

"Darren will like whatever you give him. Right?"

"Right," I said.

"Yannick, have you read this book?" Francesco asked.

"I rather have," said Yannick, with a bit of smugness. Jean-Baptiste glared at him.

"You can read English?" asked Francesco.

"Yes." More smugness, more glaring.

"What's it like?"

"You're all in it," Yannick said. "It's very good."

"How does it end?"

"Darren dies, of course."

We were quiet awhile. That remark seemed so pointless.

Yannick tried to cover up by saying, "I'm not sure I'm going to try to get to know Darren very well. There's no point. Is there."

Francesco coughed loudly. "Where *is* Darren?"

"I think he may be arriving with a friend," Jean-Baptiste said. "I get the impression he'll be arriving in some spectacular fashion."

Just then a motorboat ripped by. It tore past, bouncing like a flat, hard stone flung against the water, then U-turned in a tight arc, passing through the arches of the Pont du Carrousel, and came roaring back. It was a small, closed motorboat, and its red lights winked, on and off, in a friendly way as the motor slowed down and coughed to a stop next to us. It bumped against the dock, and we could hear a commotion going on inside. Suddenly the hatch popped open, and out came Catherine.

"Ta-DAAA!" she yelled. "What do you think?!"

We rose to our feet laughing and clapping hysterically. She looked at the shore rising and falling, and, with a brave lunge, jumped onto the stone steps. Her dress of gas-blue beads rustled and shivered as she moved, and you could see her white legs.

"Catherine. That was fantastic," said Francesco, who gave her two pecks on each cheek and one on the lips, while Marzenna observed them fondly. Jean-Baptiste looked amazed.

Francesco studied the boat. "But how is Darren going to get ashore if he's in there, in a wheelchair?"

"Isn't Darren here?" asked Catherine.

"Wait," said Marzenna, "isn't he with you?"

We all looked at each other. Catherine glanced at her boat. "Should we call him?" she asked. "I've got a phone."

"In there?" asked Jean-Baptiste. "I'll get it." He jumped into the boat. "Hey, there's a driver in here. Hello."

"The phone's next to the door," she said. "The driver can't hear you; he's plugged into his soccer match."

Jean-Baptiste appeared, the portable phone in both hands, held like a soccer ball.

"Overhead or underhand?" he asked Catherine.

"Under, please," she said, and the thing flew, and was caught, opened, and switched on in a second. Catherine dialed Darren's number at the Institut Pasteur. Jean-Baptiste, nimble as a goat, jumped out of the hatch, whipped and knotted the rope around the metal ring ashore, then jumped on land.

"Where'd you learn that?" asked Yannick.

"Oh, the colonies," answered Jean-Baptiste, blandly, but he looked at Yannick as if he needed a colonial-style lashing.

"No one's answering," she said, and closed the phone. "Where could he be?" She nibbled half-desperately at her cuticle.

"He's probably on his way," said Marzenna. "Don't worry. You look lovely, Catherine. You look lovely."

"And you, my dear." They hugged warmly. They let go and Catherine hugged Francesco.

"Hey," said Jean-Baptiste. "Don't I get a hug?"

"Jean-Baptiste!" Catherine cried. "I missed you last time! It is so good to see you!"

"*Mon amour!*" he said, laughing, and they hugged like lovers.

"Tell me," she asked. "How was Australia?"

"Orange," he answered.

"Ha!" she said, and hugged him again. "What about the furry animals? The koalas? The kangaroos?"

"I lived with a furry animal."

"Oh no!"

"But I also met a woman who reminded me of you!"

"Jean-Baptiste!"

"Only not as beautiful."

"Oh, Jean-Baptiste, I'm so glad you're back!" They hugged again.

Finally disengaging herself, Catherine asked Yannick, "Now then. Who are you?"

"Yannick," he said, and leaned forward for a kiss.

She shook his hand instead. "How do you do?" she said. Then turning to us: "Well? Shall we eat? Look what I brought." She descended the stone steps leading into the water, leaned into the boat, and the Seine licked at her beautiful blue dress. "God it's so hot. I could almost go for a swim." Her driver appeared at the hatch and gave her a carton which she carried to our picnic mat.

"Now then, ladies and gentlemen, do you know what *this* is?" she asked, opening it. We stared. It was a titanic tin of black caviar.

"What about the champagne?" asked Francesco.

"Still in the boat. We've got to let it sit awhile; otherwise it's much too fizzy. All that bouncing around. Really, the best thing to do would be to put it on the gyro, but we haven't got a gyro."

"Damn," said Francesco.

"Yes, tragic, isn't it," said Catherine, as she smoothed a luscious lock behind her ear. Her legs were folded under her to one side, she was leaning on one arm, blue beads cascading down the picnic blanket. Then she looked at me and smiled. "I remember you. You're Philippe. Darren's 'ghost writer.' "

"Hi," I said.

"Let me kiss you," she said, and she did. "*You* guys had an interesting party, I heard."

"Yes."

"Tour d'Argent? How boring. But Chet has to do everything right. He called me from Budapest tonight, you know. Regrets. Oh! Darren said you've finished the book."

"I've already got the first reviews. In this envelope."

"May I?" she said, taking the envelope gently. "Oh! It's still sealed! You mean you haven't opened it yet?"

"I'm waiting for Darren."

"Really!" she said, examining the seal. "Well, I'm sure Darren will love to see these. Feels like a lot of them. Are they good or bad, you think?"

"I asked my agent to send me all the reviews, good or bad."

She looked at me slyly. "These reviews mean a lot to you, don't they?"

"Oh, my God," said Francesco, pointing. We turned to look and Marzenna put a hand over her mouth.

It was Darren, in his wheelchair, being pushed across the heel-breaking cobblestones by a taxi driver. He looked like a skeleton encased by skin; his neck looked no larger than my wrist. Around his eyes we could see the gray circles of the sockets of his skull.

He stopped in front of us. The taxi driver looked impatient. Darren tried leaning an inch backwards, straining, trying to raise his chin, his eyes lifting out of their sockets.

"Ici," he said. Here. He looked at us with those huge, round blue eyes.

Next to me, Jean-Baptiste went white. "Darren," he said. "What happened?"

"Destiny," he whispered.

He looked so awful, we were almost afraid to come near him. "Some ending. Eh?" He observed us, amused.

"Has the taxi driver been paid?" whispered Yannick.

Catherine was shocked.

Darren bowed his head. White fingers brittle as dead twigs lifted a wallet out of his lap, about an inch above his leg.

Jean-Baptiste gently drew the wallet from Darren's fingers and opened it. "How much?" he said.

"One hundred fifty," said the cabbie.

Jean-Baptiste glanced at Darren, whose eyes were fixed on the horizon. He said to the cabbie, "Come back in half an hour."

"An hour," said Darren.

Behind Darren's back, Jean-Baptiste gestured at the cabbie to return in half an hour, and the cabbie nodded and left.

"Now," Darren said, "let's party."

"Darren," Catherine asked, "should you even be here?"

"No. I snuck out."

Yannick turned to me and said, "I'm not sure this party is a good idea. We're encouraging him to leave the hospital. And we'll be responsible if something does happen."

"Oh, shut up, Yannick," Catherine said, and Jean-Baptiste looked at him angrily.

Yannick continued. "He's out here against his doctor's orders. We're abetting his misconduct. He should not be here. *We* should not be here."

"Jean-Baptiste?" said Darren.

"Yes?"

Darren looked at Yannick. "Push him in."

And so Jean-Baptiste pushed Yannick into the river.

"Hey—WHAT!!" he yelled, as the water came up to his neck.

"Oh, no, Jean-Baptiste!" said Catherine, smiling. The water was not deep, but it was wet.

"God DAMN IT! GOD DAMN IT!!" yelled Yannick, who blubbered his way over to the shore, to the stone staircase, where Marzenna and Francesco and I helped him. Darren wore his strange smile. When Yannick got out, he was wet as a seal.

"You moron! You've assaulted me!" he cried at Jean-Baptiste. Jean-Baptiste looked at him from a safe distance, behind Darren.

"My wallet is soaked!" he said. Blazer, shoes, socks, slacks, shirt, underwear—all were sopping wet. Yannick tried to wring himself out on the quais, and we tried not to laugh.

"Gosh, Yannick, I'm sorry," said Jean-Baptiste.

"Fuck you," said Yannick.

"C'mon, Yannick," said Marzenna. "It's just a joke. Jean-Baptiste just wants you to show compassion."

"Fuck compassion."

"Yannick, don't be upset," I said.

"How am I supposed to get home? Like this? Huh?"

"We can help you," said Francesco. "We've got a car."

"Or ride with me," said Darren.

Yannick looked at him, breathing deeply, and then drew himself up and said, "Right now I'd rather go by water."

Whereupon Catherine laughed and helped him get out of his blazer.

"Hang on," she said, "I may have some spare clothing in the boat. You may have to wear a *dress*, Yannick! Oo-la-la! what would the men around here *think*?"

Catherine stepped into her boat. While she was rummaging inside, Yannick, with a calm, moon-like face, wrung his jacket; water cascaded down. Catherine waved him into the boat and the rest of us looked on as Yannick disappeared.

"It'll be a miniskirt," said Jean-Baptiste.

"No, it's going to be a strapless gown from Croirier's," said Marzenna.

"It'll be a bikini," said Francesco.

Instead Yannick came out dressed in a worker's red coveralls, and barefoot.

"Wow! How chic!" we said.

"Yannick, you know what to do," Catherine said.

He winced as he padded over the rough stones, and came over to Darren. He looked at him from the sides of his eyes. But he said, in English, "Darren, I'm sorry."

"Don't apologize," said Darren, in French. "Can't undo the past."

Marzenna said, "You must stay, now, Yannick. You must stay and drink."

"It would be a pleasure." Cunningly, Yannick was judging the distance between Jean-Baptiste and the water, but Jean-Baptiste quickly scuttled out of Yannick's reach and laughed.

"Well!" said Catherine. She held up two bottles of champagne, and gave them to Francesco to open. In his firm hands the cork hissed. Then the champagne was poured, and glasses were passed around.

"Well, Darren," said Catherine. "Here are your friends. To us."

"To us."

It was amazing champagne. We were a sight that night, next to our checkered red and white picnic blanket, a motorboat moored alongside, a cat-like woman dressed in gas-blue beads, a barefoot man in a worker's smock, a sharp young student in slacks, a sturdy nerd wearing shorts and sneakers without socks, a pastel couple holding hands, all toasting a blue-eyed emaciated man in a wheelchair. One tourist was amazed enough to ask for our picture. We wrapped Darren's neck in a shawl and toasted the camera. The flash snapped.

"And now," Catherine said, "ladies and gentlemen, please take your seats. We are about to hear the reviews for Philippe Tapon's fabulous new book, *A Parisian from Kansas*. Philippe, may I do the honors?" she asked, opening the envelope.

"Please."

She pulled something out. "Oh, look! The book jacket! But with no book. Hey, everybody! Does *this* look familiar?"

"Ooooooo!" everybody said.

"*A Parisian from Kansas.* By Philippe Tapon. And here, ladies and gentlemen, are the marketing blurbs. Let's read those first." She read them aloud.

"Powerful"
"Pins you to your seat"
"Heartbreaking"

"Oh, and this one. Ready?"

"A gay Garp."

I stood up. " '*A gay Garp*!!' " I hollered, at the top of my lungs. "WHAT?! Who put that there?!"

"Calm down, Philippe. It'll sell the book." She gave me the book jacket.

I was nearly blind with rage; I saw nothing.

"Okay! Get ready! The first review is by—Edward Gray!"

"Hurray for Edward Gray!" the others cried. "Calm down, Philippe."

I slapped the cover into Darren's lap, crossed my arms, sat down and braced myself.

"I won't read the whole thing," Catherine said. "Or it'll take forever. Just the end. Oh! it's quite intellectual. Here goes." She read:

"The literary scholars of the future are going to have a strange puzzle before them. Here is an extraordinarily self-conscious novel, rigorously planned (*très construit*), meeting all sorts of formal requirements, and where is the evidence of the struggle that went into it? Where are the letters of the writer to his friends, detailing his thoughts, his hopes, his fears? Where is the *architecture* of the novel? What has happened, in short, to the novel's scaffolding? The stubborn literary scholars will have to search hard through Mr. Tapon's deux-pièces to find such a scaffolding, because there is none. There is no scaffolding—unless the scaffolding is the novel itself. And this is Mr. Tapon's principal literary achievement. The novel is a sort of journal in which Mr. Tapon put his comments about the writing as he wrote, and in such a way, that the comments *are* the writing (what the French call *écriture*). Mr. Tapon sought to funnel all his thoughts, his hopes, his fears, *about* the novel, *into* the novel, and his autobiographical resonance is all the greater—not forgetting something that is probably quite ineffable—it is always, after all, just a novel."

"Wow!" we all called out.

"What superb writing!"

"What does it mean?" asked Marzenna, who didn't understand English.

"He's saying Philippe didn't use too many notebooks while writing."

"Is that important?" asked Francesco.

I rather liked the review, and I looked at Darren. "Should we consider this good news?" I asked.

"Kind of boring," Darren said. "Let's hear the others."

"This next one," said Catherine, "has a purple triangle stamped on top."

"Yes," said Darren. "Let's hear from the fags."

"Oh, boy," I said. My fists were clenched.

Catherine announced, "Ladies and gentlemen, the gay press." She read:

"This magazine's long-standing policy in this day and age is that there cannot be too many novels which enhance gay lifestyle awareness. But although Philippe Tapon is a promising young writer, who has written a work of authentic autobiographical scope, his concerns do not always follow the accepted program of gays and of their friends. . . ."

"Program? What program?" I asked. "Am I missing something?"

"Catherine, cut the crap," said Darren. Catherine skipped ahead.

". . . But Mr. Tapon's demented satire of gay sexuality, particularly chapter 11, "The Murphy Stavros Chapter," is the weakest part of the book. All sympathy and compassion that had been building for Darren Swenson dissolves in an unrepentant bacchanalian orgy of epic proportions. Far from creating friends for gays, this chapter perpetuates the stereotypical impression of gays as promiscuous, chronic fornicators, who put pleasure before principle and who almost therefore deserve to have the AIDS virus."

I was speechless.

"Boy, they really understood the book," said Yannick.

"Good," said Darren. "Good. Let them talk. Fuel to the fire."

"What did it say?" Marzenna asked Jean-Baptiste.

"They think Murphy Stavros shouldn't be described," said Jean-Baptiste.

"But I thought Murphy exists," she said.

"Sort of," he answered.

"Wait," said Catherine. "Here's another one. Oh boy, Philippe, are you ready?

"A PARISIAN FROM CALIFORNIA"

"Oh, as if I hadn't thought of that," I said.

"Plundering the enshrined classics of American literature, including *The World According to Garp* (!) ["exclamation point!" Catherine exclaimed], Mr. Tapon has created a novel that wallows in sex—and not even instructively. Past a parade of men in slings, leather-jacketed waiters, and sped-up parties in indecent New York discos, Mr. Tapon weaves a tale of despair, the inevitable closing in of AIDS on someone who could not but have gotten it, all the while alluding to *The Sun Also Rises*, *The Great Gatsby* (and so forth), as if to dress up his own sordid narrative.

"Jesus," said Catherine. "Philippe, they don't seem to like your book very much."

I had begun curling into a ball.

"Good," said Darren. "Add fuel to the fire. Keep reading, Catherine. I want to hear what's next."

"This one is from a New York magazine.

"Yet again, an AIDS novel. Ho hum; shall we get the energy up? Once again, young man fresh out of innocent countryside, ho hum, deedle-dee-dum, comes to New York, falls in with the devilish friends who—oh my!—fuck him without a condom. Chaos ensues. Much gnashing of teeth, et cetera. ["New paragraph."] The principal merit of Philippe Tapon's novel is that for once we get the vicarious pleasure of getting down with the doomed future AIDS cases in the heady, rockin', rollin', gay eighties. The sex is not always explicit, which will disappoint many, but at least it is more explicit than in the usual grim biographical 'novel' about an AIDS patient—a genre which is rapidly becoming as unpleasantly ubiquitous as the AIDS virus itself."

I closed my eyes tightly. How could I be so misunderstood?

"Great," said Darren. "Perfect. Philippe, this book is going to *sell*. People love sex and scandal, no matter what the critics say. Keep reading, Catherine. Read another review."

Catherine frowned and flipped through reviews.

"Read them all, Catherine."

"They're all pretty bad," she said. "Wait, here's one.

". . . A poetic novel full of the pain of living and the angst of dying—a titanic struggle between the death and life principles, symbolically represented by Darren Swenson, as death, and Philippe Tapon, the author, as life. Darren Swenson, carrying the AIDS virus and the possessor of a soul-destroying death instinct, confronts the literary man whose principal psychosexual neurosis is—"

"*Fuck* that!" I cried. "The destruction of art by sociology and psycho-fucking-analysis!"

"Philippe's right; it's very boring. Next!" said Darren.

Catherine frowned, took a quick look at me, and continued.

> "Mr. Tapon's style seems to be a Hemingwayesque parody of John Irving—or alternatively, a Fitzgeraldian parody of Kerouac. Regardless, these four authors form the literary tradition on which he draws in a magnificently failed attempt to create the Great American Novel."

I was trying not to listen anymore. Darren was laughing. "Philippe, for all the greatness you thought you had, you're going to go down as pure pornography! But at least it will sell. Excellent. More, Catherine, more!"

"Philippe, here's one you'll like. Someone liked it enough to compare you to the great American authors! And in verse! In the *Postmodernist Literary Intelligencer*."

"Do we have to listen to this?" Darren asked. But Catherine persisted:

> "Neither Fitzgerald nor Kerouac;
>   Neither Hemingway nor Irving; at the still point, there Mr. Tapon is,
>   But neither arresting nor moving. And do not call it literature,
>   Where Kansas and Paris are gathered. Neither gay movement nor conservative,
>   Neither homo nor hetero. Except for the indifference,
>   There would be no dance, and there is only the dancin'.
>   I can only say, I have read it: but I cannot say why.
>   And I cannot say, it's good, for that is to place it on the map."

"Is that it?" I asked, sourly. "Any *other* voices descanting?"

Catherine looked confused. She looked down the page. She cleared her throat and read aloud. " 'People will buy this book, if only to read the notorious "Murphy Stavros Chapter," which makes the Beats look like sissies and reveals the true lifestyle of *homo sapiens sapiens homo.*' Is that supposed to be funny?" she asked.

"Beautiful!" Darren said. "More! Read more!"

She kept reading, and I was forced to listen. It seemed to get worse. There was much irrelevant cuteness concerning what might have actually happened when Darren and I first met. Or people assumed that Darren and I were lovers, or Siamese twins, or both, or that we were the same person, really, and that I didn't live in a house at all, but in a boat that resembled a house and that under cover of night moved secretly up and down the Seine. There was an article pompously explaining why there was no wheelchair access to the Tour d'Argent. There were speculations regarding my health, and requests that I undergo a medical exam and send the results in a public letter to the *Village Voice.*

"Maybe Doctor Daly will examine you," said Darren. "Maybe he'll suggest your temper be removed."

I was becoming numb to every word, so when Catherine began reading that the novel was "a triumph for the common man—proof that you don't have to be a Rock Hudson to merit a biography," Darren whooped and cheered and clapped, although I heard almost nothing.

Darren said, "Keep reading, Catherine. This book is going to be such a success. Philippe, I got what I wanted!" He was almost shouting. The taxi driver had arrived.

"Read, read, *read*, Catherine!"

"Dear Editor:

I cannot believe that you have given space to a book which is not only about homosexuals, but about a homosexual who was a whore, a thief, who dishonored his parents and was just plain evil. I cannot believe you would give your sympathy, and one penny out of your pocket, to a man who has led such a crummy life. As far as I am concerned, Darren Swenson can go to hell, and he probably will. I will certainly not pay him the compliment of reading his book.

L.B.D., Arcadia, Kansas."

"Is that supposed to be a review?" she asked. "It's a letter from a newspaper. The *Arcadia Blade*."

"Arcadia, *Kansas?*" said Darren. "I know where Arcadia is. Hick town. Worse than Immaculatum."

"Philippe, are you all right?"

The world outside was black; I was not listening to anything.

"Are you all right? Philippe?"

"Sort of."

"I'm so *glad*," Darren said. "I'm so *glad*. Those fucking hicks are getting what they deserve. I'm *glad*."

"Darren," I said weakly. "That book *hurt*—"

"*Good*, Philippe. *Good*. Make them wake up. Good, good, good. I can go home now. Philippe, we're going to be rich. Fuck the critics."

Catherine leaned down towards me. "Oh, I'm so sorry, Philippe," she said. "Why did they send these? Maybe it was a mistake."

"Maybe the whole book was a mistake," I snapped.

I leaped up and strode away down the quais. I did not want to be near them. I strode away perhaps a hundred yards, and I put my head against a concrete wall. Out of the corner of my eye I saw Darren laughing, talking, happily. Was that it? Was that it for my book? Was that all they had to say?

The taxi driver began to push Darren, and I saw him arguing violently with the others. I could catch words of what he was saying.

". . . alone . . . !"

Then after a while I saw the sullen driver pushing Darren through the white tunnel, opposite to the dark tunnel in the Pont du Carrousel, across the river. On the other side of the white tunnel was the ramp leading to the rue du Louvre, where Darren's taxi was throbbing, waiting.

I was so angry; it seemed so unjust.

I pushed Darren away with my stare. Then the others came up to me. Yannick was stepping painfully over the cobblestones until he got back to the picnic mat.

"Philippe, don't be cross," said Marzenna.

"Yes, Philippe. Did you see how much better Darren got, just listening to the reviews?" Jean-Baptiste said.

"Philippe, you should be happy. You've made him well,

you've given him a reason to keep living. Who cares what the critics say?" Catherine said.

"*I* do," I snarled.

"Don't worry. Please?"

Catherine tried to take me by the arm, but I resisted.

"Oh, please, Philippe, don't be difficult. Life is too short. And look. Someone's arrived! Who's that? There's someone talking to Yannick. Philippe, pull yourself together. Maybe this is an important critic!" She giggled and strode away, her beaded dress flying.

I counted, slowly, morosely, to ten, then opened my eyes and looked. It was Edward Gray, in a blazer and sailboat shoes. I had invited him, I remembered. He had arrived with a sleek East-Coasty writer wearing a flannel suit. Grimly, I walked over to Edward.

"Hello, Philippe," he said.

"Hello."

We shook hands. I nodded towards his friend, who said nothing.

"Introduce me, would you?" Edward asked.

"Jean–Baptiste," I said. "Marzenna. Francesco. Catherine. And Yannick."

"Interesting costume, Yannick. Are you cruising?"

The others all burst into laughter.

"No, not really," he said.

"Where is Darren?" Edward asked.

"You just missed him. He left already."

"Did I?" He eyed us suspiciously. "Did he?"

"Yes."

"Wait a minute. Question? You can be honest. Does Darren *really* exist?"

"Yes, of course!" we answered in unison.

Edward looked around, unsure of what to believe.

"Well, I suppose he does, if you say so."

I forced myself to say, "I couldn't have written the book without him."

"Oh, really, Philippe? Really? So when's the next Darren coming along? Excuse my *mild scorn.*"

I looked at him, speechless. I felt a sudden urge to lash out, to cry, but instead I drew myself up and said, "Thanks for your review, Edward."

"No problem. A pleasure. I'll be reading the others, soon. Take care, Philippe. I have to go, another party awaits. Nice to have met you all." As they turned, his friend raised a hand in a formal gesture of farewell. Then they were off to their next soirée.

"Philippe, are you all right?" asked Jean-Baptiste.

"I'm fine."

"Well, *his* review was good, at least," said Catherine.

"Good," I said. I said nothing more for the rest of the night. But inside logs were burning and things were crumbling.

CHAPTER 20

Early the next morning I had a nervous breakdown. A nervous breakdown had been ticking in me almost since I had met Darren; and it was only the excitement of the project and the feeling that I was being timed that kept me writing so furiously. Now that the book was finished—now that I considered my attachment to Darren terminated—I found myself running down like an overwound clock. I wound down leaving my flat, and, feeling I suddenly did not have any legs, dropped on the pavement in Paris and lay there like a vagabond. Because I was well dressed someone immediately offered help. And because I knew this was only a nervous breakdown, I knew that all I needed was an intravenous feeding and complete rest. That was what I thought. What I said, speaking nearly out of my unconscious, lying on the sidewalk in front of La Palette on a brilliant morning before going to work, was some meaningless mumble about going to a hospital, getting an AIDS test, sorrow, sorrow, sorrow.

No one understood what I was saying, and it took a strong waiter at La Palette to prop me up in a chair, loosen my collar, take off my shoes, loosen my cuffs; I let this all happen, even though I was powerless to stop it, because I thought I had had enough of serving Darren, enough of being an exhausted well from which he drank and then thoughtlessly moved on. I wanted to be looked after, now. I did not feel nauseous, yet, but the world spun around and spun around, and when I raised my head, I saw that my eyelids were half shut, and my eyes could not stay focused on anything. The ambulance arrived outside, and I heard it, and I felt honored that such an ambulance should come for me, and I saw the big serious-looking ambulance men come out of the ambulance, very serious, in dark blue and in white, their hair very short and very black, and they asked me if I could walk, and then they asked the waiter if I could walk and then with what I thought was incredible fluidity they pulled out the little rolling bed they used on such occasions. The waiter left his hand on my shoulder; I noticed a well-dressed woman was holding my hand, but when I turned to thank her, the world lurched sideways, and my head fell down by my side, and I felt like vomiting instead of saying thank you; and I was very glad someone was trying to take care of me in that instant and not always me trying to take care of everyone. They put me on the stretcher, and I felt the straps go down at first gently and then snugly around my body. And a sudden feeling of desperation came over me, unable to get up from the bed, only able to turn my head from side to side, and what would I do if I had to vomit? And I saw the white cotton sheets, and how hospital-nauseous they smelt, and now I was sure I would not be able to help vomiting, and thinking how necessary it was for me not to vomit to maintain the reputation of American expatriate writers living in Paris, and thinking it would be a grand thing, wouldn't it, if I could think of a Hemingway allusion about all this, and not being able to, and being bundled into the dark ambulance, small and claustrophobically filled with all sorts of devices and principally the two big menacing-looking oxygen tanks and the even more menacing oxygen mask which I absolutely did not want lowered over my face.

I was delirious now; I was having all sorts of dreams; I saw all sorts of fragments of life passing, simultaneously, like watching three movies at once, and the ambulance bounced and rumbled beneath me; there was no ear-splitting siren at first, which was fine because I didn't want any fuss, but then the siren came on and now I really did begin at first to gag, looking straight at my taut white linen strapped down on my hospital bed stretcher, and then I actually vomited, horrible and bilious, and the attendant wiped it up, saying, "Easy, easy," as if he had been expecting it, and now I felt my sleeve being rolled up, him asking me not to move, as if I could move, yelling at his friend if there was not a stop, him saying one up ahead, and then the movement of the car stopped; the slight pain of the needle going in, me thinking that he should have done this before but perhaps I hadn't needed it, and I thought he looked like a very fine, brave boy and wouldn't Darren like to be pricked by such a handsome boy! And then I smiled and the boy smiled back, and he said, "You see, you'll be fine," and I started crying all of a sudden, uncontrollably crying, crying for all the dead I'd not been able to save, crying for all the suffering, crying for Darren mostly, crying for myself mostly, and then for my parents that might have to watch me dying, and for my brother whom I had not meant to hurt in my life, and then for Darren again, and I bawled until there seemed to be more salt tears on my face than vomit, which the boy had wiped, and I thought it was really good that I was in the hands of such fine people, because perhaps I really needed to get out from everything I was under, the writing and being so careful with Darren, all the time.

I got a hospital bed for that night. The room was designed for two, but the other bed was empty. I remembered the cavernous barracks hospitals of my military youth, which I had shared with broken sergeants and ruptured privates, lying in my compound fracture, the experience I was using to write this even now, exploiting it to some extent, but also really drawing on reserves of past and future emotions to write an overwhelming present, I thought, as I lay on the hospital bed, a dreadful hospital stillness around me, insipid prints of flowers before me, the cool blue of the walls, the gray device with buttons if I wanted to call people or if I needed anything. I needed nothing: I was happy.

But it was over. The book was over. And my relationship with Darren was over. Leave, Darren. Now. Leave. As I lay in that hospital bed, feeling the unreal silence full of hoarse breathing and emaciated bodies and formaldehyde, I wanted Darren to die. Leave, Darren; go.

I took deep breaths; I was conscious of my overwhelming bitterness, and it felt like a nauseating thought deep down; good, I thought, good; I smiled weakly, but then I vomited, more copiously this time. The more I tried to smile, the more I vomited, and I heaved until I was sure there was nothing left in my stomach, and to my astonishment more came up, until I was sure I was no longer vomiting out of my stomach, but out of my body—strange fluids, thin and horrible, and green bile everywhere that I had to wipe from the inside of my mouth, which led to more vomiting and so forth.

It was quite hilarious, in a way, and after a while I smiled every time I felt a big barf coming up. It was about getting rid of the nux vomica that had been Darren. For more than a year, I had been patiently taking it all in; now I was throwing it all up. It was a natural cycle; what comes up must come down.

Vomit. I smiled, wiped my mouth off. I relaxed, then felt it coming up again. Vomit. This is the last of you, Darren, I never wish to see you again. This is my body rejecting all your poisons; this is me rejecting all of you. Go find someone else to bear all of you, but as of now, I cannot. Vomit. I did my best: I delivered everything I could. But either because of some fault in me, or some fault in you, I cannot. Leave, Darren; go.

I felt there was some last little poison down there. Quite energetically I stuck my finger into the back of my throat, palpated the back of my tongue, pushed hard, and then my abdomen started again with the painful contractions, but nothing came out. I tried again: more palpating, more contractions, but nothing came out. I leaned back, wiped my face again, and felt empty and clean. So all this was very little—a mere side effect of being with Darren, a mere side effect of our disordered ambition.

Ambition. Darren had wanted to be a Parisian, and wanted to leave Kansas, renounce himself, become someone else. And I? I had wanted to become a writer. This is the price, I told myself. This is the bill. You want to be an artist? You want to talk about suffering? Then you have to suffer.

Yes, here is a cause of human movement. Every desire not to be who we are, moves us; the desire itself is movement; to desire is to suffer. I saw myself in the future, as a hunched-over writer publishing poem after strange abstract poem. "Why is he writing this shit?" critics would say. "Why can't he write another *Parisian from Kansas*?" Please, let me tell you all about it. Stop and listen. Let me tell you all about it.

Imperceptibly I had drifted into sleep, and now I woke up with a start. I had a new cold sensation, like the flat side of a blade being pressed against my back. The blinds were closed. I looked at a clock: two o'clock, it said. No lights, I thought, that must mean two o'clock in the morning. I was very sweaty. The flat cold metal was still on my back. Or was it my imagination? Breathe, I said; pause; wait. Control yourself. I began to recite my favorite poems—once, then twice, then over and over, until the little fingers of dawn curled around the blinds. The metal disappeared, and imperceptibly I fell asleep again.

Five minutes later, or so it seemed, I was woken up by a nurse bringing me an orange juice. I concentrated very hard on my orange juice and drank it all, and by making an effort kept it all down. Thank you, nurse. Had one day passed? Yes, one day had passed; this was my second day in the hospital. I had better call my boss, I said; I had missed a day at work. Could I have a telephone please, nurse? Oh, it's on the desk, you're right. Thank you. Thank you anyway. I dialed my work number, and my boss answered.

"Er . . . *bonjour*," I said.

"Philippe? What's going on? Where are you?"

"I'm in the hospital."

"Hospital! What happened? Not another of your nervous problems?"

"No, just a flu—a little delirium."

"Damn," he said. "Can I help in any way? Do you need any money?"

"No, not really."

"Good, because I haven't got any. What else can I tell you that will cheer you up? Oh, your literary agent called! What did he say? I forgot. Ahh . . . oh yes, he's sent you something. It should be waiting for you, at your flat!"

"Well. Isn't that fine," I said.

"That's great news, isn't it? You're in print now! Right?"

"Right."

"You can get sold, and reviews, and girls, right? That's what you've always wanted, right?"

"That's what I've always wanted."

"You sound so cheerful. Give me your telephone, before you commit suicide."

I smiled. "Here: telephone and address."

"Philippe, get well."

"Right. Thanks. *Au revoir.*"

"Au revoir." We hung up.

Oh, fuck you very much, I thought. Then I remembered Darren, in his wheelchair, probably gone to celebrate, high as a star. Why not join him? Try to be compassionate? Oh, fuck compassion, I thought.

But after a whole day of staring out the window, examining the broken fingernails on my dirty hands, I was beginning to feel miserable for my tantrum that night on the quais. I had not said the least kind word to him; instead, I had pushed Darren away with an evil, jealous stare. Somehow it seemed barbarous, that just when things were finishing, and he was nearly dead, I became sour—and because of bad reviews. Not just bad reviews, though . . . what a temper I had. I would apologize to Darren— when I left the hospital. Maybe.

Maybe Darren could be the spokesman for this book. With those electrical eyes and that canyon voice he could destroy the critics and sell, sell, sell. I could see him making TV commercials from his bed, his prophetic face leaning into the screen, hissing, "You there! Yes, *you*! *Buy*—this—*book*!" I laughed. Darren and his scary eyes, I thought.

Then I heard some voices outside my door. One of them sounded familiar.

"Aha," he said. "Yes, this is the person I am looking for."

The door opened. "Can this person visit you?" the nurse asked me.

I looked at Jean-Baptiste. "Yes," I said. "He may."

Jean-Baptiste walked in and pulled a chair up to my bed. "Well, well, well, Philippe."

"Well, well, Jean-Baptiste."

"*You* look unwell."

"Well, I am."

"Am I welcome here?"

"Yes. You are."

"What happened?" he asked me.

"I was walking along a street. And then—I fell. Nervous breakdown."

"Nervous breakdown!"

"I told my boss I had the flu. I didn't want to tell him the truth. But actually, I'm pretty wiped out. I can't sleep. I can't eat very well. I can vomit quite well, however."

Jean-Baptiste shook his head. "Nervous breakdown?"

"I just fell down yesterday morning, and now I'm here."

"For no reason?"

"For many reasons."

"I see."

"How did you find me?" I asked.

"I called the bank this morning, and spoke to your boss after you spoke to him. He seemed quite concerned about your welfare."

"Well, good for him."

He smiled. "Are you all right? You're not going to go into shock or anything?"

"I have a sweltering temperature."

He shook his head and rolled his eyes. "Our novelist," he said. "And you've been here alone, all this time?"

"Yes."

He looked at me with a strange expression which I took to be incomprehension.

I said, "I didn't feel too good that night, after the quai party. I felt pretty rotten, in fact."

He kept looking at me as if he were expecting something.

I said, "I'm sorry I was so rude to everybody. It's just . . . it's in my nature. Sorry."

He was still looking at me.

"I'm *sorry*," I repeated. "I'm sorry for everybody. I'm especially sorry for Darren."

Jean-Baptiste began to speak in a measured tone. "Darren . . . isn't very well. It turns out—after our quai party, Darren was supposed to go back to the hospital. We don't know what he actually did that night, but the police found him—in the morning, sprawled out, in front . . . in front of Notre-Dame.

Some—major hemorrhaging. Internal. Lungs filling up. Anyway, by the time they found him, he was in a coma. Irreversible. Excuse me." He turned away.

I could not say anything.

"He's back in the Institut Pasteur. In intensive care. He's—excuse me," he said, and left the room.

All my anger was sizzling off, replaced by a stranger, newer emotion.

When he came back, he said, "But you see, I'm fine," and he wiped his eyes. He even tried to laugh. "I'm well brought up, you know. I keep my dignity. I don't show emotion. I'm a tough Parisian, you know. Darren's got—oh, a little—just a little more time."

I curled my hands and touched them to my forehead.

Jean-Baptiste continued. "Marzenna and I have been in and out. We don't know whether he can still see or not. His eyes never close, but he blinks, still. It's interesting to watch him, you know? All his brainwaves are normal, and his heart is pumping away. He does need help breathing. There are lots of tubes—" He cut himself off and started crying softly.

I looked at the ceiling and tried to imagine it was a sky full of stars. When I looked down Jean-Baptiste was holding his nose tightly, with his mouth shut, trying to stop crying that way.

"Anyway. I thought you should know. Aren't I swell?" he asked.

"Yes," I said, "you sure are."

A long pause. Jean-Baptiste got up. He looked around. He walked over to the window, and then paced down the length of a wall. He looked at me with a fascinated expression, and then paced down the other wall. He did this twice. Each time he looked up with a strange smile, and it looked like he was counting. "I thought so," he finally said. "Your room is definitely larger than Darren's room. But that's all right. You can probably appreciate it much better. Oh yes. You know, Philippe—I think this room is much better than your old deux-pièces. For a start, the view from the window is better, and the walls are whiter, the ceiling is higher, and you have room service." Despite myself, I smiled. He went on. "This room is certainly cleaner. Much cleaner, in fact. Philippe, in the future, you

must not be such a slob. Slovenliness encourages mental compli-
cations. You know, Philippe, nervous breakdowns are *not* fore-
ordained. They're quite preventable. Or at least curable. In fact,
Philippe—you may be surprised to learn—that *I* have the cure
for this nervous breakdown. Yes, the cure. You must be wondering what it is."

"I'm dying to know," I said.

He looked at me, and then continued. "I had to look for it,
of course. I spoke to your boss, but he didn't have it. I spoke to
your concierge, but she didn't have it either."

"My concierge?" I asked.

"She said no, absolutely not. Fortunately . . . I had my trusty
Swiss army knife. Do you have any idea just how flimsy the lock
on your mailbox is?"

He reached into his satchel, drew out a big packet, and put it
on my lap. It pressed down on my legs.

"What is it?" I asked.

"What do you think it is? Look at the return address."

The return address was John Hawk Agency, New York,
New York.

"You should take the cure once daily," he said.

I turned the packet over and over, looking over every inch
of it.

"Philippe, if you don't open that packet right now, I'm
going to push you through the window." I smiled, and tore off
the strip to open the cardboard, then folded back the flap. There
was a white styrofoam filling which I brushed away gently. I
turned the packet upside down and let the contents slowly slip
out: one bound proof of the forthcoming book *A Parisian from
Kansas*, along with its jacket—big, bright, and beautiful.

"Well," I said.

"Yes," he said. "Well, well, well."

CHAPTER 21

Darren's last monologue:

"After the quai party, after the wine, after the merrymaking and the reviews—I got into my cab and ordered the cabbie to drive me to Notre-Dame.

"I thought, if I were to die, I would like to die here, at the point from which all Paris shoots out. Because this milestone is my true beginning. I began to imagine all the good, great things that were going to happen now. Now that Philippe had finished the book, we were going to be famous. Now, people would know me—people would call me! You're Darren Swenson! What an extraordinary life you've had, leaving Kansas, fighting AIDS, rising, rising above misfortune; yes, *you*, Darren, *you* are our hero. And the restaurants will open their tables: and the limousines will open their doors: and the mansions will open their gates: and the cathedral will open its portals, and the coffins and the ovens and the urns . . . What coffins? What doors? What? Suddenly I felt dizzy, and I looked at the gates of Notre-Dame, and I heard them swing open, and then: a grave dirge, with slow moaning, began to gather round my side, and ghosts in lamentations offered out their arms, and I turned and I saw fire, and the earth lurched. I was on the ground, every ghost gone, seeing stars twinkling. But I had only collapsed on the ground. And I thought I'd fallen asleep, but suddenly all was dark and quiet, and I could not speak."

CHAPTER 22

Anurse directed me to his room in the Institut Pasteur. Would he speak to me, I wondered; no, he could not speak, his mouth was taped shut by silence; his eyes blinked every seven seconds; blink, blink, blink, eight times a minute; his brainwaves sounded like surf; and the drip-drip-drip of his I.V. fell into an arm so thin they'd stuck the needle between the bones;

Oh God, Darren, speak to me, please say yes, forgive my anger or say no, you don't forgive but please speak, speak, speak;

Blink, blink, blink; say something, Darren, speak; what are you thinking of, Darren? Oh Darren, forgive; Darren, forgive; say something, anything; speak;

This will help you speak, this will speak for you; under your arm I commend your book; this book is yours, Darren, forever; now I must close the door;

But I stopped in the doorway. I turned to look back at Darren.

Was he speaking with his eyes? Go. Go. Go.